The Det

and

The Clergyman

* * * * *

The Adventures of

Sherlock Holmes

and

Father Brown

The Detective

and

The Clergyman

* * * * *

The Adventures of

Sherlock Holmes

and

Father Brown

Edited by
David Marcum

Belanger Books
2023

David Marcum can be reached at:
thepapersofsherlockholmes@gmail.com

For information contact:
Belanger Books, LLC
61 Theresa Ct.
Manchester, NH 03103

derrick@belangerbooks.com
www.belangerbooks.com

Cover design by Brian Belanger
www.belangerbooks.com and *www.redbubble.com/people/zhahadun*

CONTENTS

Forewords

Adventures

(Continued on the next page . . . .)

COPYRIGHT INFORMATION

Editor's Foreword:
Detective and Priest:
A Curious Partnership
by David Marcum

To paraphrase the opening of Charles Dickens' *A Christmas Carol*: "~~Marley~~ Sherlock Holmes was ~~dead~~ the Great Detective: to begin with. There is no doubt whatever about that . . . This must be distinctly understood, or nothing wonderful can come of the story I am going to relate."

Edgar Allan Poe gets a lot of credit for coming up with the detective story format. Wilkie Collins certainly deserves a lot more credit than he receives for the influences of books like *The Woman in White* and *The Moonstone*. Dickens debatably used the first private detective in *Martin Chuzzlewit*, and might have done really well with the mystery format in general had he not died in the middle of *Edwin Drood*. But it was *Dr. John H. Watson* who truly set the mystery train into motion with his recounting of the cases of *Sherlock Holmes*, the world's first consulting detective. And it's never stopped.

The original Canonical Holmes stories had it all: Adventures might be comedies or tragedies. Gothic horror or police procedural. They might be set early in Holmes and Watson's friendship, or late. Country settings or in town. And while the first two literary appearances of Holmes's cases – *A Study in Scarlet* in 1887 and *The Sign of the Four* in 1890 – didn't exactly set the world on fire, the flames began to burn hot in mid-1891 when a new magazine, *The Strand*, published "A Scandal in Bohemia", just months after Holmes was believed to have died at the Reichenbach Falls. From then until December 1893, when "The Final Problem" appeared, interest in Mr. Holmes grew exponentially – and then the world was shocked to learn that Holmes had actually died over two years earlier – or so most people thought.

Holmes's admirers were left in a dark vacuum after the events of Holmes's "death" were published – but there were other detectives with writer friends or amateur literary agents who stepped up to fill the void. Some – like Dr. Thorndyke or Martin Hewitt (whose cases, as I've shown elsewhere, were actually those of young

1

Sherlock Holmes while living in Montague Street,) are still remembered, while others are long forgotten except to students of esoteric criminal detection.

When Holmes returned to London in April 1894, the reading public was still getting used to the idea of his death, which had only been widely publicized in *The Strand* late the previous year – in fact, less than six months before. Holmes immediately reinstituted his practice in Baker Street and continued his work until October 1903, when he supposedly retired to Sussex and life as a reclusive apiarist – although in truth he was still taking on cases and doing specialized work for his brother Mycroft to help prepare England for the inevitable war with Germany.

After December 1893, Watson didn't publish any Holmes stories until late summer 1901. Over several months, from August 1901 to April 1902, the public was treated to *The Hound of the Baskervilles* – but many readers thought this was a posthumous tale, as Watson hadn't shared anything explaining that Holmes had actually survived Reichenbach, or how. It wasn't until Holmes was retired that permission was given for a new series of thirteen adventures, later collected as *The Return of Sherlock Holmes*, published in 1903 and 1904. And then, over the next few decades, Watson's writings once again became quite limited, leaving something of the same literary vacuum that had occurred toward the end of Holmes's Great Hiatus.

In 1908, the next two Holmes adventures to be published appeared, "Wisteria Lodge" in August and "The Bruce-Partington Plans" in December. Then there would be nothing until December 1910, with the appearance of "The Devil's Foot".

It's difficult to imagine when there were so few Holmes stories available, and when it might be years before another would be made public. As had been the case in the 1890's following the completion of Watson's first twenty-four stories in *The Strand*, later collected as *The Adventures* and *The Memoirs*, narratives of other detectives' cases helped fill the void.

In July 1910, nearly half-a-year before "The Devil's Foot" would be published, a modest little tale would appear in *The Saturday Evening Post* – and one wouldn't have been criticized to think that it was the initial story in a series about the famed French policeman, Valentin. Who knew that "Valentin Follows a Curious Trail", later re-titled "The Blue Cross" and republished in *The Story-Teller* (December 1910), and then in *The Innocence of Father Brown*, would be the first of more than fifty narratives regarding another who came to be regarded as a *Great Detective*. Not as great as Sherlock Holmes, of course. "~~Marley~~ Sherlock Holmes was ~~dead~~ *the Great Detective: to begin with. There is no doubt whatever about that . . . This must be distinctly understood . . . .*"

Between 1910 and 1936 – just over a quarter-century – the public came to know and love Father Brown. Of course, there were never a lot of facts about him to know. He was a short, plain, round-faced, wide-eyed Roman Catholic priest, wearing shapeless clothes and always carrying an umbrella. In "The Sign of the Broken Sword", his first name is given as "*Paul*", and in "The Eye of Apollo", his first initial is stated to be "*J.*" Sometimes he's located in London, at other times in Essex, and a lot of other places as well. He often initially appears in a story on the periphery of the action, focused on what appears to be a wrong thing at the wrong time, but his keen perception, relying on what he knows of human nature and human sin, lead him to ask the right questions of the right people, and to know what happened without the need for a specialized knowledge of cigarette ash or the tracing of footprints.

I first heard of Father Brown in the late 1970's, from two sources. My father gifted me with a remaindered copy of Otto Penzler's invaluable *The Private Lives of the Private Eyes* (1977), containing biographies of twenty-five famed detectives – Holmes, of course, and Nero Wolfe, Hercule Poirot, James Bond, Dr. Thorndyke, and others. One chapter was on Father Brown – which I skimmed, and then passed by.

Around this same time, I watched a forgettable television film, *Sanctuary of Fear* (1979) starring that old staple TV character actor, Barnard Hughes, as a modernized Father Brown, thin and elderly and relocated to current-day New York. Even at that age – fourteen – I knew that it was a forgettable effort at best, and in truth, modernizations are abysmal abominations.

I really paid no further attention to Father Brown after that, other than maintaining an awareness of who he was, for several more decades. In 2010, I purchased an oversize two-volume set of the annotated Father Brown from the Battered Silicon Dispatch Box, with the idea that one day I'd read the complete adventures. I was especially impressed that every story in that set was arranged chronologically – all of the Essex stories were together, for instance, followed by the London stories, and so on. Each story also had an accompanying explanatory essay. But I still never got around to reading these books.

However, I had met Father Brown along the way as a supporting character in several Sherlock Holmes stories. *Nightwatch* by Stephen Kendrick (2001) is a full-length Holmes novel with Father Brown playing an important role. Another is "The Adventure of Merlin's Tomb" by Frank J. Morlock, included in *Sherlock Holmes: The Grand Horizontals* (2006).

In 2010, Ann Margaret Lewis published a collection of short stories, *Murder at the Vatican: The Church Mysteries of Sherlock Holmes*. Two of these, "The Vatican Cameos" and "The Second Coptic Patriarch", have Father Brown assisting Holmes and Watson. In fact, in the latter story, Father Brown is charged with the Patriarch's murder. I've collected traditional Canonical Holmes adventures since I was a boy in the mid-1970's, and over the years, I've now accumulated and read nearly all of them – thousands of novels, short stories, radio and television episodes, films and scripts, comics and fan fiction and unpublished manuscripts. Ms. Wilson's stories were the first time I'd encountered the traditional Canonical Father Brown in a way that piqued my interest to know a bit more.

In 2013, I was finally able to go to England on the first of three Holmes Pilgrimages. If it wasn't about Holmes, I generally didn't do it. While there, I visited a number of book stores in and around Charing Cross and found a Penguin edition of *The Complete Father Brown*, marked with the mysterious price – at least to an American – of "*1-4*". Later that night, I was in Baker Street, where I was staying at the Sherlock Holmes Hotel, and I walked up the street to a Holmes-themed fish-and-chips restaurant with various Holmes-related meal combinations for sale, along with countless photos and illustrations of Holmes on the walls. I had the Father Brown volume with me, and it was in that very-much Holmes setting, on a Holmes Pilgrimage, just a moment's walk from Holmes's former home, that I read my first Father Brown story, the above-mentioned "The Blue Cross".

It was a curious experience – sitting in London, reading as Valentin tracked a thief and a priest across the city, through some areas that I had recently visited. It wasn't like a Holmes story at all, and frankly, the clues that Father Brown left so he could be followed were rather uninspiring and unbelievable. But nevertheless it was well written and fun, and I was curious to know more about Brown and Flambeau and Valentin. I continued reading the second story, "The Secret Garden", and realized that the famed Valentin was no Inspector Lestrade – and that I didn't need to plan on meeting him again.

4

Over the next few years, I continued to read Father Brown – never in a white heat to get to the end of the original fifty-three stories. Additionally, as I read them, it was in the chronological order suggested by their arrangement in *The Annotated Father Brown* – so I've never read them in either the publication order, or with each story as part of a bigger collection, such as all of *The Innocence of Father Brown* or *The Wisdom of Father Brown* at one time.

In addition to the other aforementioned meetings of Holmes and Father Brown, Subbu Subramanian has written several excellent adventures, including "The Case of the Reformed Sinner" (in *The MX Book of New Sherlock Holmes Stories – Part V: Christmas Adventures* – 2016) and "The Strange Persecution of John Vincent Harden" (in *The MX Book of New Sherlock Holmes Stories – Part XVII – Whatever Remains . . . Must Be the Truth [1891-1898]* – 2019). And Chris Chan does a great job in "The Chapel of the Holy Blood" (included in *Sherlock Holmes and the Great Detectives*, 2020).

There is also a volume which apparently includes some Holmes and Father Brown pastiches that I've long tried to acquire, but so far haven't had any luck: *Sherlock Holmes Meets Father Brown and His Creator*, edited by Pasquale Accardo and John Peterson. (I mention it for the sake of completeness, and I can't comment upon its quality, as I've yet to see it. The quest continues . . . .)

There are some meetings between Our Heroes that aren't so great. One is a 2019 play by Jon Jory, *Sherlock Holmes, Sleuth, Meets Father Brown, Detective* – a bizarre thing where Holmes and Father Brown encounter one another for the first time *in Chicago*, where they share a meal of *spare ribs* and solve a re-worked version of "The Red Headed League". (The red-headed *Mrs.* Wilson has been wasting her time copying the *Encyclopedia Britannica*.) Holmes and Father Brown are together in some other peculiar and forgettable pastiches that aren't traditional at all, including Ann M. Mackey's "The Case of the Twin Masks" (1993), "The South Downers" (a round-robin pastiche, 1993-1994), and disappointing and solution-less *The D Case* by Carlo Fruttero and Franco Lucentini (1989), in which a frankly fictional meeting of many literary sleuths from different historical eras, including Sherlock Holmes, Father Brown, Nero Wolfe, C. Auguste Dupin, Lew Archer, and Philip Marlowe, gather to discuss Dickens' *Edwin Drood*.

In my Holmes collection, I also have a 1947 pamphlet, *Some Notes on a Meeting at Chisham* by Robert John Bayer. This little volume, with a foreword by Vincent Starrett and recording a paper initially presented by Mr. Bayer in September 1947, speculates on a first meeting between Holmes and Brown, during the Canonical Father Brown story, "The Man with Two Beards" from *The Secret of Father Brown*. Bayer speculates that the detective in that story, Carver, is actually Holmes. His argument is vastly unconvincing.

Many others also try to insert Holmes, in the guise of Dr. Orion Hood, into "The Absence of Mr. Glass" from *The Wisdom of Father Brown*. Holmes and Hood were two very different people – as shown in one of the stories contained in this current volume.

In addition to the above-mentioned Father Brown pastiches in which he's assisted Sherlock Holmes, there have been some where he works alone. The best of these is Hugh Ashton's "The Persian Dagger" (2018). Not only is it the best, but it's actually the only one that is acceptable.

One of these failures is John Peterson's *The Return of Father Brown* (2015), authorized by The American Chesterton Society, containing forty-four very short stories, wherein Father Brown is inexplicably living in the United States in the 1990's – when he would have been over one-hundred years old. (Apparently, some of his admirers think that it's fine for him to be an immortal, magical being, in the way that they picture Holmes, born in 1854, or Nero Wolfe, a World War I veteran, or Ellery Queen, canonically born in 1905, still romping around among us today.)

And if that isn't enough, the Italian book, *Il destino di Padre Brown* (*The Destiny of Father Brown*) by Paolo Gulisano, has the little priest elected as Pope Innocent XIV in 1939.

There have been a number of media adaptations of the Father Brown stories. Both American and British radio have done numerous versions, all but one sticking with the original stories and setting them in the correct time period. In the United States, a 1945 radio show, *The Adventures of Father Brown*, had a current day setting – but 1945 was barely close enough to the correct era to fit, if one assumed that Father Brown was rather elderly by then.

Respected film and television versions include *Father Brown* (1934, starring Walter Connolly, based on "The Blue Cross"), *Father Brown* (1954, starring Alec Guinness, also based on "The Blue Cross"), and *Father Brown* (1974 – a thirteen-episode television series starring Kenneth More).

Besides the previously mentioned Barnard Hughes film from 1979, incorrectly updated to modern times, there has been a multi-season television series, running from 2012 to the present, starring Mark Brown, better-known to most people as Mr. Weasley from the

6

Harry Potter films. Unfortunately, while the production values on this are quite pleasing, this show is essentially about a completely different character who just happens to have Father Brown's name. (It might be tempting to think of this as "Son of Father Brown" – if Father Brown had a son.) It probably should have been called *Father Smith* or *Father Jones*, since it has nothing to do with the True Father Brown. This series is set in the 1950's – already far too late to be about the canonical Father Brown. In this version, the Father Brown of the show is a big heavy-set man towering over those around him – most unlike the True Father Brown. This one is a World War I veteran, and he's ensconced throughout the entire run of the show in the fictional Cotswold village of Kembleford. Whereas the True Father Brown of the books interacted with new people in every story – with the exception of return visits from Flambeau – this television series has a whole plethora of villagers and rectory staff and policemen whose B-plots and regular interferences take up as much screen time as what is given to the priest. And this TV Flambeau is *not* the reformed chap we know from the original stories.

Belanger Books, founded by Derrick and Brian Belanger, has made a reputation for fine Sherlockian collections, and after Father Brown's appearance in *Sherlock Holmes and the Great Detectives* (2020), they had the idea of a volume dedicated solely to Holmes and Father Brown. I was very honored to be asked to edit it. I only had one real requirement: That the stories included the Canonical Holmes and Father Brown – no modernized versions need apply.

Over the next few months, the stories began to arrive – and to my evenly mixed amusement and consternation, almost every contributor had written a story describing the first meeting between the detective and the priest. Since the stories were set at different times in Holmes's career, there was a wide range of dates. Arranging the submissions chronologically, I received a story about Holmes and Father Brown's first meeting in the late 1880's, followed by a number of first meetings in the 1890's. Then there was their first meeting in the late 1890's, and more first meetings in the early 1900's. There were several first meetings in the years leading up to the War, and then they met again for the first time in the 1920's.

Clearly, all of these first meetings would make readers' heads spin. Fortunately, all of the contributors understood the difficulties and worked to revise their stories fittingly. I ended up arranging the adventures chronologically, as I usually do when editing Sherlockian anthologies, because I'm a Holmesian Chronologist, and it pleases me, and it makes more sense when reading the books.

Although I didn't allow any first meetings, I did bend the rules a bit for Brett Fawcett's excellent story, which opens the book. Its chronological setting, early 1889, requires that Brown be a young man at the time, and it sets the tone excellently for what follows. (It too was originally a first meeting, but it was tweaked so Holmes and young Brown had at least met before this case began.)

Editing this book gave me a new appreciation for Father Brown. I very much enjoy the setting and timeframe of his canonical adventures, and that they occur when Holmes and Watson were still around. Chesterton's records of the priest's affairs are well-written and approach the solution from unexpected tangents in a clever way.

On the surface, the occasional crossing of paths between Holmes and Father Brown is a curious partnership – the logical clue-seeking detective and the intuitive clergyman would seem to contradict one another. But as these stories show, they complement one another perfectly, and their crime-solving successes are almost as satisfying as their growing friendship and respect.

There are sixty Canonical Holmes adventures, and fifty-three Canonical Father Brown tales. That isn't enough. There have fortunately been thousands more stories about the True Sherlock Holmes, but only just a few related to the True Father Brown. I urge people to write many more of them – and hopefully this book will help in that mission.

* * * * *

"Of course, I could only stammer out my thanks."
– The unhappy John Hector McFarlane, "The Norwood Builder"

As always when any new project is finished, I want to first thank with all my heart my incredible, patient, brilliant, kind, and beautiful wife of almost thirty-five years, Rebecca – every day I'm luckier than the day before, and I'm wise enough to know it! – and our amazing, funny, creative, and wonderful son, and my friend, Dan. I love you both, and you are everything to me!

Special *Thank You*'s go to Derrick Belanger and Brian Belanger. I've known them both for quite a while now, initially by emails, and then in person. They're both people, and they're doing invaluable work in the world of Sherlockian publishing. As I write this, they've both recently returned from their first trips to London – not just for fun, but as a research trip to make what they do with

Belanger Books even better. I'm very proud to be associated with them, and very grateful for the opportunities that they've provided to me.

My deepest gratitude to the amazing contributors have pulled some amazing works from the Tin Dispatch Box. I'm more grateful than I can express to every contributor who has made the effort to contribute such wonderful stories.

And last but certainly *not* least, **Sir Arthur Canon Doyle** and **G.K. Chesterton**: Founders of the Feast. Present in spirit, and honored by all of us here.

This book has been a labor of love, and I hope that it's enjoyed by both long-time Holmes and Father Brown fans and new recruits. The World of The Detective and The Clergyman is a place that I could never tire of visiting, and I hope that more and more people discover it.

And don't forget: *"The game is afoot!"*

David Marcum
April 5th, 2023
The 129th Anniversary of
Holmes's return to London in
"The Empty House"

Questions, comments, and story submissions
may be addressed to David Marcum at
thepapersofsherlockholmes@gmail.com

Foreword
by Dale Ahlquist

One of the most fascinating non-friendships in twentieth century English literature is the one between Arthur Conan Doyle and Gilbert Keith Chesterton.

Besides the obvious fact of what they had in common, G.K. Chesterton had the reputation for getting along with everybody in the literary world and out of it, including those with whom he continually crossed philosophical swords, such as George Bernard Shaw and H.G. Wells. In spite of agreeing with each other on practically nothing, they enjoyed warm friendships. But Chesterton and Conan Doyle? Nothing.

The only documented occasion of Doyle and Chesterton actually meeting was a case where they just happened to be in the same room with other literary notables. There is no record that the two even spoke with each other.

What was the reason for their non-friendship, their non-relationship? Did Doyle consider Chesterton a literary rival? Chesterton, after all, had created a rival detective to Sherlock Holmes, a character about as opposite as Holmes as possible. Holmes – the super-sleuth, the professional consulting detective, the logical machine with an encyclopedia inside his head – was quite the contrary to the dumpy, meek, nearly unnoticeable priest with the battered umbrella, who managed to be able to solve crimes by simply noticing what others didn't see even if they were staring straight at it. And to make the contrast complete, Father Brown was merely an amateur detective. No, let's make it even more complete: Holmes, the super-sleuth, had a super-villain as an arch-nemesis and an apparent dunderhead as a sidekick. Father Brown caught a master thief more than once and not only conquered him but converted him and made *him* his sidekick. Dr. Moriarty was unrepentant evil. Flambeau was a repented sinner who had the joy of reforming.

Chesterton loved detective fiction and defended it as a significant literary art form, and even defended the popular literary taste for it. "*A love of puzzles exists,*" says Chesterton, "*and men are justified in gratifying it either in mathematics or in murders.*" Critics might look down their noses at the masses who prefer bad detective stories to fine subtle and suggestive novels, but as Chesterton points out, the public also prefers good detective stories to bad detective stories, which is why Sherlock Holmes became a giant. Chesterton was a great admirer of Holmes and rightly predicted that the character would be immortal, bursting out of the pages with a life of his own, popular long past his own era. Though he is an impossible person with impossible powers, the reading public could not get enough of him because the stories succeed not just as stories, but as great literature. Conan Doyle obviously understood how addiction works. He not only makes Holmes a drug addict, he makes addicts out of all of Holmes's fans, who always need another fix from Dr. Watson. But Doyle seemed to have little affection for Holmes, and even less for detective fiction. It may explain Holmes's own lack of warmth. The author even went so far as dispose of his own child, as it were, throwing him over a waterfall and finishing him off. But he was essentially forced by his fans to bring Holmes back to life.

Ironically, Father Brown also went through a resurrection. And he had to solve the problem of his own murder, but more importantly prove that his revival wasn't miraculous. His return proved very useful to Chesterton, as he continued to write Father Brown stories to pay printing bills for his struggling paper, *G.K.'s Weekly*. The priest's continued popularity was due in part to his "incredulity" – that is, his solutions to crimes that seemed to have no natural explanation, that caused characters who were skeptics and agnostics to embrace the supernatural with alarming speed. It was Father Brown who brought them back to earth and pointed out the paradox that men who won't believe in God are willing to believe in anything.

Father Brown ushered in all manner of amateur sleuths, that "right person in the wrong place" who turns up just when needed to solve a mystery. But more importantly, he represents the advent of the underdog detective, the antithesis of Holmes. Sherlock Holmes is a super-hero. We expect him to solve the crime, and the more improbable the case – and the solution – the better. With Father Brown, we're not so sure he's up to it. Like the other characters in the stories, we barely notice when he makes his entrance, and we are more puzzled by him than impressed. Then comes the surprise. When he unveils the solution, we are not only startled at how prosaic it is, but how we could possibly have missed it. Chesterton excels at telling us what we already know while giving us the sensation that we are hearing it for the first time.

While both Holmes and Brown are master mystery solvers, they are complete contraries in nearly every other respect, from the

11

former's eccentric egoism to the latter's homespun humility. However, there is one surprising characteristic they share: They are both celibate. While the priest has taken a religious vow to that effect, the professional consulting detective steers clear of love and emotion so as not to let it interfere with his logic. But Chesterton points out that the only time Holmes is beaten, it is by a woman, because he does not know if a certain man is her fiancé or her lawyer. *"If he had been in love he might have known well enough."*

Holmes claims to stick purely to logic and facts, but Father Brown, still ever observant of material clues, also has a deep experience of human psychology. Where does this come from? How about from hearing confessions? Ironically, the only advantage Father Brown has as a detective is the one thing that everyone else considers a handicap: He is a Catholic priest. He always solves the crime, but is more interested in saving sinners than punishing criminals. For Holmes it is a game. For Father Brown, the consequences are eternal. But it makes the tales no less amusing.

If the two detectives are different to the point of being nearly opposites, so are their creators. Arthur Conan Doyle was born and raised Roman Catholic, but abandoned any credal faith on his way to becoming an ardent Spiritualist. G.K. Chesterton was not born into a credal faith, dabbled in Spiritualism as a young man, and then became a Christian before becoming a devout Catholic.

Since the two famous writers moved in precisely opposite directions, there was bound to be a collision. And sure enough, this is why there was no friendship between the two men. The fact is, Doyle did not like Chesterton because Chesterton did not like Spiritualism. As a well-known journalist, Chesterton was an outspoken critic of Spiritualism and penned several articles condemning it, not because he didn't believe in spirits, but because he did. He was not bothered by charlatans who staged séances and such, but he was genuinely concerned about the danger that comes from cavorting with demons. Very few people realize that this was a place where Chesterton had been before he came to Christianity. And he wrote a successful play in 1913 called *Magic*, a comedy with a serious undertone, where a conjurer performs tricks assisted by real spirits.

In 1924, he gave a speech in Brighton at the Brighton Dome, where he offered some lively criticisms about communicating with the dead, to a mixed crowd of Catholics and hostile Spiritualists. A month later, Conan Doyle gave a speech in the same location, criticizing Chesterton and defending Spiritualism. In 1927, in *G.K.'s*

Weekly, Chesterton wrote a sharp criticism of Doyle's book on Spiritualism, *Phineas Speaks.* Doyle fired off an angry letter to the editor complaining that Chesterton had misrepresented Doyle's views of Irish Catholicism, claiming that Chesterton had portrayed Doyle as saying something he had never said. Chesterton, very respectfully, replied and apologized for giving any offense, but then took the opportunity to present a clear analysis of Doyle's actual words. It is an insightful look at "tolerance" and at Spiritualism. No mention of Holmes. However, in 1926, in *The Illustrated London News*, Chesterton wrote about the fact that Holmes never succumbed to Spiritualism, while another of Doyle's characters did: Professor Edward Challenger, the adventurer who discovered dinosaurs in *The Lost World* and then discovered spirits in *The Land of Mists.* His transition from Skepticism to Spiritualism is utterly unconvincing, and the novel was one of Doyle's great literary failures, much to his distress.

We should add that Chesterton also wrote a short parody where Professor Challenger is deceived at a séance by a fake medium who, unveiling his disguise, is none other than Sherlock Holmes. In contrast to Chesterton using Holmes to make a fool of his own literary creator, Father Brown paid tribute to G.K. Chesterton. Father John O'Connor, the inspiration for the character of the literary sleuth, wrote a book called *Father Brown on Chesterton.*

We can puzzle over Conan Doyle's Spiritualism, just as there are many who put off by Chesterton's Catholicism, but each time we read either author, we are, one could argue, communicating with the dead. And both wrestled not only with the mystery of death, but the greater mystery of life. According to G.K. Chesterton, *"The universe presents the cryptogramic wonder of a detective story; but with this difference, that the secret is not a hidden crime, but a hidden kindness."*

Dale Ahlquist,
President
The Society of Gilbert Keith Chesterton
January 2023

The Detective
and
The Clergyman
* * * * *
The Adventures of
Sherlock Holmes
and
Father Brown

The Adventure of the
Uncommitted Murder
by Brett Fawcett

*"But [Gilbert and I] did agree that industrial disputes
would never end so long as dividends were the aim of
industry; because wages also are a dividend, and the
work-man's two hands were his investment in the
concern and much more a part of him than my loose cash
is of me . . . But obedience unto death is the soldier's
claim to everlasting life, and is the political arm of the
Cross; whilst care for the poor and indulgence of their
shortcomings is the Economic or Social arm of the
Cross."*

– Father John O'Connor
Father Brown on Chesterton

On the morning of February 13, 1889, after attending Mass and
taking tea at the Theological College of St. George's, Inspector Sam
Brown paid a visit to Mr. Sherlock Holmes. The homily was full of
warnings against falling into evil. Inspector Brown was now on a
mission to try to stop an evil from occurring.

As he traveled through the winter slush of London towards
Baker Street, Brown scratched his mustache and thought idly about
the last time he had seen Holmes. It had been a month or so earlier,
at the marriage celebration of that couple Brown met during the
surreal case of the Agra treasure. Something at Mass had vaguely
reminded Brown of the Watson wedding. His mind wandered over
the scenes from that day: The liturgy itself, the other policemen who
were present, the street urchins inexplicably seated in the front rows,
the pleasant dark-haired lady with the Scottish accent and her flaxen-
haired husband with his noble bearing and a distant look in his eyes.
Brown felt he had nearly hit upon the connection when he arrived at
221b.

While ascending the stairs, the burly, round-faced detective
reflected on an earlier occasion when he had met with Holmes. It
was a few years prior, shortly after Brown's brother, John, had begun
seminary. John was over at the inspector's house for tea when

Holmes had stopped by to thank Brown for directing him towards an interesting case which he was happy to report he had just solved. During the conversation, John had asked Holmes some penetrating questions about the nature of the evils that he had encountered in his work. The two men had conversed with such animation and comfort in each other's presence that Brown wondered if his brother had met the consulting detective before that day, though he had forgotten to ask. As he entered the flat, he wondered idly how well Holmes remembered that conversation.

The burly, round-faced detective found Holmes reading *The Times* with a look of transcendent weariness. The paper was monopolized by news of the strikes at the Carson and Conroy Artificial Kneecap Manufactory on King Edward Street. Inspired by the matchgirl protests the previous year, the factory floor's workers had taken to the streets to denounce its unsafe and inhumane working conditions. The strike came on the heels of well-publicized rumours of conflict between Lemuel Conroy and Harold Carson, the manufactory's co-owners who had famously made their fortunes as pioneers in the artificial limb industry.

"Quite dreary, isn't it, Brown?" Holmes remarked, looking up from the paper. "All the human suffering and injustice of crime, without the stimulation to the imagination which crime can sometimes provide."

"As it happens, Mr. Holmes," Brown said in the careful and deliberate way which was his manner, "there may indeed be a crime associated with those demonstrations that just hasn't happened yet."

Holmes's look of resignation immediately transformed into an expression of fiery interest. "Do tell, Brown! I only regret that Watson has abandoned us for married life and isn't here to take notes."

Brown settled into an armchair while Holmes rose to fetch the Persian slipper on the mantel. "I recently apprehended a unique kind of murderer, Mr. Holmes: A man who kills, not out of any personal animosity, but because someone hired him to do it."

Holmes nodded, digging tobacco out of the slipper with his pipe. "The assassin-by-contract. I have reason to suspect there are several such agents operating in the city."

"According to Paisley – that's the fellow I caught – you're right. The killing for which we arrested him is already solved – a sad case, that, but now all cleaned up. What brought me here was something he told us as he was being charged. When he realized his goose was cooked, he started sharing information with us. Maybe he

20

hopes that helping us catch other crooks will induce The Crown to grant him some kind of leniency. Maybe he's just hoping this will wash some of the blood off his hands."

"Either way, it's very obliging of him."

"He indicated exactly what you said, sir: There are others like him out there doing contract killings, and he suspects one of them has been hired to do a job two days from now."

Holmes puffed his pipe. Behind the smoke, his eyes shone like embers.

"Here's the story: Paisley was known to hang around the Castledown Tavern. If you wanted to hire him, your best shot was to try and find him there. Last week, a man he'd never seen before comes into the bar, sits down next to him, and tells him there's a person he needs to be rid of. He mentions that he specifically needs someone like Paisley because of his skill at breaking into, and out of, buildings without being noticed."

"A helpful detail."

"Now Paisley doesn't do work blindfolded, so he demands to know what this person did to deserve death, after warning this stranger that he knows how to spot a lie. After some grousing, the man tells Paisley that this victim has been bankrolling the kneecap strikers, and he wants them gone before the strikes end up succeeding. Paisley then asks if the job is to be done at the victim's home or at their workplace. At this point, the stranger gets *truly* irritated. That question is irrelevant, he snaps. Does Paisley want the job or not? He can offer half the money up front. After doing the job, Paisley'll need to bring the client an artifact of the killing to prove it came off successfully, and he'll get paid the rest then. Paisley asks, when does it need to be done? February 15th at eight in the evening, the man says. Paisley has to turn it down. He already has – eh – an *arrangement* for that night."

"One it appears you've prevented him from keeping."

"Thank God for that. Anyhow, the client loses his temper, checks his pocket watch, and storms out of the tavern. Paisley said this fellow seemed pretty bent on this assassination happening, and was sure he'd have hired someone else to do the job by now."

"But he never caught the names of either his potential client or his potential victim?"

Brown shook his head apologetically, as if Paisley's failure to learn these details was somehow his fault.

"So," declared Holmes, "I have a murder to solve before it occurs, and I need to identify not only the murderer, but also the

21

victim – and on a deadline, at that!" There was an unmistakable thrill in his voice. "Let's press further, Brown. How did Paisley describe this stranger?"

Brown pulled out a notebook and read aloud in his methodical fashion. "Clean-shaven, thinning hair, balding, long, dark raincoat. His watch was ocean blue and engraved with what looked like lions' heads and crosses."

Holmes was already on his feet. "This may all be so much vapour, Brown – misdirection by Paisley meant to waste the time of the policeman who nabbed him – but I shall look into this matter and see if there is any fire lurking behind the smoke. Would you kindly visit this time again tomorrow?"

Brown nodded stolidly, shook Holmes's hand, and left the flat. Five minutes later, Holmes had also disappeared from his home. In his place stood a slightly chubby manual labourer with scraggly hair and oil stains on both his clothing and his face.

This disheveled worker was soon on King Edward Street, drifting through the indignant, thickening crowd in front of the Carson and Conroy Manufactory. In front of the factory gates, a makeshift platform had been built out of Carson and Conroy shipping crates. Isaac Burgess, the factory foreman who had emerged as the *de facto* leader of the striking workers, was delivering a speech from atop this pulpit.

Burgess was a lean, muscular man in dirty overalls. His chiseled face and huge arms were covered with stains, scars, and pockmarks, and his voice warbled with sadness as he described the way loyal employees were treated in the building behind him. When he called for the workers to share ownership of the factory with Carson and Conroy, he broke into tears, and the audience erupted into riotous applause. Violent revolution seemed to simmer beneath the surface of the cheering crowd.

The dirty labourer looked around. He quickly deduced that the spectators were a collection of aggrieved factory workers, undercover policemen, curious academics, journalists, radicals of the Anarchist, Communist, and Georgist varieties – and a wide-eyed young man in a cassock, whose vacant expression suggested he was lost. The worker realized he recognized this young man as John Brown, the brother of Inspector Sam Brown. Based on his experience of the seminarian, the worker inferred that John was likely here for the same reason that he was.

Burgess dismounted the stack of boxes and was replaced by Thomas Dunn, the representative of the Socialist League. There was something of the essence of an Old Testament prophet about Dunn, who angrily denounced the factory's abuses as a classic example of the evils that inevitably flow from the existence of private property and demanded that the government nationalize the artificial kneecap industry. His long, thick beard swung violently as his furious speech practically became a fire-and-brimstone sermon. Next, the graceful but forceful Anne Flavel, whose hair and clothing were as immaculate as her precise and measured manner of speaking, ascended the podium to lament the many mistreatments of women on the factory floor and to insist to her hearers on the necessity of the suffragette movement. This received a mixed reaction from the audience.

As she spoke, the shabby-looking worker looked intently over the facade of the factory. Even from his distant position on the street, he could see a fat, ornately dressed man glowering down at the crowds from a high office window. If he was not mistaken – and he was not – the worker recognized this as being the notorious Lemuel Conroy himself.

When Flavel's speech ended, some of the crowd dispersed, including the cherubic cleric, who wandered inexplicably into a high-end hair salon, and the worker, who headed towards St. Paul's.

There are two things to consider here, the labourer reasoned. *One is that, for an enterprise to be bankrolled, it must have a bank. With whom would the organizers of this protest manage their finances? Not one of the major banks. Those are too tied up with industry to want to be associated with economic radicalism. No, they would seek out an institution with goals similar to its own.*

Thus, he found himself in the Co-operative Wholesale Society Bank, a stone's throw from the manufactory.

The second point, he continued to himself as he approached the nearest clerk, *is that this donor obviously wishes to remain anonymous. This can be used to my advantage.*

"Isaac B'rgess sent me," he stated coarsely but confidently. The clerk gave a slight nod.

My first supposition is confirmed.

"There's some confusi'n in our accountin' books," the worker continued, "an' we need to make sure our numb'rs are all c'rrect. I need to look't a recent cheque 'ssued to us and ens're we got the fig're on it right."

"Which cheque would that be, sir?"

The worker's face assumed a knowing expression as he looked the clerk squarely in the eyes and lowered his voice to answer:

23

"The big 'un, sir. The 'un from *that* don'r."

After a pause, the clerk gave another small nod, glanced around the bank, and headed into a back room.

And my second supposition was also correct.

The clerk returned with an envelope from which he gingerly removed a cheque. "I cannot let you handle this, sir, but you may look and confirm the information on it."

The worker turned his intense gaze upon the cheque, focusing solely on the signature. It was nearly illegible, but he was soon able to discern the surname.

"It was *Whitney*," Holmes announced.

Brown was sipping coffee when he heard this. At that moment, something unlocked in his mind.

"You will," continued Holmes, "recall having met Mr. Isa Whitney at Watson's wedding, his wife Kate having known Watson's wife Mary since their school days in Edinburgh. He is a barrister, and is well-known as something of a generous patron, whether that be for eleemosynary societies, construction projects, or, on occasion, the Tory Party. He thus recommends himself as a candidate for our mysterious victim – someone who gives money to pet causes, but who would have reason to conceal any pro-labour sympathies he may have adopted.

"I paid a call to their home in the afternoon. Whitney was not there, despite normal work hours having ended, but Mrs. Whitney was, and she somewhat nervously admitted me into the house. When I asked where her husband could be, she was initially hesitant to say anything, but when informed he could be in danger, she admitted that he had been spending a great deal of his private time associating with people he refused to tell her anything about. He also does not tell her where he goes, but even though they live in the West End, and his law firm is in the north, I noted soil upon their carpet that bore the odour and appearance of mud from the docks on the East End. Finally, while his study displays several awards testifying to his various benevolent contributions, his bookshelf also reveals that he has been immersed in some rather transgressive and occultic literature, and I observed some accouterments of pagan ritual discreetly secreted amongst his personal effects.

"Unfortunately," concluded Holmes, raising his own coffee to his lips, "although we have less than two days to rescue Mr. Whitney, that is all we have for now."

"It may not be, Mr. Holmes," remarked Brown finally.

24

Holmes looked up and lowered his coffee. "Oh?"

"Well," Brown said, shifting in his seat, "it's rather a long shot. You know that my brother, John, is a seminarian at St. George's. In fact, he was just raised to the order of transitional deacon. The principal there is named Father Elias Whitney. When I visited yesterday and heard Mass from Father Whitney, something about him struck me as familiar. Now I recognize what it was: He looked for all the world like a stouter version of Mr. Isa Whitney. I wonder whether they couldn't be relations, and whether we couldn't tell us anything that might help."

Holmes set down his coffee cup. "And you have chosen to share the details of this case with your brother?" he asked pointedly.

Brown started in his chair. "How did you know that?"

Holmes relaxed a bit and chuckled. "It was a less impressive deduction than yours, Inspector. I observed your priest-to-be of a sibling at the picket line and inferred that he was also investigating our future murder, which would only be possible if you had told him about it. In any event, besides sharing physical features, I know you also share a penchant for crime solving."

Brown smiled sheepishly. "Actually, sir, although police work runs in our family, I sometimes think that, while I may have a detective's job, he's the one with a detective's mind. You know that his advice has been invaluable to us more than once. In fact, I never would have caught Paisley if it hadn't been for my brother's observations."

Holmes looked thoughtful. "There seems to be a great deal of coincidental consanguinity in this case. But then, Providence does occasionally sprinkle such seasoning on human affairs. Well, Inspector, since it sounds as if you'll be appraising your brother about our progress anyhow, perhaps it is most efficient if I join you on a visit to St. George's and have a word with Father Whitney – and, of course, with your saintly brother."

"My son, one of the best practices of the medievals – you see this particularly in Aquinas – is the habit of common sense definition that is nevertheless rich in spiritual insight."

Holmes and Brown were still in the hallway of the seminary when they heard these words booming from the principal's office.

"Take the umbrella. What is it, literally speaking? The most succinct and pragmatic definition is that it is 'a portable roof'. Can you improve on this description? But now think about the definition of a roof. It is a shelter, which, by its very presence, creates a place of its own. We could thus further call the umbrella 'a portable place'. Does this remind you of anything, Paul? It is like the tabernacle of the Hebrews: The house of God, but a house that *moved*, and which, like the umbrella, promised constant protection against the dangers of this wild world – Ah, your brother has brought us a visitor!"

The office which Brown and Holmes entered was like a monastic cell in its austerity and sanctity: The walls were bare, save for a crucifix and a bookshelf stuffed with medieval treatises and papal encyclicals. Off to the side was a bed, the only indication that this office was also where its occupant lived. Brown knew his brother lived in a similarly austere but academic bedroom.

Behind the office's desk stood a golden-haired priest. He resembled a bulkier and livelier version of Isa Whitney, and was wielding his closed umbrella like a Crusader's sword. In front of the desk sat the short, blank-looking seminarian Holmes had seen at the picket line. Despite the contrast between their relative sizes, the facial resemblance between him and the Scotland Yarder was obvious.

"Mr. Holmes, this is Father Elias Whitney. You know my brother, Deacon John – though some call him by the name of his patron saint, Paul." He smiled. Deacon John Brown, who wore a smile that was identical to the inspector's, rose to embrace his brother before ensuring that the two guests were comfortably seated.

"What brings you here?" asked Father Whitney heartily, setting the umbrella on his desk.

"Would you, by chance," asked Inspector Brown in his plodding manner, "happen to be a relation of Isa Whitney?"

The melancholy that descended on Father Whitney's face was subtle but unmistakable.

"My dear brother," he answered, a little less enthusiastically.

Holmes sensed the emotion and sprung upon it. "We fear your brother may be in danger," he announced, "and are hoping you may be of assistance in rescuing him."

Father Whitney looked down and sighed. "He *is* in danger – from opium. He's been dabbling in it ever since his college days, when he read about it in De Quincey, a writer to whom he is utterly devoted. Whenever I see him, his appearance, his mannerisms, and even his comments cause me to fear he is using it more frequently and more recklessly. He'll never admit it to me, of course – he's far too proud for that – and I fear that this refusal to admit his problem and seek the necessary help will be his undoing."

Holmes and Brown shared a look.

26

"That is lamentable to hear, Father," said Holmes. "His literary tastes do run to the extreme. I observed he had been recently perusing De Quincey, as well as de Sade, Nietzsche, Blavatsky, the Decadents – a veritable library of the shocking. He was also in possession of some . . . religious material of a rather pre-Christian nature. But we believe he may be in peril from yet another source. It seems someone wants to kill him tomorrow evening."

Father Whitney's expression was now one of sorrow mixed with puzzlement.

"It seems," volunteered Brown, trying to pick his words carefully, "that, despite his position as a pillar of the community, all that bizarre literature has turned him into a political radical, and he's started putting money into revolutionary causes, like the kneecap strike. Someone wants to put a stop to that."

Now it was Deacon Brown who looked utterly perplexed. "No, no," he murmured. "That can't possibly be . . . ."

"What can't, Brother?" asked Brown.

"Hmm?" asked Deacon Brown, who seemed for a moment to have forgotten the presence of his guests. "Oh – isn't it obvious? It beggars imagination that Isa Whitney would have become any kind of left-winger."

"Do you know the man?" Holmes asked, his eyes as sharp and piercing as Deacon Brown's were wide and empty.

"No more than what you've told me, sir, but that was more than enough to make it clear he would have had no interest in a revolution. The revolutionary tends to be an ascetic who rejects the world and devotes himself utterly to change, while all these writers were nothing short of reactionary.

"People have gotten the queer idea into their heads that decadence and witchcraft lead one to reject the old social order. On the contrary, the Bohemian is the ultimate conservative. Only someone who enjoys the world as it currently is permits himself the leisure of self-indulgence. De Quincey himself was among the most unshakable of Tories, and don't you remember that de Sade was a Marquis? As for paganism, the classical pagans were the most elitist and most conservative group one could imagine. St. Augustine had to defend Christianity's revolutionary and democratic character against them. There's no reason we should expect the new pagans to be any different."

Deacon Brown turned to Father Whitney. "Your brother, as I understand it, is an aristocrat in status as well as in spirit. Nothing our friends have told us suggests anything to the contrary. He may

27

be many things, but, from what I have heard today, he is certainly no hypocrite."

Inspector Brown smiled appreciatively at this. Father Whitney's face continued to be an unreadable mixture of emotions. Holmes looked slightly irritated, but also thoughtful.

"An interesting perspective," he finally grumbled, before adding aloud, "Is there anything else you can tell us about your brother, Father Whitney?"

"Nothing likely to be of use to your investigation, Mr. Holmes. I will say this: The British Empire and the industries it produced made the Whitney family wealthy generations ago. In my experience, those of us who inherit wealth and manage to keep our consciences well-formed often feel a certain degree of guilt, and we each respond to it differently. Some feel a sense of *noblesse oblige* and try to use their money for others. Isa is the perfect example of this. Others hate being rich and attempt to rip themselves out of that world. But when one is accustomed to a certain level of comfort and luxury, it is almost impossible to really rid oneself of it. After all," he added, gesturing around at his spartan cell, "look at what I've had to do.

"That's really all I can tell you, I'm afraid, but be assured I will be praying for your investigation."

At this, everyone rose.

"Do let us know if anything else occurs to you," said Holmes to Father Whitney, "hopefully before tomorrow."

"We shall," answered Deacon Brown.

The seminarian led the investigators out of the office and down the hall. Father Whitney waited for their footsteps to fade before solemnly taking a document from his desk, exiting down the opposite end of the hallway, and slipping quietly out the back door of the college.

The rest of the day was eventful for all involved.

Inspector Brown went to Castledown Taverns. Interviewing the staff and the regular patrons served to confirm that the man who approached Paisley had only entered the bar once and had not been back since. Brown then spent the rest of the day interrogating various police informants in search of any kind of lead, all to no avail. That afternoon, in desperation, he visited his father at Laburnum Lodge. Josiah Brown had not only enjoyed a long and distinguished career as a detective for the Metropolitan Police before he retired, but also had a kindly manner about him which John had largely inherited. The elder Brown offered his son some tea and some consoling words, and the two prayed a rosary together for the intention that the case would be solved.

Sherlock Holmes visited several watchmakers and jewelers. When he had found what he was looking for, he headed to the east-side wharves, where he prowled the alleys and questioned the locals until, once again, he found what he was looking for.

Deacon Brown spent the rest of the morning working on a translation assignment for his Latin class. By noon, Father Whitney had returned to St. George's, and the seminarian was able to ask his permission to read some texts listed on the Index of Prohibited Books. Having received this permission, he left the seminary and spent the afternoon in cheap bookstores.

In a factory office filled with rare art and gold-plated appliances, Harold Carson made a decision: If the strikers did not return to work by the weekend, he would reach out to Isaac Burgess to meet in his mansion and discuss a settlement the following week. He had already contacted Burgess and his organization twice about this possibility – privately, for he knew Conroy would have no tolerance for any negotiation with his ungrateful underlings. Now, Carson would wait and see if the strike would last long enough for such a negotiation to be necessary.

In a dark, unknown room, a long-faced, short-bearded assassin sharpened his dagger.

Both Browns were at Baker Street the following morning. They found Holmes examining a dark blue pocket watch covered in stylized iconography, his smouldering pipe clenched between his teeth.

"An 1863 Patek," Holmes said without looking up. "Almost certainly the kind of watch Paisley saw his client use. One of the most expensive watches on the market. Yet for all that, not rare enough that one can cobble together a convenient short list of those who may have purchased one. We know this client is a man of means, and not much more."

Deacon Brown walked tentatively up to the watch, leaned over, looked at it closely, turned to Holmes, and remarked, "But we *do* know more than that, don't we?"

Holmes straightened and looked down at the seminarian. "*Do* we?"

Deacon Brown looked up meekly at the tall detective.

"Based on what I've read in manuals for confessors, I'd say we know quite a bit."

29

Brown wondered if the way Holmes was puffing on his pipe expressed impatience or contemplation.

"One of the great sins of our day," Deacon Brown explained, "is vainglory: The inordinate desire to be praised by others. This is so often why people purchase expensive and ornate goods rather than their less-expensive counterparts. They wish to be *seen* to be wealthy, and to win respect for it. This sin especially afflicts the *nouveau riche*: Those who are not used to being rich or respected, but who have convinced themselves they earned their wealth by their own merits and the sweat of their brow, and are thus entitled to the adoration of their neighbours. Vainglory may have sent even more capitalists to Hell than greed has. But our murderer did not flaunt his watch. Mr. Paisley said he only briefly glimpsed it. No – I don't think a capitalist in the grips of vainglory is our culprit. If that watch's owner were recently wealthy, he would surely display it for all to see."

"Unless he wanted to conceal who he was," offered Inspector Brown.

Deacon Brown furrowed his brows. "Perhaps . . . perhaps. But then why did he take no steps to hide his face? No mask, no scarf, not even turning up the lapels of his raincoat . . . a very unusual way to conceal one's identity. Perhaps he had a reason for hiding his watch, but I do not think that reason was that it was part of a disguise. Not a disguise for Mr. Paisley's sake, anyhow . . . ."

Brown scratched his mustache. Holmes blew a smoke ring, then remarked, "At best, that observation moves us away from some possibilities, but not one whit closer to any others. Fortunately, we have two-thirds of the puzzle in hand: We know who the victim will be, and we know when the assassination is scheduled to take place this evening. My investigations yesterday were not altogether fruitless: I was able to ascertain that Isa Whitney frequents The Bar of Gold opium den in Upper Swandom Lane. Mr. Paisley remarked that the question of whether the slaying would be at the victim's home or his workplace was irrelevant. Presumably, this was because it would happen at neither location. Thus, The Bar of Gold is where we will need to be at eight this evening. I will expect to see you there, Inspector, though make sure you also station a man at Whitney's home to be extra safe. If an assassin does materialize, we will be ready to apprehend him, and subsequently hope that he will betray his employer in exchange for leniency."

As the two Browns stepped out onto Baker Street, Deacon Brown turned to his brother with a confused look.

30

"Sam," he asked, "why is Mr. Holmes speaking as if we don't know who the murderer is?"

Isa Whitney, awash in the sickly light of a flickering oil lamp, was languorously draped over one of the low berths that lined the walls of The Bar of Gold. His deflated and pitiful appearance, like those of the other patrons that lounged around the opium den, was a far cry from the debonair figure he cut at the Watson wedding. He stared at the ceiling while a listless hum of intoxicated gibbering droned from every corner of the building. Across from him, and watching him carefully through the curtain of pungent smoke that hung in the air, was an overweight, disheveled labourer, who crouched on his own berth like a hunter waiting in a jungle bush.

The monotonous buzz of the place was broken by the sounds of loud coughing and stumbling as someone new came into the room and clumsily set himself down next to the worker. Despite the incongruity of his clerical outfit, the newcomer's large, vacant eyes made him seem somehow at home among the den's intoxicated patrons.

"Sam apologizes that he couldn't make it, Mr. Holmes," Deacon Brown whispered, still nearly wheezing.

Holmes raised an eyebrow. "Is my disguise unconvincing?" he whispered back.

"Oh, it's very good, sir," the deacon answered, still in hushed tones, "and I'd never have known it was you, except that I was looking for Mr. Whitney already, and noticed a man watching him who I also observed watching people at the picket line the other day. I suppose you could say I gambled on it being you."

"Hmm. So where *is* Inspector Brown?"

"He is, regrettably, preoccupied with arresting the murderer."

Whitney gave a slight moan and turned over on his bunk. Holmes chuckled in a way that was not quite a scoff.

"Your pastoral counsel must have been quite astute for him to have gleaned that information from it. Perhaps you'd deign to share it with me."

The seminarian pulled out a pair of spectacles from somewhere in his cassock. When he put them on, his eyes seemed even bigger than before. Enveloped in opium smoke, he looked like a priestly owl, perched among the forest fog.

"Well, Mr. Holmes," he began, "I was bothered right away by the fact that Paisley's client seemed to have taken no steps to hide his appearance when he approached him in the tavern. Surely, one

31

of the reasons a man hires an assassin to do his killing for him is so that he cannot be connected to the crime. But if so, why would he display himself so openly when discussing the crime in a public place?

"I am no detective, Mr. Holmes. My vocation simply calls for me to do my best to understand human motives. This was why I went to the picket line: I was trying to understand the motives of everyone involved. I find people are surprisingly open about what they want, and what they love.

"The other thing that troubled me was how the client would have known about a secret donor to the protesters in the first place. This is why I doubted our culprit was a capitalist, even before you discovered the evidence of the watch. I was sure he must have been someone involved in the protests – involved enough that he knew their success was imminent. I suppose that was also in my mind: To try to spot anything suspicious among the people criticizing the factory.

"And I did, Mr. Holmes. Surely you noticed it, too? It was the *speeches*. They were at odds with each other. Mr. Burgess was calling for private property to be more justly shared – for the workers to own the factory just as much as Messrs. Carson and Conroy did. But Mr. Dunn of the Socialist League was calling for an end to *all* private property. He didn't want the workers to own the factory any more than he wanted the capitalists to own the factory. As far as he was concerned, only the government should be allowed to own anything productive. If Mr. Burgess' strike had succeeded, it would have utterly thwarted Mr. Dunn's political goals – which were clearly as important to him as my own faith is to me.

"This raised two questions immediately. One was whether Mr. Dunn would have had the financial means to contract a killer for himself. The other, of course, was that he clearly seemed far from clean-shaven. But this prompted me to ask myself: What if a man were only ever seen in public with a beard? For such a person, being clean shaven *would* be a disguise: No one would recognize you without your whiskers. Suppose this were Mr. Dunn: If his beard is false, it is obviously of excellent workmanship – one of those elaborate ones made with wires – since it did not fly off his face even when his speech grew especially animated.

"This is why, as you surely noticed, I visited that rather expensive hair salon. I told them I was interested in artificial facial hair of Mr. Dunn's beard's description, and not only confirmed that a beard of that exact make exists, but that it is indeed one of their

32

pricier commodities. It costs more, you see, because special care has been taken to make it look even more like natural facial hair than their other products."

Deacon Brown coughed. "These poor souls," he murmured, looking around the room at the corpse-like shapes that littered the floor. "If only they were exposed to more of the fragrant incense and imagery of the Mass. Perhaps they wouldn't feel the need to find smoke and visions in this cruder form of mysticism."

"Perhaps you might continue," Holmes interrupted sharply.

"Oh – oh, yes. The next day, I did a little reading. Like I said, Mr. Holmes, I'm no detective. I don't know how to find the truth under a microscope, but I can occasionally find it in a book. *Who's Who* told me that Mr. Dunn came from a family of successful garment manufacturers, going back several generations. Surely you remember what Father Whitney said, Mr. Holmes: Those who inherit wealth often feel obliged to either use it for good or break with it altogether, but it is as hard to break an addiction to luxury as it is to break an addiction to opium, particularly without the aid of Grace. Dunn, in other words, was exactly the sort of person to purchase the most expensive watch on the market, but also to utterly resent himself for it and feel no need to let others know he owned it, just as he was the sort of man who would spend a great deal of money to acquire the most formidable false facial hair he could find, and even spend a bit extra to ensure it was so convincing that no one would ever guess that he had that sort of money to spend. I also purchased a few copies of this . . . ."

Deacon Brown fished in his cassock pockets and pulled out a thick pamphlet. On the front page, the title – *The Pathway to the Great Socialist Synthesis* – was printed in enormous font. On the back page, a photograph of Thomas Dunn had been printed above the text crediting him as the author.

"Mr. Dunn's frankness was very helpful to me in my research," he commented. "He explains here that, to achieve true socialism, the outrage of the workers against the abuses of their employers must be stoked, and given no outlet other than revolution. Any compromise with capital, or its owners, is a digression from the straight and narrow path towards a truly communal society, and cannot be tolerated by any socialist worth his salt. He is also, incidentally, no great lover of religion. He views it as a tool of oppression of the working class, and expresses special contempt for clergy. As I said, Mr. Holmes: People are often honest about their motives."

Holmes took the pamphlet and scrutinized the photograph with a magnifying lens he produced from his breast pocket.

"Truthfully, Mr. Holmes, all this only confirmed what I already learned at the picket line. But even revelation asks to be supplemented by reason. I was very sure from reading this of why Mr. Dunn would involve himself in the kneecap protests, while also doing everything he could to ensure their failure."

"It *is* a false beard," Holmes said, half to himself, as he passed back the pamphlet.

Deacon Brown nodded. "I gave another copy of this pamphlet, and this photograph, to Sam, and he made a few trips with it. He first went to the hair salon I visited, and confirmed that Mr. Dunn was one of their clients. With their help, he was able to produce a sketch of Mr. Dunn without his beard. When he saw that drawing, Mr. Paisley confirmed that it was an accurate likeness of the man he had met in Castledown Taverns. Just to be sure – Sam was always very thorough – he even tracked down the jewellry store which sold Mr. Dunn his Patek watch. That, I believe, was enough to arrest him on suspicion, and, once you catch the assassin and have his testimony, Sam suspects we will have enough evidence to satisfy even the most incredulous jury."

Holmes stared into the pungent smoke. It was not clear if he was reacting to what he had just heard, or if he was thinking about something else.

Deacon Brown coughed a bit and waved the pamphlet, trying to fan away the noxious fumes. "A strange place for a future priest to be," he remarked, "but then, Our Lord Himself was attacked for associating with drunkards."

Holmes sat upright.

"Brown," he asked abruptly, "did you have any trouble getting in here?"

"Why, no. I imagine, like many profit-oriented businesses, they're happy to let *anyone* in."

"Then why," asked Holmes, his voice becoming grave, "did Dunn want a killer who was skilled at break-ins?"

He turned to Brown sharply. "Paisley said Dunn told him the question of work or residence was irrelevant. That wasn't because the site of the killing was to be neither of those places. It's because it was going to be *both* – a place where the victim lived *and* worked."

A horrid comprehension filled the deacon's giant eyes.

Moments later, the two had abandoned Isa Whitney and were rushing through the darkness in a carriage towards the college of St.

George. Deacon Brown looked as crestfallen and guilty as a penitent in a confessional.

"Lord, what a turnip I am!" he nearly sobbed. "I failed to follow my reasoning through to the end. I knew that the reactionary is one who embraces the world and its pleasures, but forgot that the true revolutionary is the one who *rejects* the world and its pleasures – the ascetic, the anchorite, the monk. If the reactionary belongs to *this* world, the revolutionary belongs to another world – and who belongs more to Heaven than Father Whitney?"

He shook his head vigorously and beat his breast.

"Besides that, even though I knew Isa's reading would *not* make him zealous for economic justice, I should have realized his brother's reading *would* – no one denounces the rich more emphatically than the church fathers and the medieval scholastics. Why, Isaac Burgess was practically calling for us to go back to the guilds of the Middle Ages – exactly what Father Whitney would have supported! Oh, foolish me!"

"The mistake was equally mine," sighed Holmes, obviously disgusted with himself. "I knew *a* Whitney was the donor but decided too quickly which one it must have been. I did not even think to procure samples of their handwriting so as to compare them to what I had seen on the cheque. Father Whitney surely realized the controversy that would come from a Catholic seminary rector being associated with the strike and kept his involvement discreet for that reason. Blast me! It is a capital mistake to theorize before one has all the data . . . ."

Holmes realized how deeply sorrowful his companion looked. With an effort, he softened his voice. "But then," he added, "I believe it is an article of your church that we are none of us perfect and all are prone to failure. This is why we must be gracious towards others, but surely, by extension, it means we must have a certain measure of forgiveness for ourselves."

Deacon Brown looked mournfully contemplative for a moment before smiling sadly. "I accept your absolution," he said simply.

As the carriage pulled up to the seminary, Holmes spotted a figure in a dark jacket, both hands stuffed in his pockets, moving furtively from the back of the building. Flinging the cab door open, Holmes dove outwards and onto the man, tackling him to the ground and twisting both his arms behind his back in one fluid motion. A long knife clattered from his pocket onto the cobblestone street.

The cab came to a halt alongside the struggling pair. As the man snarled and writhed beneath Holmes, Deacon Brown could see that he was clutching a blood-splattered clerical collar.

The seminarian jumped out of the carriage and rushed into the building towards the principal's room, his tears already beginning to stream.

Father Whitney's body was seated behind his desk. A trail of blood traced red tree branches from his chest down the front of his cassock, but his lifeless face radiated peace and acceptance. His umbrella still lay on the desk. Beneath it was a note, written in the same handwriting as that on the co-operative bank's cheque.

Dearest Paul,

I hope this letter from Gethsemane finds you well.

Please forgive me for not correcting your friends' mistake about my brother being in danger, and letting them know that the killer's real target must have been myself. Isa's body and soul are in grave danger, but he refuses to admit to it. I knew that, if Mr. Holmes were to keep an eye on him, his habit would finally be exposed, and perhaps the help he needs would finally be forthcoming.

Do thank your brother and Mr. Holmes for letting me know when I was scheduled to die. The Church admonishes us to remember our mortality and live in the light of that fact, and it was a grace to be told the hour of my death in advance. Not only did it prompt me to make my last confession, it also gave me the opportunity to amend my will. The money which I renounced the use of in this life will be distributed to the poor, the workers, and the Church – particularly this seminary, to which I have devoted my life.

I have left you something, too, Paul – not money, out of respect to your commitment to poverty, but rather, my portable roof. May it always remind you of the importance of thinking clearly, and, more importantly, that the grace of God will cover you wherever you go.

Please do not be upset with me, my son. If the story of our college's patron teaches us anything, it's that the only way to truly slay a dragon is to follow the way of the cross.

I am honoured to have been your spiritual and academic director. Remember to pray for me. I shall never cease to pray for you.

Yours,
Father Elias Whitney, D.D.
Principal of the Theological College of St. George's

Deacon Brown's hand trembled slightly as he put the letter down and made the sign of the cross.

* * * * *

Postscript by
Dr. John H. Watson, M.D.

Because I was not present for the remarkable events you have just read, I did not feel qualified to narrate them for the general public. Nevertheless, there was so much of significance in this case that I have felt compelled to include these notes in my dispatch box, so that a record of it exists for historians who may find it of interest.

The assassin whom Holmes caught not only confirmed that Thomas Dunn had employed him, but also indicated that Dunn had found and hired him through a wide-ranging and powerful criminal network. Holmes immediately recognized this as further confirmation of the existence of a centrally controlled organization, the existence of which he had long suspected, and it served as another piece of solid evidence that he would later use against Professor James Moriarty, a point which may be of interest to students of Holmes's career.

Empowered by Father Whitney's bequest, the strike continued apace, eventually culminating in a resolution arrived at in conversation with Mr. Carson, who made concessions so distasteful to Mr. Conroy that the latter sold his share in the company and withdrew from it altogether. In his place, Isaac Burgess was promoted to a position of upper administration, which was equally distasteful to certain elements within the movement which had appointed him a leader. In my capacity as a medical man, I am always pleased to encounter products bearing the proud manufacturing label of *"Conroy and Burgess"*.

When I returned from honeymooning and learned about Isa Whitney's situation, I immediately volunteered to become his medical advisor, and did my best for the next several years to help him grapple with his addiction. Though there was much difficulty and tragedy ahead for him, he would always visit his brother's grave in his darkest moments, and these small pilgrimages inevitably helped him continue fighting, even when he was at his weakest. On the fifth anniversary of Father Whitney's death, Isa burned all his occultic literature and equipment in a great bonfire of the vanities, along with his opium pipe. He would die a few months afterwards – unhealthy but sober, and not before receiving the final Catholic sacraments. His widow took pains to ensure he was buried next to his brother.

John Paul Brown would go on to be ordained and serve in various ecclesiastical capacities throughout his ministry. Throughout this time, he and Holmes kept in contact with one another. Needless to say, this was not the last case which saw the two men uniting their distinct but considerable talents in the service of justice. You may have heard that Father Brown, as he is now known, has since had some adventures of his own that have attracted popular attention, and my understanding is that he is never seen in public without his umbrella.

The Dunderhurst Method
by Derrick Belanger

An unusual group of six men sat around a garden patio in what was, most often, a noiseless London neighborhood. However, on that particular day, it was not quiet. There were no sounds of birds nor hum of insects. Instead there was the endless slamming of sledge hammers against concrete, squeaky wheelbarrows removing debris, and shouts and calls from men completing hard labor. The boarding house we were situated behind was undergoing significant repairs. A new foundation was being added to the structure, and even some walls were being rebuilt in the interior. Hence all of the noise. It did not make for a pleasant afternoon.

The man seated to my right was Mr. Aristide Valentin, the head of the Paris police. He was unfathomably French and unfathomably intelligent. He had been compared to my dear friend, Sherlock Holmes, as both a thinking machine and a master of disguise. Whether the comparisons were deserved was, at least in my opinion, debatable. Yet, there was no debating that the man had a brain, nay not just a brain, but a logical mind, and he was using that mind of his to puzzle out why he was spending an afternoon at a noisy garden tea party and not in search of the treasure stolen by the noted art thief, Gerard Fontaine.

Speaking in French, (or almost shouting in French to be heard over the din of the construction) the man next to him assured Valentin that his men were still searching everywhere for the loot while we sat around the table enjoying a cup of Dharjeeling. *"Ne t'en fais pas. Le Yard est sur l'affaire. Nous trouverons l'art volé,"* said Inspector Lestrade sympathetically and reassuringly. A team of inspectors and constables from the Yard were assisting the Parisian police on the case.

Fontaine had made a series of thefts of a significant magnitude in Paris, most notably a collection of miniatures from the noted French sculptor Alec Toussant. The burglar was pursued by the Parisian and French authorities, and they almost had him, until he slipped through their grasp by crossing the English Channel. There was much heat on the man as the authorities from France and Britain pursued him. His capture seemed inevitable, but even sure bets can go awry.

39

Two nights before, the police were tipped off that Fontaine was hiding out in a warehouse on the Thames. The police made a raid, but they were spotted by a lookout as they closed in. Shots were fired and returned. In the end, two criminals were killed, one being Fontaine. The others who were captured did not know the location of the treasure. Fontaine had kept it a secret, and he had taken that secret to the grave.

Lestrade assured Valentin that the treasure would be found. Fontaine hadn't been in London for very long, and there were only so many places where he could have hidden the loot. "Don't you agree, Mr. Holmes?" he asked my colleague.

Sherlock Holmes, who was seated to my left, asked me to pass him the cream so he could add a dollop to his tea. He had taken one sip, winced ever so slightly, and was trying to make the offering as palatable as possible. The great detective had accepted the invitation to the gathering without hesitation, which, I confess, surprised me. It was because of the man who had sent the invitation that Holmes came, clearly intrigued by the offer. Holmes had been talking with the man who invited him, but was keeping one ear cocked in the direction of the officers, taking in their conversation and thinking through the possible solutions to the problem. He paused his conversation to respond to Lestrade. "Fontaine had been in London for several days. If he was clever, and it appears that he was, he could have done such a good job of hiding the treasure that it will never be discovered," Holmes was concerned with the facts, not with making the inspectors feel better. "You caught the thief, gentlemen. That was the more important matter, and while he didn't survive being captured, we no longer have to worry about his thefts anymore. If the treasure is never recovered, so be it. Toussant shall make more miniatures. Other artists will continue making art. The world will continue turning."

Nedley Dunderhurst, the host of the afternoon gathering, held his nose up to the heavens as if he could smell the entire universe through his thin nostrils. "Tut, tut, sirs. You have not read the map Toussant left for you to follow," he informed both inspector Lestrade and Mr. Valentin. "That is why you haven't found the stolen treasure."

All eyes turned to our host who had been taking notes while we sipped our tea and discussed the matter of the stolen treasure. That was the main reason we all had gathered.

"I'm sure they would like to hear your theory," said Father Brown, the man who had been conversing with Sherlock Holmes before the detective responded to Lestrade, and also the man who invited us all to this odd gathering at the Dunderhurst residence.

Father Brown was not a detective, at least not in the traditional sense of the word, but I suppose, neither was Sherlock Holmes. Brown came across a touch eccentric for a clergyman, and his methods of deduction were quite different from those of my partner who, at times, seemed to be a human calculator. Brown used intuition as much as logic to solve the cases brought to him, and while Holmes's scientific mind was less sympathetic to this method, my medical mind was understanding. While prescribing medications could help solve a patient's illness, my bedside manner, connecting with the patient on a personal level and building their trust, was equally important. There were occasions when I could see that a patient just needed to be listened to in order to begin healing. Finding that balance of determining the root cause of a malady and then prescribing a treatment often took an uncanny power that in some instances seemed like a sixth sense. Holmes would say this was just a different power of observation, and he could be correct in this assertion, but occasionally it felt as though there was a higher power at work, helping to guide my hand. The clergyman would concur that God assisted him on a number of occurrences. Holmes would scoff at such an idea. However, I think both men could be correct. Perhaps it was a power of observation, but perhaps it was also that God was working his magic in helping that power along.

But I digress.

The clergyman had brought about this gathering by simply inviting all of the attendees. He'd added a carrot to each of our invitations to reel us in. For Lestrade and Valentin, it had been the promise that Dunderhurst believed he had deduced the location of the stolen art. For me, it was a bit simpler. Brown explained that Mr. Dunderhurst, one of his parishioners, was an aspiring author who had some recent success getting published in American journals. Dunderhurst was an enthusiast of my own work and wished to meet me to discuss different approaches to writing. Brown had included clippings of two of Dunderhurst's publications. I read them and, while I felt that his characters lacked depth, his stories had intriguing plots, and I thought the man had merit. For Holmes, Brown had simply said he would find the gathering worth his time. Brown needn't explain more. Holmes trusted the clergyman and wrote back, replying that we'd both be in attendance.

41

Holmes and I had been the first to arrive at the party, Brown had made our invitation time a half-an-hour before the others so that Dunderhurst could speak with us uninterrupted.

"Gentlemen, this is quite the honor," Dunderhurst said, shaking our hands with a firm grip when he greeted Holmes and me at the door. At that point, it was a serene day. The air was filled with the sounds of nature. The construction hadn't yet started. Dunderhurst and his wife, Nancy, a nervous woman with wild curly hair that she tamed to the best of her ability by wearing it in a bun, led us to a card table they had set up in the garden. They apologized for the old table and the worn chairs that they had scraped together for the party. It was the best they could do on a short notice.

"Why not have the party indoors?" I asked.

"It's too cramped for a gathering," Dunderhurst explained. "My wife and I have separate rooms, you see. We rented the last two available in this house, and were delighted to find that they were the two smallest. I can barely squeeze myself into my diggings." Dunderhurst almost seemed to boast when he said this.

"There's also the noise," Mrs. Dunderhurst noted with a slight stammer in her voice. Her eyes looked downward and her body shifted slightly to the left and right. She resembled a mouse more than a human, the way that she fidgeted. "There will be construction beginning soon." Her eyes darted nervously to a couple of carriages parked by the curb. We saw a trio of men unloading sledgehammers, wheelbarrows, saws, and similar equipment.

"What's all this then?" I inquired.

Dunderhurst scoffed, perturbed that his wife had dared to show that she actually had a voice. "Bah, there've been issues with the house for the last week. Rats in the walls and a faulty foundation. The rent is reasonable, so I can't complain." We all winced as the first sound of a hammer hitting concrete echoed from the basement. "Well," Dunderhurst added, "I can't complain too much. As I said, I can afford two rooms here."

"Why would you need two rooms?" I asked.

Dunderhurst turned to me with an icy look of disdain. "And you call yourself a doctor," he quipped. He glanced to Holmes for sympathy, but Holmes returned his gaze with a look that could kill a man who was faint of heart.

Our host, who was as full of himself as though he was a stuffed bird, shook his head and then gave both Holmes and me a look of pity. "You both *should* be well versed in the scholarship on the subject of germs," he explained slowly as if we were two schoolboys wearing dunce caps.

"I believe we are," I replied curtly. "Though the topic is vast. I can't say that even Holmes here knows everything on the subject."

"Watson," Holmes interjected, "I believe Mr. Dunderhurst is driving at the belief that it is better to sleep in separate beds to prevent spouses from spreading germs to one another."

"And it's not just separate beds," Dunderhurst scoffed. He tilted his head up towards the sky so that his eyes could look down upon us. "That is not nearly the distance needed. No two people should cohabitate the same rooms. Separate beds won't prevent the circulation of diseases. That is why I make sure that Nancy and I sleep in separate rooms. It means that we will never do anything that would leave us the chance of spreading germs to one another." Dunderhurst gave a smug look to his wife. "It ensures that my Nancy here will never suffer because of me."

"You must be quite the loving couple," Holmes said. Dunderhurst didn't catch the sarcasm in Holmes's voice. I did, and from the way Mrs. Dunderhurst nervously tittered, I believe she did as well, though she looked saddened by my friend's comment.

"Yes, my wife and I are quite content," Dunderhurst explained. "The manager does want Nancy to stay in my room during the construction, but I won't hear of it. He ended up making space for her in the sitting room. Since no one goes in there at night, we had no concern about the spread of germs. The only people down there are the Mooreheads who have the large ground-floor flat. They are young newlyweds and have caused my wife no problems."

"But why was Mrs. Dunderhurst moved from her room?" Holmes enquired.

"It's because of the rats in the wall," Mrs. Dunderhurst explained. "I never heard them, and I usually hear everything," she frowned, "but Mr. Wilkins, the manager, sent a rat-catcher to inspect the house. He came to my room and said that the Italian fellow who was the previous renter had reported rats in the walls. That's why he left. I told him that I hadn't heard anything that sounds like a rat, but he brushed me aside and checked the walls. He was a muscular man, he was. Arms thick as tree trucks. I didn't stand in his way. He listened to the walls with what looked like a doctor's stethoscope and said he could hear them crawling about. That's why I had to leave my room for a while."

"Really, friends, you didn't come here to listen to my wife prattle on about a minor rodent problem. You came to discuss writing." Mr. Dunderhurst let out a *tsk-tsk*. "You're just as bad as Father Brown, encouraging my wife to prattle on and on."

"Father Brown was also interested, eh?" Holmes asked casually.

"Yes, the man came over when Nancy had spoken to him after Wednesday mass. He had a chat with the rat catcher. We thought Nancy would be let back into her room in a day or two, but Father Brown told her that they had found an issue with the floor of her room and that she'd have to stay in the sitting room a bit longer than that. Father offered to have Nancy stay in one of the nun's quarters, but I wouldn't hear of it. With all the poor and wretched people that nuns are around, Nancy would be sure to catch some disease from them."

I was going to point out to Dunderhurst that he and his wife, by attending church, would be privy to those same germs, but I thought starting an argument with him would be exhausting, so I kept my lips sealed.

Mr. Dunderhurst then pivoted to the reason he'd wanted us to be invited to the tea party: To discuss Holmes's and my methods. He wanted to talk with Holmes about his methods of deduction and to me about my methods of writing. For a quarter-of-an-hour, those were the topics. Mr. Dunderhurst had been published in the American magazines *Collier's Weekly* and *Harper's Weekly*, but he hadn't sold any stories to the British reading public. "My crime fiction has been my success. Any stories that involve a grisly murder finds an audience with the Americans. If only they paid me in sterling. Their dollar isn't strong enough for me to make a living on my stories alone," he complained.

I offered the man some advice, and even gave him Doyle's contact information. While I found the man to be egotistical and a bit odd, that made him no different from most authors. The man's stories were good, particularly his plots and pacing. His characters were a bit flat and stereotypical, but that played well with American audiences. I suggested that he study Dickens to learn how to flesh out characters and appeal to a British audience.

Next, Holmes gave a brief overview of his own methods and Dunderhurst made several notes in a journal. Dunderhurst looked a bit smug listening to Holmes, commenting with an occasional, "I see," or "Yes, I thought as much."

We would have spent hours, I'm sure, sitting in the garden, sipping Mrs. Dunderhurst's tea and discussing the financial market for writers if the additional guests for the party hadn't arrived. First was Father Brown himself. He had finished up with his morning services and had a gap in his schedule before his late afternoon mass.

Holmes often praised the priest as a genius. "His methods are quite different from mine, Watson," he explained to me one day after reading how Father Brown's advice had helped catch an opium ring, "but they lead to the same results. If I was a criminal, I wouldn't want that clergyman after me."

The priest joined us at the garden table and made note of the noise from the hammers smashing at the concrete basement floor. "I see they're still at it," Brown noted as he pulled up a chair and accepted a cup from Mrs. Dunderhurst.

"Oh yes, Father," Mrs. Dunderhurst complained. "They must think there are rats under the concrete."

"Rats under concrete?" Holmes asked.

"Yes. One of the men helping out is that rat-catcher." Once she said this, she gave a high-pitched squeal of a laugh. "Oh, how silly of me. Rats under concrete!" she giggled. "It must be that he works other jobs. He's certainly as big as the other men. All thick as mountains."

Mr. Dunderhurst apologized for his wife. "There goes Nancy again, coming up with her own theories. She's convinced the house is really infested with termites and not rats. That would explain all of the rooms being inspected. Of course, like rodents, termites don't eat cement."

Father Brown and Holmes laughed along with Mr. Dunderhurst. I remained quiet because I felt bad for the lady. Here she was, sleeping in a sitting room at night and spending her day surrounded by ear-splitting noise while serving her husband, who was certainly not a wealthy man.

Mrs. Dunderhurst excused herself to get the crumpets she had made to go with the tea. She winced before saying she needed to step away, and I could tell she was hurt by the laughter of the three men. Before she left, Father Brown said, "Just a moment, my dear. Did you happen to go for a walk around the grounds this morning I asked you to do?"

"Yes, Father, and it was as you surmised. There is a large animal walking the grounds, though I'm not sure what it could be. I found much of the grass by the pond flattened. I'd think a farmer was bringing his livestock to drink by the pond, but there's no farmer around here."

"I'm sure it's that mastiff," Mr. Dunderhurst explained. "Not sure who owns him. Sometimes we hear him at night howling as he runs about somewhere."

"I don't think so," Mrs. Dunderhurst replied. "He's locked up on that estate a street down."

"Well, I'm sure he gets out on occasion," Mr. Dunderhurst said in a tone as though he were talking to a toddler. "Now, why don't you run along and get the crumpets. I believe I see that the last of our guests have arrived."

That was when Lestrade and Valentin joined us, and that brings us back to the beginning of my narrative, with Mr. Dunderhurst beginning to explain his theory as to what happened to Fontaine's stolen treasures.

"It is quite simple, really," Dunderhurst began. "I'm surprised that Mr. Holmes and Father Brown did not already suggest it, though I'm not surprised that the Yard fell short. I concur with Mr. Holmes that the police, whether in Britain or France, appear to lack the imagination of a detective – or in my case, an author."

"You of course refer to Watson's writings," Holmes responded with enough acid in his voice to melt through irons. "While my friend here was accurate in my opinion in my early days of working with the Yard, that opinion is quite different than it stands today. Lestrade and Valentin have sharp minds, no doubt. I believe the case is in good hands."

"Hmph, well, I suppose then you are no better than the Yarders yourself, Mr. Holmes. Seeing as how the treasure hasn't been recovered, do me the honors of hearing out my theory – a theory I'm certain shall be proven true."

I wasn't sure how everyone would react to the brazen nature and callousness of our host, but Holmes responded, "You have our full attention, Mr. Dunderhurst. Please enlighten us. We'd love to know what happened to the treasure."

"Very well, then. It's quite elementary," he added smugly. "Look at the facts, gentlemen. We know that Fontaine was hiding out on the docks. The area is heavily guarded, and that it was his place of safety. Therefore, that is where you shall find the treasure."

"Do you think we have not thought of that?' snapped Valentin, who threw down his napkin and looked like he was about to leave. "This is a waste of time."

"Let's hear the man out," Lestrade suggested. He had grabbed Valentin's arm to make sure he remained in place. The Frenchman acquiesced.

"Thank you, Inspector. As I was saying, the dock was the safest place for Valentin to keep the treasure. However, it also was crawling with fellow criminals. He wouldn't hide the artwork in a place where others would have access to it. No, he was much more clever than that. He hid the treasure in the one place where no one would look. While the police have torn the docks apart looking for the stolen artwork, they haven't looked in the one place close by that most men would have no way of searching."

"*Sacré bleu!*" Valentin roared. "If you know where it is, spit it out, man!"

Dunderhurst stood from his seat, looking down at us like a judge about to issue a ruling against a defendant, explaining how the errors of his ways had led them to this position in life.

"Quite frankly, if the treasure isn't at the dock, then the treasure is most certainly *under* it."

"We've looked at the posts and beams under the dock. There's no treasure there."

"No, Inspector Lestrade, that isn't what I mean at all. I mean the treasure isn't only under the *dock*, but under the *water*. I'm certain if you dig in the ground below the dock, you shall find the treasure."

We were all silent for a moment, taking in Dunderhurst's theory. It was Valentin that broke the silence. "I commend you, Mr. Dunderhurst. You are certainly a writer of fiction, for only an author could come up with such an asinine theory!"

"Now see here," Dunderhurst began, but he was interrupted by his wife and the arrival of crumpets, cream, and marmalade.

"Sorry to take so long," Mrs. Dunderhurst began. She put the tray down before us. "I thought I'd boil more water for tea. Now don't mind me. Please continue your discussion."

"Actually, Mrs. Dunderhurst, I'm glad that you are here," Father Brown said to the woman. "You are an excellent hostess and you've prepared a scrumptious snack for us. I have one request for you."

"You only have to name it, Father," she said to the priest.

"Very well, I'd like you to take my place at the table. Have some of your fine tea and delicious scones with the gentlemen here. I must explain to the guests what is really going on here."

Everyone *sans* Holmes looked puzzled by the priest's words. Holmes looked to be having a grand time as the priest pushed Mrs. Dunderhurst toward the table after she sat upon his chair, and then the Father went around and served us before talking. At first, Mr.

Dunderhurst protested his wife joining us, but Brown reminded him that he was his priest. "You are a member of my flock, and you must listen to your shepherd," the clergyman commanded.

Our host averted his eyes and mumbled, "Of course, Father. My apologies."

When all had full plates and refilled tea cups, Brown began his story. "I first want to thank Mr. Dunderhurst for inviting us over. I'm sure you appreciate his keen flair for the dramatic and his dry sense of humor. As we all know, storing precious artwork in the salty waters of the Thames would significantly damage the materials, rendering them worthless. No one as sharp as the great Fontaine would risk the possibility of his treasure being destroyed by brackish waters. Our host was having a bit of fun at our expense," Brown concluded.

"Bravo, Mr. Dunderhurst!" Holmes called out. "I always enjoy a touch of humor to lighten a serious mood."

The officers and I didn't say anything. We looked to Mr. Dunderhurst who was seething, but as commanded by his priest, kept his tongue still. We looked to Brown who held us, his audience, in the palm of his hand. Mrs. Dunderhurst looked quite content, having the opportunity to sit down and have someone serve her.

"Now, here is where the story gets interesting, gentlemen," Brown continued. I was surprised he didn't include Mrs. Dunderhurst, as he addressed only the men at the table. "It ends up that there is a very clever mind at this table. In fact, one so sharp that even I didn't at first realize she was leading me to uncover the solution to a mystery."

"She?" Mr. Dunderhurst asked in a soft voice.

"Yes, friends, for none other than Mrs. Dunderhurst herself has used her own cunning methods of deduction to reveal the location of the stolen treasure."

This claim caused a bit of pandemonium, with Mr. Dunderhurst saying "Now, see here!", Valentin demanding the location to be revealed, and most surprised of all, Mrs. Dunderhurst, asking the priest if he had the right woman.

Holmes stood up, and with a commanding glare, silenced us all. "I for one would like to hear what the Father here has to say," Holmes said. "Pray tell, how did this ingenious woman solve the case?"

"Thank you, Mr. Holmes. Just a moment, my dear," Brown chastised Mrs. Dunderhurst. "You are the model of modesty. Please allow me to have the honor of explaining your methods."

"Of course, Father," chirped Mrs. Dunderhurst. "I'd like to hear about them myself."

"Very good," Brown said with a light chuckle in his voice. "If you wish, you may speak when I am finished, perhaps correcting any of my own errors in understanding your methodology."

"That is very kind of you," Mrs. Dunderhurst agreed, then she added, "I'd like to hear how I did it."

So the priest told us all. "When Mrs. Dunderhurst told me about the rat-catcher coming to her room, I thought it seemed rather odd. She, being an observant woman, had noted that there were no signs of rats there, no holes nor sounds of scurrying in the walls, and certainly no feces on the floor. She told me this rather nonchalantly, gentlemen – in a way that made me suspicious of this rat catcher. Who was he? If there were no rats in her room, then why was he there?

"It was a clever way for Mrs. Dunderhurst to get me involved in the case without directly asking me to be involved. She knows how busy I am with church and probably would have shooed the notion of something amiss away. She also added that the rat catcher was going to return late the next morning, a perfect time for me to visit between sermons. I tried my best to brush off the idea that something was wrong in Mrs. Dunderhurst's room, but the more I thought about it, the more questions kept spinning around in my head, and I decided that I had to see her room for myself. I finally came to the decision that I must pay the Dunderhursts a visit, inspect the room, and hopefully see the rat-catcher while he was at work.

"The Dunderhursts greeted me warmly when I stopped by unannounced. I explained that Mrs. Dunderhurst had piqued my curiosity around the rats in her room. Mr. Dunderhurst was taken aback, but I assured him that I wanted to make sure that his wife was safe and that the rat problem was being handled properly. He thanked me for my concern, and they walked me up to her room. When we entered, we found the rat catcher drilling holes in walls.

"The rat-catcher, who claimed to be a Mr. Morris Franklin, spoke with a heavy accent. He assured us that the rats were in the walls but hadn't gotten into the room and that's why Mrs. Dunderhurst hadn't seen any sign of them. 'They're cunning little fellows,' the rat-catcher said. He assured us that it wouldn't take him long to finish up and soon, Mrs. Dunderhurst would be able to return to her home. Mrs. Dunderhurst had said to me that she didn't hear the mice in the wall or under the floorboards. I didn't realize it then, but the lady here was being quite crafty.

"When we were about to leave the room, the rat-catcher asked us to extinguish the candle that was by the doorway. Mrs. Dunderhurst's room is shaded, and we had lit a candle that rests in the entryway wall when we entered the room. 'Could you close the light?' the rat-catcher asked.

When he asked this question, Mrs. Dunderhurst muttered under her breath, but loud enough for me to hear, "Spoken like a true Frenchman." When she said that, it triggered a memory I had of a few years back. At that time, a small group of Parisians had visited my parish on a tour of Britain. I noticed that sometimes the French garble their English and instead of saying put out that light, they say close the light. No doubt Englishmen make similar *faux-pas* with the French language.

"Of course, as Mrs. Dunderhurst intended, this caught my attention. Thinking quickly, I saw there was some paper and a pen by the candle. When I extinguished it, I quickly scrawled a note and put it in a corner of the room. I wanted to see if my theory – or should I say, Mrs. Dunderhurst's theory – was correct. It was.

"I put on the note the words, '*Art under floor*', although it said, '*Art under flo*' for I wanted it to look like a scrap of paper from a larger piece. I thought that if the rat-catcher started tearing up the floorboards, then Mrs. Dunderhurst's theory would be correct, and it was."

"What theory?" asked her husband. He looked suspicious of what the priest was revealing, but he was also eyeing his wife quite differently than when we first arrived at the party. There was a hint of admiration there.

"The theory that the rat-catcher was in fact a French member of Fontaine's criminal enterprise," explained Brown.

"Good show!" Holmes complimented Mrs. Dunderhurst who looked as though she just received a letter declaring her to be the Queen.

"Then, my friends, I did what you all would have done: I verified her theory. I made certain that Mrs. Dunderhurst was correct, that the rat-catcher was a criminal looking for Fontaine's treasure."

"He was?" Mr. Dunderhurst asked, clearly aghast at this revelation, and embarrassed that he hadn't suspected it.

"Of course," Father Brown chuckled, "We were both blind, but your wife saw the truth." The priest then addressed everyone at the table. "I spoke to the owner of the house and asked about the previous renter of Mrs. Dunderhurst's room. The supposed Italian, when described, matched Fontaine. He apparently was rarely in his room and only appeared at night. Then, around the same time that Fontaine was killed, the tenant mysteriously vanished and stopped paying his rent. That's when Mrs. Dunderhurst moved in.

"From speaking with Inspector Lestrade, I also discovered that the police had received an anonymous tip about Fontaine's hideout. That's how he'd been ambushed. It sounded like some members of his gang had turned on the man and set him up. They wanted the police to arrest him and then they would get his treasure. They probably knew that it was hidden away at this house, but they didn't know where. That's why they started with Mrs. Dunderhurst's room – the room Fontaine previously occupied."

"So are you saying that all the men in the basement are the remaining members of Fontaine's gang, looking for the stolen treasure?" Lestrade asked.

"Yes, and once again, we have Mrs. Dunderhurst to thank. She spoke with the landlord yesterday, interrupting him when he was speaking with the rat-catcher. She complained about hearing noises in the basement and suggested that the landlord have the foundation inspected as well. She told them it sounded like the foundation might be cracked. The landlord said he'd look into it, and the rat-catcher said he could get a team to inspect it the next day. Isn't that right, Mrs. Dunderhurst?"

She nodded in the affirmative.

"When she told me this at church yesterday, I knew it was time to strike. That's when I organized the party and wrote to you gentlemen with specific directions. You all came at the appropriate times and it appears you all are brandishing sidearms. Inspector Lestrade, if you followed through with my final request, then we should be – Ah, yes, there they are now."

We all turned to see two police wagons pull up to the curb at the house. "That should be a perfect number of officers to arrest the men in the basement. Now, shall we?"

It wasn't long before the notorious ruffians Pelletier, Gagnon, Routhier, and Lavigne were in irons. Valentin would return to his home country a hero for apprehending four of the worst men in Paris. Once the criminals were locked away in the police wagons, Valentin thanked Mrs. Dunderhurst for her clever way of alerting Father Brown.

"Madame, you are a genius," Valentin commended the woman. "Had you come to the police with your theory, they would have laughed you out of the Yard. You knew to go to Father Brown and how to, how you say, manipulate him. You had him eating the palm of your hand."

"Eating *out* of the palm of my hand," Mrs. Dunderhurst meekly corrected Valentin. "That's the expression."

"But of course. My English is not perfect," apologized the officer. "The people of France are in your debt, Madame. I shall see to it that you receive the highest commendation we can offer a non-Frenchman. My only wish is that you had also uncovered the location of the stolen treasure. We have interviewed the prisoners, and they have no idea where it could be. That's why they were so desperately destroying this house."

"I have good news for you, Valentin," Holmes said to the man. "I believe Mrs. Dunderhurst, modest as always, revealed the location of the treasure to Father Brown earlier today. She simply doesn't want to take the credit for it."

"She did?" Mr. Dunderhurst asked with nothing but awe in his voice for the actions of his wife.

"I'm not sure about that, Mr. Holmes," Mrs. Dunderhurst began.

"Don't be so modest, Madam. That pressed-down grass near the pond we all know wasn't caused by a mastiff, but by a treasure chest being dragged. I'm sure we will find some newly dug earth, under which we shall find the treasure."

And so we did. The chest was buried in a spot by a maple tree which Fontaine had covered with leaves. All the missing art was inside, and none of it was damaged.

With the last bit of excitement for the day at an end, Father Brown excused himself, as he had to rush back to the church for afternoon mass. Before he left, he said to Mr. Dunderhurst, "She is quite the muse you have there. I can see how she inspires your writing."

"Yes," Mr. Dunderhurst replied. He glanced at his wife with pure admiration and affection.

Holmes and I said our goodbyes to Father Brown, but he hushed us as we overheard the Dunderhursts speaking quietly nearby.

"Do you think, my dear," Mr. Dunderhurst asked his wife nervously, "that you might spend the night in my room tonight? We are both healthy individuals. I'm sure we'd be safe from diseases."

"I'd be delighted to," she replied with a blush.

The Disembodied Hand
by Jen Matteis

A case with low stakes, for Sherlock Holmes, is a case of high interest if it brings enough mystery to the equation. Perhaps no case better exemplifies this than the one involving a ghost in a concert hall and the unassuming priest who joined us for the adventure.

It began with nothing as sensational as a dead body. It began instead with a distraught theatre manager whose patrons were reporting an astonishing variety of missing items: Billfolds and buttonhooks, combs and coin purses, *pince-nez* and vinaigrette pendants were all the same in the eyes of the thief, who so far had avoided detection entirely. The thief's success had caused a precipitous drop in ticket sales. So too had the manner in which the items were stolen. Many of the victims blamed a ghost.

Mrs. Hudson announced the desperate theatre manager, Mr. Raymond Lewis, to us on a brisk morning in late October. The wind off the Thames had been unusually strong that day. It rattled the windows in their frames and sent stray newspaper sheets dancing in the streets. Mr. Lewis introduced himself to me and to Holmes, and then stood clutching his hat in a white-knuckled grip as if the wind still threatened to steal it. He was a middle-aged man who had a look of some refinement, though his hat was frayed on the edges and dark circles ringed his eyes.

Holmes swept him with a glance from head to toe, and then made one of those perceptive observations that has so endeared him to me and so alienated him from others.

"I see the concert hall business has not been kind to you of late, Mr. Lewis."

The man stepped back in surprise and appraised Holmes. "Have we met before? But no, I would remember it."

"It is a simple matter of observation, especially simple in this case. Every button of your coat is polished and the shirt freshly pressed, but your pants and boots are scuffed and worn. That implies an occupation where you deal with the public behind a desk or booth where only part of you is visible. Ticket selling, I presume."

"That's rather clever, but how did you know it was a concert hall?"

Holmes leaned forward and plucked two tickets from Lewis' front coat pocket. "You provided very generous clues."

"As for the last part, that the business has not been kind to me, I assume my general countenance betrays me."

"There are a thousand reasons that could lead to an agitated state," said Holmes. "I do not doubt you will enlighten us shortly. It was the hole in your boot and the poor quality of the ticket print that spoke to your financial situation."

"I am impressed you can judge it so accurately." Lewis took back the tickets and pushed them deeper into his pocket, a little brusquely.

"Many things become obvious once one simply makes the effort to notice them," said Holmes. "Now, what is it that troubles you?"

"We have had a rash of burglaries in the theatre, and I have heard you are a man who steps in when the police have tried their all and moved on."

"That is an accurate description of my work, yes. But you haven't told the whole story yet. What is it about these burglaries that you find so disturbing? Or is there something more at play? It may not take much to defeat the police, but surely there is something unusual in the matter."

"A ghost!" Mr. Lewis blushed suddenly and furiously, a red flush that ran from his cheeks, down his neck, then vanished almost as quickly as it had appeared. "Well, that is what my wife thinks, anyway."

"A ghost," said Holmes. He went and stood at the window, gazing out at the windblown streets. I could tell his attention was waning, but he waved at Mr. Lewis to continue.

"Do you have any idea how bad ghosts are for business?"

"I would think they might attract some people."

"Aye, a harmless ghost, perhaps, but not one that steals your valuables right out from under your nose. All anyone ever sees is a pale hand. No body, mind you. Only a hand."

"Hmm," said Holmes, in a slightly more interested tone. He came back and stood near us.

I found this an opportune time to pour us each a brandy. It seemed Mr. Lewis in particular could benefit from it. Lewis and I sat by the fire. Holmes stood before it, his drink already forgotten on the mantelpiece. He paced a moment and then sat, steepling his long fingers together in his lap.

"Mr. Lewis, please tell me what you have seen and heard, exactly, in your theatre."

Lewis rubbed the back of his neck, as if embarrassed. "I will, but I'm only describing what I've heard, nothing I've seen. I am not a believer in the supernatural." Despite this attempt at aloofness, he had the chair's armrests in a death grip. I did not doubt that Holmes saw it.

Holmes raised an eyebrow. "Pray, continue."

"A few years back, my wife and I bought a small theatre in the West End. Well, not right in the West End, but near enough. I had a bit of money saved up from my previous job. Evelyn had an inheritance from her father's passing. We named it The Twin Vines after some adornments on the columns. The first year went by without complaint. But it's an old building. It's always been drafty, and dark no matter how well you light it."

He paused a moment, looking uncomfortable.

"There were rumors of ghosts, I take it."

"Indeed, even before any of this started. But about three months ago, our customers began seeing things almost every night. My wife and I discounted it at first, of course. But then people's belongings started going missing. Occasionally there's an uproar and the audience runs out in the middle of a performance."

"Pickpockets are not uncommon at the theatre," said Holmes. "Why attribute it to a ghost? There is, no doubt, a natural cause."

"No doubt!" Lewis said with false bravado. "But no one has caught a glimpse of the person responsible. No ordinary pickpocket could be so talented. The police investigated but found nothing. They tracked theatregoers for several days straight but found no repeat customers on the different nights that items were taken. No one sitting next to the victims had anything on them. They even shadowed my employees for a few performances to make sure it wasn't them, which of course it was not."

"Interesting," said Holmes. "Did they provide any useful insights at all?"

He nodded. "They had a theory, of a sort. They thought it might be a copycat crime, where someone hears about a rash of crimes and then takes it upon themselves to continue it. The items are never too valuable, so the police wrote it off as a prank or a bit of youthful fun and left us to it."

"Can you describe the items that have gone missing?"

"Everything you can imagine that could be stolen from a person, even items that are utterly without value. I reckon we don't

55

hear the bulk of it. But here's the funny thing." He shifted uncomfortably in his chair. "Often nothing is stolen, but people say they saw a pale hand on their shoulder, or felt a touch on their leg when there was no one there. They'll swear blind it was a ghost."

"I would be curious to inspect this theatre of yours," said Holmes.

A look of relief crossed Lewis's broad face. "That's wonderful! I will leave you with these tickets for tonight's performance, both of you. You can take in a show at the same time you conduct your investigation. But I must warn you, my wife has gone a different way with her inquiries. She has taken the supposition of a ghost to heart and summoned a Catholic priest to deal with the matter."

Holmes laughed. "I will be curious to see what the priest makes of it. In any case, I look forward to the performance."

That night Holmes and I set out for the concert hall. A cold fog shrouded the streets and the horses' hooves echoed loudly on the cobblestones. The theatre's brightly lit marquee was an inviting sight in the darkness, despite what Lewis had told us. We had arrived an hour early, and it was empty except for us and the priest who arrived at the same time.

"Father Brown!" Holmes said warmly. Indeed, it was the meek-looking priest who had joined us on a few previous cases. He greeted us in a kindly but distracted fashion, juggling his hat and umbrella with an awkwardness that suggested he might shortly lose control of them both.

The door opened and Mr. Lewis came out. "Ah, Mr. Holmes and Dr. Watson – Welcome! Father Brown as well!" He shook our hands with enthusiasm.

"I hope you will not be put out if we don't work together," said Holmes.

Father Brown glanced up at him with watery eyes. "Pay me no mind. I will not get in your way."

"We'll do our best to stay out of your way as well."

"Please, come in." Mr. Lewis held the door for us. We entered a broad foyer that had seen more prosperous days. A strip of faded red carpet and gold railings marked the way to the performance hall. A capable-looking woman with her hair done up neatly in a bun sat at the ticket booth reading a newspaper. Lewis beamed at her. "My wife, Evelyn."

She glanced over and jumped to her feet, then ran over to greet the priest. "Father Brown! I'm so glad you could make it."

56

"Always happy to help a former parishioner," said Father Brown. Mrs. Lewis smiled at him warmly, then glanced at Holmes, perhaps a little guiltily. "Mr. Holmes, please forgive me for inviting a priest instead of trusting in your services. It is my firm belief that this is a supernatural matter. I know your reputation for solving difficult cases, but the police have already explored every conventional method of investigation to no avail."

"That is precisely what they are good at," said Holmes.

The little clergyman spoke up in a surprisingly firm tone. "I must admit, I am offended that I was summoned for a 'supernatural' case."

"Why?" asked Mrs. Lewis. "If that isn't the realm of a priest, what is?"

"Is the Holy Ghost somehow equivalent in your mind with ghosts, ghouls, witches, and other beings of that nature?" said Father Brown, shocking us with the sternness of his disapproval. "Or is a priest who believes in the former expected to swallow whole an entire panoply of superstitions?"

"Of course not," said Mrs. Lewis. "But I doubted that it was the province of an ordinary detective."

Holmes snorted.

"Please," Father Brown said. "Priests do not believe in many things, but in one thing only. My calling has nothing to do with the supernatural, and everything to do with the basic reality of man and God. I am here for the same reason as Holmes: To determine the cause of your problem, which I am certain is an earthly one."

Mrs. Lewis frowned. "I am sorry if I offended you, Father. I only wish to find an explanation for this mystery, and I have heard of your expertise in all manner of problems."

"I will help you. But I doubt there is a spiritual cause to anything involving the disappearance of physical objects, especially those with some value to living men."

I sensed something strange in Holmes's demeanor. Though he had remained silent throughout this exchange, a crinkle in the corners of his eyes betrayed that he was positively gleeful. I wondered at the odd kinship between him and the priest, a connection that still surprised me.

Holmes spoke, breaking the uncomfortable silence. "May we see the music hall?"

"Of course." Lewis led us down a dim hallway lined with flickering gas lamps. "Please do not expect a great deal from tonight's performance. It is impossible to fill the theatre lately no

57

matter what I do, so I haven't strained my wallet overmuch for the talent."

The hallway opened onto a simply adorned theatre with the capacity for perhaps a hundred. The stage was draped with a worn scarlet curtain, gold-fringed at the bottom. True to its name, two artfully carved vines of ivy crept up the columns that lined every wall, disappearing into the rafters high above. There were only two levels of seating, with a modest difference in height between them. The seats near the stage were cushioned, while the balcony had modest wooden benches. The air smelled musty and there was a strong hint of gas from the lamps. The light failed to reach not only the corners, but the rafters and the deep shadows behind each column, of which there were many. It looked perfectly the part of a haunted theatre.

Holmes was silent but absorbing everything. His gaze left no corner unexamined. The priest wandered off aimlessly. If not for our previous encounters, I would have guessed him simple-minded.

"Can you describe how the thefts occur?" Holmes asked finally.

"Certainly," said Lewis. The priest sidled closer to hear the conversation. I barely noticed him. "The disappearances always happen during the show when the lights are off. Nothing is safe. One woman had a silver hairbrush stolen from a handbag hung on the back of her seat. Another man said he felt a hand touch his shoulder during the show, and later realized his billfold was missing. Only last night, a young lady said she saw a disembodied hand flash across the seat next to her, and later realized her coin purse was missing."

"A disembodied hand?" said Holmes. "Can you be more specific? Do they see a man's hand or a woman's hand? Does it have a glove, or a ring, or any distinguishing characteristics?"

Lewis shook his head with frustration. "It's something we hear time and time again. A pale hand, a hand touching a shoulder or a leg with no one there. Nothing more specific. It's the only hint we have of the thief."

"Perhaps a white glove," I mused. "It would stand out in a dark theatre."

"Why would a thief want to stand out?" said Holmes. "No, I think another solution is in order."

"Like what?" asked Mr. Lewis.

"I don't know, but I intend to find out." Holmes took me aside for a moment. "Watson, a small request."

"Yes?"

"Please do me the favor of keeping an eye on Father Brown."

58

"What? You don't trust him?"

"You know I trust him implicitly," said Holmes. "However, I should like you to keep an eye on him."

Holmes departed before I could ask for clarification. He began to inspect the theatre, checking under the seats and in some places kneeling to examine the floor. I couldn't imagine why he wanted me to remain with the priest, but I was game to see what came of it.

Mr. Lewis returned to the ticket booth, leaving his wife and Father Brown standing near the entrance to the hall. Both were watching Holmes bring his perceptive abilities to bear on every square inch of the auditorium. Father Brown had little to say, but he radiated the sort of pleasant, friendly air that invites one to gossip. Eventually, Mrs. Lewis engaged him.

"You can see why anyone would think this theatre was haunted," she said. "It was even worse before we bought the place and cleaned it up. It creaks like a ship under full sail in the slightest breeze, and it's full of dark corners even with all the lamps on as they are now. And the mice! You wouldn't believe it. It used to be riddled with them."

The priest didn't seem to be doing anything at all, unless gazing vapidly was somehow a line of questioning.

"'Used to be'?" he asked.

Mrs. Lewis shrugged. "I haven't seen any lately. I understand you don't believe in such things, but I think the ghost spooked the mice as much as it did our customers."

Father Brown made a noncommittal noise.

"That's another reason I suspect a supernatural cause," she said, almost apologetically. "I mean, on top of what people say they saw or felt." She shuddered. "Every mouse disappearing? It's terrifying. Besides, how could it be a thief? Can you imagine a thief stealing women's hairbrushes? What would he do with them all? Besides, he's a terrible thief. He'll grab anything he can, and sometimes make off with it, other times leaving it behind on the floor."

"I have trouble imagining a thief stealing a hairbrush, but I have even more trouble imagining a ghost stealing one," said Father Brown.

"Oh, but you know how ghosts are. They are fickle – they like to play with people. Besides, belongings like brushes and snuff boxes have sentimental value. That's exactly the sort of thing a ghost would be interested in. Have you never been to a séance?"

"I have not."

She blushed furiously, as if remembering who she was speaking with. "No, I don't suppose you have."

"Watson!" I didn't see him at first, then Holmes stood up among the seats. I went to join him. Mrs. Lewis went back to the ticket booth and the clergyman made himself comfortable on a bench seat in the back, where I soon forgot about him entirely.

"What did you find?" I asked.

"Possibly something, possibly nothing. Did Father Brown get any information out of Mrs. Lewis? No, don't tell me." He cut me off before I could reply. "Let him use his methods, and I'll use mine, and we'll see where that takes us. Now, I have thought about how best to do this, and I believe I will sit against this wall, here. If you could sit by the wall opposite, then we will have a good view of the situation."

"You would have us sit on the floor?"

"I know of no better way to see under the seats."

"What is it we are looking for?"

"If I knew, I would tell you. To be honest, I am curious to see what we'll find."

"I'll make sure to keep a firm hand on my billfold," I said. "I would rather not fall victim to it."

Holmes laughed. "I shall do no such thing. I would much rather catch our thief in action."

I sat down by the wall, feeling rather foolish as patrons trickled in and took their seats. A boy came in and extinguished most of the lights, leaving only the stage illuminated. Presently a trio of elderly musicians took the stage bearing a fiddle, pipes, and a mandolin. One gentleman had a long trailing mustache that threatened to catch in his instrument. It took him an inordinate amount of time to tune his fiddle, during which he produced the most extraordinary series of discordant noises. Though Holmes was on the other side of the theatre and in near complete darkness, I could easily picture a look of amused consternation on his face.

Once the music got underway it wasn't bad at all. The trio filled the air with old folk songs, "Brave Benbow" and the like. A multitude of feet tapped out the rhythm across the hall, and I found myself distracted from my task of staring into the utter blackness under the seats. I admit I lost myself a little in the performance, except at times when I imagined Holmes's criticism and brought my attention back to bear on the matter.

In the middle of the fourth song, an argument broke out in the seats between me and Holmes.

"Are you sure you didn't leave it at home?" The man spoke in a hushed tone.

"Of course," a woman replied. "I am sure! It was right here. I had it only a moment ago."

The argument continued in lowered voices, and I endeavored to keep a better watch under the seats. However, I didn't see anything at all.

When the performance ended, the boy came back to rekindle the lights. Holmes was already making his way toward the couple in the middle of the aisle. By the time I joined him, they were gone.

"What did they say?" I asked him. "Did you see anything?"

"I heard nothing and saw nothing, but her fan was stolen right in front of us!" Holmes pronounced this with great delight, and I could see that the energy of the investigation was fully upon him. True mysteries do not often exist for one such as Holmes, but it seemed we had stumbled upon one. "She confided that she saw a white hand, but nothing more. Truly, it is odd, Watson."

I pictured a thief creeping around in the absolute darkness of the seats without a single person noticing. The hairs rose on the back of my neck. "What does it mean?"

"We'll find out. But suppress the ghost stories you're beginning to tell yourself! We'll find a flesh-and-blood answer for this, never fear. Please go see what Father Brown is up to, while I find out if anyone else witnessed anything strange."

I pushed back my misgivings and went to find the priest. He was still in the back row, chatting amiably with a young woman in a fur coat. The theatre was almost empty now.

"What do you make of it, Father Brown? Did you hear that commotion over the stolen fan?"

"No, but I had a lovely conversation with one of the patrons," he said. "May I introduce Mrs. Walker?"

The young woman smiled at us. "Pleased to meet you."

"Dr. Watson." We shook hands.

"What about you, Madame – did you lose anything?"

"No, I have a necklace that protects me against the supernatural." She held forth a small cross. "As I was telling Father Brown, I have been here several times and have never seen anything out of the ordinary."

"I appreciate your help in the matter," said Father Brown. The woman excused herself, leaving me alone with the priest. "I plan on attending tomorrow as well. Perhaps I will see you then."

"It seems likely," I said. "Tonight's performance has only deepened the mystery, I fear."

The priest nodded, not looking particularly concerned. "Then until tomorrow."

I went back for Holmes, but at first didn't see him. Eventually I thought to check under the seats, and there he was, his lean body sprawled out in an aisle.

"There is an odd scent here," Holmes said, his nostrils flaring. "Very odd, but familiar too, somehow. If only I could bottle a scent! I have done the next best thing and bottled anything unusual I could find. There may be a clue in my jacket pocket, once I have more time to think upon it. I have a plan for tomorrow, at least."

"Father Brown said he would return tomorrow as well."

"Did he say anything else?"

"Not really."

That night, Holmes spent some time at his microscope going through the samples he had collected, then settled onto the sofa in a position that for anyone else would imply that he or she had fallen asleep. For Holmes, it was instead a period of deep thought that had resulted in many of his past revelations.

"It could be an elaborate contraption," I suggested. I knew that talking often bothered him while he was in this state. I knew also that it occasionally proved useful. "Some clever tool that reaches a long distance and pries open bags. That might explain the randomness of the items that were stolen, as well, if he couldn't always see what he was grabbing."

"I've considered that," said Holmes. "I believe I have a better theory and a way to test it. But beyond the mechanism of the theft, we must find the person responsible. We must consider anyone who is present at multiple performances, from the musicians to the stagehands, and even the cleaners."

The following evening, we headed back for the same performance. Holmes and I sat together in the center. Father Brown sat again on a bench in the back. I admit he fell out of my awareness after our initial greeting.

"I was wrong last night," said Holmes.

"Oh?"

"I had us looking under the seats. This time, I believe we need to look *on* the seats."

"What exactly should we look for?"

"A white hand." Holmes laughed at my expression. "It only makes sense. People are seeing a white hand, so that's what we will look for."

"You don't think they have imagined it? You believe in a ghost?"

"I believe something is causing them all to see the same thing, and I have a theory about what it might be."

The show began shortly. This time I was familiar with its content, so I managed to keep my attention fixed on the seats around us. Not far into the third song, a man behind us let out a sudden exclamation. A moment later, I distinctly felt a hand touch my shoulder, though I knew no one was there.

"Holmes!" I cried. I looked around swiftly but saw nothing. Then, a flash of white appeared two seats over from me. Something the exact color, shape, and size of a pale hand crawled across an empty seat, then was gone.

"What is it?"

"I saw a hand, a white glove, on the back of that seat!"

Holmes leapt over me and checked under and behind the seat.

"It touched you? Did you lose anything?"

"I don't know. I don't think so."

"What did you feel?"

"A soft touch on my shoulder, like someone resting their hand there for a moment." I shivered. "I know you must have a better theory, but I have never been more convinced of a ghost in my life."

"A-ha!" exclaimed Holmes, patting me down. "It stole the dead mouse right out of your pocket!"

"There was a dead mouse in my pocket?" I felt the ground shift under me slightly.

"I thought you might not approve," said Holmes. "Cheer up, it could be worse. I still have mine."

Suddenly, a woman screamed a couple rows behind us. "A hand! A hand touched me!" Now other voices spoke up as well.

"There's a thief in the theatre!" a man exclaimed. "Stop the performance!"

"Someone touched my shoulder!" said a woman.

"Turn on the lights!" shouted Holmes. I'd seen him give the lantern boy a coin earlier. Now it paid off in the rapidity with which the lamps came back on. The musicians gamely kept playing, but the audience was now well and truly riled up, and their voices were louder.

"There's a ghost!" wailed an elderly woman. "A ghost!"

A few people made for the exit, then others followed. I saw Lewis near the exit, protesting in vain as his patrons pushed past him.

At that moment, Holmes did a stunningly athletic feat. He dove over a row of seats and came up with something small, pale, and wriggling in his hands.

Mr. Lewis screamed. "The disembodied hand!" He fainted clear away, fortunately landing in one of the well-padded seats.

To my surprise, Holmes let out a curse and dropped the object. Immediately it vanished. So, too, did Holmes, who dove under the seats in pursuit.

"What is it?" shouted Mrs. Lewis, breathless from running to her husband.

"Watson, it's coming your way!"

I knelt and peered under the seats.

"On top of the seats!"

I looked up just in time to see a white blur heading straight for me. I shouted, held up my hands, and fell back onto the floor.

By the time I regained my feet, the theatre was mostly empty. Alone in the back, I noticed the priest lost in a private paroxysm of laughter. I took it to mean the situation was safe, whatever it was.

Holmes waved me back into position. "Get on the other side, over there!"

I clambered over a row of seats and crouched down on the opposite side. Suddenly, a flash of white shot past me, heading to the back benches.

"Follow it!" cried Holmes. He was holding one hand in the other.

"Holmes, you're hurt! By God, what is it?"

"We'll see in a moment, I have no doubt."

We ran down the aisle, checking each row of seats as we went. Finally, we ended up at the very last row of bench seats. Father Brown was there, deep in conversation with a young woman. They were laughing and chatting as if they were the most intimate of friends.

"Father Brown," Holmes addressed him.

"Oh," said the little priest, blinking rapidly as if surprised to see us. "Mr. Holmes. I was wondering when you'd make it here."

Holmes took one look at the clergyman's companion and burst into laughter. "I see you beat me to it."

Father Brown shrugged. "I took the direct path, and you took the indirect one. They both brought us to the same place."

I was lost. "What is that?"

"May I introduce Miss Julia Haversham," said Father Brown.

"The thief?" I asked, dumbfounded. I couldn't draw a connection between the disembodied hand careening around the theatre and the woman standing before us.

Holmes and Father Brown shared a cautious smile, like two canny generals who might be the best of friends were it not that they happened to fight under different banners. I felt I was being left out of some enormous joke. "Not exactly," said Father Brown.

"But he isn't far, I'll wager," said Holmes. "Watson, put all thoughts of ghosts out of your head and look merely at what is in front of you."

I looked again at the woman. She was fair of skin with shoulder-length dark hair, about the same height as Holmes – very tall for a woman. She wore a ruffled periwinkle dress of the style that was popular, with an ermine fur stole wrapped stylishly around her neck.

The stole caught my eye. It was the exact color of whatever Holmes and I had been chasing. I leaned in for a closer look. It consisted of dozens of white stoats stitched together, complete with a clasp of one stoat's mouth biting another's tail. It was a horrible thing, really, and it became a hundred times more so when one of the miniature heads turned to face me.

"Good Lord!" The tiny beast let out a sneeze, breaking whatever spell it had held for the moment.

Father Brown doubled over in laughter, and I could tell Holmes was enjoying himself immensely. "I see you have spied the thief at long last."

"A stoat?"

"Notorious thieves," said Holmes in an admiring fashion. "I suspected as much from the hairs I found last night, though it was impossible to tell if they had come off a living animal. May I?"

Miss Haversham nodded. He reached out a hand and gently plucked the creature out of its grisly complement of dead brethren. It squirmed briefly and then settled down in Holmes's hands.

"Did you train the animal or was it born a pickpocket?"

"A bit of both, I admit. I am sorry for all the trouble Sebastian has caused, really. Once it began, my sisters and I were far too amused to deny him something that caused him so much enjoyment."

"May I see the glove?" Holmes asked.

Miss Haversham took a white glove out of her pocket and showed it to Holmes. The fingers had been cut off partway down. It

65

was in effect a miniature costume for the stoat. "Eliza made this. She's talented with a needle, unlike myself."

"You were right about the white glove, Watson," said Holmes. "Sometimes the simplest explanations are the best."

"I wouldn't call this a simple explanation," I said with a laugh. "What a strange affair!"

"I confess we took much delight in this pastime of ours." Miss Haversham let out a peal of laughter, which ended abruptly as Mr. Lewis came storming up to us red-faced. He glanced at the stoat in Holmes's hands, then at Miss Haversham holding the glove.

"Delight? I've lost many a potential patron to your pastime." He did not look amused at his accidental alliteration. Indeed, he was turning an even deeper shade of red.

Miss Haversham blushed, a pale reflection of the burning orb of Mr. Lewis' indignation. "We meant to return everything when the fun wore off. It just never did."

"How many sisters do you have?" asked Holmes.

"Three, all married. I'm the only Miss Haversham. We take turns at the theatre. We knew someone would be onto us otherwise." She turned to Lewis. "I swear to you, we had no evil intention. I admit it became a bit of a contest between us, about what Sebastian could bring back. I realize we took it too far, and I am sorry for the trouble we caused. We never thought about the impact it would have on the theatre."

"The lady is repentant, if the beast is not," said Father Brown. "We've agreed to go together and return the stolen items with all haste. I intend to speak with her sisters as well."

"I will accompany you," said Holmes.

At the same time, Lewis said, "You will let her walk away after all this? I cannot let that happen."

The priest replied to them both. "Please, you successfully caught the thief, which was your goal. You have him right there. My realm is the thief's conscience, which in this odd matter resides somewhere else entirely. I will be speaking at length with Miss Haversham and her sisters. No real harm has been done, and much may be averted if this is dealt with right. The future of several souls is at stake."

Lewis made to say something, but his wife drew him aside and whispered in his ear.

Holmes bristled, then visibly calmed himself. "Very well. But tell me before you go, what brought you to your conclusion?"

"Oh, I simply looked for someone who was bored," Father Brown said modestly.

"Bored?" I asked, amazed that a man with his demeanor had the perceptive skills to rival Holmes.

"Indeed. The thief had to be a repeat patron. I sat in the back, where they would have the best view of their mischief. Then I looked for the person who was least interested in the performance, as he or she had likely heard it many times before."

"Sixteen," said Miss Haversham, barely able to stifle her laughter. "I've seen it sixteen times. I can barely stand to hear it again, except that Sebastian's hobby is so entertaining."

"Mrs. Lewis also confided that the theatre had formerly been infested with mice, but they vanished with the ghost's appearance. I knew it had to be an animal of some kind. When I saw the ermine stole appear for the second night on a young lady who was completely ignoring the performance, I knew I'd solved our mystery."

"Father Brown, you again have my admiration," said Holmes. He handed the stoat back to Miss Haversham. It vanished into the stole. This time, I knew to look for two bright eyes peeking out. The two men shook hands, then the priest and the woman left together, chatting like old and dear friends.

That night, I asked Holmes how the priest had beat us to it. He took the question quite seriously.

"I observe and draw conclusions based on my observations," he replied. "That can take a significant amount of time, especially if done thoroughly."

"And Father Brown?" I asked.

"Faith is the realm of priests. He had a hunch and went with it, and it paid off for him." Holmes leaned back in his chair. "He had another advantage as well. You surely recall how I dressed as a simple clergyman to gain the sympathy of Irene Adler." His brow furrowed as he remembered that case. "Father Brown permanently has that advantage. Criminals tend to confide in priests, and I suspect Miss Haversham's conscience was beginning to weigh heavily upon her, despite her flippant attitude."

We sat in silence for a moment, watching the fire send sparks up the chimney. The wind of the past few days had died down, but a chill still lingered. The blaze provided a welcome warmth.

"I do have one trick up my sleeve, Watson," he announced a moment later.

"What is that?"

67

"Criminals will often confide in a doctor as well."

The Order of the Flood
by Jason Half

The lives of storms, like the lives of people, can take many forms and run many courses, causing much damage along the way. There are sudden intense storms, brief and tempestuous, that surprise with their arrival and their fury. There are storms that are all flash and thunder but fail to deliver on their heavy promise, and there are the quiet storms, underestimated, but building a slow and steady accumulation of rain. Of the three strains, the quiet storm was the most common to be found in the small, damp seaside village of Benford.

Jonah Starkwell, self-proclaimed leader and prophet of The Order of the Flood, had taught his followers well. On a wet Thursday afternoon, the congregation of nineteen souls gathered along the rocky cliff shore to worship. Led in prayer by Tobias Barnes, the prophet's one-time assistant, the congregants then broke as a group and took their familiar positions along the coast, standing sentry and praying as the sea's waves battered the rocks below.

During these vigils, Prophet Starkwell had always insisted that no weakness be shown against the elements. The acolytes were forbidden to shiver or move or wipe the mist from their eyes. Permitted only a thin oilskin robe to wear over their clothes, the silent outdoor service was as much a testament to the miseries on Earth as it was to the rewards of Heaven.

Now, despite her leader's certain disapproval, nineteen-year-old Marie Rowley yielded to an involuntary shudder that coursed through her body. Her face flushed hotly against the wind from an immediate sense of guilt. Her thoughts were never far from Leader Starkwell and the transcendent state of grace in which his worldly body had been found only a week ago. The memories filled her with warmth and renewed her devotion.

One mile inland, a disapproving housemaid ushered two men into Sir George Rowley's home. Had the servant possessed the powers of observation credited to one of the visitors, she might have surmised from the coat of the somewhat shorter man that the pair came not from London, but from nearby Hensgate, as a box of matchsticks advertising an industrious publican there could be found in its pocket. Only three of the thirty matchsticks were absent, which inferred a recent acquisition.

But the housemaid, not being the consulting detective Sherlock Holmes, did not discover this fact, and indeed was content to remark to the undermaid that, "the tall one seems ready-made for the stage".

In his study, Sir George Rowley rose from his desk and crossed the modest but tidy room to greet his visitors.

"Mr. Holmes! I am so grateful that you have decided to come." Rowley shook hands first with the detective and then with his smiling companion.

"It is fortunate that your telegram found us at the Hensgate Inn before we began our return trip to London. I introduce my friend and colleague, Dr. John Watson."

Sir George indicated two chairs placed near an inviting fire. "Do take a seat. I am sure you're chilled from traveling in this weather. I hope your previous case was resolved satisfactorily?"

It was the doctor who answered.

"A rather knotted affair involving a necklace, a disgraced acrobat, and a curious powder from South America."

Holmes permitted a tight smile at this account. "My biographer is already considering how best to memorialize it in print, I fear," he commented.

"It is an adventure worthy of your reputation," countered Watson.

"Regardless," said Holmes, "that mystery is over and a new one is now before us. Sir George, kindly begin your tale."

George Rowley took a deep breath and began.

"My family is a small one. My wife died shortly after delivering our second child, and I have raised Stephen and Marie on my own. I hope it is apparent that I love them both in equal measure." He paused and then continued.

"Stephen has always showed promise. As a child, he was quick with sums and very affable, and so is especially suited for his post as a junior clerk at the village bank. Indeed, he is engaged to a lovely girl who happens to be the daughter of Charles Simmons, the bank's manager."

"That's a fortunate set of circumstances," noted Dr. Watson.

"Stephen's future prospects are now in jeopardy," explained Rowley. "He has been arrested for the murder of a charlatan named Jonah Starkwell. Have you gentlemen heard of his organization, The Order of the Flood?"

70

"No mention of this order has yet reached London," answered Holmes. "It appears to be a regional rather than a national group."

"It should not exist anywhere," said Rowley darkly. "It is surely a twisting of Christian tenets and morality."

"Please tell us how your son came to be connected with Jonah Starkwell's death."

Rowley took another inhalation of breath. "Stephen was always a sunny, clear-eyed lad. By contrast, his sister Marie cultivated a different outlook. My daughter, it saddens me to say, has always been moody and melancholic. As a child, she was reluctant to make friends and would find excuses to isolate herself from others. Six months ago, Marie started to take an interest in a new religious group that was building a following. It appears that Starkwell had arrived in Benford for just this purpose. At first, I thought her participation might do her some good. After all, she began to meet with others and seemed to find a purpose in attending.

"But two warning signs soon took shape. First, this order and its worship schedule consumed our Marie. She would leave the house at all hours and in the worst kinds of weather to join her group on the cliffs for prayer. I forbade her from attending, and Stephen would argue with her to stop this nonsense and resume Sunday services at our church. I fear our demands only strengthened her resolve."

Sir George fell silent as the taciturn housemaid entered with a tray of tea and cakes. Once cups were filled and a plate passed around, the servant exited. The speaker resumed his tale.

"Shortly thereafter, Stephen learned that Jonah Starkwell had cast himself as a prophet and encouraged his followers to worship him as much as they would their Creator. I am certain they were happy to oblige. Marie clearly regarded him as a mystical figure, and I admit he had the looks for it. Nearly six feet tall, with wild grey hair and beard framing a pair of ice-blue eyes."

"You have met him then?" asked Holmes.

"I saw him walking into town, staring ahead and taking great strides."

"What was his purpose in town? Do you know?"

Rowley shook his head. "I do not. I asked Stephen if Starkwell was a customer at his bank, and he said he had never known the man to enter the building."

"So when did your son cross paths with this prophet?"

"I will tell you, Mr. Holmes. On the afternoon before Jonah Starkwell's death, there came a rain every bit as cold and miserable as the one plaguing us today. Stephen, who happened to be at home due to the bank's Wednesday half-day, noticed Marie preparing to leave in that thin robe and hood that passes for The Order's worship costume. The pair began to argue, and the exchange became heated. I reached the hall to see Stephen grab Marie's arm, attempting to keep her here. But she pulled away and rushed out the door.

"Stephen reached for his coat and turned to me and said –" Here Sir George faltered. Meeting Holmes's dispassionate eye, he continued. "He said, 'This needs to end, Father. That scoundrel is ruining Marie.' With that, he also rushed out into the storm. He returned two hours later and told me this account.

"Stephen had resisted his initial instinct to overtake Marie and return her to the house forcibly. Instead, he followed her to the gathering on the cliff. The entire group was assembled – Stephen counted twenty, including Marie and the prophet – and their leader, Starkwell stood in front of them, his eyes closed as he held a cleft staff before him. He was offering up some prayer, his lips moving as rain poured down his face and water dripped from his beard. And there was Marie, head bowed in supplication to their leader just like the rest of them. The sight was enough to make Stephen as mad as a bull.

"He raced towards the group, consumed by anger. He passed Marie and charged straight at Starkwell, and in that moment he might have come to blows with the older man. But he did not. He stopped right in front of him. Stephen says that the prophet's eyes were now open, and those cold, ice-blue eyes were fixed directly upon him. But it was the wood staff that stopped Stephen from advancing. That staff could have felled him if Starkwell had the mind to make it a weapon. He stopped his charge, and a good thing too. But then he spoke the words that brought him to his current state. He looked at Jonah Starkwell and in front of nineteen witnesses he said, 'If you don't let Marie leave this cult at once, I swear to God I will kill you!'"

Sir George Rowley lifted his cup to his lips and swallowed some tea. A tremor in his hand caused the cup to chatter when he replaced it on the saucer. He concluded his story.

"Starkwell never took his eyes off Stephen. He said, 'My children can leave The Order whenever they wish. Sister Marie, do you wish to leave The Order of the Flood?' Marie said no. So Stephen returned to the house, wet through and alone. That night a letter arrived saying that Marie would stay indefinitely with other members of that infernal church." Rowley paused, the memory of that message clearly stirring up sadness and pain. "The day after that, Jonah Starkwell's body was found on the floor of his church chapel. That wood staff lay beside him. Constable Wren tells me he died from a blow to the back of his head. And although no rain fell that day, the church leader's body was drenched in water from head to toe."

Sherlock Holmes leaned forward, his eyes alert and his mouth curving into a thin smile.

"And that, Sir George, is what I wish to investigate."

"It really is the most curious thing, Mr. 'Olmes," said Francis Wren, the village's only constable. "'Course, we sometimes find an unfortunate soul drowned at sea, but this is the first one found soaked right through in the middle of the room."

"It is unusual," Sherlock Holmes admitted. "Have you requested assistance from Scotland Yard?"

"No, sir, on account of we already arrested the murderer."

"Which is all very well, provided the man you arrested is in fact the murderer of Jonah Starkwell."

Constable Wren pulled on the reins and the speckled roan trotted to a halt in front of an unassuming, low-roofed cottage on the outskirts of the village. A wooden sign affixed to the door read simply *Chapel – The Order of the Flood*. Wren jumped from the seat of the wagon and helped his passengers down.

Sherlock Holmes allowed his eyes to search and commit this new location to his remarkable memory. John Watson knew the detective's methods well. Quite likely, Holmes wasn't looking for any specific elements within the tableau, and yet his mind, sharpened through years of intense and exacting observational exercise, could recall the smallest details weeks later if it benefitted his investigation. Watson tried a similar scrutiny but soon abandoned it to speak with the constable.

"What evidence do you have against Stephen Rowley?" asked Watson. "Surely your case is more than just a sharp exchange of words between suspect and victim."

"That exchange was a promise by one to kill the other, remember. And within a day, that threat 'ad been carried out. But there is more than that. Old Starkwell was last seen alive around two o'clock that afternoon. After that, 'e vanished from sight until Tobias Barnes and that church group returned from the cliffs and found 'im in the chapel around a quarter-to-five. Well, it just so 'appens that Stephen Rowley was away from 'is 'ouse during those exact 'ours.

73

No one can vouch for 'im during that time – not 'is father nor the bank manager nor anyone."

Dr. Watson frowned.

"How did Mr. Rowley spend that time, then?"

Wren offered a sardonic grin.

"'E *says* 'e left the bank and went searching for 'is sister, who was staying with some of those Flood followers. Very convenient that 'e went on the search at that very time. I asked 'im, 'If you looked in on all those people, someone can speak to seeing you, surely?' And 'e says to me that no one saw 'im because 'e went around stealth-like, peeking in at windows and going 'round by the back lanes. Said 'e didn't want the church knowing 'e was looking for 'is sister so they couldn't raise the alarm until 'e found 'er."

Dr. Watson looked doubtful. "Still, the presence of motive and absence of an alibi isn't evidence of a man's guilt. Wouldn't you agree, Holmes?"

Having completed his survey of the surroundings, Holmes now stood by the chapel door.

"Gentlemen, I lack relevant information. Once I acquire it, I can speak conclusively about Stephen Rowley's innocence or guilt. Shall we enter?"

Constable Wren knocked. Receiving no answer, he opened the door and the party entered the chapel.

The cottage had been purposed into one large room, ascetic and strangely primitive in its spare furnishings and adornments. The walls were a rough surface of whitewashed stone and plaster. On the west and north sides, two clear glass windows allowed weak beams of sunlight to enter the room. Three unlit oil lanterns hung from crossbeams supporting a simple thatched roof, while the wood-planked floor seemed to consist of long, narrow boards of cedar and birch.

At the back stood four rows of pews, spaced tightly and stretching from the back wall to the middle of the room. The pews faced the front wall, which supported the two most singular attractions in the spartan space. Leaning upright against the wall was a large forked staff, a heavy branch of solid wood as tall as the prophet who once wielded it. On the floor beside it sat a large ornamental basin filled with water. Its flattened metal back was secured to the chapel wall while its deep bowl curved out into the room. Directly above it, a miniature emblem of the forked staff was affixed to the wall.

"Sacrilege and 'eresy, if you ask me," said Constable Wren, scowling at the staff. "Where a proper cross should go, you 'ave this sorry piece of driftwood."

Dr. Watson walked over to study the icon. "Reminds me of a giant divining rod. That connects with the water worship, anyway." The doctor turned back to the room to find his friend on his knees, closely examining the rough wood floor. Holmes addressed the constable.

"Tell me where Jonah Starkwell's body lay in this room."

"Well, 'bout where you are right now, Mr. 'Olmes. On 'is back like, with 'is feet pointing to the door and 'is 'ead nearer to the pews."

Holmes nodded. "Observe, Watson, the slight discolouring of these center planks from being soaked with water. The amount must have been considerable if these boards are still damp to the touch."

"That's right," said Wren. "Both the prophet and the floor looked like they'd been dunked proper."

"Where is the man's body now?"

"Well, sir, from the moment old Starkwell was found, those followers of 'is 'ave refused to let 'im leave this chapel. Said it would be desecration and the like. The man had no relations, so I couldn't appeal to family. In the end, I sent someone to fetch Doctor Danbury from 'Ensgate to come over and take a look. 'E shooed everyone out and examined 'im *in situ*, as they say. Decided that death was from that blow to the back of his 'ead."

Still kneeling on the chapel floor, Holmes had opened a penknife and was carefully scraping its blade between two boards. He gathered a minute pinch of residue onto the knife's flat surface and tipped it into a waiting envelope. Then he stood, pocketed his findings, and crossed to the staff and basin.

Over his shoulder he said to Wren, "I shall speak with this doctor, but such a cursory examination is unfortunate. I will be very interested to prove or disprove another means of death."

"Another means?" asked Wren. "What would that be?"

"Drowning." Holmes kneeled once more, this time in front of the decorative basin. The detective's thin fingers followed the bowl's curved lip and then moved down to trace a small, flexible tube concealed along the side. Holmes smirked as he discovered a tiny rubber bulb at the basin's base and could not resist squeezing it several times.

"Observe, Constable. Bear witness to the mighty power of the Flood."

75

At first, nothing happened. Then after a moment, a tiny trickle of water began to pour from between the cleft of the miniature staff mounted on the wall. As the liquid dripped from the staff, it fell back into the basin below. Constable Wren frowned at the water feature but Dr. Watson, more mechanically minded, stepped in to study the crude siphon more closely. Then another thought struck him, and the doctor turned around to address the constable.

"Did you say the staff was found beside the body?"

"It was," answered Wren.

"And that it was also wet to the touch?" The constable nodded. Watson inhaled sharply. "Surely, Holmes, you recognize the significance of the staff's shape?"

Holmes permitted himself an enigmatic smile. "I believe *you* recognize a significance, and your theory is tenable enough."

"Which theory is that now?" asked Wren. Holmes, who had moved on to examine the upright wooden staff, gave a curt nod and Dr. Watson explained.

"Someone could have used that forked staff to hold Starkwell by the neck and force his head, face up or face down, under the water until he expired."

"But the blow to his 'ead – ?" Wren noted stubbornly.

"Delivered first, as a means to stun the man. Or possibly it was received while fighting for his life as he was held down. What do you think, Holmes?"

Before the detective could answer, a sharp bleat of protest issued from just outside the doorway. A small, aggrieved figure entered the room and addressed Constable Wren.

"Here! You've no right entering this chapel! This is a private place of worship and needs to be respected as such. Mr. Wren, with the removal of Leader Starkwell, you have no more business here." The man turned to the other visitors. "Gentlemen, if you wish to join The Order, I shall be happy to speak with you. If not, I must ask you to leave."

"This 'ospitable young man," said Wren, "is Tobias Barnes, Prophet Starkwell's assistant. Barnes, this is Mr. Sherlock 'Olmes, the well-known consulting detective, along with 'is associate, Dr. Watson. They, too, should be treated with respect, so keep a civil tongue."

At this, much of the assistant's righteous anger seemed to leave him. He moved to the middle of the room and stood before the empty pews.

"Forgive me. This is our church, and I am understandably protective of it. I will help you within reason, but I thought the investigation into our dear leader's demise had finished."

"Stephen Rowley is still under arrest, if that's what you mean," said Wren. Now, however, Tobias Barnes's attention had also been arrested.

"Say! Who started the fountain? That is reserved for Order ceremonies!"

Holmes stepped forward, appearing contrite.

"My apologies, Mr. Barnes. We are surely intruding and you are a busy man. I have three questions for you, and upon receipt of the answers I will take my leave. First, was there any acrimony between Jonah Starkwell and any member of his flock?"

"Acrimony? Certainly not. We are a peaceable congregation, and everyone revered our leader."

Holmes nodded as if he expected this response. "Second question: When you and your colleagues returned from the cliff and found your prophet's body lying in the chapel, what was your reaction?"

Barnes frowned. "I'm not sure I understand you. We were stunned and saddened, naturally."

"But your reaction *as an order*? You are worshipers of the Biblical Flood, are you not? How do such worshipers react when they find their leader in the middle of the chapel, his staff beside him, drenched in water? Was that sight blasphemous? An offense to your faith?"

The young man's expression changed. He looked up, his face a mix of wonder and growing pride.

"No, sir. It wasn't blasphemous. On the contrary, it was a miracle. Leader Starkwell hadn't shown up to lead us in prayer – a highly unusual oversight – so we were forced to carry on without him. When we returned to find him here, covered in water, it was as if he had been anointed in the Holy Waters of the Flood."

Again Holmes nodded. "My third question: Where is Jonah Starkwell's body now?"

Quiet wonder gave way to a smug smile of rectitude. Tobias Barnes, short of stature, straightened and answered with a gleam of triumph in his eyes.

"It was a transcendent ceremony. Four boats for the believers, with every member of The Order in attendance. I was honored to act as minister. The Flood of Noah has reclaimed our leader, and we have returned him to the sea. It is the blessed ending for us all."

77

Before they left the chapel, Constable Wren had managed to extract a list of names from the prophet's assistant. Wren knew about most of the members on the list, but a few names had surprised him – upstanding villagers who had been taken by the Flood, as it were. Before they were situated in the cart, Wren handed the list to the detective.

"Nineteen in all, Mr. 'Olmes. Will you tackle each in turn?"

Holmes studied the list and made a decision. "The men and women listed here could be considered the dead man's inner circle. I'm more interested in tracing those in Jonah Starkwell's outer orbit."

"And how do you wish to do that?"

"Let us start by visiting the village parson. The official one. Please take us to the rectory."

Ten minutes later, the horse-drawn cart came to a stop beside the worn stone steps of Saint Matthew's Catholic Church. In contrast with the modest cottage that acted as church and chapel for the Flood worshipers, the conventional edifice of stone and cement, as well as its recognized shape and purpose, offered some comfort to Wren and Watson, who shared more orthodox views of religion.

A closer look revealed that the courtyard was overgrown and needed weeding, while one side of the tiny rectory building had been steadily covered by clusters of unflattering vines. The attending clergyman was found neither in the church nor the rectory. The visitors found a slight, bespectacled, unremarkable man in clerical collar behind the buildings, looking up to study a weather-worn bell tower. A woman stood beside him, delivering a monologue in an admonishing tone, her hands occasionally flying upwards towards the tower. His back to an untidy cemetery, the cleric looked uncomfortable and out of place, but he blinked and started to smile when he saw the approaching men.

"We are destined to meet once more," announced the priest, shambling forward to greet his visitors. "Look, Mrs. Crayle, a detective, a doctor, and a policeman!" He shook hands with Holmes and Watson, who were pleased to encounter their friend Father Brown in this isolated seaside village.

"Are we disturbing you, Father?" asked Constable Wren. Mrs. Crayle, the church secretary, stepped forward and answered for him.

"I was just showing Father Brown all the repairs and tasks that need managing before Father Shively returns next month. As you can imagine, the list is extensive."

78

"Knowing Father Shively, I can imagine," said Wren.

"Did you know there is a family of ospreys nesting in the bell tower?"

"It isn't a surprise, if they don't mind the noise."

Unamused, she turned back to the priest. "You will have to attend to it while you are here, Father, along with mending the gates and removing the creeping vines on the north walls."

"And those front steps could do with a patching," added Wren.

"Do you have a moment to talk, my friend?" asked Holmes. Father Brown, grateful for the reprieve, ushered his visitors into the rectory.

Father Shively's cluttered office, made even more cluttered by Father Brown's residency, was covered in sermon collections, books on theology, and miscellaneous papers and correspondence. Surfaces were cleared and the men settled in the little space as best they could. The detective's first question was met with more blinking and head shaking from the clergyman.

"I know very little about The Order of the Flood, I'm afraid. You see, I arrived only two weeks ago, and am conscripted to attend to this parish until Father Shively returns from sabbatical."

"Perhaps you have formed an opinion of this sect through interactions with your own parishoners?"

Father Brown shrugged. "I understand it to be a religion that, like other religions, takes its own singular path to finding purpose in life's work through devotion to God. In that respect, the Flood worshipers are little different from us Catholics, or indeed from the Protestants or the Adventists."

"You haven't interacted with Jonah Starkwell or his followers?" asked Holmes.

"I witnessed one of their clifftop services when I first arrived. An intriguing ritual, if a physically uncomfortable one for its participants."

"It's heresy, if you ask me," said Mrs. Crayle, who had not been asked. "That Flood lot is not true Christian, despite what this one says. Father Shively preached against them, and I dare say he has the right outlook. Of course, no one in the village could stand that Starkwell. He would stir up bad blood everywhere he'd go."

"That is why I wished to call here," explained Holmes. He turned to his friend. "Any illumination you can provide me regarding Jonah Starkwell and the citizens of Benford may prove invaluable."

But the little priest just shook his head. "That is light that Father Shively could have shed. I fear I have very few details to share, and fewer opinions." The church secretary cleared her throat.

"It so happens that I know more than some about this town and the people in it. While I would never wish to gossip, I may be persuaded to share my views of that Starkwell and the toes he stepped on."

"Excellent!" said Holmes. With Dr. Watson taking notes and Father Brown looking distinctly uncomfortable, the detective guided Mrs. Crayle through her observations. In no time, the doctor had filled half his journal.

He had the forethought to start a new entry each time Mrs. Crayle discussed a new subject, and as he reviewed his writing that afternoon, the dossiers of a dozen people took shape. Sherlock Holmes reviewed the pages while smoking, a blue cloud surrounding him within their room at the local inn. He held a small pencil and periodically added a checkmark to the top of a page. Finished, he closed the journal and handed it to Watson.

"Your notes are admirably effective. I have marked the names of four persons well worth pursuing."

John Watson turned the pages, pausing at each checked name. In the order of Mrs. Crayle's rather breathless testimony, the detective's choices were these:

- *Charles Simmons, Manager, Bank of London, Benford branch. Motive: Dispute with J.S. over land deed for chapel building and grounds. S. had threatened Simmons in public and railed against the bank.*
- *Samuel Batterby, Grocer, Batterby and Sons. Motive: Starkwell routinely stole bread and port from the grocer's store. When confronted, J.S. claimed the items should be donated to the church. Great argument at store last month. S. not seen on premises since.*
- *Thomas Donner, Miller. Motive: Donner was challenged by J.S. at his mill, who accused him of slandering the church to win back his apprentice. Simon Green left the mill after a dispute with Donner.*
- *Roger Jones, Carpenter. Motive: Jones's wife was an early convert to the Order. She returned to Jones but died months later. Known grudge against J.S. and his church.*

80

"Interesting," said Watson as he finished reviewing the entries. "All of your candidates are businessmen, and all are labourers, except for Simmons the bank manager. You have no suspicions of the other men and women who have tangled with Starkwell?"

"It is the manner in which the prophet was killed and disposed. Others in the village might well have wanted the man dead, but few would have done so in quite this way."

"You refer to the blow to the back of his head."

"I refer to the water and the staff and the fact that the man was found on the floor of his chapel. Our question is *Why?*"

Watson waved his journal. "And you think one of these men will provide an answer?"

"I'm certain of it. Come, Watson. we shall first hear the miller's tale."

Constable Wren had arranged the hire of a cart and driver for the visitors to use as needed. The driver, an elderly field farmer named Mattis, arrived atop a harvesting cart that had weathered several seasons. Cart, driver, and horse proved slow but dependable and conveyed Holmes and Watson to the lowlands, where the riverside mill of Tom Donner was situated.

Stepping from the cart, Sherlock Holmes moved fleetly across the road to examine a squat but wide delivery wagon. Six large burlap sacks of grain flour were stacked on one side, and a thick weather-treated muslin canvas stretched across the frame, shielding the goods from wet weather.

Holmes noted the width of the wagon's wheels and the pattern their metal rims had cut into the damp ground. Satisfied, he moved to the mill's open door and waved for Watson to follow.

Inside the mill, the atmosphere was gloomy but active. Tall, high openings along the building's river wall invited the available sunlight of this cloudy day. A man in an apron stood near a revolving top stone in the center of the room, using a blade to scrape and gather crushed corn grain into a pail. The top stone, lifted and pinned, was spinning its slow revolutions at a height beside the miller's head.

"Mr. Donner? I know you're busy, but we would be grateful to speak with you. My name is Holmes, and this is my associate, Doctor Watson."

Tom Donner left the millstone, wiped his dusty hands on his apron, and stepped towards the two men.

"What's this about?"

"I'm enquiring into the death of Jonah Starkwell on behalf of Sir George Rowley. You have heard that his son, Stephen, stands accused of Starkwell's murder?"

"I heard as much," replied Donner. "I'm sorry for young Stephen. I'm not sorry for that scoundrel, Starkwell."

"Could you tell me the circumstances under which you and the scoundrel last spoke?"

The miller opened his mouth to respond when a woman's harsh voice boomed from the doorway.

"He will not speak a word to you, you meddlesome devil! Tom, don't be a fool. They're only looking for someone else to hang in Rowley's place!"

The men turned to acknowledge the new arrival. A short, wiry woman, her blouse and dress incongruously colorful and her black hair tucked under a red kerchief, stood defiantly on the threshold. Holmes responded with a courteous bow.

"Mrs. Donner, I assure you I am not searching for a scapegoat, but only for the truth."

"So you say. Leave our mill and let us alone." She took two steps forward, the hem of her dress raising tiny clouds of flour dust as it swept against the floor.

"Sarah, I can speak for myself," said the miller. His voice was weary, as if reluctant to argue.

"You do and it will do no good, only harm," his wife replied.

"If I may," suggested Holmes, his voice a model of *politesse*. "I know already of the many grievances between the residents of Benford and Jonah Starkwell. That includes your own complaint: The fight over your apprentice Simon Green, and the prophet's accusation that you and Mr. Donner have spoken out against his church. I wish to hear your side of that story. Whether you want to tell it or let others tell it for you, that is your decision."

After this brief speech, Sherlock Holmes waited. The millstone rotated, and Watson observed Holmes's keen eye studying its thick edge for an entire revolution. Sarah Donner, meanwhile, had moved from protective anger to a more philosophical view.

"Go ahead, then," she said to her husband. "They already know the worst of it." With permission given, Tom Donner told his tale. It was an uncomplicated and simple one.

The mill was of modest size, and for years Mr. and Mrs. Donner had managed it on their own. Three summers ago, the millers arranged to take on a slow-witted but strong apprentice, the oldest boy of the Green family. Simon Green had responded well to the labour and proved to be a reliable and cheap worker, with his family willing to collect his pay in the form of sacks of grain and animal feed.

Then, last summer, Leader Starkwell had received him into his church. From that moment, Simon Green became an unreliable assistant. He often absented himself from the mill when The Order called a service, which, according to Mrs. Donner, was "too bleedin' often to count", and would abandon deliveries if he encountered his fellow congregants *en route*. He also started to proselytize on the cleansing waters of Noah's Flood, and these amateur sermons irritated Tom Donner and maddened his wife.

This had led to arguments both within Simon Green's home and at the mill. The talk stirred anger but no action, much of it directed at Jonah Starkwell and his intrusive church. The situation remained in this unhappy state until two weeks ago, when the prophet descended upon the Donners at their mill. He was full of Old Testament fury and was ready for battle. The exchanges were fiery and unpleasant, with Starkwell accusing the Donners of slandering the church throughout the village. ("Which we never had done, Mr. Holmes," said Tom Donner in their defense. "Honestly.") Still raving, the wild-eyed Starkwell finally departed after proclaiming that Simon Green would devote himself fully to The Order and would never work at the mill again.

"And he never has," added Sarah Donner. "Which I'm beginning to view as more of a blessing than a curse."

Returning to Farmer Mattis and his cart, Watson added some lines into his journal. As he positioned himself along the uncomfortable bench seat, he turned to his companion.

"That seemed instructive. We know more about Starkwell, at any rate – his character and his temper."

Holmes nodded, his brow creased in thought. Mattis swiveled his head a fraction and gave a grunt of enquiry.

"To Jones's carpentry shop, I think," said Holmes. The old farmer flicked the reins and the cart began to move.

"And then to the others?" Watson asked. "The greengrocer and the bank manager?"

"They are looking less and less like our quarry, Watson."

"But surely Simmons, the bank manager, is worthy of an interview. For one thing, it is a fact that Stephen Rowley worked under the man."

"That is a fact, you are correct on that point," agreed Holmes. "The world is full of facts. It is our job to determine which ones are valuable."

But Watson persisted. "Why? Why not the grocer and the banker?"

"The grocer, possibly. The banker, most unlikely. My decision to exclude them is simple: They aren't engaged in the right professions."

The detective would say no more, and the journey continued in relative silence.

In front of the open barn that functioned as the woodworking shed of Roger Jones, the proprietor was bent over a sturdy wooden door that reclined horizontally atop two standing frames. He tapped a beveled chisel to gouge a panel groove parallel with the door's edge. Then he sensed his visitors and looked up.

"Gentlemen," said Jones curtly. Holmes introduced himself and Watson.

"We wish to learn about the life and demise of Jonah Starkwell."

"Then talk to Constable Wren." Jones tapped the chisel again.

"We have done so," answered Holmes, "and also to Sir George Rowley, whose son is accused of murder." The tapping stopped and the carpenter looked up once more.

"I don't know what I can tell you."

"When was the last time you interacted with Prophet Starkwell?"

Jones straightened up and cracked his neck. "I suppose it was six months ago, maybe more. Me and your prophet don't get on."

"Your wife was once a member of The Order, yes?" For a moment, anger flashed in the carpenter's eyes, but soon dissipated.

"She never joined it fully. She flirted with it, though, and attended a few of those blasted sermons by the sea. That was a year ago now, and she soon came to her senses. Starkwell wasn't pleased, but I offered to put out the lights of him or anyone from that church who pressured my Elizabeth again. They left her alone after that."

"And that is when villagers heard you threaten Jonah Starkwell's life."

"Yes," said Roger Jones, studying the chisel in his hand. "But that was long ago."

"Not so long ago," corrected Holmes. "And when did your Elizabeth die?"

Jones kicked at the shavings on the ground. The question was clearly an uncomfortable one.

"In November of last year. She had been taken ill, you see."

The detective changed the subject. "That is a handsome barn. It is where you store your lumber?" He strode to the building's open door, and Jones set down his tools and followed him. Holmes's gaze traveled from the dusty cement floor to the work bench, and then up to the loose boards stacked and resting against the wall. Among the boards hid a figure who, once spotted, moved instinctively back.

"Hello," said Holmes. "I didn't see you there."

"This is my assistant, Micah," explained the carpenter. "It's all right. I don't need that board, my boy." The shy young man moved away from the boards but kept his distance from the strangers.

After asking a few more questions, Holmes left the barn, with Watson following. On his way, he took a moment to observe the woodworker's handsome delivery wagon, closely studying its wheels and the cargo inside. As he took his seat in the cart, Holmes leaned towards Mattis's stoic frame.

"Will you take us to the home of Simon Green?" The old farmer gave a grunt of assent and the cart's weathered wheels began to turn once more.

"Please take a seat, Sir George, for I have information that will interest you."

Sherlock Holmes gestured towards the front pew, and Sir George Rowley dutifully took his seat. That morning, the chapel of The Order of the Flood was hosting a strange and contradictory assembly of people. At the detective's invitation, the accused man's father had accompanied Holmes, Watson, and Wren to the small cottage. They had been met at the door by a civil but frustrated Tobias Barnes.

"I hope this will not last long," Barnes complained. "There is a meeting of The Order later today."

"You will have your place of worship restored very soon," remarked Holmes. Barnes strode from the men back to the fountain near the door. The heavy wooden staff stood to the side, just within the newly elected church leader's reach.

The pair of visitors who next entered the chapel caused Barnes to visibly react, and he reflexively took a step backwards. In the doorway stood Simon Green, the miller's former apprentice, tall and sinewy, and behind him was a short, frowning woman who peered into the room with suspicion. Holmes crossed to greet them.

85

"Mrs. Green, your attendance is most welcome. Please come in and sit with your son over there."

The stout lady moved to the front pew on the aisle opposite Sir George. Simon Green, his face bowed more in embarrassment than in reverence, followed in her wake. Tobias Barnes moved quickly to the tall man and whispered to him.

"What is this, Simon? Why have you come here with your mother? Answer me!"

"Simon," called his mother sharply, and the miserable young man ignored the church leader. He sat beside his mother as the pew creaked in protest.

Giving up, Barnes turned to discover another unwelcome visitor inside the chapel. Father Brown, Benford's interim cleric, stood blinking at the staff and basin as if trying to divine their purpose.

"Now see here," said Barnes to Holmes, although he faced the rival clergyman. "I agreed to let you use the chapel to conduct your business, but I take exception at inviting a Catholic priest!"

Father Brown's blinking hesitated and then cleared. "You will be succeeding Prophet Starkwell as the leader of your church?" he asked.

"If you must know, yes, I will be," answered Barnes. Father Brown nodded, but his brows furrowed in concern. Still nodding, as if working out some troubling thoughts, he ambled to the rear of the room and seated himself at the edge of the back pew.

"I am glad you are here, Father," said Holmes. "Will you take a seat, Mr. Barnes?"

"I prefer to stand," Barnes said coldly. Holmes nodded.

"Very well. Gentlemen, Mrs. Green, I am prepared to explain exactly how Jonah Starkwell met his death. Doing so, I will also prove that Stephen Rowley is not guilty of the crime with which he is charged."

Holmes pivoted to Barnes, and his tone became admonishing. "The solution would have been apparent if you and your church hadn't disposed of the body at sea."

"That action runs according to our creed," said Barnes defensively.

"That action could have caused an innocent man to hang!" Holmes shot back, then tempered his speech. "Regardless, enough evidence remains to extricate Stephen Rowley. First, we have a witness, however reluctant, who will speak in his defense." Holmes turned to Simon Green, who stared at the boards of the church's

86

floor. "Mr. Green, will you tell Constable Wren what you saw on the afternoon of Leader Starkwell's death?"

A moment of silence held, broken by the sound of Mrs. Green shaking her son by his shoulders.

"Go on," said the woman. "You speak and you tell the truth." The young man stirred and spoke in a low, flat voice.

"I seen that Stephen Rowley outside my bedroom window. He was a-hidin' behind the rose brambles, peekin' around 'em. He didn't know I seen 'im, but I did."

"When did you see him?" asked Sherlock Holmes.

"'Twas late, maybe comin' on to four o'clock that day. I know on account of we was havin' a meetin' soon and I didn't want him to foller."

"Stephen Rowley has maintained that he spent the afternoon trying to locate his sister Marie, who was staying with a member of The Order. As he was spotted outside the Green farmhouse while trying to conceal his presence, that surely lends weight to his story."

"Thank God," whispered Sir George Rowley from his pew.

"But this sighting alone may not be enough to convince Constable Wren to release his prisoner. So let us determine who murdered Jonah Starkwell and brought his body to this chapel, for I am certain that the man wasn't killed here."

There was a clatter from the pews as Father Brown dropped and then retrieved his umbrella. When the noise subsided, Sherlock Holmes continued.

"A key question, of course, is motive. But other aspects are even more curious. If Starkwell was killed elsewhere, why was he brought back to the chapel? Why was his body drenched in water? And why was the staff lying beside him also wet?"

This time the noise came not from the visiting clergyman but from the domestic one. Apparently as tribute to his departed leader, Tobias Barnes had chosen that moment to start up the fountain.

"As I explained earlier," he answered, facing the detective, "the dousing of the body with water, as we found it, and the placing of the staff showed how much our leader was revered. It is a fitting memorial for the founding member of The Order of the Flood."

"Perhaps," countered Holmes, "but would it not have been more fitting to commit the body to the sea, as your church ultimately chose to do? If so, then why was he returned to the chapel?"

Tobias Barnes was about to reply when the detective held up a hand in warning. The room grew silent and another sound, this from outside, reached the listeners. A wagon was pulling up beside the cottage, its horse brought to a halt.

The silence held as two pairs of scuffling footsteps grew louder. "Hello?" a voice called out. "Mr. Barnes?"

"Do come in, Mr. Jones," said Sherlock Holmes.

The village carpenter stepped through the doorway, his apprentice Micah following behind. Roger Jones stopped when he saw the assemblage of people. They all stared back at him.

"I beg your pardon," said Jones. "I received a note asking me to come and assess the church for salvage lumber as it's going to be disbanded. I have come at the wrong time."

Sherlock Holmes offered a tight smile. "Your timing is propitious. I wish you and your assistant to stay."

"I can come back," began Jones.

"I must insist. Constable Wren?"

The constable stepped behind the two men and shepherded them to the first pew, where they sat uncomfortably beside Sir George. Holmes approached the new arrivals.

"I apologize for the deception. The message that summoned you was my own creation, and the disbanding of The Order is perhaps premature. But I wanted you in attendance, Mr. Jones, for I was just asking why Jonah Starkwell's murderer chose to return the dead man to this chapel and douse him with water. Mr. Barnes thinks it was a gesture of religious reverence. I believe the reason was a practical one."

The detective crossed to the wall where a steady trickle of water now dripped into the curved basin below. He bent down and traced a finger along the reservoir's rim.

"Even with his body absent for analysis, I knew that Starkwell didn't die by drowning in this fountain, with or without the forked staff used to pin the man down. This basin is made of a decorative soft metal that would never withstand a violent struggle without damage. Rather, the man was struck a deadly blow at the base of his skull. But there are few surfaces within this chapel where the victim could have fallen and acquired that wound. The pews are too narrowly placed for a fall, accidental or deliberate. And although it might have been just possible, the large staff would have proved a most cumbersome murder weapon.

"We must surmise that the blow occurred away from the church, and that the body was brought here. And again I ask: *Why?* How would this move benefit the murderer? If Jonah Starkwell was killed at a person's home or workplace, then by necessity the body would need to be conveyed elsewhere."

Holmes paused and looked directly at Roger Jones, who sat as still as a statue.

"On Thursday afternoon last, Jonah Starkwell called on you at your workshop, did he not? Once there, you entered into an argument that ended with you or your assistant striking him down inside your shop."

The carpenter met Holmes's gaze.

"Go on. You know so much."

"After some deliberation, you decided to place the man's body in a trunk or crate, load him into your wagon, and convey him to the cliffs where you could throw him over and into the sea." Jones looked up at this but Holmes merely shrugged. "It would be the most economical way to dispose of the dead man."

"And then what?" challenged Jones.

"And then, as the cliffs came into view from the path, you saw that the entire range was occupied by The Order's followers, all holding vigil and staring out at the sea. You had no choice but to find another means of disposal. And with everyone from the church worshiping out of doors, it was logical to return the prophet to his chapel. You and your assistant carried Starkwell into the empty church and –"

"It was just me," Jones interrupted. "Micah wasn't at the shop that day. He had nowt to do with it."

Sherlock Holmes studied Micah, not unkindly, before returning to Roger Jones.

"It's a kind gesture, but it's a lie. However, if your assistant didn't strike the blow –"

"He didn't. I hit Starkwell with a newel post that was lying on a work table. He had turned around when Micah entered."

Holmes nodded. "The judge will likely be lenient when considering Micah's role."

"That church of his killed my Elizabeth," said the carpenter. "She had only attended a couple of those infernal services by the sea, but the damage was done. She came down with chills and fever from being out in that damp, cold air and never found her health again. And then, after all these months, this Starkwell had the nerve to come to my shop and accuse me of slandering his church among the village. I never did! But he carried on with his shouts and accusations. He saw red and so did I."

There was another noise from the back pew – Father Brown had dropped something again – but no one took any notice. All listeners seemed intent on catching every word of the craftsman's confession. But it was Sherlock Holmes who spoke next.

"You needed your assistant for the following. Once inside the chapel, you realized you couldn't leave the prophet to be discovered because the condition of his clothes and hair would incriminate you. So you used the forked staff to lift the body upright in the center of the floor – for you are easily the stronger of the two – while Micah retrieved the pail from your wagon and poured water repeatedly over Jonah Starkwell."

"But why, Mr. Holmes?" asked Mrs. Green, bewildered enough to speak out. "Why should he do that?"

In answer, Sherlock Holmes reached out a hand and gently gathered the cloth of Roger Jones's shirt.

"Look closely, Mrs. Green. Do you see?"

The woman leaned across the aisle and stared in concentration at Jones's shirt. Sir George stared also. On the fabric Holmes displayed, minute flecks of sawdust were just visible, along with one thin but definite curl of wood shaving caught among the cloth."

"When he landed," explained Jones ruefully, "he fell on the shop floor. I didn't notice all the sawdust his clothes and hair had picked up until we got him here. With luck, it would've washed away into the floorboards."

Watson recalled the residue Holmes had saved from the chapel floor.

Jones turned to Sir George, his eyes sad but sincere. "I wouldn't have let your Stephen hang. If he was found guilty, I would've done the right thing."

Sir George offered a sad smile. "I believe you. And I'll see to it that you get good counsel. Your Elizabeth wasn't the only one affected by that false prophet." Tobias Barnes, new acting leader of The Order of the Flood, pursed his lips and said nothing.

Later, after Constable Wren had left the chapel with his quarry and the other guests had finally taken their leave, Barnes stood and watched the clouds forming in the stormy southern sky. The clifftop service that afternoon would be a strong one, and with luck a steady rain would fall on the worshipers and commingle with the mist from the sea.

Still thinking of The Order and the alignment of nature, he entered the chapel to find, to his surprise and frustration, that the room wasn't empty after all. The rumpled little Catholic priest was

90

at the fountain, pinching the small tube that siphoned water from the basin to the icon above. The clergyman frowned at the apparatus.

"It is a manufactured miracle," he said. "There is no divinity in it,"

"Divinity be d----d! – Get away from it!"

But the little priest held his ground. "We should all seek divinity, but we should never manufacture it. It is what separates the faithful from the fallen."

"Away with you. You have no right to be here." Barnes stepped forward to run the cleric out, but the man's next words stopped him.

"It is truly sad. From the little I know of Leader Starkwell, I believe he was inspired. That is, he tended his flock out of genuine conviction and for the right reasons, as misguided as those reasons might have been. He was a zealot but an honest one. But you, you aren't a zealot. You are merely a mercenary."

Caution and confusion crept into Tobias Barnes's face.

"What are you talking about?"

"For whatever reason – pride, perhaps, or envy – you have cast yourself in the role of leader, but you will not be able to truly lead your followers. Jonah Starkwell led from his heart and his soul, while you have only your intellect, which is really a low cunning. And that, in the end, will not be enough."

"Nonsense. The Order has cast ballots. I have been elected the new leader."

"Elected, not divinely called." Father Brown was now studying the wooden staff. "It is all manipulation to achieve a goal, calculations that mean nothing. One day, Prophet Starkwell confronts Tom Donner and accuses the miller of slandering his church. Then he argues with Roger Jones, another adversary who Starkwell also believes is attacking him, and that confrontation ends in bloodshed. The prophet is a zealous man, as I said, and would argue and accuse the moment he believed that he and his church had been maligned. And above all I wonder this: Who fanned the flames of persecution? Who told this prophet that others had attacked him and his faith when both men asserted that they had not?"

The priest stopped speaking and silence filled the chapel once more. Father Brown looked now at the rows of pews, empty and unwelcoming.

"It is such a cowardly thing. Perhaps you meant only for your leader to find disgrace and not death in these heated confrontations, but your actions and intent are still mercenary. Just as you cannot hide sin, you cannot hide weakness. You may think yourself a leader, but without redemption, those whom you lead will surely be following a false prophet."

His listener did not reply. The priest studied the interior of the small church. Passing clouds had robbed the room of any sunlight and the atmosphere was now dark and oppressive.

As Father Brown stepped out of the chapel, a distant rumble of thunder sounded. He was glad he had brought his umbrella.

The Adventure of the Canterbury Tale
by Craig Stephen Copland

As I look back on the year of 1895, I note that it had been an exceptionally busy one for Sherlock Holmes. In addition to helping Miss Burnet escape the clutches of Don Juan Murillo, setting young Gilchrist on a straight path, rescuing Violet Smith from the horrors of a forced marriage, solving the murder of the impaled Peter Carey, and sending Hugo Oberstein off to prison, and – if that were not enough – he helped Scotland Yard put away a dozen more criminal men, three gangs of miscreants, and yet another winning woman.

All these cases took place before the welcome arrival of Christmas and the lull that always accompanies the festive season.

The week between Christmas and the New Year has always been a quiet one for me. The English tend not to become ill during the holidays.

Crime is also diminished following Christmas. Some of the rich-but-not-wise families vacate England for the Algarve and take the family mastiff with them. They are then relieved of their silverware, plate, and paintings, many of which are copies and thus a nuisance to the otherwise hard-working burglar.

Regardless, it all left Sherlock Holmes with little to do to occupy his restless mind. Thus, he busied himself at his chemistry table whilst I took a book off the shelf and read in front of the cheerful hearth.

The volume I chose – there was a reason for it – was *The Canterbury Tales* by Geoffrey Chaucer. I hadn't read them since I was a schoolboy and laughed at the ribald humor of *The Miller's Tale*, but on this day, it seemed appropriate to re-read them. This day was the twenty-ninth day of December.

"Do you know," I asked Holmes, "what took place on this day exactly seven-hundred-and-twenty-five years ago? On 29 December, 1170?"

"No, and quite frankly – "

"I'll give you a hint. Someone was murdered. Now, can you guess?"

"No, and furthermore – "

"The book I am reading was written because of it. Does that help?"

"As I have neither any idea what you are reading nor interest in knowing, no. Now, if you don't – "

"*The Canterbury Tales.* Surely you recall why they were written."

"So that an entourage of pilgrims could amuse themselves as they rode to Canterbury. There. Are you done? Now, kindly – "

"Ah, but what had happened *at* Canterbury that made it a shrine for pilgrims?"

He uttered a sigh of exasperation. "The Archbishop, Thomas Beckett, was murdered in the cathedral by four knights who were inspired by a debatable comment of King Henry and, by all accounts, drunk. Since that day, the murder of priests has become rare, as they have been very diligent in preaching of the eternal damnation that is visited upon anyone who dares do so. I have yet to hear of such a murder in England, although some would argue there are cases in which it would be justifiable homicide. Now, please, desist and let me get back to my – "

A loud banging came to the door in Baker Street. We heard Mrs. Hudson open the door and the unmistakable gruff voice of Inspector Lestrade as he apologized for bumping past her. He walked into our front room a few seconds later.

"Mr. Holmes, get your coat on. You better come too, Doctor. There's been a murder a couple of hours ago in St. John's Wood. It's an odd one. Right up your alley. Come along."

Holmes couldn't repress a grin as his eyes sparkled, and he hastened to shut down his chemical experiment so it would neither asphyxiate Mrs. Hudson within the hour, nor explode.

"Pray tell, my dear Inspector," he said as he turned the gas down under his Bunsen burner, "Where in St. John's Wood?"

"St. Monica's Church on the Edgware Road. You know it?"

"I have been there before. And do you have a name of the victim?"

"Name's Thomas Delaney O'Dowd. Better known as Father Tom, the parish priest of St. Monica's. Now, come along. A crowd of prurient gawkers is already standing around the door of the church."

* * * * *

94

In the bold blue brightness of a December morning, a crowd of curious commoners had congregated on the concrete near the door of St. Monica's Church. A phalanx of uniformed constables barricaded the entrance to the narthex and insisted that everyone keep his or her distance.

"'Ow did he get done in?" one of those standing around asked of the others. The man who asked was an old man with a scar on his left cheek and a face almost as grey as his mustache.

"The choir says he had his head split open," said Silas Lapsley. He had dark flowing hair, an eagle nose to rival Dante, wore a black cape, and fancied himself a troubadour. He lived out his assumed identity as a decent bass in the choir of St. Monica's.

"You're in the choir, aren't you?" the grey man said to Silas.

"Indeed I am, and would that I, rather than one of our tender-hearted sopranos, had been the one to discover the body. Dear Mrs. Ordiway followed the trail of blood down into the crypt and screamed and fainted when she saw him."

Overhearing this piece of information, another man, one of the tenors in the choir and therefore being high-strung and having a high voice, whispered, "Is it true Father Tom didn't have a stitch of clothing on him when she found him?"

"Utter nonsense, Hayurst. He was still wearing his shirt and trousers. Only his cassock had been removed, and it was lying on the floor in the apse where, going by the blood on the floor, it looks like he was killed."

The small choir of St. Monica's, consisting of four men (two tenors and two basses) and eight women (four each sopranos and altos) had arrived at the church for a special Sunday afternoon choir practice. It was special because they would be singing two hymns at the evening Vespers Service. That service was special because the homily was to be delivered by the Most Reverend Herbert Vaughan, the Archbishop of the Archdiocese of London.

Needless to say, the Vespers Service had been cancelled and the Archbishop and the Secretary of the Diocese, on hearing of the tragedy, had departed. Before they did so, however, Archbishop Vaughan paid a nearby bicycle boy to run a message over to the Catholic Church of Our Lady on Lisson Grove. The message demanded that the visiting priest, who was most likely taking a nap in the spare room in the manse, come immediately to St. Monica's.

None of the growing crowd on the steps of the church, including the members of the choir who hadn't returned to their homes after the shocking experience of finding a dead priest in the

95

crypt, as well as nearly fifty local residents who had come running when they heard the sirens of the police wagons, had noticed when a short, stocky figure with a round face like a Norfolk dumpling and dressed in a dull cassock and carrying a heavy umbrella arrived and worked his way through the crowd and up to the constables who were guarding the door.

"Oh dear, do pardon me," he said to a constable, "I am required to perform some sacred duties in the church. Terribly sorry to inconvenience you."

With that, Father Brown, the former parish priest in the village of Cobhole in Essex, entered St. Monica's, noticed that the crypt was already filled with important-looking people doing important things and talking importantly, and he spent the next twenty minutes meandering slowly up and down the north and south aisles of the church, pondering the relief sculptures and paintings.

* * * * *

Inspector Lestrade's police carriage stopped in front of St. Monica's Church, and he and Holmes and I stepped out and elbowed our way through the crowd on the steps and up to the door.

As we worked our way through the mass of bodies, all huddled together to protect themselves from the December cold, I heard a deep voice say, "Blimey, if that ain't Mr. Sherlock Holmes, the detective. Scotland Yard must have sore puzzlers if they're bringing in Sherlock Holmes."

I chanced to look at the chap who had said these words. He was tall and powerfully built and although the shape of his facial features was Caucasian, his skin color was dark. He wasn't African dark, but not far off. Maybe North African.

He managed to put his large frame in front of me, blocking my way. "And would you be that Dr. Watson, the one what writes all those stories about Sherlock Holmes?"

I acknowledged somewhat curtly that I was. Before pushing on past him, I reminded myself that Holmes had always maintained that any piece of data, no matter how small, can be significant.

So I asked him, "And who might you be, sir?"

"Name's Simon Martin, sir. If there's anything I can do to be of help, you just have to ask."

"We'll do that," I said and hurried on into the church.

There was no one in the nave. Two uniformed constables were stationed by the side of the altar, blocking the way into the ambulatory and the apse. They moved aside to let me pass, and I caught up to Holmes and Lestrade. At the foot of a pillar in the apse, I saw a pile of cloth that I assumed was the priest's cassock. Beside it was a large pool of drying blood, in which were scattered some particles of flesh.

"Ah, Doctor, there you are," said Holmes. "Would you mind taking a look at these pieces and telling me what they are?"

I knelt down and, with my multiplex knife, picked up a piece and took a close look at it. My initial horrified suspicions were confirmed.

"These are brain matter," I said.

"Precisely what I feared. Now, please follow me down into the crypt."

More constables were standing guard, and they also moved aside to allow us to descend the narrow staircase beside the Lady Chapel. The light was poor, but it was enough to see a body lying on the floor in an awkward, twisted position.

Holmes first inspected the crypt itself and the floor around the body. Apparently convinced that there was nothing of significance to be found there, he asked the constables to perform the unpleasant task of carrying the body up and into the Lady Chapel where the light streaming through the stained-glass windows would allow an immediate examination.

"The wound on the back of this man's skull," said Holmes, "could only have been inflicted by a heavy weapon with a long blade. Has anyone seen such a weapon?"

"Begging your pardon, sir," said one of the constables, "but there's a broad sword lying right back there across the altar. Has a bit of blood on it. You can see that up on the wall, above one of the grave markers, there's a helmet, and underneath is where there should be two swords crossed, but there's only one there. It's a match to the one on the altar."

"Excellent, Constable, thank you. There are two other matters that require an explanation. The first is that the man isn't wearing his shoes. One does not walk around a church in one's stocking feet, so would a couple of you constables mind going to look for them? They cannot be far away, and there must be a reason they aren't on his feet."

Inspector Lestrade nodded to two of his men to start a search for a pair of men's shoes.

"Right, and what's your second thing?" he then asked Holmes.

97

"He has a deep cut in the palm of his right hand. In usual deaths wherein a man is attacked, he faces his attacker and tries to defend himself with his hands and forearms. These often are attacked and bear cuts, abrasions, and bruises."

"That makes sense," said Lestrade. "Whoever murdered him came after him with a broadsword and a dagger. Stabbed him once with the dagger in his hand as he tried to defend himself, and then split his head open with the broadsword."

Lestrade pursed his lips and nodded, seemingly satisfied with his logical deduction.

"A very reasonable conclusion, sir," said Holmes, "and unfortunately, it cannot possibly be true. If he had been facing his opponent and defending himself, his head would have been split from his forehead and not from the back. And I suggest you try lifting and wielding the broadsword. You will find that it requires two hands. It is impossible unless one is an enormously powerful man to run with it in one hand and a dagger in the other and then to use it to strike a powerful blow when holding it with only one hand."

"All right, then, Mr. Holmes," said Lestrade, "what happened?"

"Inexplicable though it appears, it is possible the stab wound in the hand was inflicted after the *blow* to the head. Don't ask me why someone would do that, but it does fit the data we have observed."

"All right, I won't ask," said Lestrade. "Anything else you can tell us?"

"The head wound begins on the top of the cranium and continues down around the back side of the skull. This priest is as tall as I am. In order to inflict a wound with a sword that extends to the top of the skull, the attacker would have to be even taller if he were to raise the sword and bring it down at that angle. Were he shorter, the wound would be mainly to the back of the head."

"All right," said Lestrade. "We're looking for a tall fellow who kills a priest, stabs his hand, removes his cassock, and then drags him to the entrance of the crypt and throws him down. Shouldn't be too hard to find. We can start in by seeing if anyone has escaped from Bedlam."

"Somehow, I don't believe whoever did this is insane. However, it is too early to form any conclusions. Oh, did anyone find his shoes?"

There was no answer, and the constables who had been sent on the search shrugged with their palms up and open.

"They must be somewhere not far away," said Holmes.

"Have you looked in the confessional?"

This question came from the quiet voice of a small man who had been standing behind one of the large constables. He now stepped forward and bowed ever so slightly toward Holmes.

Holmes looked up at him and gave an equally small bow in return.

"Hello, Father Brown," he said. "I suppose I shouldn't be surprised to see you here. The Archbishop sent you?"

"Yes. He tends to demand my presence when crimes take place anywhere in his ecclesiastical domain."

"It will be an interesting experience to work with you again," said Holmes. "I have fond memories of our last cooperative effort."

"Oh, oh yes, so do I. I was so awfully impressed with your singular ability to observe physical evidence where no one else had noticed."

"And I with yours to see what could have transpired in a man's heart that I lacked the insight to understand. The heart, you informed us, has its reasons that reason knows not of. I believe Dr. Watson wrote that one down and gave full attribution to you."

"Oh dear, I hope not. I'm afraid I merely borrowed it from Pascal."

* * * * *

Over five centuries ago, the Knights Templar (the English division) established themselves in a forested area two-and-a-half miles northwest of Charing Cross. In 1312, the property was transferred to the Order of the Knights of the Hospital of St. John of Jerusalem (also the English division) and was eventually sold off as housing lots and became an expensive residential suburb of London. It retained the name of St. John's Wood, although trembling trees and wooded areas had become scarce, with the exception of a small woodlot, which is all that remains of an overgrown cemetery.

On this Sunday afternoon in 1895, the residents of St. John's Wood walked and wandered their way through the winter weather to wonder at the wretched waste of the life of their parish priest, the Reverend Thomas Delaney O'Dowd of St. Monica's Church on Edgware Road.

St. Monica's Church in St. John's Wood was named after the marvelous mother of St. Augustine who must have spent many sleepless nights making plans to marshal her miserable son into moral improvement and finally force him to forget about the few pears he stole as a child. She succeeded, and the baptized boy

99

became a saint, and his writings have been bitterly argued over by his Augustinian devotees and the tried-and-true Thomists ever since.

As we enter this fine church on this final Sunday of 1895, we see an empty nave and a cluster of men emerging from the ambulatory, led by a short priest whose countenance is chubby and cherubic. He considered taking them down the south aisle but then stopped and elected to take his followers down the center aisle.

"We mustn't disturb anything of importance," he said although only those immediately behind him could hear him.

He then cut back through the pews and approached the confessional booth from the other end of the south aisle.

"If you will look into the priest's compartment of this dark box," he said to one of the constables, "I expect you will find the missing shoes."

The constable opened the door of the center section and there they were, two well-worn shoes lying irregularly on the floor.

"All right, Father," said Lestrade, "why would the killer take the man's shoes and throw them in the confessional box?"

"Oh no, sir. They weren't taken. Reverend O'Dowd left them there. We men of the cloth don't let on about it, but sitting in the dark box for an extended time is horribly uncomfortable. We cannot be seen, and so it isn't uncommon for a man to doff his shoes and loosen his belt whilst listening to a confession. I'm afraid I do so all the time."

"Right, so he's listening to someone go on about their sins and suddenly he bolts out of the door, *sans* shoes, and goes up to the apse where someone whacks him. Is that what happened?"

"Oh, I don't think so, Inspector. If you look at the hymnals and prayer books lying in the aisle between here and the altar, it seems more likely he was running from the moment he left his box. As he was running in his socks, he most likely slipped, knocked those things to the floor, and got up again and kept running."

"From what?"

"Oh no, Inspector. From *whom*?"

"All right, who?"

"If we can answer why first, sir, we are on the road to answering whom."

"Fine then. Why?" asked Lestrade.

"We don't know yet, but most likely because of whatever the penitent, who entered the confessional box whilst armed with a broad sword, confessed to."

"So the priest hears something and that causes him to flee in panic, chased by a killer wielding a broad sword. He runs to the back door. There's a door beside the Lady Chapel, right?"

"Yes, there is, and I do believe that is a reasonable reconstruction. Oh, and if you look along the aisle between here and the altar, you might find a woman's scarf or shawl."

One of the constables walked up the aisle, peering down at the pews as he went. At the third pew from the front, he leaned down and retrieved an elegant purple shawl.

"Here it is," he said and he brought it back to where Father Brown, Inspector Lestrade, Sherlock Holmes, and Dr. Watson were standing.

"Thank you, Constable," said Father Brown. "I believe you will find it belongs to one of the members of the choir. She will be standing outside with the other women from the choir. They will be in tears. And her name will be Veronica."

* * * * *

Holmes spent a few minutes inspecting the confessional booth and the aisle leading to the altar. He then walked back down the south aisle toward the front door of the church and I followed him. The constables must have taken pity on the crowd, for they had allowed them to come in from the cold and stand in the narthex.

"Holmes," I said when we were out of earshot of the others, "what did you think of Father Brown's saying the woman's name would be Veronica?"

"I expect he is right."

"But how could he know that? Do you suppose as a priest he has some special revelation from the Almighty?"

"Oh, please, Watson."

Obviously, no ghosts need apply, or spirits for that matter, holy or otherwise. I let the matter drop but remained somewhat perplexed.

"Enough of all that," said Holmes. "It's time to begin our interrogation of the suspects."

"There must have been fifty people standing around. Maybe closer to a hundred by now."

"We were told that the only people in or near the church at the time of the murder were the members of the choir, the organist, and the priest. That reduces our list. Assuming the killer was strong enough to wield a broadsword, sufficiently fleet of foot to keep up with a fleeing priest, and tall enough to land a blow on the top of his

101

head, we are down to six. The men. The organist, the tenors, and the basses."

"Oh, yes, well, I suppose that does cut down the numbers. Anything else?"

"The Archbishop paid a visit. That is of interest."

"You don't suspect him, do you?"

"No, but his visit raises other suspicions. He brought the Secretary of the Diocese with him, did he not?"

"Yes, they do like to have their underlings around to support them. It makes them look important, wouldn't you say?"

"The Secretary of the Archdiocese of London isn't a mere underling. He has oversight of all the business, financial, and administrative affairs of the Diocese. As a business, it is larger than all but the largest commercial firms in the city. There are hundreds of employees, scores of properties, and it has assets and transactions in the realm of a million pounds a year or more."

"So what was he doing here if all the Archbishop came for was as a guest to deliver homily?"

"My dear Watson, clearly he doesn't tag along with the Archbishop if His Grace came to do no more than preach for twenty minutes. His presence tells us there is some other matter of concern taking place in this parish. I am assuming whoever murdered Father Tom did so for reasons that may be connected to whatever brought the Archbishop. I shall now pursue that line of inquiry until proven otherwise."

I looked over the crowd who were standing around chatting. The members of the choir had been told not to leave. Those who weren't members had been encouraged to leave. Some did. Many did not. Such is the irresistible attraction when something macabre takes place all too close to home.

"Who are you going to interrogate?" I asked. "Several of the men from the choir, including the tenors, are quite tall. I wouldn't know where to start."

"Then we shall not start with the men. We shall have a friendly chat with one of the women members."

"A woman? Which one?"

"The fairer sex is your department," he said. "Cast your knowledgeable and experienced eye over the lot of them and tell me which one you can tell, by looking at her, is the most likely to be the confidant, the keeper of the secrets, the font of knowledge concerning the church and Father Thomas."

102

If I had learned anything from my years as a doctor with many female patients, it was that infinitely more is learned by listening than speaking. For several minutes I regarded the gathered sopranos and altos as they engaged in animated conversation and watched to see who amongst them was competing to be heard and who was listening.

I settled on a plain-looking soul of around fifty years of age who was looking directly into the eyes of an energetic and voluble much younger woman and saying next to nothing. I walked over to the two of them, apologized for interrupting their conversation and requested that the older woman come with me.

"Scotland Yard and Mr. Sherlock Holmes are beginning their interviews with the choir members," I said.

"Well, then, I should come too," said the younger one. "Our dear Hazel is a very close friend, but her mind isn't as sharp as it was when she was my age."

"It's quite all right, Harriet," said the older woman. "Let's just do what the police are asking."

"Oh, I don't think that would be a good idea. You never – "

"Madam," I said, "you are asking your friend to violate police procedures. Scotland Yard takes a very dim view of those who obstruct their investigation. Now, if you will excuse us."

I led Hazel back into the nave where Holmes was waiting for us. He smiled and greeted her graciously, and the three of us sat in chairs along the back wall of the nave where Holmes began his questions.

* * * * *

Father Brown had also ambled out of the nave and into the narthex. Once there, he gazed around the crowd, looking for the one distinctive head of a Gascon of gigantic stature and enormous strength. He had given Flambeau instructions to do something at which Flambeau was exceptionally good. He told him to find out everything.

He spotted him. Flambeau was standing near the middle of the room and was surrounded by a half-dozen doe-eyed darlings who were driven to devote their time to this powerful giant with the irresistible French accent.

Father Brown approached his colleague from the posterior and gave his derrière a firm smack with the handle of his umbrella.

103

"*Mon Dieu!*" cried Flambeau, "Who do you think . . . oh . . . it's you, Father. What do you want?"

"It seemed that once again a good-looking woman has called you off the assignment I gave you. Have you found out anything about this priest, Father Thomas Delaney O'Dowd?"

"But of course. These lovely ladies have told me very much. I would to tell you everything I learn."

He turned back to his attractive attentive audience and bade a gracious and flattering *adieu*, giving each of them his card before turning to the somewhat impatient Father Brown.

"Well, well, what to you can I say?" said Flambeau. "This priest, he was respected but not, how shall I say, *sympathetique*. He is very strict, they tell me. If you don't come to Mass and confession, he comes to find you and tell you to make better. When you come to do confession, he doesn't just listen and say to you encouraging things. He chastises, he reprimands, he lectures. If you try to make a confession that is only in part, he knows. He asks questions. Many questions. It's as if he knows what is your sin before you confess and he drags the truth from your heart."

"Goodness, why would anyone come to confession if he treated them like that?"

"I ask to them the same. They say – What is the word you use? *Cathartic*. Yes. One *jolie fille*, she say to me, it is like when you are sick in the morning and you feel terrible in your stomach, but then you vomit and you feel better."

"Oh, well, that is an interesting analogy."

"You think so? I didn't think so. But they all agree he is to them like Christ driving the money lenders and bankers out of the temple. He is like Our Savior when he came to Saint John on the Isle of Patmos and is holy and righteous and terrifying. His homilies make them feel so bad they go home and resolve to be better. So he is a good priest, even if he isn't a friendly priest."

"Such a shame he's gone. Very well, then, Flambeau, come. We need to have a chat with the inspector and Mr. Sherlock Holmes."

* * * * *

"Thank you kindly for helping with our investigation," said Holmes to the woman I had introduced to him as Hazel. "And is it Miss Hazel, or Mrs. Hazel?"

"It is Miss Hazel Hubble, and I live in Briony Lodge. I am employed by the Board of Inland Revenue. I am forty-eight years of age and I sing alto in the choir. Do you need any further information about me?"

I scribbled furiously and Holmes replied.

"No, Madam, that is sufficient. Please accept our condolences for the tragedy that occurred here this afternoon."

"Thank you, Mr. Holmes. Now then, what do you wish to know?"

"Was there any animosity toward Father O'Dowd? Did anyone in the parish, or anywhere else for that matter, have a strong dislike of him? And, if so, why?"

She responded with a silent pause and a serene smile. "Mr. Holmes, as a devoted Catholic, I make it a practice to not speak uncharitably of anyone behind their backs, and especially, I do not speak ill of the dead."

"A most admirable way to live," said Holmes. "However, I am assisting Scotland Yard in a murder investigation. In such a situation, unpleasant though it is, one must tell the truth. It is much easier to do so here when Dr. Watson and I can guarantee complete confidentiality than in open court where there will be none. With that in mind, Miss Hubble, please do your best to help the investigation."

"I suppose, if you put it that way, then I have to be frank. Nobody liked Father O'Dowd."

"Can you be more specific? Did anyone dislike him so greatly that they would do him harm?"

"Obviously, someone did, Mr. Holmes. Every member of the choir has an opinion, but no one could come up with any name of anyone who would want to *kill* him."

"Had there been any threats against him?"

"Yes."

"Oh, could you please elaborate?"

"Three weeks ago, one of the choir members – a tenor, Mr. Lebrun – had some words with Father O'Dowd. He accused him of – well, not exactly being an adherent of Americanism, but of failing to condemn it sufficiently. But nothing came of it. Well, almost nothing."

"Yes? Go on."

"Well, we don't know if there was any connection, but the following Sunday, after Mass, as we were all milling around outside the door, where Father O'Dowd always stands and reminds us to live righteously, someone – and no one saw who it was – gave him a push and he tumbled down the steps."

"Ah, and was he injured?"

"Yes. He hurt his knee and strained his back and had some nasty scratches on his head. Simon Martin helped him up and took him to the hospital. That would be the St. John and St. Elizabeth Hospital over on Circus Road, just north of Lord's. He spent the rest of the week in that hospital."

"I am familiar with it. Go on."

"The ladies from the women's auxiliary sent him some flowers and sweets, mostly chocolates, and cards telling him were praying for him."

"And how did he come along? I assume you all visited him regularly."

"Well, no. Not a one."

Holmes raised an eyebrow. "That seems rather uncharitable, does it not?"

"You could say that, I suppose. However, we have no choice but to have a conversation with him when we endure confession. No one would voluntarily submit to an additional admonition he would be sure to give you, even from his hospital bed. Well, I shouldn't say no one. We heard that his mother came to see him several times."

"As one might expect a mother to do," said Holmes. "Thank you, Madam."

Over the next hour, having been denied an opportunity to look at the body of the dead priest, the curious and prurient drifted away. Holmes and Inspector Lestrade interviewed other members of the choir, and I noticed that Father Brown and his tall friend were doing likewise. When statements had been taken from everyone who had been anywhere close to the location of the crime, Inspector Lestrade requested that we come into the vestry office for a strategic meeting. He made a point of asking Father Brown to join us.

Father O'Dowd's spacious office was, not surprisingly, spotless, spare, and scrupulously well-ordered. One wall was entirely lined with bookshelves on which sat copies of the volumes penned by St. Augustine, St. Thomas Aquinas, St. Anselm, St. Theresa of Ávila, and Ignatius of Loyola. Well-thumbed editions of both Foxe's *Book of Martyrs* and Butler's *Lives of the Saints* sat on the desk where, I assumed, they were consulted when preparing the weekly homily.

On the other walls hung paintings depicting Biblical scenes. The largest was a miniature copy of the massive altar wall of the Sistine Chapel where Michelangelo painted the Last Judgement. There were also prints of Samson tearing apart the lion, Christ clearing the temple, an entire triptych of Hieronymus Bosch's *Garden of Earthly Delights*, and a rather primitive one of St. Peter cutting off the ear of Malchus after the fashion of Caravaggio.

Any space on any wall not covered by a painting was adorned with a crucifix.

"All right," said the inspector to the attendees of his meaningful meeting. "Let us pool our knowledge and decide where the evidence leads us. Right, you start, Mr. Holmes."

Sherlock Holmes recounted his conversation with Miss Hazel Hubble and her revelation about Mr. Lebrun and Father Thomas O'Dowd.

"Is he one of the tall ones?" asked Lestrade.

"He is indeed."

"Good to know. Anything else?"

"Yes. I have previously imparted my deductions as to how the murder took place and any pertinent data I extracted from my interrogations. However, I did return to the south aisle and the ambulatory with a question in my mind: Why did he fall? Had he not, even running in his stocking feet, he might have made it to the rear door and escaped with his life. I observed that in both places where he fell, partway up the aisle and by the pillar in the apse where he died, the floor had been polished with a fine coating of wax. It was treacherously slippery in those places and not in others."

"That's interesting, Mr. Holmes," said Lestrade, "and if I am following your thought, it looks like whoever did this planned it out in advance."

"Precisely. He fell twice."

"Three times," said Father Brown.

Everyone turned to look at him.

"You said he also fell down the stairs, or at least he was pushed. That would make three falls."

"It would," said Sherlock Holmes, "if you choose to add an event that took place a fortnight earlier."

"I'm afraid we must if it is to all fall into place," said Father Brown. "You said he was taken to the hospital, but you didn't tell us who took him and who helped him after he toppled down the stairs. Is it possible his name was Simon?"

"Yes, it was, but how did you know that?"

"And his mother came to visit him in the hospital. Her name must have been Mary?"

"Correct," said Holmes. "May I ask how you deduced that?"

"And while you're at it," said Inspector Lestrade, "just how did you know that shawl belonged to a woman named Veronica?"

"Because it all fits. Everything fits."

"Fits what?" said Lestrade. "Now, look here, Father, I mean no disrespect, but you seem to know quite a lot about what went on here. How about an explanation?"

"It was all around you in the nave and the ambulatory. Did you not see them?"

"See what?" said Lestrade, the volume of his questions rising.

"Why, the Stations of the Cross. Everything that took place was planned to correspond with the Stations of the Cross. Whoever did this terrible deed organized it in accordance with the fourteen stations."

"All right, Father," said Lestrade, "that might make sense to you, but I was raised as an occasional Presbyterian, and we didn't have any stations. So kindly explain."

"If you will bear with me, gentlemen," said Father Brown. "At the first station, Our Lord was condemned – that would be the accusation of Americanism. Then he was forced to carry his cross, which matches metaphorically with the burden of expecting to have to defend himself in front of the Archbishop and the Secretary. The push down the steps was the first fall. Those are the second and third stations. Our Lord then met his mother, Mary, and was helped by Simon of Cyrene. Those were out of order but they were fifth and the fourth. Veronica used her shawl to wipe Christ's brow, and then he fell a second time. Stations six and seven took place in the aisle between the confession box and the altar. The women of Jerusalem, who are played by the ladies in the choir, were weeping. He fell a third time when he reached the apse. Stations eight, nine and ten. Our Lord was stripped, his hands were nailed to the cross and he died. He was taken down from the cross and placed in the tomb. Those are the remaining stations. The priest's cassock was removed, his hand was pierced, he died, was taken away, and thrown into the crypt. It's all there."

His explanation was followed by a long, stunned silence.

"If I understand you correctly," said Sherlock Holmes, "you are telling us that this murder was planned out as a re-enactment of a religious ritual. The murderer has re-created the stages of the crucifixion. Is that right?"

"Yes, quite thoroughly, and we must not forget the most immediate event."

"And just what would that be?" said Lestrade.

"The martyrdom of St. Thomas Beckett. He was murdered whilst clinging to a pillar in the apse of the Canterbury Cathedral. His head was split open with a broadsword."

I glanced at Holmes. He was scowling and had taken out his cigarette case and lit one of them.

"Father Brown," he said, "I have been privy to no end of bizarre cases, many of them complicated murders, but I have never heard of anything so strangely plotted and carried out as what you have described."

"I have no doubt of that, Mr. Holmes. But neither have you sat in a confession box and listened to men's – and one or two women's – imagined ways they would take revenge on their enemies. By comparison with the evil that takes place in the mind, the evil that is carried out pales. Horrifying acts beyond our most debased imaginations are laid out in a man's thoughts. By the grace of God, they are seldom transferred to reality. Once you have listened to so many of them, it isn't difficult to put yourself inside the mind and soul of a murderer and see what he sees."

I had to ponder what he had said. It occurred to me that whatever confidences had been shared with me by a patient in my surgery concerning hair loss, unwanted hair growth, bowel obstructions, loss or acquisition of bodily fluids and the like were of little consequence to what a parish priest must endure hearing about whilst on the other side of the confessional screen.

Inspector Lestrade broke the awkward silence.

"Mr. Holmes, this tall tenor who had the barney with the priest – What was his name?"

"Lebrun. Joshua Lebrun."

"He's tall, right? And something of a zealot, right?"

"Right on both, Inspector."

"Then he's at the top of my list. You agree?"

"It is still somewhat premature, but it is plausible."

"Good. But I suppose he's gone home. Do we know where he lives? I'll bet there's a record of all the choir members' addresses somewhere in this office. Let's start looking."

"Allow me to suggest a more efficient route," said Holmes. "I hear the organ playing."

"What? Are you now hearing voices from God hidden in the Curious?"

"I believe you are referring to the *Kyrie*. And no. I am assuming the choir organist knows where all the members live, and all we have to do is ask him."

Unlike the great cathedrals of Europe where the organ sits high above the back of the nave, the organ in St. Monica's, being more modest, was nestled in a niche near where the nave met the ambulatory. An exceptionally ordinary man sat on the organist's bench, his long legs pumping on the pedals, rehearsing Bach's *Mass in C Minor* and Prince Albert's *Te Deum*. He didn't appreciate being interrupted, and Holmes did not care.

"As you know, sir, we are investigating the murder of your priest and need your assistance. Would you kindly tell us your name?"

"Olivenstein. Otis Olivenstein. Please pose your questions quickly so I can get on with practicing these pieces. They will be wanted at the funeral."

Holmes asked his simple question, and in response was given an address for Joshua Lebrun close to the intersection of Abbey Road and Grove End Road, a few minutes north of St. Monica's.

"Jolly good there, Mr. Holmes," said Lestrade. "I'll go and chat some more with this crazy conservative Catholic and see what he has to say for himself. I'll wager now he has no alibi for what he was up to when the priest got his head hacked."

"I look forward to hearing what he has to say," said Holmes.

"That won't be necessary. You've done what I wanted you to do here, so you and the doctor may as well go back home. Same goes for you, Father, and your Frenchie friend."

Holmes, I knew, wouldn't like being left out, but there was little he could do, and so we turned on our heels and headed back to Baker Street, where the indefatigable Mrs. Hudson fussed over us with a late lunch.

We spent the rest of that afternoon reading and sipping sherry. By five o'clock, it was dark outside, and I was ready for a cup of tea.

"Would you like one as well?" I asked Holmes.

He nodded and kept reading.

"Do you suppose Scotland Yard will want you to do more on this case? Or is that the end of it?"

He put down his book and lit a cigarette.

"It had the marks of an interesting investigation, and I admit I was looking forward to the pursuit, but it is out of my hands. All I can do is wish the inspector good success and a happy New Year."

"Do you agree that this Lebrun chap is the likely suspect?"

"I neither agree nor disagree. I would have waited until significantly more data had been gathered before moving to an arrest. Although I must give Lestrade credit – had he waited, it's possible Monsieur Lebrun would have made a run for it. He is French, of course. Perhaps there was some wisdom in acting quickly. We shall see . . . and speak of the Devil!"

A familiar rough knock pounded on our door and, a minute later, Inspector Lestrade entered the room.

"How kind of you to come for tea, Inspector," said Holmes. "Please join us."

"Don't have time for that, Mr. Holmes. Unlike you gentlemen of leisure, a policeman's job is never done, Sunday evening or not. I just came by out of professional courtesy to thank you for your help this morning."

"It is my calling and duty to provide such assistance as I'm able to," said Holmes.

"Right, and again, not being in any way obligated to do so, you understand, I thought you might want to know what has happened since this morning."

"Very thoughtful of you, Lestrade, as always," said Holmes.

"Right. So I took one of my constables with me, and off we went to where this Lebrun chap lives, up at Abbey Road and Grove End Road. First thing I see when we get out is some bloke wearing a black suit and walking across the road in his bare feet. It's winter, and some of these strange Catholic monks are into mortification of the flesh, correct? Well, that isn't him. It's only some Bohemian musician, but I ask if he knows where Lebrun lives and he says, 'I imagine he's in that block of flats,' and it turns out he's right. Right?"

"And you knocked on his door and there he was," said Holmes. "I imagine it was easy to do."

"Right. I go in and start with chat-chat and such and ask him some questions. Well, he acknowledges he's part of some movement of devout French Catholics, and yes, they are upset about what they call this *Americanisme* – that's French for Americanism – spreading through the Church."

"And just what is that?" said Holmes.

111

"Well, that's what I asked him, and he says it all the thing in America, where the bishops and priests are watering down Catholic doctrine to make it more appealing to all those independent, individual-minded Americans who think their devotion to their flag and constitution and civic duty come before their obligations to the Church. And in France, they say it's a heresy. And, well, you know what the French do to heretics, right?"

"They burned Joan of Arc at the stake did they not? Back in the Thirteenth Century? Three centuries before they had their revolution – Isn't that correct, Watson?"

I said nothing and only nodded, anxious for the inspector to get on with the story he appeared to be enjoying delivering.

"Well, and yes, he admits he and Father O'Dowd had a few words about it three weeks ago after the priest said something in his homily about loyalty to the Crown. But he says there were no hard feelings, and he and the Father often had arguments after Mass. Well then, I hit him between the eyes and demanded that he account for where he was just before choir practice, and he says he was standing out behind the church having a cigarette, a *Gitanes*, or maybe it was a *Gauloises*, but he can't remember which it was. And was anybody with him? Could anybody vouch for him? Nope, not a one. So then I lower the boom, and tell him we now know he's the one what killed the priest. Well, he gets all huffy, you know, the way the French do, and denies everything, but I can see through him and arrest him and so off he comes with me to the Embankment, and we put him in jail, and Bob's your uncle."

"An unparalleled accomplishment," said Holmes. He looked ready to say more, but Inspector Lestrade turned toward the door.

"And a Happy New Year to you, Mr. Holmes. And you too Doctor." And with that, he departed.

Holmes sat in silence, puffing on his cigarette.

"You aren't convinced, are you?" I said to him.

"It is too early to tell," he said. "However, I may make a few discreet inquiries on my own time."

* * * * *

It is half-past four in the afternoon on the first day of the New Year and the sun has already set. It is cold but not windy and the streets are quiet. Many English families have adopted the ritual of sitting down to a cooked goose, enjoying each other's company, and announcing those resolutions which they have no possibility of keeping.

We see, slowly walking north on Baker Street from Marylebone and using his umbrella as a walking stick, the unmistakable round shape of Father Brown. He looks at each door number as he strolls past and comes to a stop at the one marked *221*. With the handle of his umbrella, he gives a quiet rhythmic tap on the door. It is answered by a woman of a certain age.

"Blessings on you for the New Year," he says to her. "May I ask if this is the residence of Mr. Sherlock Holmes?"

"For sure it is," she says, and then gives him a look up and down. "Must say, you're an odd one. What crime have you been accused of that you're needing Mr. Holmes?"

The look on his face says he finds her question amusing.

"They say I murdered, cooked, and ate my last landlady, but I got off because the evidence had disappeared."

The look on her face says she didn't find his answer amusing. She stands back and points to the stairs.

"He's up there."

The priest enters the front room, where Dr. Watson is sitting, reading, and Mr. Sherlock Holmes is pacing back and forth the length of the room. They welcome him and Dr. Watson rises, walks to the sideboard, and pours their visitor a glass of brandy.

"And here's to the New Year of Our Lord, 1896," says the doctor, raising his snifter. The priest raises his in response. Sherlock Holmes does not bother. They sit quietly and sip.

"The possibility of your coming for a social visit is nil," said Sherlock Holmes. "Pray tell, to what do we owe the honor?"

"I have walked here from the offices of Scotland Yard. It took some time and allowed me to examine my thoughts."

"I presume," said Sherlock Holmes, "that you weren't so much visiting the offices as you were the cells in the cellar, and furthermore, you were paying a visit to Monsieur Joshua Lebrun. Correct, Father?"

"Oh my, yes. One would have to get up awfully early in the morning to evade your deductions, Mr. Holmes. Yes, he and I had a chat, and then I offered him the Sacrament of Confession."

"And what did he tell you?"

"Of course, I am forbidden to reveal what he said during the sacrament, but when we were only chatting, he was quite vociferous in denying he had murdered Father O'Dowd."

113

"Without knowing what he then said during his confession," said Sherlock Holmes, "it's impossible for me to judge if he were telling the truth."

"Ah, an excellent insight, Mr. Holmes. I would be violating my vows if I were to disclose what he did confess, but I don't think I would be in too much danger if I happened to let slip what he did *not* confess."

"And that would be, Father?"

"He did not confess to being a murderer."

"Would any man?"

"Oh, yes, they do. I have heard it three times during my years, and those of my order who labor in the prisons hear it all the time. When a man is facing the gallows, he is quite eager to seek absolution, hoping his time in the next life will be easier than this one."

"Listening to such men make a confession as they are about to meet their Maker is not something I have experienced. Pray tell, Father, what, if any, conclusions did you reach?"

The round little priest transferred his umbrella to his left hand and with his right hand crossed himself.

"I believed him."

Sherlock Holmes said nothing and stood and resumed pacing back and forth the length of the room. After two complete circuits, he stopped and lit a cigarette.

"I consider your insight significant," he said to the priest. "What are you going to do about it?"

"Oh, no, Mr. Holmes. The question is not what am *I* going to do about it. It is what are *we* going to do about it? As a man who has given his life to the service of the Almighty, I have no choice but to continue the path I find myself upon. You sir, as a man who has devoted his life to the pursuit of justice, have no choice but to join me. Would you agree, sir?"

Sherlock Holmes stubbed his cigarette in the ashtray, somewhat forcibly.

"Agree that I have no choice? Well, I suppose I don't."

"Oh, and allow me to remind you that you will not be paid a farthing for your efforts, but the rewards to your soul will be beyond earthly value."

"Fine. Then let us get to work. But no sermonizing and no appeals to the supernatural."

* * * * *

I sat in one of our chairs with my pencil and notebook at the ready. Holmes, his pipe lit, sat in his familiar armchair and looked steadily at Father Brown, who occupied the sofa, his umbrella standing straight up in front of him and held in place by his interlaced fingers resting on the handle.

"I have been giving this matter considerable thought," said Father Brown, "and I must confess, I am somewhat befuddled about one or two matters. Would you mind, Mr. Holmes, if I asked for your insights on them? It would be very helpful."

Holmes smiled and nodded, but I had seen the look on his face and the subtle roll of his eyes often enough to tell that he gave short shrift to any possibility Father Brown was indeed befuddled.

"Please, Father, pray share these matters with me."

"Why, thank you, sir. Let me begin with my seeing that the killer staged his foul deed by mimicking the Stations of the Cross. However, the first station, if we may call it that, took place three weeks earlier. The second, third, and fourth were also some time before the day of the murder. Therefore, we can conclude our villain was a regular attendee of the church. He was on the inside, as they say. Would you agree, sir?"

"Entirely. If we accept your Stations of the Cross insight, your conclusion is inevitable."

"Oh, good. It is always nice to get off to a good start. All right, then. The next curious item is the murder. Had our villain wanted to murder his priest, it would have been far easier just to open the door of the confessional box and shoot him as he sat there. He could have done that with little fuss and escaped out the back door by the Lady Chapel. But he chose not to do that."

Holmes nodded. "I agree. Do go on."

"He entered the confession and, at some point during the confession, he told Father Tom he was going to kill him. Otherwise why would Father Tom have bolted out of the box and run for his life? Something must have taken place during the confession that wasn't known for certain before the confession."

"But the killer appears to have taken the broad sword off the wall and taken it with him into the confession. He was prepared to kill the priest."

"Oh, indeed he was, Mr. Holmes. Indeed, he was. But had he made his confession and received absolution and was assured of inviolable confidentiality, there would have been no need to kill the priest. He could have walked away and put the sword back on the

115

wall. Therefore, I have tried to put myself inside the heads of both the killer and the priest and see what they saw and hear what they heard whilst in the confession box."

"An interesting exercise, Father," said Holmes, "but as what was said can now never be known, how does that help us?"

"Oh, yes, of course, that is quite right, sir. We cannot *know*, but some things can be *inferred*. Every priest is bound by Ecclesiastical Law and privilege and cannot divulge what he is told during confession, not even in a court of law. But there are exceptions. If the penitent confesses to a horribly hideous crime – say, perhaps the violation or murder of a child, or the assassination of a prime minister in such a way as to start a war – the law and Rome require such information to be divulged, in confidence, to the police."

"I am aware of those possibilities, Father. Please continue."

"If such a crime had been committed and the criminal confessed and received absolution, there would be no need to kill the priest. Therefore, it seems reasonable to conclude that, having been told of the monumental crime, Father Tom not only refused absolution, but informed the villain he would have to take what he had been told to the police. And now the villain proceeds with his well-laid plot to rid himself of this meddlesome priest. Do you follow me, Mr. Holmes?"

"Yes, but I'm not aware of any such horrendous crime having been committed of late that would qualify for such an exceedingly rare exception. And I assure you, I follow the news of crime both in England and on the Continent closely."

"Ah, and your doing so leads to the next conclusion: The villain confessed not to a crime he had *already* committed, but to one he was *planning* to commit. Of course, no absolution can be given for such a confession, as absolution requires acknowledgment of sin, remorse, commitment to go and sin no more, and some form of penance. That is not available for a sin that has not yet taken place."

"You are confusing me," said Holmes. "Surely no sinner, and most certainly no criminal, confesses to something that hasn't yet taken place. What is the use of that?"

"Oh, my dear Mr. Holmes, it happens quite often. Think of it as an insurance policy. It is particularly prevalent amongst those men who plan to do something wrong that poses a danger to their lives if the plan fails. They could be killed whilst engaging in crime and sent on their way to appear before the Almighty having been neither absolved nor given the Last Rites."

116

"That makes sense, but you left out the re-enactments of the events."

"Oh, yes, those. The murder of Thomas Beckett and the Stations of the Cross. Had our killer chosen *one*, I might have believed he was a religious zealot and consumed, indeed obsessed. But two? Doesn't that seem to you, Mr. Holmes, to be one too many? I reached the tentative conclusion that they were a blind, a distraction to lead us to accuse Mr. Lebrun."

"They worked."

"Yes, but Inspector Lestrade is a Presbyterian, so we cannot expect him to be familiar with historical events that are sacred to the Church."

Holmes leaned back and puffed away on his pipe for a full minute.

"If I understand you correctly, you are saying that a regular adherent of St. Monica's is planning to commit a horrific crime. He goes to confession in advance, hoping to be absolved, just in case. He knows there is a possibility Father Tom will not only refuse absolution but, on hearing of the intended crime, let it be known that he must inform the police. Whereupon the killer withdraws the sword he has taken into the confession, just in case. Father Tom sees the danger and dashes out of the box and toward the door. The killer runs after him, catches up when he falls, and kills him."

"Oh, very good, Mr. Holmes. You have such a gift for organization and clarity. Very good."

"All well and good. But what then is this expected enormous crime that would justify breaking the confidentiality of confession?"

"Oh, dear, I'm afraid I don't know. That was as far as my mind took me. Can you think of anything?"

* * * * *

Dr. Watson, Sherlock Holmes, and Father Brown sat in silence pondering the conclusion the well-fed little priest had just revealed. The doctor stood, made his way to the mantel of the hearth, and retrieved the decanter of sherry. After refilling three glasses, he returned the bottle, sat down, and exercised his gift of silence.

Sherlock Holmes then put down his sherry and started to pace the length of the room, rounding at the chemistry table, and returning to a place where he could gaze into the hearth. After giving the coal and ashes a stir with a somewhat less-than-straight poker, he turned back to Father Brown.

117

"I am no more aware of any enormous crime that is planned than I am of one recently committed. However, I do know one or two things *about* crimes. A single man alone – or a woman, for that matter – can plan and commit a murder. From what you have said, however, this anticipated crime must be likely to bring about calamitous results well beyond the loss of one life."

"I fear so," said Father Brown.

"Crimes of great magnitude," said the detective, "invariably require more than one criminal to take part. There will be one who is the leader and several who are the henchmen and assigned to supportive roles. If they all work together, the crime will be finely orchestrated and carried off."

"That does seem reasonable, sir," said Father Brown.

"There are two things in our favor when facing a conspiratorial gang. The first is that if they are beyond five members, factions will form, and the unity will be broken. The second is that criminals planning a crime that would inscribe their names in the annals of the most outrageous events of our time can never resist bragging about what they're about to do. They will seek to impress other criminals, or perhaps a woman who is attracted to the proverbial bad boy."

"Oh, why yes, Mr. Holmes. Someone, or some two or three, out there knows something, and it is highly probable that at least one of them will not be able to keep his mouth shut, and will let the cat out of the bag. But how are we going to hear about a planned crime in time to prevent it?"

"I have a network of reliable informants. Some of them may not be of the highest moral character – otherwise, they wouldn't have access to the dens of iniquity where secrets are shared amongst the criminal class. My brother also has a network of agents, also known as spies, who inform on those who are wealthier and hold higher office, but who are every bit as venal."

Dr. Watson looked up from his notebook. "Mustn't forget your Irregulars, Holmes."

"Quite right you are," said Sherlock Holmes. "And what about you, Father? Do priests have spies and tattle-tales amongst the populace?"

"Oh, my goodness, yes. Almost every barkeep, cab driver, beer delivery man, bookmaker, navvie, and scullery maid can be called on. Almost all those good people are Irish and therefore Catholic. Oh, yes, Mr. Holmes, I can put the word out straight away. Someone will have heard something."

118

* * * * *

By the end of the following day, Sherlock Holmes and I had met with a dozen people and each of them had met with a dozen more. Holmes was able to chat briefly with Shinwell Johnson, Langdale Pike, Wiggins and the Irregulars, Billy, and, of course, Mycroft. I went for my medical colleagues and was able to pay visits or send wires to Doctors Trevelyan, Mortimer, Meek, Barnicot, Armstrong, Wood, and Belcher.

We assumed that Father Brown had put the word out to all the faithful Catholic workingmen and women in London and the Home Counties.

The problem when one engages so many sources is that the volume of data that comes in can be overwhelming. It isn't without reason that the unacknowledged official practice throughout the city amongst those who wished to be perceived as "in the know" is *if you haven't heard a rumor by noon, you start one.* Snippets of conversations overheard in the pub and innuendos whispered in the ladies' sewing circles delivered a deluge of hints about possible crimes, mostly petty.

But there was one recurring ominous warning.

Some great and foul deed was about to be visited on the monarchy.

A singular set of rumors suggested something dreadful was going to happen to a member of the Royal Family. The problem we faced was that every possible person who was in any numbered position in line for the throne had been named.

Unlike the rumors of planned burglaries, thefts, muggings, and the like, these hints of some danger to the Royal Family didn't originate east of Aldgate. They came entirely from the establishments of the West End, Knightsbridge, Oxford Street, and Park Lane. Whoever was privy to whatever epic event was in the offing had money and position.

More sobering yet was the repeated use of one word: *Kidnapping.*

Over the next two days, the data continued to pour in. By the morning of Monday, 6 January, we had received several hundred tidbits that were meaningless, but there were some thirty that led us to believe a possible kidnapping of a member of the monarchy was coming soon.

Other than comments like, "That'll teach those nobles and royal blighters a lesson," we were as blind as a mole as to *why*. Not only

119

that, but we had no idea which member or members of the Royal Family were targeted. A warning could be sent to Scotland Yard advising them to increase the guard, but as Father Brown observed, that would do little good.

"All those sons and daughters and grandchildren of the Queen," he said, "to say nothing of the multitudes and multitudes of cousins who aren't going to sit inside because there is some rumor of danger to them. They love being seen. They are endlessly parading themselves at the theatre and in the shops, and praying in that other church."

"And to make matters worse," said Holmes, "Lestrade remains convinced he has arrested the right man and cannot be persuaded that the danger persists and is far beyond some deranged religious revenge."

"Oh dear," said the priest, "I'm afraid our plan of asking every one of our informants has worked all too well. There is just too much data to sort through. Can you suggest a solution, Mr. Holmes?"

"I can, Father, and I already have put it into practice."

"You have? Well, thank Heaven for that. Please tell me . . . even if it involves activities that are beyond the usual boundaries of priestly comportment, I will do anything I can to help."

"Nothing underhanded at all, Father – unless you judge employing children as informants as not entirely indicative of high moral standing."

"As long as they weren't required to act immorally themselves, that is quite acceptable."

"Good, because I have had my Irregulars hard at work, but not to listen to rumors and boasts in the pubs. They have been following and dogging every member of the St. Monica's choir for the past four days, and I'm expecting Wiggins to arrive with their latest report within the hour."

Ten minutes later, the young fellow who Sherlock Holmes referred to as his dirty little lieutenant entered the room. With an air of lounging superiority, Wiggins, the leader of the Irregulars, touched his forelock and stood in front of us. He gave a glance to Father Brown as if to say *What the deuce is a priest doing here?*

"Welcome, Wiggins," said Holmes. "Allow me to introduce you to Father Brown. Should you ever convert to anything even vaguely resembling Christian faith, I recommend you make use of his services. Now then, what have you to report on our choir members?"

120

"Reporting I am, Mr. Holmes, sir. Like you told us, we followed all the choir members. Like you said, we had our sisters and cousins and a few of the local girls who have an eye for us lads follow the women from the choir. The four who you said were sopranos, meaning Mrs. Riddle, Mrs. Normington, Mrs. Ordiway, and Miss Durston, they are all good friends, and every day the four of them got followed. Two of them have nannies who came with them, and they had to push the prams, in which our girls assumed were babies, and buy the flowers, except on the third day when Mrs. Ordiway said she would buy the flowers herself. They followed those ladies real close."

"Good. And where did they go?"

"They never left St. John's Wood, sir. Every morning around half-ten, all four of them, and also the nannies and the babies, would arrive at The Holly Tea Room up the far end of the St. John's High Street, and they'd sit there and order tea and sweets and talk and laugh. Not the nannies, though, seeing as they had to push the prams up and down the street whilst the ladies were sipping tea and chatting."

"Did anyone ever get close enough to hear what they were chatting about?"

"Oh, right, sir, but it didn't seem important enough to bother reporting on, sir."

"Every piece of data may turn out to be important, Wiggins. What did they talk about?"

"Well, sir, the two what were already mothers talked about lying in, and labor pains and giving birth and feeding their babies, and they complained about the help and said some mean things about their nannies, and talked about where they could get decent vegetables this time of year, and about getting the carpets cleaned and all that. But twice, they chatted about the church and choir and how inconvenient it was for the priest to go and get himself killed and ruin the chance to perform in front of the Archbishop. But that was all, sir. Nothing no way that sounded suspicious. Like I said, it weren't important."

"I do believe you may be correct," said Holmes and he sighed. "Very well, then. What about the rest of the women?

"You mean the altos, sir?"

"If the first four were the sopranos, then yes, the remaining four must be the altos, Wiggins. Pray, report on them."

"Those ladies – well, those birds were older and they were also real tight with each other. Every day, they meet at the other end of

121

St. John's High Street at this fancy place what calls itself *Poutine's* and says all they serve is French food. Right, so Jimmy's big sister, Rose, she gets hired to work there taking all the dirty dishes and such back to the kitchen and she can listen in on what those birds are clucking about. And all they can talk about is bragging about their children, each trying to outdo the other, and complaining about their governesses, and gushing about their latest bottle of wine or their last trip to Italy where they almost got to see the Pope."

"Nothing at all about any impending crime? No consorting with shady characters?"

"None at all, Mr. Holmes. But the men, those tenors and basses, they were a different kettle of fish."

"Ah, pray tell."

"Well, wee Georgie, he followed the skinny tenor, Mr. Hayhurst. He teaches music across the river in Barnes at St. Marks, and he isn't married, and every day when classes are done, he slips into a cab and spends his supper and evening at a club of sorts, sir."

"What club? Where?"

"Carburton Street. It isn't like all those toff clubs in Pall Mall. It's in a house like the one that used to be over on Cleveland Street."

"I know of the establishment," said Holmes. "It is quite secretive and although its members may be known for engaging in some practices the law foolishly deems illegal, they tend not to engage in conspiratorial criminal machinations. Who was next?"

"The other tenor, sir. Mr. Lebrun. We never saw nothing of him. Waited every day he never once came out his flat."

"That isn't surprising, as the man is still in jail. Fine. Move on to the basses."

"Oh, all right. Well, the first bass is Mr. Foxwell. Freddie was assigned to him, and you have to give Freddie a few more pence, sir, seeing as he had the hardest work of all of us."

"Did he? And why was that?"

"This Mr. Foxwell, he's what you might call a righteous sort, sir. Every morning at six o'clock, his wife kisses him at his door and he's out of his house and walks to St. Monica's for the morning Mass. And then he's off to his employment across the city, and at the end of the day he's back straight away to his wife and family in St. John's Wood."

"Where is he employed?"

"At the Whitechapel Mission, sir. They feed the hungry and let those folks who would otherwise have to sleep rough sleep in their basement."

"He is employed there?"

"Not exactly, sir. He's in charge. He's the General Secretary."

"Very well, move on to the second bass. What about this Silas Lapsley fellow?"

"Oh, he's quite the gambler, he is, but . . . umm . . . can we do the organist first, sir? He's next on my list."

"Fine. I met him. Mr. Otis Olivenstein. His Mozart was rather good. What about him?"

"He lives just north of the Park, sir, on Avenue Road, in a terrible posh house like what some of the rich bluebloods do. We – that would be Nigel and me – we deduced, as you call it sir, that he must be getting his money from somewhere else, 'cause even we know that no organist is paid enough to stay in a big posh house. Do you agree with our deduction, Mr. Holmes?"

"Well done. Now do get on with your report."

"Jolly good, sir. We thought you would like it. This Mr. Olivenstein has a wife and two children and all the governesses and servants a big house needs, or so we been told. Nigel goes to one of the windows that's open a little, and he peeks in and listens, and he says the mister and the wife are speaking in a language that isn't English. But he says it sounds like they're clearing their throats all the time and coughing and doing that thing people do before they're about to spit out a big one, if you know what I mean, sir."

"I do. We call that speaking German. Go on."

"That's what Nigel and I deduce as well, Mr. Holmes, but he made it easy for us by going on Saturday morning and walking all the way to Belgravia and going into the building what has the big black eagle on the front of it, and we ask around and we're told it's the Embassy of Germany."

"Very interesting. No doubt making no end of *Geld* by importing high-grade German steel as well as strudel. Continue."

"On all the other days, he goes to St. Monica's and practices on the organ, but twice, during the afternoon, he quits early and goes walking, and I follow him from St. John's Wood down to Notting Hill and you would never guess where he goes when he gets there."

Holmes looked somewhat impatient but went along with Wiggins.

"Fine, let me guess. He has a mistress, a large German woman named Brunhilda? No? Well then, he visits a Bavarian coffee house

123

where they serve delectable strudels and coffee of sufficient viscosity to seal macadam? No? All right. I give up. Where does he go?"

"He goes to Wormwood Scrubs, sir. He visits the prison. Me and Nigel, we're deducing maybe he has some friend or relative who's in there and he's being a decent, kind fellow – several of our lads' fathers and uncles are in prison, sir, and so we appreciate those blokes who make a regular visit. It means a lot to those chaps behind bars – and he's paying a visit to some poor bloke who's serving his time and – "

"Stop there!" said Holmes. "Come, Watson, Father – We have our man."

He rushed to don his coat and tossed mine and Father Brown's to us. As the priest and I nearly stumbled down the stairs behind him, the clergyman called back a brief *Thank you* to Wiggins, who had looked awfully disappointed with not being able to deliver his full report.

"Doctor," said the priest, "what is he doing? Why did he cut off the boy's report? I confess, I felt the behavior of the male choristers was getting interesting."

* * * * *

The three men, to the varying degrees they were able, ran down Baker Street toward the nearest standing cab. The January cold bit into their hands and faces and the frigid air assaulted the lining of their lungs. First Sherlock Holmes, then the doctor, and finally the slow-moving priest clambered into the cab.

"Good heavens, Holmes," said Dr. Watson, sputtering to catch his breath. "Where are we going?"

"To that prison."

"Would you mind telling us why?"

"To warn them."

"Of what?"

"Do you not recall who we helped send away there just last November?"

"Of course I recall. Hugo Oberstein."

"And what was the name of the organist?"

"Otis Olivenstein. Oh, you think perhaps they are related?"

"*Oberstein* is from the same family clan as *Olivenstein.* Merely a shortened version. The Germans do that. Hugo Oberstein may have put the invaluable Bruce-Partington plans up for auction in all the

124

naval centers of Europe, but we must conclude that the most successful bidder could only have been the Kaiser. Germany alone had the burning desire for superiority at sea and the industrial wherewithal to copy the plans and manufacture the submarine."

"And you think that . . . What are you thinking, Holmes?"

"I cannot yet be certain, but there is a strong likelihood that the Germans want to retrieve Oberstein from prison. He is too-skilled an agent to allow to rot in a cell for fifteen years."

"Are they planning some sort of armed assault of Wormwood Scrubs?" asked Dr. Watson.

"Of course not. They're planning to kidnap a member of the Royal Family and hold him, or her, for ransom in exchange for Oberstein's release."

"Is he that valuable to them?"

"Any man who could obtain the plans that would render naval warfare impossible is worth a squabble with the British Government. All transactions would be kept secret. The press and the public would never hear a peep about it."

"Well," said Dr. Watson. "This is a surprise. Who would have suspected the organist?"

"I did," said Sherlock Holmes.

"Oh, come now, Holmes," said the doctor. "How could you possibly – "

"The music. He was practicing Mozart. His Mass is wonderful but not popular at English funerals, and the *Te Deum* he chose was composed by a member of the Royal Family, the now departed Prince Albert. These were only hints, but the minute Wiggins told us about the visits to the prison, that sealed the question."

"If he has a troop of German agents helping him, how are you going to stop them? Do you know who they are going to kidnap?"

"No, at the moment we do not," said Sherlock Holmes.

"Oh, I think we do," said Father Brown.

Holmes and Watson looked at the priest sitting quietly in the corner of the cab.

"Would you kindly explain?" said Sherlock Holmes.

"The infant. The queen's great-grandson. The little tyke is only eighteen months old and quite the charmer. His full name, if you recall from the notices in the press, is Edward Albert Christian George Andrew Patrick David. But his parents and the rest of the family all call him David. He's the fourth in the direct line for the throne of the British Empire."

125

"And why," asked Sherlock Holmes, "do you suspect the infant *David* will be kidnapped?"

"The other piece the organist was practicing. He was also playing *Der Herr ist Mein Getreuer Hirt*. It's the cantata composed by Bach for the Shepherd Psalm. That psalm is attributed by everyone – well, except for the German biblical professors who refuse to attribute anything to anyone anymore – to the shepherd boy, *David*."

"It might behoove us," said Holmes, "not to play that card yet. Better that Mr. Oberstein and his ilk smugly assume we do not know."

On arriving at HMP Wormwood Scrubs, Holmes asked the governor if he could visit with Mr. Hugo Oberstein.

"Blimey, if he's not the popular chap. Hardly just arrived here and he's got visitors coming almost every day."

"Would you mind, sir, telling us who else has been to see him?"

"What with all the reforms they been passing for Her Majesty's prisons, we're supposed to keep all that confidential. But I would be guessing that if Sherlock Holmes wants to know something like that, he's going to find out anyway, right? I may as well tell you. His cousin, an ordinary-looking bloke, comes every other day. Then there are those two chaps from the German Embassy – can't recall their true names, so we just call them Fritz Number One and Fritz Number Two. And there's been three *Fräuleins* who we're not sure if there are his paramours or secretaries, and a Mr. Adolph Meyer. Meyer is the only one we suspect of anything. The others seem harmless enough."

The dusty, musty prison cell that was occupied by Mr. Oberstein and occasionally by a friendly visitor must have been a long way from his luxurious lodgings in the Hôtel du Louvre on Rue Rivoli in Paris. He was reclined on his cot and reading when we arrived.

"Good day, Mr. Oberstein," said Holmes. "We never did have the opportunity to meet face-to-face, but I expect you know who I am."

"And good day to you, Mr. Holmes. Of course, I am aware of the person who foiled my brilliant plans. You led me into a trap, and I fell for it. My hat is off to you, sir."

126

"It is regrettable that you and your colleagues, your *agents* I should call them, didn't learn their lesson and are planning yet another scheme. I assure you, sir, it will also fail."

If Hugo Oberstein was alarmed by what Sherlock Holmes had said, he gave not the slightest indication. Instead, he merely shrugged and looked befuddled.

"Another scheme, you say? Would you be so kind as to tell me what it is? I am terribly in need of amusement in this awful place. Please indulge me."

"Your plans to kidnap a member of the noble class in the hope of exchanging her for you will come to naught. We are on to you. You will not get away with it. All you will accomplish is having your sentence extended for another five, or maybe seven years. I suggest to you that you call it off. It is hopeless."

"Whatever are you talking about, Mr. Holmes? When you have the time, do put this fantasy in writing and post it to me. Oh, and if I can no longer be found at my current address, have the letters sent to me care of the Hôtel du Louvre in Paris. I will have them forwarded."

"Did you wish to confess whilst we are here?" asked Holmes. "I do believe Father Brown would be happy to listen to you. We can wait outside."

Oberstein laughed.

* * * * *

Once we were out of the prison and strolling along Notting Hill, Holmes lit a cigarette, puffed several times, and smiled.

"He has fallen for it," he said. "He assumes that we are lacking in details but are onto him. He is now under some pressure, and will go ahead and tell his agents to proceed with the plan forthwith."

"Are you going to let them try to kidnap the infant prince?" I said. "You must try to stop them."

"Doing so would allow those conspirators to walk free. By permitting the attempt to go ahead, we should be able to capture the lot of them, including our nasty organist. Without any firm evidence against him, we run the risk of allowing him to escape without even being charged. Better to put him away for attempted kidnapping than let that happen."

"But you are putting a child in danger!" I said. "That cannot happen. What would his mother, or father, or his great-grandmother say?"

127

"I expect that when they know they have helped foil a plot to do damage to the Empire, they will play along."

Play along they did. At first, the mother of the fourth-in-line to the throne, the eighteen-month-old prince known as David, objected. Her motherly concerns were understandable. However, she was given word from a certain gracious lady that any future king of England would have to have a resolute spine and soul and better he start young.

Every day – rain, snow, sleet, or the occasional sunshine – Princess Mary (formerly known as Mary of Teck, and informally known as May) walked out of Kensington Palace along with two ladies-in-waiting and a governess and, taking turns, they pushed a pram with the future king of England along the paths of Kensington Gardens. On the afternoon of Sunday the twelfth of January, in the year of Our Lord 1896, the entourage was set upon by six men. Five of them restrained the princess and the other women, whilst the sixth grabbed the pram and began to run pell-mell toward the Bayswater Road.

The little boy in the pram had never had such a fast, bouncing ride and clapped and gurgled and shouted in glee. Witnesses reported that he was shouting, "More! More!" but these reports are considered less than reliable.

Regardless, the entire lot of would-be kidnappers were tackled by no less than twenty Royal Marines who had been disguised as groundskeepers, sweepers, food cart vendors, fathers pushing their own prams that were filled with large dolls and – the most coveted role – lovers strolling arm-in arm with paid actresses from the theatre.

As would be expected, the miscreants, when given the chance to lessen their punishment, sang and implicated both Oberstein and Olivenstein and several officials at the German Embassy. Those having diplomatic immunity were sent packing back to Berlin, and the others were tried and convicted of attempted abduction.

The entire affair was kept out of the press.

* * * * *

On Sunday afternoon, 26 January of the same year, Sherlock Holmes, Dr. Watson, and Father Brown sat together in 221b Baker Street, sipping sherry and enjoying a plate of excellent shortbread lovingly provided by Mrs. Hudson, even if it was left over from Christmas.

128

"My dear Mr. Holmes," said Father Brown, tapping his umbrella on the floor as if to signify that he was about to say was important, "in my prayers this morning, I thanked God for the singular gift of logic and deduction he bestowed upon you. It was a blessing to be able to work alongside you."

"And I dare say, Father," said Sherlock Holmes, "I sit at your feet, as St. Paul did Gamaliel, and seek to learn more about the workings of the inner minds and souls of men. But pray tell, what will you do now that this assignment has been completed?"

"Oh, yes, well, the Archbishop has told me I have to take over responsibility, temporarily, for St. Monica's. As it's only a few steps from your home here, I should be happy to see you there."

"Would you now, Father? And can you give me a good reason why I might start going to church?"

"For starters, you really should consider confession."

Sherlock Holmes was apparently not expecting that reason, and for a minute looked thoroughly nonplussed. Then he smiled and replied.

"I suggest you not hold your breath waiting for me to enter the box, Father. And allow me to further suggest you remove the broad swords from the wall."

"I already have."

Bigger Fish to Fry
by Gustavo Bondoni

Just south of Twyford, the River Itchen wends its way between the trees in what is reputed to be the most magnificent collection of fishing streams in all of England. Having no interest in the life of an angler, I was hurrying south to the chemist in Eastleigh when I realized I was no longer alone.

A short man in grey, ill-fitting clothes, carrying an unnecessary umbrella was attempting to catch me on the lane. To judge by his labored breath, he found my pace a challenge.

As I was in no hurry other than from a desire to get my blood flowing, I stopped and waited at the top of a slight rise.

"Hello," I said as the man reached my side. I admit I wasn't paying much attention to him, as I was studying the path ahead. It had rained some days earlier, and I was keen to avoid muddy patches.

"Hello," he wheezed. Then he held up a hand as if to say '"Give me a moment," and proceeded to regain his breath. "Thank you for waiting."

"It's my pleasure," I replied. I noted that, beneath the shapeless grey coat the man appeared to be wearing the robes of a Catholic priest.

Suddenly alert, I studied his face and smiled.

"Father Brown!" I exclaimed. I tried not to let my concern show. Could it be a coincidence that another famous investigator would chance to be in the vicinity just as Holmes was closing in on a case?

"Hello, Dr. Watson. I'm happy to see you again. I'm staying in Eastleigh. Father Santos is unwell, and I've been asked to assist during his convalescence."

"Nothing too serious, I hope."

Father Brown shook his head. "A broken leg, I'm afraid. He had a nasty fall in these very woods while attempting – and here I must trust that a man of God wouldn't fall into the trap of exaggeration – to land a trout that measured at least two feet. Slipped on a tree root and fell awkwardly."

I'd spent the past week observing the river and the fishermen on my long walks, and I knew most would have been delighted with a specimen half that size. I kept that knowledge to myself, however. "Well, I'm delighted to see you again, although I can't imagine why I'd be important enough to chase through the woods. Unless you need a medical opinion in the matter of Father Santos' leg."

"Nothing of that sort. I'm more concerned with your . . . amateur pursuits. Such as the one that I assume is taking you to Eastleigh as we speak."

"Of course. Holmes is always on about how you should have been brought to trial as an accomplice for all the times you permitted Flambeau to escape, when one timely word from you would have seen him incarcerated once and for all. He is quite puzzled by *your reticence in that regard.*"

He replied quietly, without any rancor. "I'm not surprised that Holmes sees my activities in this way. He is famous for analyzing the facts of every case to understand the logical sequence of events." We walked a few more steps in silence. I felt he had more to say on the matter. "Unfortunately, his scope is limited to the plane of human laws and human facts. I strive to serve a different justice."

"And you preferred to speak to me than directly to Holmes."

"I didn't think he would appreciate my interference," Father Brown replied.

I laughed. "I don't think Holmes would care about your interference. He is normally unaffected by anything happening around us. Most of the time, he seems to be doing one thing and then suddenly reveals that his actions were aimed in another direction altogether. It would take a particularly brilliant mind to interfere with his methods. Or a particularly unfortunate coincidence."

"Then he would have continued on his course even if I stated my concerns that some crimes are better left unsolved?"

"You would have more success attempting to turn aside a railway locomotive by pushing it with a long blade of grass," I replied. "Holmes arrives at his own conclusions and leaves the moral issues to the law."

"Perhaps the law shouldn't be the final arbiter in those things."

The woods gave way to a famer's field and the river arrived at a road. We left the path and walked along the pavement for some moments. "Do you think there is anything I can help you with?"

"No. I would have liked to feel that there was some hope to appeal to Holmes's better nature, but I fear we'd have a very different opinion about what, exactly, comprises a person's better nature."

"I have never found Holmes to be particularly heartless. He is logical and perhaps a bit inflexible in his methods, but he is not a monster." We had reached the outskirts of Eastleigh, which was much more of a town than the tiny hamlet of Twyford where Holmes and I were lodged. "I would never assist him otherwise."

I didn't know why I clarified that final part. For some reason, I felt the small cleric's opinion of me was important. I would have preferred a strong disagreement from a fire-and-brimstone type to his nonjudgmental acceptance.

"The chemist says he hasn't had wine in stock for a year. Ever since the brickworks closed down and the owner died."

"Thank you, Watson," Holmes replied. He was sitting in a leather chair beside the empty fireplace. The summer evening, though not as warm as the previous day, didn't justify lighting a fire. The smoke from his pipe filled the room.

I half-expected him to mention my meeting with the priest. He had the knack for knowing everything that happened around him. But how could he know? By happenstance, Father Brown had located me in a place where few could observe us, and then walked with me in the very direction I was headed. The few minutes more that I'd taken because of his slightly less vigorous pace were negligible in the long distance I'd walked. I went to the same places I would have visited had he not been there . . . and I took the same amount of time.

Or had it not been happenstance?

Since no mention of my encounter appeared forthcoming, I moved to the next item on my list. "He also told me that the best place to buy port wine in the vicinity is in Southampton. There is a wine-seller who brings it in from Spain."

"Very well," he replied. "We must dress for dinner."

Thirty minutes later, I was just heading down the stairs when the first gong sounded, and I saw Holmes enter the dining room just as I came into the hall.

Our host sat at the head of the table. Sir Brian Glouth was a tall, gangling man who, though sporting no beard or mustache, found himself in possession of a set of quite amazing sideburns that reached his jowls. His small mouth gave the impression of being slowly crushed between the two masses of hair. This mouth smiled as I sat.

Other guests trickled in. Amaelia Hunt, the American heiress, sat to our host's right. Despite being dressed to the height of

132

decorum, her mere presence, unencumbered by a female chaperone, gave the event a racy air. She was a pale creature who would grow into a plain woman if I were any judge of such things, but still had the rounded beauty of youth about her features.

Two young men were also present. They would remain present until Miss Hunt decided to leave, and they would always be present while she was in residence. One was a young Lord from Essex, and the other was the second son of an impoverished Earl. Both of them were involved in the pursuit of the one thing that could turn a family's fortunes around: American dollars. From what I could tell, they were somewhere in their middle twenties, at that age in which young aristocrats find themselves adrift after finishing or abandoning their university studies before ending up in parliament. These two appeared to be more responsible than most: Chasing Miss Hunt showed considerable foresight.

The final man was a local merchant named Wellington Da Silva, whose family had emigrated from the Continent at some point in the eighteenth century and who, apparently, felt obligated to choose patriotic names for their children in in order to make up for a lack of Anglo-Saxon blood that only they cared about.

I let my gaze rest on Mr. Da Silva for a moment. He was in his mid-thirties, wore an impeccably-tailored brown suit and had a soft, deep voice.

The final guest was Mrs. Tyne, Sir Brian's widowed aunt, who was quite a bit older than the rest of the party – I judged her to be in her seventies – but who still had a spark in her eye and spoke rapidly and evenly.

Embarrassed at being the last to arrive, I hurriedly sat and joined in the conversation.

Sir Brian spoke once I was settled. "Holmes tells me you spent the day hiking down to Eastliegh. Quite a walk, I'd say."

"Just over five miles there and back," I replied. "Although, to be honest, I found the journey more pleasant than the destination. Eastleigh is not one of England's scenic towns."

"That's why I stay on the grounds whenever possible. And if I must leave, I limit the excursions to the stream. In fact, I was planning on doing some fishing tomorrow morning. You should come along. Now that you've seen the eyesore of the county, I feel it's my duty as a host to show you its glories."

"Unfortunately," Holmes interjected as I racked my brain for a suitable excuse, "Watson and I will be back in Eastleigh tomorrow.

I have an audience to speak to the Catholic priest there, Father Santos."

I wondered if Holmes saw me jump. Normally, he misses nothing, but in this particular instance, I believe he was looking in another direction. Still, it was an effort to get my breath under control. There was nothing I could do about the flush I felt rushing on my cheeks.

"Oh," said Mrs. Tyne. "You know old Santos?"

"Only by correspondence," Holmes replied. "I was hoping to get to know more of him tomorrow."

"He's a good egg, for a Papist," Sir Brian said. "One of the few men I'd fish with any day, rain or shine. He knows the importance of silence when you're after the cagey ones."

"If he paid more attention to his duties and less to the fish, he'd have avoided his accident," Mrs. Tynes interjected.

Sir Brian guffawed good-naturedly. "How much sharper than the serpent's tooth . . . I don't think he is derelict in his duties, Aunt Mirtha. At least I haven't heard anything of the sort. Winchester, you're Catholic, aren't you? What do you think of your priest?"

"He is a good man," Da Silva said. "He should be a bishop by now. If he were Italian or Spanish, he would be. But he is merely Portuguese, so must toil twice as much as most men."

"Well, at it's a good thing you got him assigned to Eastleigh," Mrs. Tyne exclaimed. "Otherwise he'd still be in some flyspecked little chapel in the Portuguese mountains."

"Aunt Mirtha!" Sir Brian censured.

But Da Silva didn't seem offended. "When my family explained that he had taken it upon himself to feed a family of four orphans until they reached adulthood, and found them positions in the communities, I knew he was the man to have, although I admit that I expected there to be more difficulties."

"It isn't as if Eastleigh is such a prize," Mrs. Tyne said.

"It will be when Santos is finished with it," Sir Brian said. "The orphanage is coming along splendidly, from what I hear."

"It is," Da Silva agreed, lowering his eyes to the table. "It's a triumph. Father Santos has touched the community deeply."

I listened to this conversation with deep interest, waiting to see if anyone mentioned the fact that Father Brown was officiating during the local priest's convalescence. I was particularly interested to see whether anyone would connect the little man with the rumpled clothes to the figure mentioned so often in *The Illustrated Police News*.

134

None of the diners appeared to be aware of Father Brown's presence in the parish, so my attention drifted to the three younger members of the party. They seemed completely immersed in their own conversation, and I wondered what connection they had with Sir Brian. I assumed that at least one of the young men would be a relation, which likely meant that he'd invited the others. Although not as beautiful as some country seats, Sir Brian's Estate was charming enough in its own way, and the ample, wooded grounds were ideal for courtship purposes.

Delighted with this minor act of deduction, I turned my attention back to the discussion of Father Santos' suitability for his position.

But, somehow, the talk had turned back to the quality of fish one found in the River Itchley, so I decided to focus on the excellent soup which had just arrived.

The Catholic Church in Eastleigh, Holy Cross, was a weathered brick edifice across the paved street from a small, wooded park. Holmes asked Sir Brian's coachman to wait for us, and we stood on the pavement and surveyed our surroundings.

"Grim place, isn't it?" I observed.

Holmes chuckled. "I observe that you have little patience for all but the smallest and largest of human dwelling-places. You overlook the pollution and crowds of London because the city offers so much in exchange for those inconveniences. And you will excuse the remoteness of Sir Brian's country seat because of the beauty of its lands. But the happy middle ground . . . you do not enjoy."

"There's some truth in what you say," I replied. "Market towns aren't a place I'd live in by choice. But I would also argue that Eastleigh is a rather unfortunate specimen of the type. And this church is a prime example."

The building was an unimposing structure that rose a little over three stories above ground level at the highest point of its triangular façade. Brick covered everything but three tall, thin windows above the door. Those were surrounded by grey stone, as was the arched doorway itself. We entered to find the interior dark. A woman in a light grey habit approached us.

"Can I help you gentlemen?" she asked with a smile. She appeared to be about fifty years old, plump and round-cheeked, and seemed to radiate a sense of well-being, a feeling that everything would be all right in the end. Hers, I assumed, must be a peaceful existence.

135

"We're here to see Father Santos," Holmes replied. "We're expected."

"Oh, yes. This way, please," she said, clapping her hands as if someone asking to see Father Santos was an unusual and delightful surprise. She led us towards a door to the right of the church. "As you must know, if he's expecting you, Father Santos is an invalid at the moment. An unfortunate accident, most unfortunate. But we've set up a place for him to rest by adapting a classroom. It's inconvenient for the pupils, of course, but it's only temporary."

The doorway led into a stark white corridor which gave me the sense that I'd left the church proper and entered a different ecclesiastical world. My experience with Catholicism was limited, but had this been an Anglican outpost, I'd have considered these rooms part of the vicarage. I would have expected the living area to be separate from the house of worship itself, but perhaps the Catholic usage was different. It certainly appeared that way in this particular case.

The woman kept up a running commentary. "Normally, Father Santos would sleep upstairs. But stairs do trouble him so in his condition."

We entered another room, also painted in white. This one held an iron bed and a crucifix, complete with a painted Christ figure, on the wall at its head.

A man whose red hair was just beginning to show streaks of grey sat propped on pillows against the head of the bed. A plaster cast immobilized his leg to the hip, which was modestly covered by the white sheets of the bed. He wore a black frock that, unlike the clothes of his helper, Father Brown, was immaculate and looked as if it had just been dyed. Fortunately, that worthy wasn't present, as I wasn't in a mood to explain how we'd met previously.

"Ah, Mr. Holmes, I think," the priest said as we entered the room. "Forgive me if I don't stand to shake your hand. He spoke English with an unmistakable accent. Had I not known he was from Portugal, I would have guessed Spain.

"That is quite all right," Holmes said. "It is kind of you to see us at such short notice."

The priest laughed, an open, unembarrassed sound. "As you can see, I am not able to move. Having visitors is a blessing. You said you wanted to speak to me on an important matter. Please sit down."

We sat down on two straight-backed chairs of dark-stained wood brought in by the woman in grey.

Holmes leaned in and spoke softly. "I'm afraid that's true. In fact, though the main thrust of my inquiries has to do with smuggling, there have been whispers of murder."

"That is very bad," the priest said. "Of course I will help with anything you require."

"A man of my acquaintance has asked me to look into the illegal arrival of wine from the mainland into this country. He has a large import concern, and has lately been losing custom to inexpensive Spanish wines that he has been unable to trace back to a reputable importer. The low price, combined with the high quality of the product, made him suspect that the wine must be smuggled.

"My inquiries have uncovered little hard evidence thus far, but all the whispers I've collected point in one direction: To the Port of Southampton."

The priest appeared saddened by this news. "It wouldn't surprise me in the least, my son. The docks are . . . well, they are typical of docks everywhere. Violent, uncontrolled except by criminal gangs, and even that control is susceptible to bribery. Many of our orphans were created by those conditions. And most of my work with the children is aimed at keeping them away from that life."

"That's admirable," Holmes said. "And I'm glad you feel that way. Perhaps our investigations will remove one of the scourges from the docks." He glanced at the woman.

"Sister Charity is absolutely in my trust," the priest said. "Anything you might say, she can hear."

"I was going to ask you about the wine you use for the communion," Holmes said.

"Ah. There is no secret in that. It comes from my countryman, Mr. Da Silva. He is most generous in his donations."

"And does he give anything else to the church? Perhaps for your own personal consumption?"

Father Santos smiled. "I see you have been warned about me. Yes, you are right. He also provides the port I drink with my meals."

"And too often between-times," Sister Charity interjected.

"Sister Charity objects to the glass of port I take before bed. But I assure you I drink only a small glass before bed to help me sleep. And besides, Mr. Da Silva knows it is for me, and he only sends us a small quantity." The priest smiled benevolently at us, then turned serious. "But I'm afraid my testimony won't help you too much. Mr. Da Silva, as you've probably already learned, is a saint of a man. He spends every penny he has to spare on the orphanage."

"He didn't look particularly poor to me," I interjected. "In fact, he was expensively dressed at dinner just last night."

"Oh, no," Father Santos replied, holding out his hands. "He cannot afford to look like a poor man. He must present himself to the world as a wealthy benefactor . . . or he will not be held as a serious man. You must understand this."

Holmes nodded reassuringly. "Of course. And I also understand his storage warehouse isn't near the docks but at the Smithling Crossroad."

"Yes," the priest said eagerly. "It would be awful for him to be involved in the goings-on at the seaport. A man of his stature must keep his hands clean of such things."

"Surely most of his wine comes through Southampton?" I asked.

The priest shook his head. "I know little of these matters."

"He was the one who brought you to England, was he not?" Holmes asked. "How did you meet him?"

"He came looking for me. I used to help a few children in the mountains, and Mr. Da Silva heard about this. So he journeyed to find me . . . and now I help a hundred children. Your orphanages in this country can be quite grim, but ours attempts to be good for the boys."

"He's just being modest," Sister Charity exclaimed loudly. Then she looked around and seemed to realize what she'd done. Color rose in her cheeks and she looked down at her feet. "I apologize, but it's true. You should see the little angels. They smile, they're well-fed, and they know we'll do whatever we can to see them in good homes. You don't see that often. Not at all. And it's all because of Father Santos. And Mr. Da Silva, of course. Judging from them, Portugal must be a land of love and generosity, even if Da Silva pretends to be an English gentleman. I wish everyone was more like them."

"Now, now, Sister," the priest said softly. "I have told you many times. Portugal is a land of men, with all the good and bad that comes with that. There, too, we can only try to rise above our frailties."

The sister harumphed at that and bustled off. The priest followed her with a fond gaze.

We exchanged a few more pleasantries and, with every passing moment, my anxiety increased because I hadn't mentioned the presence of Father Brown to Holmes. It was nice to have information he hadn't managed to deduce yet, but it also made me feel slightly guilty and question why I'd held it back. It would have been particularly unfortunate had the man wandered in just as we were speaking.

But Brown must have taken his duties as substitute quite seriously – or else he was out in the woods accosting other hikers – because he failed to appear before we said goodbye.

"What did you think of the priest?" Holmes asked as we strode the streets of Eastleigh while we waited for our carriage to return.

"He appears to be a solid fellow," I replied, "but I think Da Silva has him hoodwinked: A little wine and the money for a good deed goes a long way. I can't think of many character witnesses stronger than a priest. It seems to me that any attempt to take action of a legal sort against the man would run into all sorts of local objections. The police would have to move against the will of the townsfolk. They would have to be quite convinced of what they're about before take any action against Wellington Da Silva."

"Indeed," Holmes nodded, and then gave me a smile. "Fortunately, my friend, we are not the police. I believe tonight will be an interesting evening. If you'd care to participate in the events, I ask that you meet me after the party disperses. Wear dark clothing."

The night was dark and overcast, with only diffuse light from the full moon managing to make its way through the clouds to afford me a minimum of vision once my eyes acclimatized.

It was no surprise that Holmes materialized by my side without my knowing it. He could move as silently as a mouse when he set his mind to it, and was such a wizard with his makeup that he was often quite hard to spot, even in broad daylight.

This time, however, he had eschewed any exotic disguises and simply appeared carrying a shuttered lantern, which he gave to me, and wearing his cape and cap.

We walked in silence as far as the road, where he asked me to unshutter the lamp. I was curious to see how he would contrive to have us travel the miles that separated us from our objective.

When I saw it, I smiled.

"A hansom?"

"It was available," he replied.

There would be more to it than that. A cab, while ubiquitous and suited for work in the city, wasn't a species native to the wilds of southern England. I suspected this conveyance had been chosen not so much for the cab itself, but for the discretion of its driver, a man whose features I couldn't quite make out: All I could see of him was his enormous bulk, the burning ember of his pipe, and a battered hat of the kind referred to as a *titfer*. I assumed he was here to pay off some previous debt accrued in one of Holmes's earlier cases.

We drove through Eastleigh, no more attractive in a dark and shuttered state than it had been in the daytime, and descended beside the road a half-mile south of town.

"This way," Holmes said.

We walked through an empty field, negotiated a stile, and came to a low building set among a stand of trees, illuminated by a lamp burning in a small guard cottage. We shuttered the lantern as we came to the trees.

"Stay here," Holmes whispered. "I will deal with the guard."

"Guard?" I asked.

But he was gone, a shadow in the inky night.

I waited, peering uselessly into the dark and listening for the inevitable sounds of violence or alarum. None reached my ears, but I maintained my attentive vigil, certain that some sign, some evidence of Holmes's actions would reach me. A quarter-of-an-hour passed.

"It's done," a whisper beside me announced, nearly making me jump out of my skin. "You can uncover the lantern."

I did so to find Holmes standing at my side. He showed no signs of agitation.

"What did you do?" I asked.

He just smiled enigmatically. "Temptation is stronger than any action I could take."

With that, we walked toward the building which, I could now see in the lamplight, was of solid brick construction, likely built to hold wool and now repurposed as a wine deposit. Inside the open door of the guard's cottage, I saw a man slumped over a table, a bottle held in his hand.

"Did you poison him?" I asked.

"Nothing so dramatic," Holmes replied. "I merely put a few drops of a chemical that induces stupor into a bottle of brandy and placed it where he would find it. The rest . . . he did to himself. Come. The effects of the draught aren't scientifically predictable. I think we should have twenty minutes at least . . . but that is just an estimate."

We hurried past the guard cottage and approached the door of the warehouse proper. Holmes extracted a large iron key from his cloak – doubtless taken from the incapacitated guard – and we pushed the thick door, wide and tall enough to drive a wagon through, aside. Barrels sat on racks within, as well as demijohns and even some bottles, ready to be shipped locally.

"What is it we're looking for?" I asked. "I only see what I'd expect from a place of this sort. How can we possibly know whether the contents are legitimate or the product of smuggling? I very much doubt they would label their illegal produce as such."

I couldn't see Holmes's expression in the darkness, but his words seemed amused as he said, "Perhaps we should look beyond the obvious."

The long building held four rows of solidly-built wooden shelves. It was on these that the several containers of liquid were arrayed by type. Some areas held barrels, others glass containers. There was a small sector of small casks. "The priest's port, I assume," I said softly.

"You are most likely correct," Holmes replied. Then, holding his hand up for silence he looked around the building.

We stood in the exact center of building, in the aisle between the second and third row of shelves and exactly half the length of the building from the door to the back wall. Holmes rotated his body, studying everything in sight, including the roof and the floor as he did so.

I watched the rafters, which cast deformed shadows as the lamp swayed in my grip. I tensed as something moved near the door, but then relaxed, reassured that, once again, I was witnessing the effect of the moving source of light.

In order to avoid the illusions of movement, I watched Holmes. Past experience taught me that his mind, relentlessly trained to observation, would see the same things I did, but notice details I would miss. He would then reconstruct things as they were. That this method invariably functioned was the most surprising thing about him.

His motion arrested, Holmes turned to me. "Would you consider it normal to place a guard on a warehouse such as this one?"

"Of course," I replied. "Wine is a tempting target, even if you disregard the cost."

"In a city, I would agree with you, but out in the countryside? The door appeared thick enough to deter most burglars. You would have to know where the merchandise was stored and obtain a horse and wagon. Thieves, of course, are well-known for making enormous efforts for their plunder which often put honest men's work to shame, but the difficulties in this one might be a little hard to overcome. And then there would be the issue of defeating the lock

141

and the thick door. A guard, in those conditions, would seem an unnecessary precaution, would it not?"

Logically, he made sense, but I was a man of the city. I would never leave any valuable unguarded. If I owned a warehouse such as this one, I'd likely have assigned two guards, on the off chance that one became incapacitated or was in league with criminals. I said nothing.

Holmes walked ahead, slowly. I followed, illuminating his way.

"Have you noticed the floor?" Holmes asked.

"It's just dirt," I replied. "Da Silva should take better care of his product."

"But he does. You see how the racks hold the barrels a few inches above the floor? This is a very well-constructed storehouse, as long as the wine doesn't remain here for too long. A cellar would be better, of course, but lowering barrels into a cellar is much more difficult than simply driving a wagon through the door."

We reached the rear wall of the storehouse, rougher brick than the outer skin of the building. Unlike the front of the building, which had some empty space for wagons to maneuver while entering each of the passages, the shelves in this section met the far wall. Holmes stood beside one of them, another rack of casks of port, and raised his eyebrow.

"If you wanted to hide something in this warehouse, where would you do it?" he said. He seemed unconcerned that the guard had already been asleep for a good seven or eight minutes.

"Well, you can't bury it," I replied.

His eyes widened. "Very good. Your powers of deduction are most certainly improving. You realized that digging up the floor would be obvious to anyone who came here."

I stomped my foot. The dirt was packed hard. "Yes. It seems like this has been here for some time. You'd need picks to break it effectively." I pointed to the bad brickwork beside us. "And if you hide it in the bricks, you would have to break down the wall. This is old work. Rough, but solid. You could never move things in and out of a hiding place like this one without anyone noticing." I smiled and pointed triumphantly upward. "So I'd hide it among the rafters, if it was small enough."

"Pity," Holmes said. "You came tantalizingly close to arriving on the right road. There are two problems with your deduction. The first is that for the rafters to be used, the guard outside would have had to be complicit in whatever was happening – something which I think we agree would be risky. The man doesn't strike me as particularly reliable." He gestured to the shelves around us. "No. The only safe place to hide something is on the racks, in plain sight, perhaps in a barrel, perhaps in a cask. Not in a bottle – there is always the possibility of its being seen through the glass, or of a breakage. And it occurs to me that this rack in the center of the room furthest from the door, is the most secure place in the entire building."

He rapped on a cask of port. "Did the priest strike you as a drunkard?"

"Not particularly. He seemed lucid and capable. His face didn't show signs of excessive drink."

"That was my impression, too. Regardless of the Sister's remarks, he certainly didn't appear to be the kind of man who could consume this amount of port in any reasonable period of time." He gestured towards the racks nearest us, where a good twenty casks sat awaiting shipment. "Which begs the question: Who is drinking all of this in Estleigh and surroundings? Sir Brian is the largest potential customer in the vicinity, and as you have seen, he is a man whose tastes tend to wine and sherry. These casks, like the ones nearer the entrance, hold port. So who is drinking it?"

"Perhaps someone further afield? If he's bringing it in from Portugal, he could be selling it anywhere. In London, even."

"That's true, and perhaps some of it is being sent further afield. That wouldn't concern us. But what does concern me is the fact that Da Silva gifts it to the priest in the first place. Why would he do that? The wine for communion is perfectly understandable, and that is something he very openly bottles at his estate. But the port?"

"I don't understand what you're getting at. And we don't have much time for explanations."

He nodded. He loved to make explicit his deductions – and I was certain he had deduced what was happening – but our twenty minutes were fast coming to their end. We needed to act.

Fortunately, Holmes was able to act as well as he was able to pontificate, and he simply said, "Very well. It's my belief that the port is given to the priest just to prove that the barrels contain port."

"What else would they contain?"

"I have a suspicion, but we'll have to look." He studied the casks on the shelf before us and rapped one on the second shelf with his knuckles. Unlike the ones on the bottom shelf which were simply lain on the wooden molds shaped like the bottom of the casks, the ones on the upper shelf had another set of casks piled above them. "Yes, I think these are the ones that concern us. No one would ever move these by accident."

From the pocket of his cloak, Holmes extracted an implement which, in the darkness, I first confused with a stiletto, until I realized the metallic portion was circular, not flat. It wasn't a blade, but some species of awl with a long, sturdy spike. He held a wooden mallet in his other hand. Before I could ask what he was planning, he placed the point of the awl against the face of the casket and applied two solid blows with the mallet.

When he pulled the metallic blade from the wood, I stepped away instinctively, expecting my shoes to be showered with port. Instead, as he carefully removed the needle-like point, nothing happened. In fact, Holmes simply held up a tiny cork for me to inspect, dark like the barrel itself, which he proceeded to press flush with the surface. He inspected it and said, "There, that should keep our ministrations undiscovered for some time."

The spot he'd picked to make his incision was well-chosen. The face of the barrel had text branded into it just above and below the hole he'd made. The repair would be impossible to see.

"And now, we should make good our escape," he said.

I burned to ask what he'd discovered, what meaning he ascribed to an empty barrel, but my anxiety about the guard's slumber stilled my questions. I followed him out and helped him to close the door.

We stealthily approached the guard cottage – the last place my frayed nerves wished to approach – in order to return the key to its rightful position, and found the man within quite motionless. His breathing was deep and restful, and he didn't stir as Holmes crept past and replaced the key upon its peg.

The woods beyond the edifice, and the blissful darkness of the clouded night, brought my breathing back to normal. If we were discovered now, we could simply state that we were out for a night-time walk, and no evidence could point to something else.

But only when I discerned the dark bulk of the hansom waiting on the side of the road did I truly begin to relax.

"What was that all about?" I asked Holmes as we climbed into the cab's interior.

In response, he pulled out the spike he'd buried into the casket and placed it before my face. I studied it, but was unable to see much in the dim interior of the cab. All I could discern were brown streaks along the grey of the metal.

I assumed they must be from the wood or a residue of the port, and I sniffed at it. But instead of the sweet wine-like scent I expected, a bitter ammonia-laced odor, with only traces of flowers in it assaulted my senses.

144

Having been with Holmes on a number of cases, I knew the smell quite well. "Opium," I said.

He nodded. "It's the evidence we needed."

"Opium isn't illegal," I pointed out. I knew he was perfectly aware of the fact, but I thought a gentle reminder wouldn't be amiss. He sometimes went off on moral crusades when something made him angry. And Holmes's experiences in any number of opium dens had created a strong conviction in him that no good could come of it.

"This opium is. The novel method of shipping it would suggest that the officers of Her Majesty's Customs are ignorant of its presence on English soil. In fact, I'd bet that the very port it was supposed to be hasn't been taxed either."

"Why would anyone do that?"

"Because no one would suspect smuggled goods to be hiding less-savory smuggled goods inside," Holmes replied calmly.

"Can you never find a simple solution to these cases?" I exclaimed in exasperation. "Must it always be a complex thing of layers upon layers?"

He chuckled drily, once again amused by my frustration. "You forget, my friend, that it isn't I who ideates the crimes. I merely apply my mind to disentangling them." He paused to look out the window. "And in this case, all the evidence points to our erstwhile dinner companion, Mr. Wellington Da Silva, as the mastermind behind the operation." Then, without taking his eyes from mine, he continued. "But before we send in the constabulary, I believe we should talk to Father Brown. He seems to have a very strong interest in this case. Strong enough that he took some remarkable risks to ensure he could keep us under surveillance. Truly remarkable. Oh, Watson, close your mouth or you will soon have horseflies buzzing around inside." He laughed now.

I tried to ask him how he'd known, but found it nearly impossible to emit a sound. My shock was more profound than at any other time in our acquaintance.

Holmes seemed to understand. "Perhaps it would save time if we simply spoke to him, and I'll reveal what I know. I'm deeply interested in what he is trying to achieve." He knocked on the roof of the cab and the vehicle came to a stop.

"I don't think we shall be very welcome if we pound on a priest's door at this time of night," I said, thinking he was about to tell the mysterious cabbie to head for that destination.

145

"There will be no need for that," Holmes replied as he opened the door and stepped out into the summer night.

Shrugging, I followed with the lamp, to find the cabbie descending from the roof of our hansom.

I realized immediately that it wasn't the same person who had driven us to the warehouse.

That had been a hulking brute of a man whose size was visible even through the clothes. The man who descended from the driver's position was slight and short, and he was dressed in grey. I recognized him immediately.

"Father Brown," Holmes said, "it's a pleasure to meet you, as always."

"At your service, Mr. Holmes," the priest replied, holding out his hand.

Holmes shook it solemnly and I wondered at the tableau. Could there have been a more fitting place for these two legendary detectives, so beloved by the press, to meet again than a desolated stretch of road on a dark night near a warehouse full of smuggled goods? I couldn't think of many.

"You have been following our progress," Holmes said. It wasn't a question, but a statement of fact, as if commenting on the weather.

Brown nodded. "I have."

"And you are intent on stopping us. That is why you approached Watson."

"Of course. He didn't tell you about that, did he?" Brown gave me an understanding look. "I didn't think he would. But I had to attempt it."

"I can see why," Holmes said. "But perhaps the time has come for us to speak openly."

"Honestly, I would have preferred to leave that for tomorrow. I wasn't intending to confront you now, only to hear what you'd found in the warehouse."

"Yes. I know. But since the coach runs quite differently when Old Meecham drives it than when a smaller man does, I decided that, since I had you at such close quarters, we should talk now." Holmes looked around at the empty night. "Although to be honest, I wouldn't mind holding our discussion somewhere more congenial. Is Meecham far?"

"He said he'd be waiting for the cab outside Sir Brian's property," Brown said.

"Good," Holmes replied. "We should head to the house, then."

146

"I think not," Brown replied. For the first time, I saw the determination that had made this unassuming little priest such a formidable adversary to criminals both domestic and international.

Holmes seemed unmoved by the sudden iron in our interlocutor's will. "I'd be interested to understand why not."

"Because," Brown replied, "the crime goes a bit further than you've discovered thus far."

Holmes waved his hand. "Oh, I imagine there are details on the operation side that I have yet to uncover. I shall leave those to the police, who have the men and the patience to study the methods used by smugglers. I'm satisfied to have uncovered evidence enough to convict the master criminal."

"But you haven't. You've only got enough to put an innocent man in jail."

"Hardly innocent," Holmes insisted. "You saw us investigating. Heard us discussing this. The opium in that warehouse goes to London dens. How many lives has it ruined? I can tell you of at least one: Meecham's wife, who fell in the river from one of the docks while in a semi-stupefied state." He shook his head. "How you were able to convince him to hand over his cab without suffering a beating is beyond me, but I am quite certain you didn't use force or poison."

Brown smiled. "God has given me other tools than force or poison. He has given them to you as well, from what I hear. In this case, compassion born of his own grief moved Meecham to yield. And you might feel the same." Father Brown sighed. "You have tracked down the source of the opium brilliantly. You've solved the *Why* and the *Who* of the crime in just a few short days, but it will take you a lot longer to understand the *Why* of this. Only one man knew that before I convinced him to tell me about it. Perhaps it would be best if you learned it, too. But not at Sir Brian's house. Would you accompany me to the church? Meecham trusts me to return his cab."

"Of course," Holmes replied. "And I trust you not to warn our quarry regarding what we've found."

Brown nodded, and I realized that nothing could induce him to break the bond implied in that simple gesture.

He returned to the roof, and within minutes the lights of the village came into view. We entered the church and waited while Brown lit the lamp in the office, which turned out to be a cozy, unassuming room furnished with a wooden desk and several chairs surrounding a small round table. Father Brown sat at one of the chairs. "Please sit down."

We sat and Holmes removed his pipe from another pocket in his coat and lit it. At the second puff, he faced the priest.

"I suspect you've brought us here to try to convince us that Mr. Da Silva isn't guilty of smuggling."

"On the contrary. I'm quite convinced that Wellington Da Silva is a smuggler. In fact, I knew it long before you did."

"How?" Holmes demanded.

"I'm not at liberty to say," Brown replied.

I had a sudden inspiration. "Is it because of the secret of confession?"

"If it were, I wouldn't be able to tell you that, either. Suffice to say that, knowing that Mr. Da Silva was guilty of that crime, I wondered why he would do such a remarkable thing."

"I expect the profit motive would suffice," I said. "Untaxed opium must yield a certain amount of financial gain."

"I have no doubt about that, except that I also know that Wellington Da Silva donates nearly all his profits, including every penny from the opium, to the orphanage. He only keeps enough back to maintain appearances, feed himself and his family, and pay for the upkeep of his house and grounds – which are quite modest by the standards of wine merchants I've encountered before. And, though I know you will want to verify that assessment for yourself, believe me when I tell you that I am absolutely certain of it."

Holmes and I pondered this in silence.

Father Brown smiled gently. "So you see, I have an advantage over you, even though I'm not a fabled intellect. I knew all the facts before you started digging for them, which gave me the opportunity to ask myself: *Why?* Why would a man who has no interest in profit, a man whose sole concern appears to be to live a Christian life and to help others, import a poison used to send men astray? Because, as you suspect, and as I know perfectly well, the opium in that warehouse isn't destined to become hospital morphine. It is taken to an opium den, once a fortnight, by a team of ruffians from London."

"I would say he's likely imbalanced," I replied. "Do you know if he suffered any strong shocks? Or perhaps a blow to the head? His actions aren't those of a sane man. Or perhaps he needs to dabble in crime to keep the orphanage from failing?"

"The orphanage is in no danger of failure. The money is for improvements and growth at this point."

Holmes said nothing, but I could almost sense the millwheels of his mind grinding this new information to powder to reach the bare essence of what the priest was saying. "It isn't his decision,"

148

Holmes said. "He is under coercion." He looked at the priest. "Blackmail?"

"Yes," Father Brown said sadly. "And it's a sad story indeed, because the blackmailer himself isn't a bad man, just a man under quite a bit of pressure. Family pressure in his case."

Holmes snapped his fingers. "Of course. This is why you didn't want us discussing the matter at Sir Brian's home. He is the blackmailer."

Brown nodded, his eyes conveying the depth of his concern. "It's quite easy to understand once you know his history."

"Which we don't," I objected. "To what are you referring?"

"Sir Brian has a cousin who is an MP," Holmes said quietly, "but who is also an addict. I assume these shipments make their way to the London den that supplies his needs discreetly. Unfortunately, that same den also makes the opium available to anyone with the price of a pipeful. People like Meecham's wife."

"No one wants it that way," Brown said. "Except the owner of the den, who demands his profit for the risk he takes. He's threatened to go to the authorities if Mr. Da Silva attempts to deliver the drug to the poor addict himself. Or if anyone else does so, for that matter."

"A hollow threat," Holmes said. "He would expose his own part in the plot. It would be much more effective to go to the press. Or to the man's political enemies."

I was horrified at the simple brilliance of Holmes's suggestion. Not so much at the elegant solution, but at the velocity with which he created a better crime from a flawed one. I thanked my stars that Holmes was on the side of the angels. He would be a terrible enemy to society were it otherwise.

Father Brown didn't appear to be thinking of those things. He just shrugged. "It's as you say. The only true criminal in this entire affair is the man from the den. He is the only person profiting. The rest are sad souls doing what they can to avoid censure."

"And Da Silva? Why is he helping? You mentioned blackmail. I've heard nothing about his past that might invite censure."

"Da Silva isn't protecting himself. He is protecting Father Santos." Brown mumbled down into the table. "Unfortunately, there was a slip. As a youth, he fathered a child before entering the seminary. His family raised the child, but the church was never told. Now it would be a scandal, and he'd be expelled from England. Da Silva is taking this risk not for himself, not even for father Santos, really. He is doing it for the children. For the orphans."

"And Sir Brian is doing it to protect his kinsman," Holmes said.

"Exactly. As long as Sir Brian thinks you suspect Da Silva, he knows he is safe. Da Silva will not talk. He'd rather go to jail than risk the orphanage by exposing Santos – which would happen if he exposed Sir Brian."

"This is quite convoluted," I said.

"No," Holmes said. "It's quite clear. Everyone is a victim, to some degree or other, excepting the criminals on the docks that own the den. But that means very little. The flow of opium must be stopped. It's already claimed one life that we know of – Meecham's wife – but must also have damaged countless other lives."

Father Brown hung his head. "Then do what you must. I shall not stop you. I had hoped to make you understand why I believe the crime should be forgiven. But you are free to do as your conscience dictates."

"Forgiven, perhaps," Holmes said, "but it can't be allowed to continue."

A fortnight passed, and Holmes and I had returned to Baker Street when we received the post from Eastleigh. A newspaper clipping fell from the cover along with a note.

"It's from Father Brown," I said after inspecting the paper. "He's sent us the clipping from *The Illustrated Police News*."

Holmes harumphed. He was never much impressed with the more sensational weeklies that I favored. "And the note?"

I read it aloud:

Dear Holmes,

I wanted to express my sincere admiration at how neatly you solved the crime without involving either Father Santos, Wellington Da Silva, or Sir Brian.

Having the police intercept the shipment as the wagon arrived was, of course, expected. But to be honest, I thought the trail would eventually lead back to Da Silva. In that sense, having a well-known dock figure step forward as a witness to say it had been unloaded in the night from a darkened ship on the Thames was a stroke of genius. I assume it was Meecham giving the testimony, even if I was unable to recognize the name given.

150

But more than genius, it was a clear sign of a moral man. A man with a soul as well-formed as his intellect.

I had my doubts. But you have restored my faith in mankind and showed me I was wrong to approach Watson first. While I still consider him a paragon of virtue, I will gladly admit to being wrong about you.

Yours Sincerely,
Father Brown

Holmes took a puff of his pipe and looked out the window for a few moments. Then he sighed.

"A most irritating fellow, wouldn't you say, Watson?"

I kept my own council, preferring to omit the fact that, over the course of our occasional meetings, I'd grown rather fond of the little priest. And that I'd rather enjoyed seeing someone force Holmes to think beyond the purely intellectual challenge of locating the criminal.

Perhaps Holmes wasn't a force of nature after all. Perhaps he was human.

But he had a long way to go if he wanted to be as human as that little priest.

We all did.

151

The Loyal Retainer
by Paul Hiscock

It was early evening, and Holmes and I had just sat down to eat a light supper when we heard a disturbance downstairs, followed by heavy footsteps on the steps. A few moments later, the door to our rooms was flung open, and a stout man with a florid complexion stepped inside, followed by a visibly distraught Mrs. Hudson.

"I'm sorry, gentlemen," she said, "but this man insisted on seeing you immediately, and would not even wait to be introduced."

"I can introduce myself," said the intruder. "My name is Mr. Raymond Murray, and I require the services of Sherlock Holmes."

I bristled at the man's dismissive treatment of Mrs. Hudson, and would have thrown him back out into the street. However, before I could suggest such a course of action, Holmes invited him inside and directed him towards the visitor's chair.

"You will have to excuse Mr. Murray, Mrs. Hudson," Holmes said. "His brusque behaviour is no doubt a response to having recently suffered a bereavement, and I'm certain that under other circumstances he would have been more considerate."

From the way Murray snorted when Holmes said this, it was clear that his lack of manners had nothing to do with grief. Mrs. Hudson left us to deal with our disagreeable client.

"You know who I am, then?" he said, once the door had closed behind her.

"Indeed. Your uncle, Sir William, was a notable figure in the business community. His death was reported in all of the newspapers, as was the identity of his heir."

"Very good. In that case, I can get straight to the point. I believe I may have been robbed, and I require your assistance to identify what was taken, and to bring the culprit to justice."

"*May* have been robbed?" I asked. "Surely you must know, one way or another?"

"That might be the case for a person like you or me," replied Holmes. "We are here, in our home, surrounded by all our worldly possessions. However, I don't think Mr. Murray is talking about the items that he has acquired over the years, but rather to the property that he inherited yesterday when his uncle died."

"You are correct, Mr. Holmes. Although it was always determined that I should inherit my uncle's estate, seeing as he had no children of his own, I spent very little time with him while he was alive. He had no interest in supporting me, stating that I would have plenty of time to waste his money once he was dead. I honoured his wishes and kept my distance, building up my own successful shipping business in Liverpool.

"I hadn't visited my uncle for at least five years before he died, and while you may think me uncaring, I feel little grief at his passing. However, I am mindful of my responsibilities, and came promptly when I heard, knowing that his widow and servants would be worried about their future. Yet when I arrived this morning I found a household, not in mourning, but in uproar. During the night, someone had broken into the house and forced their way into the safe in Sir William's bedchamber."

"What did he keep in there?" I asked.

"That's the problem. I'm not sure. Sir William apparently behaved as though that safe was of grave importance. However, he never talked about its contents."

"What about money?" I asked. "He was reputed to be a rich man."

"I don't believe so. He preferred to keep his money in the bank, and for his daily expenses, he had a second safe in his bedroom, where he kept a small amount of cash. I checked it myself this morning, and the money was still there, along with a ledger accounting for every shilling and penny."

"What else might have been in there, then?" I asked.

"There was some jewellery," replied Murray. "Lady Barringford told me that he would take it out for her to wear on special occasions. However, the burglar discarded these items and they were found on the bedroom floor."

"That is strange," I said.

"Not really. I looked at them and they were just costume jewellery – nothing of any value. Anyone who had seen Lady Barringford wearing them in public would have known that they weren't worth stealing."

"Did anybody else have access to the safe?" asked Holmes.

"No. He wouldn't allow anyone else in the room when he opened it, and the combination was only written down in one place – a sealed letter, held by his solicitor, which I am due to receive as part of my inheritance. The only person other than Sir William who ever saw inside the safe was his faithful servant, Harrison, and then only by chance on a couple of occasions, from the doorway. He told me that he thought he might have seen a small box in there once, but otherwise the safe appeared to be almost empty."

"Is this Harrison trustworthy?" I asked.

"I would consider Harrison above suspicion. Sir William was a difficult man, and miserly in spite of his wealth. Most servants couldn't stand him, and few stayed in his service for more than a year. Yet Harrison became Sir William's manservant before I was born, and I never heard him say one word against my uncle, even when provoked. Furthermore, he was always kind to me, and never expressed any unhappiness at the fact that I would inherit the estate one day."

"Have the police examined the scene?" asked Holmes.

"Yes. In deference to my uncle's status, they sent over a detective inspector. Apparently the Commissioner of Police insisted upon it, and sent his particular condolences to me, even though I don't believe we have ever met. The inspector seemed to do a thorough job. Not only did he examine the location of the crime, but he also questioned the whole household closely regarding visitors to the house in the weeks preceding, and especially regarding their movements the night before last, when my uncle died."

"Did the inspector suggest there was anything suspicious about Sir William's death? It is my understanding, from the newspaper reports, that he passed away peacefully in his sleep."

"That was my understanding too, and the inspector didn't contradict it. Yet I began to wonder if some foul play might have taken place, and that was when I decided that I should engage your services."

"Very well," said Holmes. "I would like to see the house, and this safe for myself. I know it's late in the day, but if it is convenient, Watson and I will accompany you there now."

Murray nodded in agreement. "That would suit me well. I have my own business to return to, and no desire to stay in London longer than is absolutely necessary."

Sir William's house was far less grand than I would have expected from a man of his standing. It was a small townhouse, located in a respectable, but not fashionable, neighbourhood. Furthermore, by comparison with its neighbours, the house hadn't been well maintained. The walls were grubby and in need of a fresh coat of whitewash, while the paintwork around the door and windows was peeling in multiple places.

154

Murray rang the bell and we waited for a minute, but nobody came to let us in.

"Where are the d----d servants?" he asked, before hammering on the door with his fist.

This time we heard some movement inside, and after a moment a maid answered.

"I am sorry to have kept you waiting, sir," she said. "I was attending to Lady Barringford and her guest."

"What about Harrison? Where is he?"

"I don't know, sir. He left the house shortly after you did, and he hasn't returned."

"Did he say where he was going?"

"No, sir."

"He will not be coming back," said someone behind us. I recognised the voice immediately as that of Inspector Hopkins.

"Inspector," said Holmes. "I didn't expect to see you here, investigating a simple burglary."

Hopkins smiled.

"Ah, Mr. Holmes and Dr. Watson, what a pleasant surprise! I should have expected that you might become involved. After all, there is nothing simple about this case. However, you have come too late. Employing all the investigative techniques I have learnt from you, I have already found the solution. "

Holmes looked sceptical. Despite Hopkins's enthusiasm for deductive reasoning, he had demonstrated a tendency to leap to erroneous conclusions in the past.

"I am pleased to hear you say that," said Murray, "but why will Harrison will not be returning? Have you arrested him for the theft? He was such a loyal servant to Sir William. I really cannot believe him capable of such a betrayal."

"Indeed not," said Hopkins, "but I think it would be better if we discussed this inside with everyone present." He then turned to the maid. "Please could you take us to Lady Barringford?"

The maid led us inside, as instructed. She guided us down the corridor by the light of a small candle, and it was hard to see where we were going. There were light fittings on the walls, and when she stumbled on the threadbare carpet, I asked why they weren't lit, as it would make her work considerably easier and safer.

"The master – that is the *old* master – wouldn't allow it," she replied.

"Well, I told you that I wanted them lit," replied Murray, whose foot had just caught in another hole.

"Very well, sir," she said, but she didn't stop to rectify the situation, and instead continued to lead us through the gloom.

I whispered to Holmes, "It seems that, even after his death, Sir William casts a long shadow over this household," and he nodded in agreement.

When we reached the sitting room door, the maid knocked softly, then opened it without waiting for an answer.

"Excuse me, my Lady," she began, "Mr. Murray has returned with – "

The inspector pushed past us in the corridor, so that he could enter the room first, and interrupted her.

"Lady Barringford, I am here to arrest you on charges of theft and murder!"

"What?" said a woman from inside the room. "You cannot do that! I have done nothing wrong!"

I stepped into the room myself, eager to see who was speaking. I was surprised when I saw her. Knowing how elderly Sir William had been, I had expected his wife to also be frail and infirm. However, the lady who sat, sobbing, in one of the armchairs by the fire wasn't that many years older than her nephew, Mr. Murray, and still seemed to have plenty of life left in her.

"This is preposterous," said Murray. "Look at my aunt. Surely you can see that she is quite incapable of murdering anyone."

"In my experience, anyone can commit a murder, if they have sufficient motive and the right tools," replied Hopkins.

"It wouldn't have taken much strength to kill an old man like Sir William," I agreed.

"No, Doctor," replied Hopkins. "While I have no doubt that Sir William was murdered, it was subtly done and I cannot prove it – yet. However, Lady Barringford's complicity in the murder of Mr. Harrison is undeniable."

"Harrison?" said Murray. "Don't be ridiculous! The man is alive and well. I saw him for myself, in this very room, just this morning."

"I am sorry to inform you that you are wrong," replied Hopkins. "The unfortunate man was murdered, barely an hour ago, in an alleyway not far from here."

There was a quiet cough from the other side of the room, and I remembered that Lady Barringford had been entertaining a guest. I looked around, and saw that there was a small man dressed all in black sitting opposite her. He had been concealed by the high winged back of his chair, but now he stood, and I was delighted to see the face of an old friend.

"I am sorry, Inspector," asked Father Brown, "but did you say Harrison was killed within the last hour?"

"That is right."

"Only, I have been sitting in this room with Lady Barringford for at least two hours. May I ask why you think she was involved?"

"An alibi from a priest? I suppose you thought that would save you, my Lady. Father, I'm sorry to inform you that this woman has taken advantage of your unworldly nature."

Holmes exploded with laughter, startling the assembled company.

"Inspector, you must be careful not to judge by appearances. This 'unworldly' priest's understanding of the criminal mind rivals my own. If you're lucky enough to happen upon Father Brown at the scene of a crime, I would listen very carefully to what he has to say."

"Well, in this case I'm afraid he has been fooled," said Hopkins. "However, he shouldn't feel bad. Even I didn't initially realise the depths to which this woman would sink, and if I had, an innocent man's life might have been spared."

"I will leave it to God to determine who is good and evil," replied Father Brown. "I am more interested in understanding the deductive process that led you to this conclusion. What evidence do you have that Lady Barringford was involved in this murder?"

"I should explain that I had my suspicions even before I arrived at the house this morning. The Commissioner would never usually concern himself with anything so trivial as a simple burglary. However, he insisted that I should keep him informed at every stage of the investigation. The obvious conclusion was that he believed the theft, just one day after Sir William's death, made the first event look suspicious. It would have been a black mark against the reputation of the police if it turned out Sir William had been murdered and we hadn't even bothered to investigate.

"The events surrounding the burglary were straightforward. There was a pane of glass broken in the kitchen door to make it look like someone had broken in, and the broken glass had fallen *outside*, not *in*, which is something we detectives look for, as it is a common mistake that less-intelligent criminals make when trying to conceal an inside job. However, I was still certain that someone from within the household was involved. Who else would have known about the safe in the bedroom?"

157

"But there was nothing of value in there," said Lady Barringford.

"Or so you would have us believe. Yet there were your jewels."

"Which the thief left behind because they were worthless. You saw them for yourself."

"Indeed, I did see them, but while I might only be a humble detective, I do know a little about the habits of the gentry, and am aware that they often commission copies of their valuables, so that they might wear them in public without the fear that they might be stolen. I put it to you that the real jewels were kept in the box that Harrison saw in the safe, and that, as the owner of the jewels, you were well aware of this fact."

"This is preposterous, Inspector! I should call the Commissioner this moment, and have you removed from the case, and from this house! I have no doubt that, as a friend of my husband, he simply expected you to offer your condolences to our family, not carry out a witch hunt in pursuit of me."

"The Commissioner was your husband's friend?" asked Holmes.

"I believe so," she replied. "He called upon my husband regularly, although sadly, being a busy man, he was always in a hurry to get away and was never able to stay and dine with us."

"It is interesting that you should mention visitors, Lady Barringford, as one of the things I was keen to learn was who had called at the house in the days preceding your husband's death. One caller stood out – a Mr. Belmont. He visited the day before your husband died, did he not?"

Lady Barringford nodded, hesitantly.

"Your maid told me that she heard Mr. Belmont arguing with your husband while he was here. Sadly, she couldn't tell me what it was about, as the study door was closed, but she did see Mr. Belmont slam the study door when he left. She also saw him go straight to this very room, where he then spent at least fifteen minutes alone with you. I believe that's when you conspired to kill your husband."

The maid took a step back towards the wall, to cower in the shadows, trying to escape the unwanted attention. This was clearly a house that had been run on fear. It was obvious why servants didn't stay long, and it made me wonder why Harrison had been an exception to this rule.

Lady Barringford didn't seem angry at her maid, but her voice dripped with distain as she replied to Hopkins' accusations. "Mr. Belmont is an old friend of my family. There is nothing strange

158

about us spending a few minutes together. You seem to be implying that there was some sort of inappropriate relationship between us, which was the cause of the argument and our motive for murder. Yet you have no evidence to back these scurrilous accusations, and will never find any, because they aren't true. Mr. Belmont's argument with my husband was about a business matter. I don't know the details, only that Mr. Belmont felt that his trust had been abused and asked if I might intercede on his behalf. I did so, after he had left, but my entreaties were rejected. My husband was a shrewd businessman, but believed every man should look after his own interests. He wouldn't hesitate to take advantage of any opportunity, even at the expense of a friend or colleague. I assume that is what happened in this case.".

"It is a nice story, Lady Barringford," replied Hopkins. "We probably would have believed you, if it weren't for the theft. I understand why you felt you had to steal the jewels immediately, but it was your undoing."

"Well, I don't understand. Why would I steal my own jewellery?"

"But it wasn't *your* jewellery, not legally. It was your husband's, and after his death it became the property of his heir. You probably expected it would be a few days before Mr. Murray came to inspect his new property, but when you learned that he was going to be arriving today, you panicked, and had to risk arousing suspicion by getting Mr. Belmont to break into the safe for you. If your plan was to succeed, Mr. Murray would never know that the real jewellery ever existed."

"That is a very interesting theory," said Father Brown. "However, none of it explains what happened to Harrison."

"I was coming to that, Father. Having deduced all this, it was clear that the best way to prove it would be to find the real jewellery. Lady Barringford wouldn't have wanted to keep it in the house, knowing that the burglary would lead to a thorough search of the premises. It was most likely that her accomplice, Mr. Belmont, would hold on to them, and after the appropriate period of mourning had passed, they would sell them and use the money to start a new life together. Therefore, after I reported back to the Commissioner, who was still very concerned by the case, I decided to visit Mr. Belmont and search his house. However, as I approached, I saw him leaving the premises, and decided to follow him instead. If the jewellery was in the house, it would keep, but if he was going to hide it somewhere else, it might never be seen again."

159

Holmes nodded in approval at this particular decision, and Hopkins beamed with pleasure.

"I followed him around town for an hour or more as he performed various errands. Eventually, he turned into a narrow alleyway, and I was left with the difficult decision as to whether to follow him down there, as I feared he might spot me. However, then I realised he had stopped, so I decided to watch from a doorway opposite.

"I wondered if he might be planning to hide the jewellery there. It seemed like a very public location, but he might have known of some secret hiding place. However, he seemed to just stand there, and a few minutes later another man joined him. At first, I didn't recognise him, but then I realised it was Mr. Harrison."

"Why didn't you recognise him immediately?" I asked.

"Well, he looked very different. He was wearing a much smarter suit, and his posture had changed too. I had thought he was a short man, but now he was standing up straight and looked a lot taller.

"At first, when Mr. Harrison entered the alleyway, Mr. Belmont greeted him cheerfully, but soon they started arguing. I moved closer, in order to hear what they were saying. I was just in time to hear Mr. Belmont shout, 'I won't let you reveal everything!' before he raised his cane and struck Mr. Harrison across the side of the head.

"I rushed into the alleyway to help the poor man, but I was too late. The metal head of the cane had crushed his skull, killing him instantly. Mr. Belmont knelt down beside the body and started crying uncontrollably."

"It sounds like the assault wasn't planned, and that he regretted it instantly," I said. "Surely you can't hold Lady Barringford responsible for that."

"It wouldn't have happened if her Ladyship hadn't manipulated his affections. He has loyally chosen not to say anything since his arrest, no doubt fearing that he might incriminate her. However, I believe she should still be held responsible. It will be up to a judge and jury to decide if they agree."

"Why was Mr. Belmont meeting with Mr. Harrison?" asked Holmes.

"That is the great tragedy of the case. I believe that loyal servant, who had served Sir William for so many years, was trying to persuade Mr. Belmont to quietly return the jewellery and prevent a scandal that could have threatened his master's posthumous reputation. He didn't deserve such a violent ending."

Holmes grunted in acknowledgement of the reply, but I could tell he wasn't entirely satisfied with the explanation.

"Did Mr. Belmont have the jewellery with him?" I asked.

"Sadly not, but I've sent a constable to his house to search, and I'm sure it will be found soon.

Having made his case, Hopkins stepped towards Lady Barringford, obviously intending to follow through on her arrest. Before he confronted her, he turned to Holmes, obviously seeking his approval. However, it was Father Brown that spoke up.

"Are you sure about the suit?" he asked.

"What suit?" replied Hopkins irritably.

"The one Harrison was wearing. You said it was smart?"

"Yes, I noticed how shiny and new it was, because the one he had been wearing earlier had been so threadbare. He must have kept it for special occasions. However, it was nothing outrageously expensive, if you were thinking he might have already sold the stolen jewellery and used the proceeds to pay for it."

"I was thinking no such thing," said Father Brown. "However, I've been visiting Lady Barringford for years, and I've never seen Harrison wearing a suit that wasn't on the verge of falling apart from years of wear, even on the most formal of occasions."

"I might be able to answer that," said Murray. "This morning when I arrived, I paid both the servants two weeks wages in advance from my own pocket. I didn't want them to have to suffer while they waited for the estate to be settled. I imagine that Harrison used that money. He probably wanted something smart to wear to the funeral."

"That might be the case," agreed Father Brown, but he didn't look entirely convinced.

We waited in silence for a moment, to see if he had anything more to add, but the cleric seemed lost in his own thoughts, and Hopkins once again turned to Holmes for his verdict.

"It is an interesting theory, Inspector, although built more upon conjecture than deduction. I would like to examine the evidence for myself, most especially this mysterious safe in the bedroom, before you arrest anyone else."

"Very well, Mr. Holmes. It wouldn't hurt. As keen as my eyes are, I know I don't have your extraordinary faculties. You might well spot something that will help prove the case."

Father Brown emerged from his reverie and said to Hopkins. "If you wouldn't mind, I would like to – "

161

Hopkins cut him off before he could finish. "Yes, of course. We have no need for you here. You may return to your Psalms and Canticles, and safely leave the detective work to us professionals. The rest of you, if you would be so kind as to follow me? That includes you, Lady Barringford. I have no constable here to leave watching you."

Then, without waiting for a reply, he opened the door and set off down the corridor towards the stairs. I glanced back, just before we left the room. Father Brown seemed to be making no move to leave, but instead stood there watching us intently.

Upon entering the bedroom, Holmes headed straight for the safe. The rest of the company stood back, next to the walls, leaving him space to work.

I could see why they had been sure there had been a robbery, even though it wasn't certain if anything had been taken. The safe hadn't been opened gently by a skilled cracksman, but had been forced open violently. We could see the marks where the thief had first tried to force his way in with a large tool, and where he had eventually succeeded, the metal door was twisted and bent.

"Was Mr. Harrison a heavy sleeper?" Holmes asked.

"No," replied Lady Barringford. "The slightest thing would disturb him. There was one time that a tree outside started tapping at his window. It would keep him awake all night, and he pled with Sir William to have the branch trimmed. My husband refused. He didn't think it was worth the expense, and in the end Harrison climbed the tree and cut it off himself."

"Did it disturb you?"

"No, I have a preparation prescribed by my doctor to ensure that I sleep well. My maid gives it to me every night before she goes home."

Holmes seemed satisfied with this response and returned to his examination of the safe.

"Where was the cheap jewellery found?" I asked.

Murray pointed to the carpet in front of the safe, "That's where it was. However, it's now on the nightstand over here."

"It's a pity that it was moved," said Holmes.

"I am responsible for that," said Hopkins. "I examined the scene carefully first, but I needed better light to examine the items properly."

"Very well," said Holmes, but it was clear that the Hopkins had disappointed him once again.

162

I went to look at the jewellery, which consisted of a simple diamond pendant and a small pair of earrings. They weren't that impressive, and I wasn't sure that even the real jewellery Hopkins believed they were copies of would have been that valuable.

Holmes came over to stand by me, but he barely spared the jewellery a glance.

"As Mr. Murray informed us before this, it's poor quality costume jewellery. I can see why the thief discarded it. However, you should come and look at the safe."

He led me across the room.

"Tell me what you see," he said, and I could detect a note of eagerness in his voice.

My first impression was that it was very large for such a small amount of jewellery. I looked inside, expecting some great revelation, but the space was empty.

"There's nothing there," I said.

"That's right," said Hopkins. "The thief was very careful not to leave any traces. Now, if you have seen everything, Mr. Holmes, I would like to take my suspect back to the station to interrogate her further."

Holmes ignored him, "Look again," he said to me.

I did as he instructed, but still couldn't see anything. "It is just a metal box, with a sheet of felt in the bottom. The manufacturers will have put it there to protect anything placed on the hard surface."

I looked at Holmes, and he nodded in approval, so I turned back to examine the sheet of material in more detail. There didn't seem to be any hairs or other trace evidence on the soft black surface. I ran my fingers lightly over it, to see if I could feel something that wasn't visible. There was nothing there, but I did realise that the surface wasn't entirely smooth. I traced a slight ridge in the felt running around all four sides of the safe.

"There is an impression in the felt," I said. "Something heavy pressed into it."

"No doubt that was the jewellery box Harrison mentioned," said Hopkins.

"I don't think so," I replied. "It is far too big. Something large and heavy was kept inside that safe, and for quite a while to have time to make such a mark."

Holmes nodded in approval. "I see the shape of things now. Inspector Hopkins, if you had examined the safe more closely, you would have realised that Mr. Harrison lied to you. I am afraid that your entire case has been built upon a faulty premise. Lady Barringford is completely innocent."

I could see Hopkins turning over the facts in his mind, trying to understand where he went wrong. Eventually he said, "I am sorry, Mr. Holmes, but I cannot see why you think that. You will have to make your case properly if you wish to change my mind."

"Very well," replied Holmes, "but I think we should return to the sitting room. I believe Father Brown has reached the same conclusion that I have, and that we would benefit from including him in our discussion."

"But the Father has already left," complained Hopkins. "Do you expect us to wait while we send for him?"

I remembered the look on the priest's face as we left the sitting room. "I don't think that will be necessary," I replied.

As I had suspected, Father Brown was still in the sitting room when we returned. He was standing by the fire, stirring it with a poker. I wondered why he was doing this, as he already looked flushed by its heat.

"I thought that you would take longer," he said.

"And I thought you were leaving," replied Hopkins.

"No. I realise that is what you thought. However, I only wanted to suggest that I didn't need to see the safe."

Hopkins harrumphed slightly at this, but he couldn't deny that he had made an incorrect assumption.

Father Brown put down the poker and returned to his armchair. The rest of us also found places to sit and waited for Holmes to explain what he had discovered.

"When Mr. Murray came to us, he presented us with the mystery of what was in Sir William's safe. Although the investigation of the theft has been superseded by the desire to bring a murderer to justice, the contents of the safe remain the key to this entire affair. Mr. Harrison tried to mislead us. He might not have had access to the safe, but he knew what was inside. He lied, and told everyone about a small box, to encourage us not to look so closely. I'm not sure that he intended to implicate Lady Barringford by doing so, but his lie certainly fed the flames of the inspector's suspicions."

Holmes paused, and to the surprise of most of the people in the room, Father Brown took over the explanation.

"Inspector Hopkins, you described Harrison as a tragic figure. I'm afraid that you were more correct than you realised. As I said before, I met Harrison many times over the years while visiting this house. You assume that he loved his master because he stayed here for so many years, when others did not. However, if you had witnessed them together, you would have seen that Sir William was dismissive and often cruel to his servant. Though they wouldn't say it in public, the whole household feared Sir William."

Lady Barringford gasped, and Father Brown reached out his hand to hold hers.

"I don't intend to reveal anything you have confided to me," he told her, "but I will tell you that you are free to share the truth with these gentlemen. It cannot harm you now."

"What is this?" exclaimed Hopkins. "Did Lady Barringford confess to you before we arrived?"

"No," replied Father Brown, "but even if she had, you know I couldn't have shared it."

Lady Barringford sighed. "Are you sure, Father?" she asked.

"I am certain."

"Very well. A few years ago, I confided to Father Brown the dark secret of my marriage to Sir William. Having decided that he wanted me, he forced my father to approve the match by blackmailing him over some past business dealings. I wasn't privy to all the details, and I would never reveal them even if I was. However, because of the threat, and to save my father from disgrace, I endured a loveless marriage for over a decade."

Holmes nodded. "I wondered if you were one of his victims," he said. "When Mr. Belmont asked for your help, you immediately agreed to intercede for him. It suggested that you sympathised with his cause, rather than your husband."

"I suspect that Sir William tried to gather blackmail material on almost everyone in his circle," said Father Brown. "Certainly his files of evidence were thick enough."

"Files?" asked Hopkins. "What files?"

"Why, the heavy stack of papers which he kept in his most secure safe beside his bed," replied Holmes.

"We know that they must have been heavy, because of the indentation they left in the felt," I added.

"While I don't know what the files said," continued Father Brown, "I'm certain that one of them concerned Harrison. He didn't stay here all these years out of love for his master, but out of fear of having his secrets revealed, and Sir William took cruel advantage of this fact. Not only did he keep Harrison from seeking employment elsewhere, but he also used the threat to avoid paying his manservant more than the smallest pittance. Harrison always wore shabby suits

165

because he couldn't afford to replace them. That's why, when he was paid his proper salary for the first time in years by Mr. Murray, the first thing he did was to go out and buy a new suit."

"He used to wear old clothes that Sir William passed down to him," said Lady Barringford sadly.

"Inspector Hopkins," said Holmes, taking over again, "you were correct in one important regard: The early arrival of Murray accelerated matters and led to the clumsily executed break-in. Harrison knew that Sir William kept his blackmail materials in that safe, and that they were to be passed to his heir in the case of his death. I would like to think that Murray would have been as disgusted by them as we are, but Harrison couldn't afford to take that chance. He had no time to manage the matter subtly, but he knew that Lady Barringford took a sleeping draft every night, and since she would be the only other person in the house, nobody would hear him. Once he had safely removed the files, all he had to do was stage a break-in and suggest that something far more innocuous had been taken."

"And that is where I wish the matter had ended," said Father Brown, sadly. "Are you familiar with the Parable of the Uncompassionate Servant?"

The sudden change of subject caught me by surprise. This didn't seem the appropriate occasion for a sermon.

Father Brown didn't wait for anyone to answer, but continued, "If I had known what was going to happen, I might have told it to Mr. Harrison, and possibly saved his life. In the parable, a master forgives his servant's debts. However, the servant responds to his newfound freedom by cruelly demanding the repayment of another debt owed to him by one of his fellows.

"Harrison could have destroyed the blackmail files, freeing everyone who had been held under Sir William's thumb, but instead he chose to use them against his fellow victims. I don't know why he chose to start with Mr. Belmont. Maybe it was because he had been the most recent visitor to the house, but regardless, we are all aware that, just like the servant in the parable, Harrison paid the price for his actions in full."

"That might explain the altercation between Harrison and Belmont," said Hopkins. "It also explains why Belmont is refusing to explain why it took place. He is clearly afraid his secrets will still be revealed if we know that he was being blackmailed. However, you still haven't told us who killed Sir William. It seems that everyone had a motive."

"They may all have had a motive," said Holmes, "but like Harrison, they will all have been afraid of being revealed if the files passed to someone else. No, I don't think Sir William was murdered. He simply died of old age, as anyone who lives long enough is bound to do eventually."

"So where are these files now?" asked Hopkins. "We should begin a search immediately."

"I don't think you'll find them," said Holmes. "I doubt anyone will. If Harrison was prudent, he would have hidden them far from here, where none of Sir William's other victims would have thought to look. If that's the case, then the secret of their location will have died with him."

"Nevertheless, we must conduct a thorough search," said Hopkins. "For all we know, they are simply under a floorboard in his room. I'll fetch some constables and we'll start this very night."

Father Brown started to cough.

"Is something the matter?" asked Hopkins.

Father Brown cleared his throat. "No, not at all. However, I was wondering if you would you grant me a small favour, Inspector? I would like come to the police station and speak with Mr. Belmont tomorrow."

"Whatever for?" asked Hopkins. "Mr. Holmes has already set out the facts of the case. What more is there that you want to know?"

If Father Brown was offended that Hopkins didn't acknowledge that he had also seen the truth that Hopkins had missed, he didn't show it.

"Mr. Belmont has committed a terrible act. I'm afraid that his life, or at least his liberty will be forfeit. However, while there is nothing I can do to save him in this life, I can offer to save him in the life to come."

"Very well. If he will see you, I will allow it. I'll tell the desk officer to expect you."

"And please send our regards to the Commissioner," added Holmes. "I am sure he'll want to know how the case was resolved."

"Indeed. Good evening, gentlemen, and your Ladyship."

As soon as he had left, Lady Barringford said, "If that horrid man is going to be bringing back officers to ransack my house tonight, then I don't want to witness it." She gestured to her maid. "Go prepare my medicine, and bring it straight up. I intend to be fast asleep by the time he returns. Mr. Murray, please will you help me up to my room."

167

Murray picked up a candle to light their way along the gloomy corridor and offered his arm to Lady Barringford to help her out of her chair.

"Thank you for your help, Mr. Holmes. I knew I could rely upon you to resolve this matter swiftly."

Lady Barringford placed her hand on Father Brown's arm. "Thank you all, gentlemen, for believing me. I don't know what I would have done, had you not been here."

"You can see yourselves out?" asked Murray.

"Of course," I replied. "Do not concern yourself."

Once they were gone, Holmes stood, and I thought he was preparing to leave, but instead he walked over to the fireplace. He took up the poker and stabbed at the ashes in the grate.

"Harrison would never have succeeded as a blackmailer," he said. "He wasn't nearly cautious enough."

"No," replied Father Brown, "but I'm glad about that. He wasn't a bad man, just one who had been abused. I pray that will be taken into account on the Day of Judgement."

"I am also glad we resolved the matter in this way," said Holmes, poking at the fire once more. "It is far better that Sir William's files are never found."

"But what if someone stumbles across where Harrison hid them?" I asked. However, even as I was saying the words, I noticed a scrap of paper float up from the fire, provoked by Holmes's prodding.

The Blood of Hailes
by Chris Chan

Sherlock Holmes had endured his guest's presence for much too long. The man had invaded his Sussex cottage twenty minutes earlier and Holmes wanted to get back to his bees. "Sir, you are going around in circles and getting nowhere. Every time you speak, you contradict yourself in the next sentence. Do you want me to investigate a mysterious death or not?"

"Well, I'm trying to tell you," Mr. Shennan explained. "I'm not sure that you can call them deaths or not, as both of the deceased have made a full recovery."

"If they're still alive," Holmes snapped. "They weren't dead in the first place."

"But they were," Mr. Shennan insisted. "The blood brought them back."

"This is the fourth time you've mentioned blood with reviving powers. Are you talking about some kind of transfusion?"

"No, sir, it's some kind of magical blood. Not that I believe in that sort of thing myself, but it seems to have that effect on dead people."

Holmes made no attempt to hide the incredulity in his voice. "This is blood that can raise the dead?"

"Yes."

"What – does someone take a hypodermic syringe and inject it into them?"

"No, it's a little phial of blood in a fancy crystal bauble. It's waved over the dead person, and then when it touches them, the person comes back to life."

"What kind of blood is this? Human blood? Or some sort of mythical creature?"

"Well, it's a religious relic. Supposedly, it contains some of the blood of Jesus Christ. I believe they call it 'The Blood of Hailes'. People are saying it's saved the lives of two people so far. The first was an electrician. The second was a fisherman."

"How long were they dead?" A bit of curiosity flashed across Holmes's face.

"Not long at all. Just a few minutes. I don't think it works if the bodies have started to decompose. Though who knows? Maybe it

169

could make flesh and hair grow back on skeletons. I suppose you never know until you try." Mr. Shennan giggled a bit. It was not a pleasant laugh. It was more supercilious than mirthful.

"I should like to know how the electrician and the fisherman died, Mr. Shennan. Or perhaps it would be more accurate to ask: How did they *allegedly* die?"

"They both died as a result of their work, I suppose. The electrician was working on some wires at one of the big houses at the edge of the village, and he must have made some little mistake, and he got electrocuted. Well, the doctor came by and pronounced him dead, and then Sir Bartholomew – this odd elderly man with an interest in antiquities, he's always boring people at village functions droning on and on about local history – he comes by with that so-called relic, and he wanders into the house just as they're preparing the body to be carried away. He takes whatever-it's-called out of this little box he was carrying, and he started chanting some made-up words."

"I wouldn't be surprised if it was Latin."

"No way for me to know. I don't know Latin, and I wasn't there. I heard about it second-hand."

"Who told you about this?"

"It was my sister. She's a bit of a busybody around the neighborhood, and in a small village like ours, news circulates faster than you'd ever imagine. The doctor's assistant overheard what happened to the electrician, and she told a bunch of people who told plenty of other people, and before you know it, it was common knowledge in the area. That's how Sir Bartholomew Cornwallander heard about it. One of his servants was doing some shopping in town, and she heard the news, dropped her bag of vegetables, and rushed back to the Grange to tell him about it. Moments later, Sir Bartholomew leapt into his dog-cart and raced over to the house, right after the doctor pronounced the poor fellow dead. Then Sir Bartholomew did his mumbo-jumbo, touched that little blood bubble to his forehead, and – *Hey Presto!* – the electrician was alive again. Amazing."

Holmes's face was impassive, unlike his guest, who was smirking with a self-superior air. After a moment, Holmes asked, "What of the fisherman?"

"Ah, him. Well, I don't think I mentioned, but our village is in Gloucestershire. A good portion of the community went down to the seashore as part of a community picnic. I wasn't there. I don't care for that sort of thing, but my sister went along. She's quite the social butterfly. Anyway, Sir Bartholomew was with them, and he brought his little artifact with him. Apparently he's afraid to leave it out of his sight, or perhaps he wants it handy in case of emergencies. In any case, he was justified in bringing it, at least in his own mind. While they were all eating their sandwiches by the beach, some fisherman none of them knew fell out of his boat, and he was retrieved by some other fishermen and brought to shore. But apparently it was too late. He'd drowned."

"Did the doctor pronounce him dead?"

"No, there wasn't a doctor on the trip. But my sister says he wasn't breathing. At least, not until Sir Bartholomew did his little ritual. He said his words, he tapped the drowned fisherman with the blood, and a moment later the man spat out a gallon of seawater and was gasping for air."

"Your sister told you this?"

"She did. And she's subjects to flights of fancy and an overactive imagination, so bear that in mind, but still, I'm convinced there has to be a rational scientific reason for what happened."

"And you want me to do your investigation for you?"

"I – *ahem* – I cannot afford to pay you very much, but I'm sure that a man of your intelligence and dedication to the truth will consider this a worthy challenge."

Holmes pursed his lips. He didn't care for Mr. Shennan. There was something in the man's personality that he found off-putting. After a moment's reflection he was just about to send him on his way, when Shennan spoke again. "I should let you know that your presence in this investigation will help offset the meddling of someone who will no doubt stoop to shady means to tell the world this blood magic is genuine. A Catholic priest has been called to investigate, and I'm sure his validation of the supposed miracles are a foregone conclusion. This priest, Brown – "

"Eh?" Holmes's demeanor altered instantly. "Father Brown?"

"Yes! You've heard of him?"

"I have. He's an old friend of mine, and I can assure you that his integrity, honesty, and investigative skills are beyond reproach."

Mr. Shennan's face sank. "Then you won't help me?"

"On the contrary, I shall take the next train to Gloucestershire. But it will be to catch up with Father Brown, not to question his work . . . ."

Later that evening, Holmes stepped off the train in Gloucestershire. He had been compelled to share a compartment

171

with Mr. Shennan, and he had not enjoyed the experience. Mr. Shennan had been given many opportunities to lapse into silence, and he had taken advantage of none of them. Holmes was making a considerable effort to keep his face impassive, when he felt a sudden shock when he saw Mr. Shennan running towards him wearing a long auburn wig and a tweed jacket and skirt. A quick glance to his right assured him that Mr. Shennan was still standing next to him, and a moment's reflection led Holmes to the conclusion that this was Mr. Shennan's sister.

Incredulous at the family resemblance, Holmes endured Miss Shennan's garrulous introduction of herself and, after several minutes, the only comment of hers that he was willing to commit to memory was the fact that her first name was Aerona.

"I'm so glad you're here, Mr. Holmes!" Aerona gushed. "You've come just in time!"

"Why is that, Madam?"

"Oh, haven't I mentioned it? I haven't, have I? How silly of me. It's completely slipped my mind. I have a habit of leaving my head in the clouds, don't you know? Anyway, there's been a murder!"

The more Holmes pressured Aerona to focus, the more vague and talkative she became. After some gentle guidance, she gradually made it clear that the victim was a young man named Brice Bardalph, a not-particularly-well-liked fellow who ran the most successful pub in the village alongside his much more popular brother, Bramwell. The latter was the elder by a year-and-a-half, and the two bore a marked resemblance to each other, with similar hair and eyes, though it was not enough for them to be mistaken for twins.

The brothers had inherited from their late father, and Bramwell was more than happy to spend his life serving his friends and neighbors drinks. Brice, in contrast, had dreams of travelling the world, but only had enough money on hand to make it to Wales, and insufficient cash to make his way back. Shortly after their father's burial, Brice had pressured his brother to sell the pub, so that they could split the funds and pursue their own interests. Bramwell flatly refused, saying he would never allow the family business to fall into someone else's hands.

Undaunted, Brice asked his brother to buy out his share of the pub. Bramwell was much more amenable to that possibility, but that plan was hindered by Bramwell not having enough money to perform the suggested transaction. Bramwell had been speaking to a local bank about the possibility of a loan to pay for his brother's half of the family business, but seeing as how the profits from the pub were enough to provide a sufficient living for the brothers and little more, the lenders were reluctant to offer Bramwell the money.

"And Brice is the one who's dead?" Holmes asked.

"Yes. He was found shot dead about fifteen minutes ago, in the middle of the pub. It was Bramwell who shot him, you see."

"How do you know that?"

"He left a signed confession. Apparently Brice had gotten increasingly insistent on getting his half of the inheritance in cash so he could leave the little town where he'd lived for all his life and start the travels he'd always wanted, and it had spiraled into an increasingly violent argument. Bramwell had broken his usual abstemious habits and had a couple of drinks, so he wasn't as controlled as he normally is. He grabbed his father's old revolver from behind the counter and fired it at his brother's head before he realized what he was doing. He panicked as soon as he realized what he'd done to his own flesh and blood, but he felt so guilty he had to write a note explaining himself to the authorities. And then he fled."

"He can't have gone far," Holmes observed. "The train which carried us here is the only one to come to this village until the morning milk train, and I didn't see anyone climb aboard before it left the station."

"Perhaps he came around the other side and slipped on without being noticed," Mr. Shennan suggested.

Holmes managed a level of balefulness in his glare that he had never previously achieved. He despised it when near-strangers suggested that his observations had been insufficiently thorough. "I suppose that anything is possible," he admitted with a firmly clenched jaw.

Mr. Shennan continued to theorize about where Bramwell might be hiding as the three of them climbed into a waiting automobile, and after a bit of arguing between the two siblings, Aerona drove them into town towards the pub. About half-a-mile from their destination, as Holmes was resolutely ignoring Mr. Shennan's ideas on what foreign country Bramwell might be fleeing to as he spoke, Holmes interrupted him with a sharp, "Stop!"

Aerona stomped upon the brakes and sent them all lurching forward. As Mr. Shennan asked why Holmes had called out, Holmes, without answering, stepped out of the car to greet a small clergyman who was strolling along the side of the road. "Father Brown!"

The priest smiled, and the two friends greeted each other with the usual pleasantries. After a rapid explanation of what he was doing in Gloucestershire, Holmes offered Father Brown a ride to the location of the crime, which Father Brown had been heading towards when Holmes spotted him.

"Father Brown, what is this Blood of Hailes?" Holmes asked. "I know it's supposedly a relic, but I'm unaware of the history behind it."

Clearing his throat, Father Brown provided a historical overview. "According to some narratives, when Jesus Christ was being crucified, Joseph of Arimathea – one of Jesus's disciples who oversaw the funeral arrangements – collected a quantity of Christ's blood as it dripped from his wounds. This was bottled and some of it was enclosed in a small phial – some scholars believe that it was a little crystal globe. For centuries, it was one of the crown jewels used in coronation ceremonies for the Holy Roman Emperors, but in 1270, it was brought to Gloucestershire's Hailes Abbey, where it was placed in a bejeweled shrine, and became a popular pilgrimage site, especially for those seeking its renowned curative powers, which were believed to include healing illnesses and even, on occasion, bringing the dead back to life."

"Preposterous," Mr. Shennan snorted. His sister jabbed an elbow against his ribs.

Father Brown cast a vaguely amused look at the back of Mr. Shennan's head. "You may mock the story, but the fact remains that Hailes became one of the most popular destinations for pilgrims for centuries, rivaled only by Canterbury Cathedral. While the Church rarely makes official pronouncements on the genuineness of certain relics from centuries ago, there are many cases where people visited Hailes and were healed of their various ailments. There are documented cases of unexplained phenomena connected to the Blood. A priest from Shropshire became convinced that the supposed relic was a fraud, and he started preaching against pilgrimages to Hailes. Soon after he made his pronouncement, at his next consecration of the Eucharist, the chalice containing the Blood of Christ started bubbling, as if it were placed on a fire to boil. That changed the priest's mind. Another skeptical priest saw one of his religious texts start to bleed, leading to a change of heart. Whether or not people came back from the dead thanks to it is more controversial."

"If this Blood of Hailes is so wonderful, and so historically important, why did the Church lose control of it?" Aerona asked. "How did Sir Bartholomew gain possession of it?"

174

"Did the Church misplace it? Sounds careless to me," Mr. Shennan quipped.

"It was stolen," Father Brown explained. "After Henry VIII broke from Rome, he and his cronies made a point of seizing every bit of land and every valuable item they could grab. The monasteries were dissolved, and the King's allies turned the properties into their own estates. Churches were transferred to royal control, and priceless artworks were confiscated. Altarpieces housing the relics of saints were snatched because they were decorated with precious metals and jewels. The money went to the Crown and those working for the King. The Blood of Hailes was no exception. It was protected by a fantastic altarpiece that was seized and dismantled for profit. The abbey at Hailes was almost completely destroyed, though portions of the ruins still exist today. The Blood itself was taken by the new Church of England authorities, and was repeatedly denounced as a fraud. One Protestant minister claimed it to be duck's blood."

"How could he possibly have known that?" Holmes sniffed. "I know from my own experiments how hard it is to tell the difference between blood and similar-looking substances without complex chemical tests. They didn't have my personal reagent then. How they possibly tell what kind of blood it was?"

"A point that had occurred to me, and one which calls into question the efficacy of their analysis," Father Brown replied. "Other authorities of Henry VIII's new church called it an 'unctuous gum' or 'honey mixed with saffron'. Whether this was true, or whether this was simply a falsehood meant to discredit the monks and Catholic Church practices in general is a point hotly debated by scholars. In any event, at some point, the little phial of blood disappeared, and no one knows what happened to it."

"Until Sir Bartholomew gained hold of the relic," Aeorna added.

"I can make no pronouncement on whether or not Sir Bartholomew's possession is the real Blood of Hailes or not," said Father Brown. "I've been asked to look into these alleged resurrections. I've just heard that Sir Bartholomew is heading to the tavern where that poor man was shot, trying to bring him back to life."

"Why are you investigating this if it's now a Protestant relic?" Aeorna asked.

"First of all, the Catholic Church doesn't consider it a 'Protestant relic', especially since The Church of England tried so hard to discredit the Blood. The Catholic Church still believes the preservation of The Blood of Hailes to be its responsibility, and in any event, not many ministers in the Church of England are experts in these antiquities. I happen to have some knowledge of relics in England, and as I happened to be in the area, I was asked to investigate."

At that moment, the car reached their destination. Holmes was the first one to enter the pub, followed by Aerona and her brother, with Father Brown being the final one to pass through the door. There, they saw Sir Bartholomew, a tall, lanky man with wild white hair and a similarly disheveled beard, kneeling on the ground in an expensive but rumpled suit. He was leaning over a body lying face down in a small pool of blood. The victim was wearing a shabby brown clothes and had matching hair, worn rather long.

A constable tugged gently Sir Bartholomew's collar. "Sir, I really think you need to – "

"Quiet!" Sir Bartholomew's voice was like a cannon exploding. "Let me finish!" He resumed his chanting.

"His pronunciation of the Latin is a bit shaky," Father Brown murmured.

Presently, Sir Bartholomew pulled a little velvet case out of his pocket, and withdrew a glittering little crystal bottle out of it. Even in the poor tavern light, the liquid inside glimmered and gave the impression of being a fantastic ruby. Sir Bartholomew's voice raised dramatically, and he placed the phial upon the back of the dead man's head.

Scarcely had the phial touched the corpse, when the body began to twitch and shake. After a moment, the once-still figure rolled over upon his back and started gasping, his blood-stained face partially but not completely masking a look of utter bewilderment.

"I . . . I'm alive? Where's my brother?"

Most of the people in the pub started screaming, aside from Holmes and Father Brown – and Sir Bartholomew, who looked triumphant.

The man on the floor staggered to his feet and stumbled towards the large glass mirror behind the bar. He picked up the cleanest-looking cloth in a messy pile, soaked it with water from the tap, and washed his face clean. There was no trace of a wound. Without the blood, his face was much more pleasant to look at, and Aerona squealed and ran up to him.

"Brice! It is you! You're all right?"

"Of course I am. Why wouldn't I be?"

"Well, for a man who was just fatally shot in the face, you're in remarkably good health."

"Hmm? Oh, yes. I forgot about that for a moment. I must have hit my head rather hard on the floor after falling."

"Do you remember what happened to you?"

"Of course! My brother started an argument with me. He was absolutely nasty, telling me that I was betraying our father's memory by wanting to go out for myself and pursue my own interests and make my own life. Well, I told him that I wasn't about to waste my best years in a tiny, dark pub until they stick me in the ground, and Bramwell growled and said, 'That may happen sooner than you think!' and, without any warning, he pulled out a revolver from his jacket, pointed it at me, and fired. The next thing I know, I'm on the floor here and my face is a mess. I always knew Bramwell had a temper, but I never expected him to come at me with a deadly weapon."

"Luckily, I was here to bring you back from the brink, old boy," Sir Bartholomew chuckled.

"Balderdash!" Mr. Shannen snorted. "There has to be some mistake. He must have only gotten a flesh wound when he got shot, and then fainted or something, and you all just thought he was dead."

"Mr. Shannen, I can assure you that it is you who is talking balderdash." The icy reply came from a spare man with sandy hair and a pencil moustache. Judging from the black bag he was carrying and the stethoscope sticking out of one of his coat pockets, Sherlock Holmes and Father Brown deduced that he was the village doctor. "When one of my neighbors heard yelling and a shot coming from inside the pub, she tried to come in to see what happened and she found the door locked. She ran to get me, and then we came in through the back door and found him here. I examined the body and I can assure you that he was completely dead. I saw the damage done to his face. It wasn't a 'flesh wound', as you call it. It was a fatal and destructive bullet hole. Your theory is wrong. He was indeed dead." The doctor glared at Mr. Shennan, silently challenging him to try to contradict him. Mr. Shennan had no reply.

"And you were here the whole time?" Holmes asked.

The doctor reflected for a moment. "Actually, no. The woman who brought me here went out to fetch a constable, and a few moments after she left, I smelled smoke and went out back. An empty liquor crate had caught fire. I believe some fool had tossed a smoldering cigarette upon it. It didn't take long for me to put out the flames, and then I went back inside. My neighbor returned with the

177

constable a couple of minutes later, and pretty soon half the village was coming to see the body for themselves. I tried to turn them out but they wouldn't listen." He glared balefully at his neighbors.

"Clearly no one's bought a drink here yet today," Father Brown commented.

A few of the other people in the pub shot him quizzical glances, as if they thought his comments weren't quite appropriate at this moment.

"What makes you say that, Father?" Holmes asked, with none of the judgment expressed by the others.

"Take a look. No used glasses. No freshly washed glasses. They're all dry, and the bottles are nearly lined up on the shelves, all dusted and in alphabetical order. Very orderly. The two of you must be very organized young men."

Brice dismissed the comment. "It's Bramwell who's obsessed with keeping things orderly. I'm not nearly so fastidious as he is."

"Is he really that fastidious?" Father Brown crossed over to a document lying on the corner of the bar.

"Is that the confession?" Holmes joined the clergyman, having previously examined some small brown marks on the far corner of the wall, three yards from where Brice's feet had been pointing when he lay on the ground a few moments earlier.

"It appears to be, yes." The two men read through the document.

"Why did you ask about my brother being fastidious?" Brice asked.

Father Brown turned around, looking a trifle apologetic. "It's the handwriting, you see. It's quite sloppy. Quite hard to read, really. Not entirely illegible. The narrative matches what Miss Shennan told us – " He gestured over at her. "Of course, it's understandable that a man mightn't be thinking about his penmanship when he's dashing down a confession before running away. But why would he take the time to write out a note at all if he was planning to flee? Why not escape to safety as soon as possible, without missing a moment, and then, once he was out of the country, he could write a confession in the safety of some hotel room and then mail it back to England?"

Brice looked a trifle unsteady. "Perhaps he wasn't thinking clearly. When Bramwell became flustered, his mind didn't work as smoothly as it usually did."

"That is a possibility," Holmes admitted. He turned to the constable. "Do you mind if we take a quick look around?"

"By all means, sir. It's an honor to have you here, Mr. Holmes."

"From my observations of the outside of this building, there is no floor above this one, and this room here appears to take up almost the entirety of the ground floor. Therefore, there must be a cellar where you keep your stock. I presume we'll find the stairwell if we go behind that door in the corner?" Brice nodded, looking rather frightened. As Holmes and Father Brown crossed the room, Holmes leaned over to the constable and whispered a few quick words into his ear. The two men descended into the cellar, ignoring the sound of a scuffle upstairs as they reached the bottom of the staircase. The light was dim, so Holmes struck a match and set a lamp upon a shelf alight. There were several rows of wine bottles (all of them cheap vintages), and six open crates of different bottled beers. The cobwebs and the grime made it clear that the basement hadn't seen the touch of a broom or a duster for at least a year. A thick layer of dust covered the floor, though it was sprinkled with footprints and scuff marks, and the disturbance around the large barrel that, from the smell of the small puddle beneath it, contained an inferior grade of rum.

After they climbed the stairs, Father Brown told Holmes, "Odd, isn't it, how the ground floor of the pub is so tidy and organized, but the basement hasn't received the same level of care?"

Aerona overheard and informed him, "That's not surprising. Bramwell had a fall a year-and-a-half ago, and injured his back. Not seriously, but he couldn't go up or down stairs without pain, and he certainly couldn't carry heavy objects up and down stairs. The brothers divided the labor. Bramwell would keep the pub organized, and Brice would bring items up and down from the basement, and he was also supposed to keep the cellar tidy, but I'm not surprised that he devoted very little time to cleaning."

Holmes nodded. "I see. Well, I believe that explains everything. Do you agree, Father?"

"Yes, Holmes, I do."

An hour later, Holmes and Father Brown were seated at the sergeant's office at the local police station as they explained the different paths that they had made towards their deductions.

"It was fortunate that you told my constable to keep an eye on Mr. Brice Bardalph," the sergeant said. "Mr. Bardalph declared that he was going out for a breath of air, and the moment he stepped out the door he started sprinting down the street."

"Thank you for catching him," Holmes smiled. "I trust that you didn't have to run too far?"

"Well, I have to admit I prefer my criminals overweight and out of shape. Mr. Bardalph had a good fifty yards on me before I left the pub. Fortunately the roads aren't very even, and he managed to catch his toe in a little depression and stumble to the ground, giving me just enough time to catch up to him. I suppose you might say the foot of Providence stuck out and tripped him, eh, Father?"

"That was indeed fortunate, Sergeant."

"So gentlemen, would you please be good enough to explain how you figured out what had happened so quickly?"

Holmes and Father Brown looked at each other briefly, and Father Brown gave a little gesture, encouraging Holmes to go first. Clearing his throat, Holmes began to speak, saying, "It was obvious through simple observation what had happened. Please excuse my skepticism, Father, but from the beginning I doubted very strongly that this was a case of a miraculous resurrection."

"How do you explain the two previous people being brought back from the dead?" asked the sergeant.

"I don't believe they were dead. Plenty of drowned people appear dead for a short while, only for their bodies to suddenly manage to expel the water blocking their lungs, bringing them back to the land of the living. And it's also common for electrocuted people to have their hearts stopped, enough to convince even a doctor that life has expired, but they make a full recovery after a little pressure on their chests."

"As for me, I haven't had sufficient time to complete my investigation of the two earlier incidents," Father Brown added, "and while I cannot rule out any possibility, I also consider that Holmes's suspicions are likely. Certainly the words Sir Bartholomew spoke were barely Latin – his pronunciation and grammar were atrocious, and I doubt that any ritual so inaccurately spoken could possibly have any supernatural effects."

Holmes nodded. "I noticed the blood spatter from the shot didn't match where the body fell – I saw some brownish marks on the wall, and though I didn't have the opportunity to perform a proper test, I'm quite sure they were bloodstains caused by a gunshot.

"It was quite apparent to me that the man on the floor had never been shot. But if that were the case, then how did the doctor examine a dead body? It soon became apparent to me that it was *Brice* who shot his brother *Bramwell* over an argument, almost certainly over the money Brice wanted. Given the nature of his plan, I doubt that it was premeditated. Brice developed his plan on the spur of the

180

moment. He quickly scribbled out a confession in his brother's name, blaming Bramwell. When the body was first discovered, Brice hid outside, and after he lit that fire to draw the others out, he grabbed his brother's body, dragged it into the cellar, hid it, smeared some blood on his face, and lay down on the floor. But where did he hide it? The only hiding place nearby where he ran no risk of being seen by a passerby was the cellar, which is why I searched there immediately. The disruptions in the dust on the floor told me at once that Bramwell's remains had been hastily concealed in a cask of low-grade rum. I believe that was a once-popular means of shipping the bodies of the dead home from the West Indies."

The sergeant nodded. "Father Brown, does that match your thought processes?"

"Not quite. I noticed a discrepancy in the confession. If Bramwell had been drinking, as it said in the confession, there'd have been a glass with residue out, and perhaps an open bottle. I suspect the untidy handwriting was the result of Brice writing very fast. Also, I thought it rather odd that a man who had supposedly come back from the dead wasn't more amazed by what had happened to him. I've met people who've been through potentially miraculous situations, and most of them are so blindsided by the immediate aftermath that they're absolutely discombobulated for quite some time. There wasn't any wonder or awe at being brought back from the dead, no comments on anything he'd seen after allegedly dying, just a flat accusation of his brother and an attempt to send the police after him. That was the flaw in his planning. He tried to create a fake miracle, but he forgot to *act* as a person might when he comes across something potentially miraculous."

"It was a rather foolish plan, but I don't believe that Brice is a criminal mastermind," Holmes noted. "How did he know Sir Bartholomew would show up with The Blood of Hailes? For all he knew, Sir Bartholomew could be indisposed with an upset stomach and couldn't come to his rescue. It would be a very awkward situation for him. He couldn't lie there forever before someone noticed his breathing. He was lucky enough that it worked for a short while, but he could just as easily have been exposed within minutes. It wasn't a premeditated crime and he came up with a rather silly idea on the spur of the moment."

The sergeant thanked them, and after a few more questions, the pair were allowed to go. As they left the police station, Holmes asked, "Father, what do you think of The Blood of Hailes itself? Do you think it could be the genuine article?"

"I'm no expert in ancient relics, but I think that a team of experts ought to spend some time scrutinizing it. There's no shortage of fake relics, though that in no way invalidates the object in question. A great many rare and important items vanished during the seizures of Henry VIII, and antiquities are often discovered in the oddest places. The Church rarely makes a firm pronouncement on the validity of any alleged relic, and much more study would have to be done regarding its supposed healing and resurrection powers. Hopefully, Sir Bartholomew will give us the opportunity to study that little phial."

Unfortunately, Father Brown never got the chance to get a closer look at the supposed Blood of Hailes. Sir Bartholomew balked at allowing the Blood to be touched by anybody but himself, and the negotiations went on for a few months before Sir Bartholomew passed away suddenly but peacefully in his sleep. He had left The Blood of Hailes in his safe, and by the time a workman was hired to open it, Sir Bartholomew's body had already been cremated. In any event, no one else seemed to know the words to the ritual Sir Bartholomew used. His heir was only interested in the cash value of his relative's many possessions, and they were all quickly sold off, despite the protests of Church authorities who pointed out it was sacrilege to sell relics, or even suspected relics. The Blood of Hailes was purchased by a wealthy eccentric in the American Midwest, where nothing more was heard of it for some decades. Holmes and Father Brown returned to their regular routines, and the truth behind that small crystal phial remains a mystery.

NOTE:

The fate of The Blood of Hailes is a reference to John Bellairs' book *The Dark Secret of Weatherend*, where I first heard the story of the relic. – C.C.

The Four Detectives
by John Linwood Grant

The coastal town of Scarborough, in Yorkshire, has long been famed for the restorative, if rather acidic, spa waters, which spring (with a little human assistance) from the cliffs thereabouts. With the added blessings of soft, forgiving sands, a ruined castle, and many entertainment halls, it is a popular destination for all levels of society. Less well known, perhaps, is that just above that great headland which juts defiantly into the North Sea, there stands a small church by the name of St. Mary's-without-the-Castle.

Likely of Norman origins, this church is of the Old Religion, that which pervaded England before the displeasure of King Henry VIII, and indeed, it is an old building, with all an old building's flaws. Such flaws, in fact, that every few years the diocesan authorities draw up plans for a new establishment somewhat closer to the town centre – and with a roof which would more permanently dissuade the rain from trickling down the necks of its limited congregation.

In the meantime, however, responsibility for both the souls of those who attend St. Mary's and for the tin buckets strategically placed in its aisle, falls to one Father Brown, who is, at a casual glance, no more remarkable than his church. Small and round, he can often be seen bicycling through the streets of the town, his cassock flying, with one hand gripping his clerical hat rather than the handlebars. Such forays might as often be prompted by the needs of a venerable parishioner as by some sudden notion as to how ship's tar might temporarily seal the vestry from the ravages of a winter blow. "For was not our Saviour Himself humble enough to embrace carpentry?" he reminds himself as he puzzles over one or other failing in the fabric of his church . . . .

It was in this latter, quite earthly cause, on one early autumn afternoon in 19--, that Father Brown came to be outside the consulting rooms of Dr. Orion Hood, in a wealthier part of town, not far from the seafront. Knowing the eminent criminologist to be away, his purpose was to beg Dr. Hood's housekeeper that her son might clamber once more onto St. Mary's precarious roof the next morning.

As he paused to gather himself for his plea, untangling his cassock from the bicycle chain and straightening his broad-brimmed hat, he happened to look out over the bay. From this elevated parade could be seen not only the foreshore below, where a trickle of late visitors were braving the elements, but the road down to the main promenade, where strode – to his considerable surprise – a tall, solitary figure with a quite distinctive profile.

"My goodness," the bicyclist said to himself. And, "Well, bless me."

It is said that when two Great Minds first meet, there is by their very nature a moment of appraisal, as fighting cocks might cast a beady eye on each other when placed in the ring. (Not that the little priest approved of such things.) Father Brown, who did not consider himself to be of any outstanding mental capacity, needed to conduct no such appraisal. He was already moderately acquainted with the approaching figure. More puzzling was why they should encounter each other again here, on the Yorkshire coast, in dank October.

Letting his bicycle clatter to the pavement, he went down to meet the newcomer, accidentally scattering a number of liquorice lozenges in his wake.

"My dear Mr. Holmes!" he said with warmth, extending one hand.

This other Great Mind, the consulting detective of note, stared at the priest's hand as if unacquainted with the custom, and then shook it.

"Hmm . . . Brown. A pleasure."

Father Brown smiled. Holmes had never been comfortable uttering the clerical title.

"And a surprise."

The lean, hawk-nosed face of the slightly older man seemed to settle into a more welcoming expression.

"I confess, I didn't know that this was your latest parish, though I remember now that you had been despatched to some Northern outpost."

"Yes, I was here many years ago. Like Hadrian's unfortunate soldiers, Holmes, we poor priests must also serve on the edge of Empire. For who knows when the Presbyterians might march down from their misty Scottish glens?" And he chuckled at his own very little joke. "But to find you up here . . . ."

"Watson's orders," said Holmes, without enthusiasm. "Even in my retirement he is the mother-hen. He visited me in Sussex after one of my bronchial attacks, and prescribed a break from the muggy

184

heat of an Indian summer which clings to the south coast. 'Brisk, bracing air,' he demanded. It was easier to comply than to remain under his watchful eye. And besides – "

"You thought it would afford you the opportunity of calling on the renowned Dr. Orion Hood. Who is currently on a lecture tour of the Midlands, I'm afraid. His only absence this entire year."

"Ah. No matter. I had no express purpose for meeting him."

"Oh, I'm sure that you would have had much to discuss. He, too, is officially retired, but is not averse to a little debate."

"You know him well?"

"We are acquainted. We worked together on an amusing little puzzle long ago, and his housekeeper, Mrs. Strachan, is a parishioner of mine. That is where I was headed. Do come inside anyway – you might enjoy a glance at his consulting rooms, replete as they are with relevant texts and a considerable amount of scientific equipment."

As they walked up the road, a passer-by would have concluded that no stranger pair could have been found on stage at the Theatre Royal. The short black-clad priest with an almost playful shamble, and the tall, sharp-eyed detective in his sombre, conservative over-coat, with a long stride which had diminished little with age.

Father Brown examined his fallen bicycle, and finding nothing amiss, propped it against the house wall. Satisfied, he went to the front door, which was set back at the side of a series of large French windows, and knocked.

The big blue door was opened with surprising alacrity, revealing a lady in her fifties with a straggling lock loose from her grey hair – and a distraught expression. Seeing her visitor, she gave a small gasp.

"Oh, Father Brown! Thank guidness ye're here. Ah sent Rory for ye not ten minutes gone."

The priest blinked. "Is someone ill?"

"There's summat amiss, is what, and Ah'm at ma wit's end o'er it."

"Then you must tell me more. Um . . . May I introduce Mr. Sherlock Holmes . . . ?" He waved one hand in his gaunt companion's direction.

"If I can be of assistance, madam?" said Holmes.

Wide-eyed, the woman ushered them in, and down a utilitarian corridor to a small parlour.

"Holmes, this is Mrs. Strachan, Dr. Hood's housekeeper," Father Brown explained as they walked.

"I imagined so. She seems distressed."

185

"Distressed?" The housekeeper gave a muted wail. "Mr. Holmes, Ah'm at a loss, for there has been a terrible theft, and Dr. Hood no' here."

Of Scottish extraction but clearly long resident in Yorkshire, Mrs. Strachan's accent was a marvel in its own right. At times, her ancestry prevailed. At other times, even before a sentence could be concluded, the flat tones of a Yorkshire matron would take over.

"This afternoon, this very afternoon, someone has entered and tekken up the maister's tantaliser! Spirited it away, aye."

Father Brown sat down gingerly in an old armchair, and a bright look came into his eyes. "You mean Dr. Hood's tantalus, the one in his consulting rooms?"

"Aye, of course. His tantaliser, with silver clasps an' all."

"How odd. Have you informed the police?"

"The polis?" Her upper lip curled. "And bring shame to the hoose, that Dr. Hood, an' him a proud criminalist, was robbed?"

The two men looked at each other.

"Perhaps," said Holmes, "We might hear the precise details of the, ah, crime?"

Mrs. Strachan, after being persuaded that neither of the visitors required refreshments, was happy to oblige. Plunging her hands into her apron pocket, she began her recitation, which is best recorded without the idiosyncrasies of her delivery:

Not long after noon that same day, she said, the coalman called round, to inform her that Dr. Hood had placed an additional order, and required the coal cellar restocked before the weather turned to its usual autumnal chill. There outside was the horse and dray, with its sacks heaped with black nuggets. Here in the house was a depleted cellar. But there was an annoying problem. It appeared that Dr. Hood had placed a padlock upon the street hatch down which the coal should flow – why he had done this, the housekeeper could not imagine, unless he feared some scamp might creep in. Nor had he left her the key.

Puzzled, she granted that the coalman could come through the old tradesman's entrance, which offered a shorter route to the coal cellar. Such a solution would, as she pointed out, additionally minimise the "black stour" that the coal sacks would shed on her carpets. He duly drew his dray to the rear of the house, and hauled his load that way, not without considerable complaint.

The last sack emptied, he was about to leave when he called out to her from the main passage. He was sure he had heard someone

186

muttering by the open front door, which gave access not only to the kitchen and servants' domain, but also to Dr. Hood's consulting rooms.

Mrs. Strachan duly emerged from her parlour, only to hear a voice by the door, which was round a bend in the corridor, cry out, "Run, 'Arry!' We's been rumbled!"

Naturally, she ran to the entrance, but could see no one there – though the town council's habit of planting trees and bushes along the streets to "improve the panorama" did not help. The coalman followed not long after, and despite a cursory search of the area, could offer no suggestion as to where possible intruders might have gone. Nor did either recognise the voice they had heard.

Given that Scarborough has no fewer and no more troublesome youngsters than any other borough, Mrs. Strachan returned to her domain, signing the coalman's docket and dismissing him.

As the dray rattled away, it struck her that she should ensure there had been no minor vandalism inside the house, or dirty fingermarks that would require attention. Had not someone scrawled "*Buffoon*" across the mayor's festival poster only last month? All seemed well until, glancing into the "Maister's" suite of rooms, she realised one terrible thing: A single item, resident in its place for some years, was missing!

"I have seen it myself, Holmes." Father Brown took advantage of the housekeeper's pause for breath. "A handsome enough object, much as the usual tantalus – three crystal decanters in a walnut frame, with silver trimmings on the bar which secures the decanters and requires the owner's key to allow access."

"Aye, so it is," she confirmed.

The older man nodded. "An expensive item?"

Priest and housekeeper could give no certainty on that account, and Holmes's brief interest seemed to fade.

"I had hoped," Father Brown murmured, "That Mr. Holmes might be allowed a glance at Dr. Hood's ingenious collection of criminological equipment, but under the circumstances . . . ."

Mrs. Strachan leaped at the suggestion, insisting that, as the same room was the location of the crime, it would be entirely appropriate. Accordingly, she led them across the passage and opened what seemed to be a service door, for a dark velvet curtain hung on its other side. This entrance opened onto an elongated suite which faced the sea, a generous space lit by late sunshine streaming through the aforementioned French windows.

187

Books aplenty lined the walls, whilst comfortable leather chairs were placed ideally for study and for consultations. A set of plain but well-made tables at one end displayed a plethora of almost alchemical wonders – alembics, flasks, and test-tubes. Reagents, tongs, and spatulas. Holmes ignored these, however, in favour of a finer table by the window, which held boxes of cigars – and between them, an absence.

"The tantalus stood here," he said, examining the surface of the table. "The felt base has protected the top from sunlight, and left the wood a slightly darker colour."

Mrs. Strachan agreed. As her accent varied between Scotland and Yorkshire, so her attitude seemed to shift between her alarm over the theft and her excitement at having *the* Sherlock Holmes at her side.

"No dust, of course, to leave any other tell-tale marks," he added, a remark which she clearly took to be a testament to her housekeeping, but which Father Brown thought evidenced a certain disappointment on Holmes's behalf.

"Cleaned every day, sir."

Having confirmed that the "public" door at the far end of the suite could easily be accessed from the front entrance, and that it had been unlocked when the coalman called, there seemed little more that could be done at that juncture.

"Enough that I ha' had the chance to tell you twa fine gentlemen," said the housekeeper. "And the maister canna say that I did nowt, nor hid the truth!"

"I'm sure he will not hold you in any way to blame," the priest assured her.

Holmes made a cursory examination of shelves and equipment. "Nothing else seems obviously disturbed. An opportunistic theft, seeing the coal dray, and that the household might be distracted – or had this Harry and his confederate been in wait for such a moment?" He shrugged. "The result is the same."

Mrs. Strachan was adamant that she would not speak to the authorities until she could discuss it with Dr. Hood, which was not for two more days. Holmes remarked only that the police would no doubt ask amongst dealers in such things, if the missing item were distinctive enough.

The little priest wandered over to the fireplace, the hearth almost spotless.

"Another fortnight or so," he said, "And I suppose that we shall all be enjoying our coal – wherever we may obtain it." He smiled at

188

Holmes. "The wind from the sea can be a little *too* bracing in Scarborough when October comes."

The two men took their leave, the priest promising to return the following day and offer any spiritual comfort that Mrs. Strachan might require.

A sea fret was building outside, that coastal fog which so often shrouded the ports of the Yorkshire coast, and the two men stood, considering the haze as it moved in towards the land.

"'Wherever we may obtain it,'" said Holmes. "Did you have some point to make with that remark, Brown?"

A bland, harmless expression met the detective's gaze. "These are thrifty folk, an admirable Yorkshire trait," he replied. "Sea coal may occasionally be gathered on the shore further up the coast, whilst the Tyneside barges often off-load small quantities at a more than favourable price – without the company being informed, you understand – as they head south. And then there is the matter of the funicular railway."

"I have seen it – that arrangement which conveys passengers from the top of the cliff to the lower parade. What of it?"

"It is steam powered, you see, the engines fed by coal. One of my parishioners was telling me that the storage shed there was tampered with a couple of nights ago. An inconvenience – not a major loss, mind you, and not the first time such has occurred, I gather."

His companion was about to respond when the small man knelt down in the street, peering at something. Holmes walked over.

"Do you see this?" asked Father Brown, pointing.

Holmes regarded the pavement, where a wooden hatch was set into the flagstones immediately before the house of Dr. Hood.

"The coal hatch, for deliveries."

"But padlocked."

"As we were informed by your Mrs. Strachan."

The priest got awkwardly to his feet. "But what precisely do you observe, Holmes?"

"A padlock. A standard, inexpensive model, not new, nor in terribly good condition."

Father Brown looked somewhat doleful. "Oh dear. No, that will not do."

Nor would he elaborate upon his remark, but bid Holmes farewell – the one to return to his modest parochial quarters, the other to his rooms at the Grand Hotel . . . .

Early the next morning, the town's habitual purveyors of deck-chairs and bathing apparatus made an unexpected discovery. Not a tantalus, or anything of immediate relevance to anyone else, but a peculiarity – a horse and cart had turned up on the foreshore, much to the displeasure of some early bathers. Munching on seaweed and the odd tuft of rough grass at the high-water line, the beast regarded onlookers with an amicable disinterest, and was reluctant to be moved. When the priest arrived, a constable was attempting to lead it – and its attached cart – onto the main thoroughfare.

Father Brown, who had been informed of this oddity by his usual network of loquacious parishioners – he tried to avoid the word "gossips" – patted the horse absently and examined the waggon. Was that . . . yes, the plain wooden base was soiled with exactly what he might have expected.

He wiped his hands on his cassock and ambled slowly up from the shore, the impressive bulk of the Grand Hotel before him. For, according to a panting bell-boy who had run from that esteemed establishment, a guest – one Mr. Holmes – wondered if the priest might spare him a moment.

The older man was on the great balcony which overlooked the sea, taking morning coffee.

"I saw you down there on the beach," said Holmes, rising. "And believe you might be like to examine a certain curiosity which I received late last night, hand-delivered." He took a folded piece of paper from his jacket and passed it to the priest, reaching over a tray of untouched scones.

Father Brown, who had not yet broken his fast, eyed the scones with interest, but forced himself to attend to Holmes's offering. Unfolded, it was no more than a single sheet of cream paper, on which had been drawn – in black ink – a number of black dots. He turned the paper this way and that in his fingers, but could make nothing of the pattern.

"Is this one of those odd codes that Dr. Watson used to record in your adventures?"

Holmes snorted.

"Not a code, Brown – a representation."

"Of . . . ?"

"A hunter who once had a dog by the name of Sirius, if I remember my Greek from school."

The priest regarded the piece of paper from several angles again, and his face cleared.

190

"The constellation Orion! Yes, here is the belt, of course, and the broad shoulders. Fanciful, really, but no more so than some of his kind. I never could fathom how they made out Cassiopeia, for example – "

A wave of Holmes's long hand interrupted him.

"It must surely refer to our acquaintance Dr. Orion Hood."

"A reasonable assumption," Father Brown agreed. "Though I seem to remember Dr. Watson remarking that astronomy was not your field?"

Holmes looked away. "If you really must know, I was out on the balcony at a late hour, considering the note which had just been handed to me. On glancing up, there stood the constellation in the night sky. Of course, I observed the similarities, and formed my conclusion."

"God's gentle way of reminding us how much we need His guidance," chuckled the priest. "But that the note should be sent specifically to you, Holmes . . . Is it widely known that you are in town?"

"As widely as *The Scarborough Mercury* is read." Holmes had a sour expression. "It appears that an employee of the Grand saw fit to inform them, when I arrived on Friday. I have already turned down several entreaties – pleas over a supposedly mysterious elopement, a begging letter from a man who wishes to become a 'consulting detective', and even a woman who has lost her 'dear little Samuel'."

"A child?"

"An over-fed Siamese cat."

The priest failed to repress a smile. "And do we know who delivered the astronomical reference?"

"A well-dressed man, possibly in his late twenties or early thirties, who called late last night. Top hat, and somewhat formal evening dress. The desk clerk could not bring to mind any other particularly distinctive features."

"Late from his revels, possibly."

"Possibly." Holmes's shoulders sagged. "I have retired, Brown. I am here to take the air, and then return, reporting that – however I truly feel – my lungs are much, even miraculously, improved. I am not here for minor mysteries."

The small, black-clad man abandoned self-control and took up a scone. Nearby was fresh butter, and *My!* – A brand of marmalade far more sophisticated than the parochial house would ever see.

191

"How *do* you feel, Holmes?" The scone received appropriate adornment, and headed closer to eager lips.

"Older. More prone to this wheeze in my chest, and rheumatic. Less patient with folly and frippery. A bracing North Sea wind will not cure the vagaries of age, whatever Watson and his peers profess. And I feel disinclined to follow missing ornaments, well-dressed strangers, or star-maps."

To which there was no response – could be no response, for the priest's mouth was otherwise occupied. A waiter, unsure, arrived with an additional cup, just in case, and the two men sipped coffee in silence, until Father Brown was sure that every crumb of scone had been despatched.

"It was, you know, a very ordinary padlock."

Holmes glanced up.

"Dr. Hood," continued the priest. "Of independent wealth, semi-retired, but still feted for his wisdom and his former cases, decides that for some reason his coal cellar must be made more secure. To which end, he utilises a rusty old padlock – one which would surely not be difficult to open with a mere bent wire – and takes the key with him on a lecture tour, rather than leave it with his housekeeper . . . ."

"A reasonable point. Your conclusion?"

"You are the . . . ah, detective, Holmes."

His friend tested the coffee pot, and found it wanting. "Very well. Let us suppose that the padlock was applied by another. To what purpose? To make it necessary that the coalman must use the rear entrance, distracting attention from the front door and offering easy – if brief – access to the consulting rooms. A basic knowledge of the interior would be required."

"Housekeeper, maid, and daily are beyond reproach," said the priest. "Not that they lack the usual human failings – I mean only that they are dutiful and well-satisfied in their employ."

"No matter. It would take little time to learn the customs and layout of the place. As to the specific nature of the theft – the tantalus was obviously the most valuable and portable object that could be snatched in such a short time. Little profit could be made from a random armful of books, cigars, or test tubes and flasks."

Father Brown rose to his feet, satisfied that he had engaged the detective's interest, even if briefly.

"Alas, I have Tuesday Mass to organise – and a Sacrament for the Sick, always popular with the older members of my flock. Though I suspect that the tea urn and the free biscuits afterwards

192

may be the most substantial reason for their attendance. Possibly we could meet at Dr. Hood's later today?"

A time was agreed, and the two men parted.

The Sherlock Holmes who stood in Dr. Hood's rooms that afternoon was a taller, more-intent figure than he had been the previous day. His gaze was sharp, his manner brisk.

"As it appears that someone wishes me to take notice," he said, as soon as Father Brown entered, accompanied by the housekeeper. "I have made a few enquiries – a telegram to Dr. Hood, in Birmingham. He concurs that any official action should await his return. An exchange by telephone with a fellow in York who is familiar with the antique dealers, and so forth. He will listen out for any news of such a tantalus. And . . . ." He paused for what the priest could only believe was "effect". "No, no local coal merchant made a delivery to this house yesterday, nor had they any order to do so from Hood."

"No," said Father Brown. "I rather imagined that would be the case."

Housekeeper and consulting detective stared at the little man, who looked quite apologetic. Mrs. Strachan's face took on a rosy flush.

"Ah beg yuir pardon, Father, but Ah was here. Did Ah not see the dray, and watch him carrying his mucky sacks in and oot o' this very house?"

"You did, in a sense. But there is the funicular, you see," he murmured. "And the horse on the beach. You saw a cart with coal on it, obviously a delivery dray, and someone in workman's gloves and apron. All well and good – but the horse and cart were borrowed, its load was purloined from the shed at the funicular railway, and your visitor was not a coalman."

"The cart you were examining on the beach this morning?" asked Holmes.

"Yes. There was coal dust on the boards."

The housekeeper confessed that she had not seen that particular individual before, but who pays attention to delivery men?

Had he been tall, or broad, or with distinguishing marks? No, if anything she supposed that he was a little smaller, less burly, than the usual sort. His face? Ordinary, without moustaches or beard. She did not (a slight sniff) pay much heed to him, being annoyed about the unexpected inconvenience of it all. She was certain that he carried nothing away with him – his final sack was empty, and he had no bag or other means of taking away such a large object as the tantalus.

"So an imposture," said Holmes. "To distract."

Father Brown nodded. "Oh, it was. The more ordinary, routine, the imposture, the less it is noticed. Why, how often have you yourself posed as a tradesman, Mr. Holmes, in the pursuit of your cases?"

The detective cleared his throat. "I give you that, Brown. But why not a button salesman at the back door, or a hasty, if invented, message to draw Mrs. Strachan away for a moment?"

"I am puzzled by that aspect." Father Brown stared at his scuffed shoes, barely visible to him beneath his rotund form. "And why the note sent to you, to ensure that you paid attention to the event? A trap to ensnare the great Mr. Sherlock Holmes – an old foe brooding on vengeance? A bitter rival . . . or some form of taunt?"

Holmes responded with a snort of derision. "Most of my 'foes', as you so romantically put it, are dead, imprisoned, or reformed. Besides, a missing piece of silverware is hardly a matter of life and death, or a troubling affair of state." He paused. "But it could, I suppose, be connected to one of Hood's previous cases. The criminologist is also a detective, in his way."

Such an addendum did not serve to calm Mrs. Strachan. Instead, it propelled her into a somewhat muddled line of thought which involved miscarriages of justice, men hanged for a crime which was not theirs, and so forth. Was Dr. Hood in danger? Or was Mr. Sherlock Holmes to investigate her faultless "guid maister". (The lady's Scots side was in full flow by this point)?

Seeing Holmes's growing irritation, Father Brown suggested that a cup of tea might be of value, and such was the housekeeper's ingrained hospitality that she took herself and her wilder fears off to the kitchen.

In her absence, Holmes drew the priest to one side, well away from the door to that mysterious world in which servants ensure the survival of such households.

"I did not wish to mention the fact in front of Mrs. Strachan, but I was given this ticket, Brown, not half-an-hour ago, on the promenade. A hunched fellow in nondescript clothes, with his cap low, pushed it into my hand, and promptly lost himself behind a party of brewery workers on what I assume was a late charabanc outing."

He handed over a faded theatre ticket, its provenance being the Empire Pavilion in Scarborough.

"The, um, ticket has not been clipped, yet it is dated for a performance from last September," said the priest.

"I had noticed." The detective's tone held a touch of reproof. "If you examine the back . . . ."

The pattern of the constellation Orion was clearly visible, made with a soft pencil or charcoal stick.

Father Brown rubbed the side of his nose. "Your attention is once again being drawn to this affair, it seems. What will you do?"

"Do?" He took the ticket back from the priest. "I shall enquire at the Empire Pavilion to see if this, or the date upon it, has any especial significance, and then, when Hood returns tomorrow morning, I shall put everything I know into his hands, and relieve myself of any concern over the matter. If Hood wishes to look into it, or communicate with the constabulary, it is up to him."

Holmes, having displayed something of his old self not half-an-hour earlier, appeared to be tiring once more. He announced that he had sea air to consume, and left the little priest to tend to his parishioner and disabuse her of her wilder notions.

After a cup-and-a-half of strong tea with Mrs. Strachan, Father Brown – a competent smoother of troubled waters – was eventually freed to ponder, and to re-examine the scene of the theft, a task which produced yet another line of thought.

"Tantalus – I wonder . . . ."

After which he made his way to the Grand Hotel once more.

The evening clerk was just taking up his duties at the hotel's front desk when the priest struggled into the lobby, catching his umbrella in one of the doors and almost losing his clerical hat for the fourth or fifth time that day.

"I understand," said Father Brown, re-furling the rebellious umbrella, "That a note was hand-delivered for Mr. Holmes last night, around eleven of the clock."

The young man smiled, smoothing back hair which had seen a little too much oil. "Why, yes, sir. The number of enquiries we have had since the great man arrived, and letters – calling cards!"

"But this particular note," pressed the priest. "Was there anything at all unusual about the man who delivered it? For example, was he tall, stout, or possessing any other obvious qualities which might identify him?"

The clerk, seemingly unsure as to how he should deal with an unexpected Catholic priest asking peculiar questions, vacillated between "Sir", "Father", and "Monseigneur" as he tried to answer. No, on reflection the man with the note had not been tall, although a large top hat had made it seem so at first, nor had he been well-built, despite a dress coat which amplified his frame . . . .

As he listened to himself, the young man's face began to screw itself into perplexity.

"Everything was a bit too large, too ostentatious," he said at last. "Too – "

"Theatrical?" suggested the priest.

Which produced a beam of agreement on the clerk's sallow face.

"Yes, Father!"

When Holmes entered the lobby of the Grand, he was greeted by the unusual sight of a priest oiling his bicycle chain in full view of the other visitors. Behind the desk, the assistant manager and the evening clerk looked on in discomfort, but the Head Porter was in eager conversation with the priest – gear ratios seemed to be the topic – and any passing guests seemed more amused than discomfited.

"I did not relate, Holmes" said Father Brown, "the details of the small incident which introduced me to Dr. Hood."

Holmes conceded the truth of this statement, and the priest spoke on.

"A matter of an impending marriage, you see, where Mrs. McNab had grave doubts as to the desirability of her daughter's suitor, a Mr. James Todhunter. Strange muffled conversations in his room (he boarded with them), an occupation concealed, and so forth. I consulted Dr. Hood, and we –"

"This is pertinent, Brown?" said Holmes, stiff-faced.

"I would say so." Father Brown returned the oil can to the man from the hotel and thanked him. "We found young Todhunter tied up in his own room, but tied up by his own hand, as it turned out, and surrounded by playing cards and other paraphernalia. He was, you see, secretly practising to be – "

"An escapologist, one might assume . . . or, a stage magician," said Holmes. "At the Empire Pavilion."

"Precisely!" The priest beamed. "Then your visit to them was informative?"

"That ticket was issued for a performance by '*Zaladin, the World's Greatest Conjurer, Contortionist, Ventriloquist and Human Kangaroo*'. The last performance, the theatre manager informed me, as the conjurer did not live up to his epithets, drawing only modest audiences at best. I assume that Todhunter was Zaladin?"

"He was. The marriage went ahead, after Hood and I had explained the innocent reason for the young man's peculiarities, and he did indeed take to the stage."

"You are implying that Todhunter had something to do with the theft of the tantalus. That he was one of the men who entered Hood's domicile whilst the housekeeper was distracted by the supposed coalman."

"Something along those lines," said the priest, wiping his oily fingers with a grubby handkerchief. "We are – You must surely admit? – being pointed in that direction."

Holmes conceded that such could be the case.

"But why anyone should be trying to leave such trifling clues eludes me – unless there has been a falling out amongst thieves. Still, Hood can confidently instruct the police to seek out James Todhunter, and resolve the matter. The tantalus may have been sold by now, but it should be traceable."

"Oh, that would be a hasty act." Father Brown looked alarmed. "Todhunter is surely not a thief, dear me, no. What is that phrase? Yes – '*Method in his madness.*' Hamlet, was it, or perhaps the old retainer . . . I seem to be thinking of polony sausage. Ah, Polonius! It was he who said it."

"I marvel," said Holmes, "that you fill your mind with such clutter, Brown. I myself preferred to retain only that which might be of service in the pursuit of justice."

"Clutter? That clutter is *Life*, Holmes." His smile was gentle. "There is no tapestry, without God's myriad threads from which it is woven."

"Hmmph."

Dr. Orion Hood returned with the first spatter of rain the next morning, having sent a telegram alerting his housekeeper to the time of his arrival. Tall and grey-haired, he was the very picture of an eminent and respected criminologist. Were he to rise in court to give his considered opinion on a case, he would have the members of the jury nodding with suddenly acquired wisdom. "Hood, of course, was the final nail," the lawyers would mutter afterwards.

His performance upon returning to his Scarborough apartments, was not so much authoritative as mildly curious. The stolen object, he confessed, was of some value, yes, but not so much that its loss would inconvenience him greatly. He held no personal affection for it. More interesting was the presence of both Father Brown and Mr. Sherlock Holmes in his home.

197

"We have not met before, Mr. Holmes, but I used to follow your cases with great interest." He shook the consulting detective's hand warmly.

"And I had a number of occasions to peruse your various scientific monographs, Doctor" said Holmes, adding in a tarter voice: "Had the gentlemen of Scotland Yard done likewise, I am sure that more of their cases would have been resolved."

"Kind of you, Holmes. And you, Father – a pleasure to see you again, naturally. It does seem that you have the knack of involving yourself in the oddest little affairs."

The priest confessed that such seemed to be his lot in life.

The master of the house was introduced, over a cup of coffee, to such facts as had been gathered. He was shown the rusting padlock, the note bearing his constellationary namesake, and the theatre ticket. Finally, he was introduced to the absence of the tantalus.

"Most strange," he murmured. "'Behold the coalman cometh.'"

Holmes raised an eyebrow. Father Brown looked amused.

"Matthew, the parable of the wise and foolish virgins," explained the priest. "Though admittedly it was oil in their lamps, not coal."

Hood stared out of the French windows, observing the restless sea. "So we have a theft, engineered by James Todhunter and unknown confederates, one of whom is called Harry. Might Todhunter have been coerced, or threatened? It may be that he was not outside, waiting for his chance, but played the part of the coalman himself. A stage magician is also an actor, after all. If so, then why would anyone seek to draw Mr. Holmes's attention to the matter?"

The little priest's round face was wrinkled with concern. "A guilty conscience, or a hope that they might be extricated from events beyond their control?"

"Would Todhunter be familiar with your household arrangements?" asked Holmes.

"Familiar enough, I suppose. And Mrs. Strachan is acquainted with his mother-in-law, Mrs. MacNab, through the intricacies of these Celtic lineages. He has certainly been to these rooms, earlier this year."

"A social call?" asked the priest.

"I seem to remember that I offered him a glass of sherry, to which he demurred, and he made enquiries as to the range of my work and studies. I found him intelligent and affable, though he is

198

largely self-taught, not a college man. Admirable in its way, of course."

"An easy situation in which to get caught up with dubious enterprises," said Holmes. "Are the Todhunters in pecuniary need?"

Father Brown blinked, turning his clerical hat in his hands.

"Dear me, Holmes, most of my parish is in 'pecuniary need', as is St. Mary's itself. That does not mean that we all resort to criminal activities." His gaze settled, with a certain weight, on the older man. "Some of the greatest scoundrels I have known were college men, and peers of the realm."

Hood smiled. Holmes narrowed his eyes.

"You still do not consider Todhunter to be the villain here?"

"I don't consider him to be the villain *anywhere*. I do suggest that, rather than bother the constabulary, you and I seek out young James immediately, in order to discover the full story."

"I will come with you," said the criminologist. "if my second visit is as illuminating as the first, it will at least provide amusement in my dotage."

And despite the others' protestations over the term "dotage", Dr. Hood drew on his outdoor coat once more and proclaimed himself ready.

The ruins of Scarborough Castle stood proud on the headland, much as the broken indicator of a monstrous sundial might, casting its shadow over a relatively calm sea. To its north, the town seemed to lose its civic cohesion, the orderly streets of villas, terraces and shops being replaced by a sprawl of workman's cottages, fishermen's huts, and the occasional relic of a manor or estate. Past St. Mary's-without-the-Castle, the buildings became lower and more solitary, though a number had brightly painted doors and thriving kitchen-gardens.

Dr. Hood pointed out the cottage where he and Father Brown had last called, the home of the widow MacNab.

"The Todhunters live two doors down," said the priest, "a situation due more to Mrs. Todhunter's admirable loyalty to her mother than to the young couple's hopes and dreams. James is, I think, of a mind to make more of himself, and thus, in turn, his family."

"Two doors down" was a comfortable-looking, two-storey fisherman's cottage, with washing on the line and – at the back – a fine crop of cabbages, penned in by a wooden fence.

Mrs. James Todhunter, *née* Maggie McNab, seemed entirely unsurprised to find Father Brown. Mr. Sherlock Holmes. and Dr. Orion Hood at her door.

"I knew it!" she said as she ushered them in. "I just knew it!"

Father Brown, holding his broad-brimmed hat in one hand, patted her shoulder.

"What did you know, Maggie?"

"That James has done something stupid. Mother warned me – said his comings and goings at odd hours again boded ill, and that she had always had her doubts, as well I knew." To her credit, though her eyes glistened, no tears were evident. "Is he . . . is he injured, Father?"

The priest's round face took on an expression of surprise. "Not that I am aware. But we were rather hoping to find him at home."

"He was," she said, "but when I entered the back parlour a few minutes ago, where he keeps his books and paraphernalia, I found the room empty, and blood upon the sill of the open window! I was fearful, wondering if I should tell Mother and set about searching for my husband."

To everyone's surprise, the priest smiled.

"Good, good. I believe that all will be well, then."

And he trundled down the passage to the back parlour, gesturing that his two companions should follow him.

The small room in question contained a chair, a large black stage portmanteau, and a few shelves stacked with various tricks and a few battered books. Dr. Hood peered at the volumes.

"I see that Mr. Todhunter has a copy of my *Essentials of Criminology*."

"I suspect that he is a great admirer of yours," said Father Brown. "And of Mr. Holmes."

Holmes was by the window, looking out onto the back garden and the grass-tufted dunes beyond. "No one in sight. This does look like blood on the sill. Smeared as if a wounded man had left the room this way, or been dragged outside. The glass is intact, nor are there any sharp protrusions to cause such a flow. Although . . . Hood, does this not look a little *too* much like blood?"

The two men edged round each other, both examining the window-frame. First one, then the other, touched the ruddy stain and brought finger to lips.

"Glycerine," said Holmes.

"With Carmine Red dye in it, and perhaps a little sugar syrup," agreed Dr. Hood. "Theatrical blood."

Father Brown's smile grew wider, wrinkles forming around kindly eyes. He turned to the portmanteau and spoke with unexpected authority.

"Misdirection, as I expected. The game is up, James. Both your principals are on stage, though, so you may not yet have lost."

To the obvious surprise of the two criminological stalwarts – and of Maggie Todhunter in the doorway – the large black case split open, revealing a pleasant-faced, clean-shaven young man in his shirtsleeves, crouched in such a manner as only one of his age might achieve for long.

"I concede, Father," said James Todhunter, unfolding and showing himself to be a slim fellow of no great height. "Dash it, I should have realised that you would get involved. No wonder I've been caught so soon, given that mind of yours."

Consulting detective and criminologist exchanged what might have been an aggrieved look.

"Oh, hardly, James," the priest said quickly. "Professionals such as Mr. Holmes and Dr. Hood examine both evidence and circumstance with a cool, intellectual rigour, as is proper. I merely have a fertile imagination. But whilst I could now, with that imagination's assistance, reconstruct your path over the last few days, I remain unsure as to its purpose."

The young man sat down on his portmanteau, and his expression became one of gloom. "The truth is, Father, I wasn't terribly successful as Zaladin the Magician. I had some of the gifts required by a stage magician, but none in any measure which would have provided for us properly." He glanced at his wife, who seemed genuinely dumbfounded at the turn of events. "I was, in short, dismissed at the end of last season. Then, reading of your own exploits in the past, Father, and having met Dr. Hood by your good graces, I saw what I should do. I was intelligent, observant, and had drive – I should start a detecting agency!

"I approached Dr. Hood, but he held out little hope of me entering the field of criminology, given my limited formal education. Those police officers of whom I enquired treated me even less kindly, offering only scorn. I was losing courage, and then I heard that *the* Mr. Sherlock Holmes was in town. Well – such an opportunity! I naturally wrote to him immediately, begging that he advise me, perhaps recommend a way in which I might follow in his footsteps."

"Ah," murmured Holmes. "One of the letters I received at the Grand."

201

"To which you did not reply, sir." Todhunter shook his head dolefully.

Holmes made a noise which might almost have been one of embarrassment. Dr. Hood seemed deep in thought. Only Father Brown was in good cheer.

"So you undertook the one act which might draw their attention," he said. "You planned a crime, followed by clues to tease and make them take note."

"I did no real harm, Father," Todhunter pointed out. "I even left coin by the coal shed at the funicular, but some rogue, presumably the night-watchman, seems to have kept that part quiet."

Hood frowned. "Might I assume, then, that your confederates, this Harry and his friend have the tantalus safe?"

The priest giggled in a manner which would have turned up the nose of his bishop.

"There were no confederates, Dr. Hood. 'Zaladin, the World's Greatest Conjurer, Contortionist, Ventriloquist'. You threw your voice, did you not, James?"

Todhunter looked pleased. "Yes, Father, I did. It's relatively easy to make a voice sound as if it comes from a distance, and my audience – Mrs. Strachan – was primed to expect sounds from that direction."

"But the tantalus – " repeated Hood.

Holmes coughed again, this time apparently to draw attention, and all looked to him.

"Let us consider, gentlemen." He tapped his fingers on the windowsill. "Mr. Todhunter must have used the servants' door to the consulting rooms, whilst the housekeeper went in search of intruders. He dashed in order to remove the tantalus from its usual position, but had little time, and the item was too bulky to conceal about his person. Therefore, Hood, it must still be somewhere in your rooms."

The young man nodded. "It is, Mr. Holmes. Quite safe in hearth and home, for actual theft was never on my mind."

"I assume," said the priest, "that you were the man with the note for Holmes that night, the one with Orion upon it – dressed in your Zaladin outfit? And that you passed him the theatre ticket on the promenade the next day."

Todhunter agreed that he had been.

"I was trying to introduce mystery, you see, enough to draw Mr. Holmes's interest, even encourage him to investigate. I had intended to play the game out a day or so longer, and then leave another trail,

202

but . . . Well, here we are. May I come and show you where your tantalus is concealed, Dr. Hood, as the last act of my foolish play? After that, I will accept your judgement, harsh as it may be."

A half-hour saw the four men standing in Dr. Hood's consulting rooms.

"Holmes," said Father Brown. "I don't think that we really need James's guidance here. Shall you do the honours?"

"I believe so." For the first time that week, Holmes showed a twitch of humour. "Safe in 'hearth and home', you said earlier. And one 'thief', one miscreant only. There are many ways of concealing missing items in a room, but few allow for haste. Books that are moved may be noticed, cupboards searched. A coalman enters, and has only a few seconds to act . . . ."

Holmes strode to the fireplace, examining the grate. "A little soot-fall, a scrape in the patina of ash on the floor of the hearth . . . yes." He looked pleased with himself. "I would venture that the tantalus is lodged upon the smoke-shelf of this very chimney, barely out of sight. Might you save an old man from bending and reaching, Mr. Todhunter?"

The young man was swift to comply, kneeling by the grate, thrusting his hands up into the chimney and . . . .

The object within, partially wrapped in a hessian cloth, was revealed. Todhunter placed it almost reverentially back on its table, brushing it with his sleeve to ensure it was spotless once more.

"Yours, I believe, Dr. Hood," he said, with the tone and flourish of a magician.

The faces of the other men retained their composure, but surely more than one eye was touched by an inner gleam of amusement.

"I thank you. This has been, I must say, an over-elaborate scheme," said the eminent criminologist.

"More a fanciful stage entertainment than a reflection of true crime," added Holmes, his tone now one of mild disappointment.

Father Brown chuckled, his small round frame shaking.

"Gentlemen, this over-elaborate, fanciful young fellow has had two of this country's foremost experts on crime, pillars of society, who are not unused to audiences with princes, paying serious attention to him. Does it not strike you that he is worthy of wiser guidance, even a small degree of patronage? Dear me, were I a detective, I would want him on my side, so to speak."

Todhunter waited, hardly drawing a breath.

"And if you wish more evidence of a sharp mind," added the priest, "might I re-introduce the venerable Greeks?"

203

"What?" Hood looked puzzled.

"Orion . . . and Tantalus. Orion being a hunter. You yourself once, Doctor, in your former professional role – and Mr. Holmes, naturally. Tantalus being a man who could see what he wanted, but never reach it. Mr. James Todhunter, of course. His exploit with the tantalus, rather than with a valuable book or other object, was quite deliberate. Symbolic, one might say."

The little priest was not entirely sure on that last point, but if it served a good purpose, he hoped that he might be forgiven for a little embellishment.

In the kitchen beyond, a kettle began its soft whistle. Outside a gull shrieked, oblivious to the ways of crime.

"It is true," said Hood at last, "that I do have a modicum of free time in my retirement." He glanced at Holmes. "There might be occasion for me to expound on some of my more interesting cases, to a small, attentive audience – and to take questions pertinent to those cases. And if such an audience wished to be guided through the more useful texts in my field, well . . . ."

Whether from generosity of spirit or from a lingering sense of professional standing, Holmes admitted that he still had a number of contacts in the field of investigative endeavour. Some of those gentlemen might – possibly – be persuaded to make themselves known to a bright young fellow who sought to swim in those same waters. And yes, there were certain routine case-notes, retained at his Sussex farm, which a trustworthy student might borrow for instructive purposes . . . .

"Under the circumstances," said the criminologist, "I suppose that I should offer you gentlemen a drink from my now famous tantalus – but truth is, the key has been lost for years! I shall have Mrs. Strachan find some sherry. Holmes, I have long wanted to ask you – what was the true resolution of the Musgrave case, rather than the version which you allowed Dr. Watson to publish?"

"Ah, well," murmured Holmes, "If what I tell you goes no further . . . ."

Father Brown began to edge discreetly towards the door, for it seemed to him that James Todhunter had acquired, by fair means or foul, the very patrons he desired. Collecting up his umbrella, he tipped his hat to Mrs. Strachan and headed out into the Scarborough evening, already designing, in his head, a method by which he might keep the pulpit of St. Mary's dry long enough to finish at least the sermon, if not the readings.

Behind him, clustered around a forgotten tantalus in the consulting rooms of Dr. Orion Hood, three detectives stood deep in conversation.

Little more need be said, except to add that in the fullness of time, it afforded Father Brown no small amount of pleasure to observe in the pages of *The Scarborough Mercury*, just below an offer of Plinny's Patent Colic Mixture (*"Only 4d a bottle!"*), an equally modest box which read:

> *Todhunter and MacNab,*
> *Enquiry Agency*
> *Discretion Guaranteed*
> *As Recommended by the*
> *Famous Consulting Detective,*
> *Mr. Sherlock Holmes*

The little priest cut out the advertisement and placed it carefully in a kitchen drawer. He would keep this memento, but decided that – under the circumstances – he would *not* forward a copy to the Great Detective himself . . . .

Deadly Dog Days
by Robert Stapleton

Speaking for myself, John H. Watson MD: I am a physician of the body. This has for many years been my occupation, my concern, and indeed my source of income. However, I have always been aware that a person's state of mind can have a profound effect upon his or her body and its well-being. I have recently become aware of a new and developing interest in the study of the mind, and even of the subconscious, and the influence that these can have upon the physical state of an individual. I tend to view with great caution much of that nonsense currently emanating from Vienna. On the other hand, the story I am about to relate has given me a great deal to think about, and challenges me to consider the place of the subconscious, and the emotional feelings of patients in my own on-going medical care of them.

It so happened that, one day during the second week of August, I was attending an evening social gathering at a town house in the city of Peterborough.

The gathering was being held at the home of an acquaintance of mine, from my time in the Army. In civilian life, this man had become a highly successful businessman, although this success had stood neither the test of time nor that of rival market forces. After leaving Afghanistan, we had kept in touch over the years. However, the reason for this evening's gathering hadn't been made clear to me, nor was I happy about being there. The stifling hot weather seemed singularly inopportune for such an occasion. I would much rather have been walking beside the River Nene, which flowed through the city, on its way toward the North Sea.

My recent contacts with Sherlock Holmes had been few and far between but, although he was by constitution in no mood for such a gathering, he had agreed to attend this evening, out of consideration for myself – a decision he now deeply regretted.

The guests, perhaps thirty of them in all, had gathered in a room decorated in a pale shade of green. These people were standing around, eating sandwiches and other such appetizers, drinking glasses of some unidentifiable white wine, and attempting to remain cool. Even with all the downstairs windows open, the guests generally appeared to be suffering in that unaccustomed summer heat. The men were dressed in smart gray suits, whilst the ladies were all festooned in the latest summer fashions, in the lightest possible fabrics.

A bevvy of young waitresses bustled among the guests, distributing food and drinks.

Our host, a sturdy and resolute man by the name of Major Nahum Edmundswell, had been doing the rounds of his guests and sharing mindless small-talk with everyone he met. Apart from a means of renewing acquaintances, this pointless gossip seemed to me a complete waste of time, so I could imagine what Holmes was making of it. On the other hand, I am well aware that such discussions are part of the oil which lubricates the machinery of human social interaction.

Our host eventually made his way through the crowd to join us, accompanied by a young woman.

"Dr. Watson and Mr. Holmes," said our host. "It is very good to see you both here this evening. I'm glad you managed to take time off from your busy lives to be with us."

I nodded graciously, whilst Holmes maintained a gloomy silence.

"I should like you to meet my younger daughter, Violet," said the Major, turning to the young woman beside him. "She looks after the house, as well as caring for me. Violet is also my personal secretary – an extremely talented young woman."

Miss Edmundswell seemed embarrassed by such an accolade.

"It is indeed good to meet you," I told her.

She smiled and nodded.

"Are you staying locally?" the Major asked us.

"We have rooms at an inn near the city center," I replied.

"Splendid," said the Major. "In which case I hope you'll feel able to remain after the other guests have all departed."

"Really?"

I could sense Holmes on the cusp of rebellion.

"I should be very much obliged if you would come up to my bedroom before you leave," said Major Edmundswell. "Violet will bring you. Please don't let me down. I have something extremely important that I wish to discuss with you regarding a matter of life and death."

The mention of death aroused my companion's attention, and his ears pricked up at our host's insistence that he wished to converse with us further.

I could see immediately that our host wasn't a well man. His smart clothing seemed to hang off him in no flattering manner. His face appeared haggard. The tone of his skin was an unhealthy pallor. I had seen dead men looking more wholesome than did the Major that evening. I tried to be tactful as I expressed to him my concerns about his health, but he merely smiled – rather sadly, I thought – so I wasn't at all surprised when, shortly after our discussion, he excused himself from our gathering and retired to his bed, escorted once more by his daughter.

A knowing look from Holmes confirmed that he shared my unhappiness about the man's health.

My legs felt cramped, so I left Holmes for a moment and wandered through the room until I reached the doorway connecting it with the rest of the house. The sound of raised voices reached me from along the corridor. Being of an inquisitive nature, I followed the sound and found myself at the door of the kitchen. The severe-looking cook was berating one of the staff, a young woman, who had apparently absented herself from her duties for a few minutes. The young kitchen maid appeared suitably chastened and humbled.

By way of explanation, she simply replied, "I had to run an errand."

"An errand?" demanded the cook. "Whoever for?"

"I'm not allowed to say," replied the young woman, with a touch of defiance in her voice.

For a moment, and from the look on her face, I imagined the cook was about to slap the young woman across the face for her insolence, but at that moment a pan of water began to boil on the kitchen range, and her attention was diverted.

The young woman at the center of the row turned to her duties and noticed me standing in the doorway. She gave me a secretive grin, put her finger to her lips, and tapped something in the pocket of her uniform. I caught a fleeting glimpse of what appeared to be the corner of a banknote – a five-pound note, most likely. Whatever the young woman had been doing that evening, it had made her instantly wealthy compared with her fellow kitchen staff members.

I returned to the main room and rejoined Holmes.

Violet Edmundswell followed me in, collected another woman by the arm, and led her in our direction.

"Dr. Watson. Mr. Holmes," she said, "allow me to introduce you to another member of my family. I am the youngest of three children, you understand. With our mother having passed away some six years ago, my brother Jonathan is now the head of the

208

household." She pointed to a sandy-haired man standing beside the drinks cabinet at the other end of the room. "The other members of the family tend to leave me to look after the daily affairs of the house, but they are close by when needed. This is my sister, Bella. She is married to a very sweet man, Horace Wattling. They have one child, a little girl of eleven years."

I smiled. "It is very good to meet you, Mrs. Wattling."

"I'm sorry my husband couldn't be with us tonight," she told me. "Our little girl is unwell, so he has stayed behind to look after her."

After the two women had moved on to speak to some of the other guests, I wandered across the room to converse with the brother, Jonathan.

"Thank you for coming this evening, Dr. Watson," he said. "And I see you have a friend with you."

"Mr. Sherlock Holmes."

"The famous private detective?"

"That's right. But he is retired nowadays, and lives in Sussex. Tending bees."

Jonathan chuckled. "Bees?"

"Oh yes," I explained. "But your father made a point of asking him to be present this evening."

"Is that so?"

"Certainly. His appearance here is by special invitation."

After a little more conversation, I collected another glass of wine and made my way back to where Holmes was standing.

I noticed that, throughout the gathering, Holmes couldn't remove his eyes from one of the other guests: A man standing at the far side of the room. I knew that look of old. He had used it on countless occasions during the years of our acquaintance. I knew he was making a detailed scrutiny of someone.

I looked in the same direction, but all I could see was a small, round man, dressed in the black cassock of a Roman Catholic priest. He was standing alone, holding his somewhat disheveled black umbrella in one hand, and a broad-brimmed hat in the other. Then the priest was looking toward us, and I chuckled to myself as I realized that we had met this man before: Father Brown.

Leaving them to their scrutiny of one another, I watched as Miss Edmundswell returned to the room and continued to circulate among her father's guests.

Later, as the guests dispersed and made their various ways home, Miss Edmundswell reminded me of her father's request that I should stay behind, along with Holmes.

"Before that," she said, "I should like you to meet another acquaintance of ours. Not that we are Catholics, you understand, but this is Father Brown." She ushered us toward the small priest. "He lives and ministers locally."

"We have met before," said Holmes.

"A number of times," added the priest.

"Father Brown," continued Holmes addressing the little priest, "I see that you have recently been traveling in France." To the astonishment of those around him, he added, "You have the stub of a French Railway Ticket protruding from your hat-band."

"That is true," said the little priest. "But we are both experts in the observation of people. For instance, I can see that Mr. Holmes is writing a book on beekeeping." In response to our questioning glances, he added, "He has two recent bee-stings on his left hand, and a number of ink stains on the skin of his right hand."

"I cannot deny it," said Holmes. We all laughed.

"Now I should like all of you to see my father," said Miss Edmundswell. "He told me earlier that he is very keen to talk to all three of you. In confidence. There is something he wishes to discuss with you."

"Certainly," Holmes replied. "Kindly lead the way."

We all three followed the young woman upstairs and into the bedroom of her elderly father.

The room was arranged oddly, I thought. Violet gasped. "Somebody has been in here. Only in the last hour or so. The bed had been turned to face the door!"

The bed had indeed been pushed into one corner of the room and had been turned to face the door. The man in the bed lay silent and still. An expression of anxiety showed on his face.

His daughter hurried over to the bedside.

"He's dead," she gasped, in a quivering voice. "I know he is."

Holmes turned to me. "Watson."

I stepped forward and examined the man. It was a formality, but it confirmed what I had initially suspected. I shook my head, trying to be gentle as possible with the harsh news. "Heart failure is my best assessment," I said, "although that would require further corroboration."

"What's going on here, Mr. Holmes?" demanded Violet Edmundswell.

210

"And why tonight?" came the small voice of Father Brown.

Sherlock Holmes turned to Miss Edmundswell. "I think you should call for your family physician to come, as soon as possible. He will have to confirm the cause of death, and write out a death certificate."

Now in tears, the young woman nodded, turned, and left the three of us alone in the bedroom.

"Quick, Watson!" said Holmes as he began to search the bedroom, examining every inch of the place in as much detail as he felt he had time for. "Look around!" Almost immediately, he knelt down on the carpet at the far side of the bed, took out his notebook, and recorded a number of observations.

The door opened again and Miss Edmundswell came back in. Her eyes were now even more red and swollen than they had been before, and her face was buried in a huge handkerchief.

"Doctor Hamble tells me he will be here in a few minutes," she said, her voice cracking.

"Then perhaps we should be on our way," said the priest. "My companions here will have arranged their overnight accommodation, as have I."

"But first, some questions," said Holmes.

"I think perhaps we should leave that for the morning," insisted Father Brown. "After all, this young woman has had a terrible shock tonight."

"In that case, Miss Edmundswell," said Holmes, "would it be in order for us to return tomorrow morning to talk with you further?"

"I don't see why you should need to," she returned. "This isn't a police investigation, is it?"

"Not at all," said Holmes. "But your father did say he wanted to tell us something in particular, and we should very much like to find out what he wished to say."

"Very well, then," said the young woman, looking doubtful. "But I shall have to be busy for much of tomorrow, so you had better come early."

With that, we felt ourselves dismissed, so we made our way downstairs and outside into the refreshingly cool night air.

"Well, Watson," said Holmes, lighting up his pipe, "what did you see in that room?"

I tried to remember all that I had observed there. "I saw a man lying on his deathbed, which was set at a peculiar angle. I saw a glass of water standing on his bedside cabinet. I noticed a row of document folders standing in a row on a shelf. Oh, and I saw his

211

wardrobe standing beside the window on the far side of the room. And a dressing table standing against the wall opposite the bed. I noticed a calendar hung on the wall above it. I think that's about all."

"Excellent," returned Holmes. "You managed to see only half of the things that were on view, without observing anything at all."

I felt hurt by his rebuff.

"Really," I told him, "that is a rather harsh judgement to make."

"Not at all, my dear fellow," he replied. "For you, it is just about average."

"And as far as I am concerned," chipped in the priest, "I saw the scene of a murder."

It was after midnight by the time Holmes and I reached our overnight accommodation. The night porter let us in, handed us our keys, and wished us both a good night.

But I was in no mood to sleep. My mind was in turmoil. What had I missed in that bedroom? What further questions did Holmes have in mind to ask Miss Edmundswell? And perhaps above all else, what had made that harmless little priest, Father Brown, conclude that the Major's death had been murder? I had no answers to any of these and, even over breakfast I could make no further sense of the matter.

Holmes was no help.

"Wait and see," was all that my companion could suggest as I returned with him to the Edmundswell home. I followed him as he approached from the rear. A gate opened from a narrow cobbled lane serving the back of the property. Fortunately, it was unlocked, so we made our way quietly into the back garden. A stone-paved footpath then led us from the gateway toward the house.

At one point, Holmes stooped down to examine the earth on either side of this pathway.

"You may remember," said he, "that last night I took particular notice of the floor on the far side of the bed."

"I do," I told him, "but at the time, I could scarcely make out why."

"My interest was aroused by a footprint I discovered there, indented into the carpet. It was clearly made by a man with a larger-than-average size of boot, and I noticed traces of garden soil beside the print. I also noticed that it carried a distinctive design on the heel. *This* design," he announced as he pointed to the ground. "It seems this man has been using this pathway quite a number of times in recent days."

"The gardener?"

Holmes shook his head. "Not with boots like these."

I looked down and saw what he meant: An imprint made by a particularly solid heel, of a larger than normal size, and with a distinctive design.

Holmes proceeded to follow the pathway, stopping occasionally as he came across another indentation. This path led us to the rear wall of the property, directly below a window.

"That," declared Holmes, "is the window of the bedroom we visited last night – Major Edmundswell's room. You will notice that the window is unlocked, and stands slightly open."

"They must be airing the room."

"There is more to it than that."

I thought for a moment. "Are you suggesting that somebody entered that room through the open window?"

"That is precisely what I'm suggesting. It's highly likely that it was this Big Foot himself. He has been using the wooden ladder that I can see hidden away among the garden foliage."

Now I also noticed the ladder. "But why? For what purpose?"

"In order to gain access to Major Edmundswell, without anyone else knowing."

"Again I have to ask, for what purpose?"

"Why, murder of course."

We made our way round the outside of the building and reached the front doorstep just as Dr. Hamble was returning to the house. We were all shown into the drawing room together. There we found Father Brown, already sitting beside Miss Edmundswell and talking quietly with her. They rose as we entered. We greeted each other, and then sat down in a gathering around the young woman.

"I have come to bring you the completed Death Certificate," the physician announced. "I agree with Dr. Watson's initial conclusion that the cause of death was heart failure."

"Indeed," said Holmes. "He looked very ill when I saw him earlier in the evening. But you had been treating for heart trouble, is that not so?"

"Certainly," said Dr. Hamble. "A fairly strong dose of digitalis, in tablet form, taken with water twice per day."

Holmes turned to the young woman. "And you made sure that he took those tablets."

"Of course. Twice a day. Ten o'clock in the morning and then ten o'clock in the evening. I would take him a glass of water and place the tablet into his hand."

213

"Then you left him alone, relying on him to take his medication."

"Of course. Why would he not do that?"

"It would be the natural thing to assume," mused Holmes. "And afterwards, you took away the water left behind in the glass and disposed of it."

"Naturally."

"But are you sure that he had taken his medication?"

"What are you saying, Mr. Holmes? Are you suggesting that he deliberately stopped taking those tablets, and intentionally speeded up his own demise?"

"I'm not sure what to make of it," replied Holmes, rubbing his chin. "But last night, when we entered your father's bedroom, I noticed a glass of water standing beside his bed. And I saw the remains of a white tablet in the bottom of the glass. I took the liberty of removing the glass and its contents in order to have them forensically examined."

He turned to Miss Edmundswell. "I hope you will forgive the subterfuge."

"I suppose you know what you're doing, Mr. Holmes, so of course. If it will help."

"The results should confirm the presence of digitalis," said Dr. Hamble.

"I should be greatly surprised if it were otherwise," replied Sherlock Holmes.

Dr Hamble looked deeply concerned. "I have given the cause of death as heart failure. Are you suggesting, Mr. Holmes, that it was something different?"

"It isn't my place to suggest any such thing," replied Holmes. "If both you and my friend Watson agree that it was heart failure, then I'm happy to concur. But I wonder if that is the full story."

Father Brown interrupted the discussion. "Miss Violet has been telling me about her family."

"Yes," said Holmes. "She introduced us to her brother and sister yesterday. She also told us about the little girl who is unwell."

"Indeed, she is extremely sick," said Bella. "Some kind of wasting disease."

"So it seems," agreed Dr. Hamble. "I have done all I can for the child, but with little lasting success. My consultations suggest, however, that some time spent at a special sanatorium might be her only hope. I have one such place in mind, but a course of treatment there would be extremely expensive."

214

Holmes slapped his knees and stood up. "I should like to visit the bedroom once more," he announced.

"Certainly," said the young lady, and led the way upstairs.

Once more in the bedroom, I looked around with eyes more alert to the things I had failed to notice on the previous evening.

"The bed is now empty," said Holmes, "but I remember there being a red scarf on top of the sheets, held firmly in the Major's hands."

"Oh, yes," said Miss Edmundswell. "I tidied the place up after you had gone, and put the scarf back into the wardrobe."

"May I please see it?"

"Of course."

Holmes opened the wardrobe door, reached inside, and took out a scarf of distinctive and exotic design. How I had failed to notice it on the previous evening, I could scarcely imagine.

"May I borrow it?" Holmes asked.

"Certainly, if you think it might be of any help."

"Thank you. I hope that it will."

It was Father Brown's turn to look around the room.

"Tell me, Miss Edmundswell," said the priest. "was your father a particularly superstitious man?"

"I have to admit that he was, Father," she replied. "Perhaps obsessively so. He used to spend a fortune on purchasing horoscopes."

"I noticed a horseshoe hanging above the entrance to this house."

She nodded. "That was his doing. And he could never abide having black cats around the place. He also had a lucky sixpence attached to his watch chain."

"For that matter," I declared with a chuckle, "so do I."

"More seriously," said Holmes, "he seems to have had a distinct dislike for the number *thirteen*."

"Yes, that is true."

"See, Watson, that row of document files on the bookshelf. They are numbered in sequence, and the number thirteen is missing."

"I see it now," I replied. "But there doesn't seem to be a gap in its place."

"That is because there never was a number thirteen there. And the calendar above the dressing table. Can you see that the number thirteen has been erased? Violently crossed out."

"Yes. How could I have missed it?"

"And a row of dates on the calendar, each having been circled in red. They include most of July, and the first eleven days of August. Ending with yesterday's date: The eleventh."

"Great Scott!" I exclaimed. "Those are the Dog Days, when traditionally the Dog Star, Sirius, rises with the sun."

"They are usually reckoned to be particularly unlucky," added Father Brown. "Generally recognized as running from the third of July to the eleventh of August. The hottest and most unhealthy days of the summer."

"And therefore unpropitious."

"Particularly so for a highly superstitious man such as Major Edmundswell."

"Some regard those as the most likely days for a death to occur."

I took the chance to cross the room and examine the carpet where Holmes had discovered the footprint of Big Foot. But so many people had come and gone during the night that I failed to make it out.

"Where did your father have his study, Miss Edmundswell?" asked Holmes.

"Oh, the study? That's on this same upper level, down the corridor, Mr. Holmes. Would you like to see it?"

"Certainly, if possible."

Once there, Miss Edmundswell pulled open the window coverings to allow some light into the room, and Holmes continued to examine the room with great care.

"What have we here?" he exclaimed. "The furniture appears to have been moved around. And only recently, judging by the indentations in the carpet."

"The furniture?" asked Miss Edmundswell. "Oh, yes. Only last year my father had a man come in and help him to rearrange the furniture. He told me it would enhance the good fortune of the household, and of his business."

"Was this man Chinese?"

"I believe he was. Somebody from London whom my father had come to know through his business dealings."

"But this isn't how the Chinese man left it."

"No. It looks as if somebody has been moving it around again."

Holmes tried to move the furniture back to where it had been until recently.

"This furniture is heavy," observed Holmes. "It must have taken a particularly strong or determined man to move the items apart."

"We certainly had to bring some workers in to arrange them in the first place," said Miss Edmundswell, "so if another person were to rearrange them on his own, then he would certainly have had to be particularly strong."

"The arrangement of furniture in a room is a major principle of the Eastern system of *Feng Shui*," said Holmes. "I came across it years ago when I was traveling in the East. *Feng Shui* is based on ancient Taoist principles. The idea is to arrange buildings and objects in such a way as to enhance balance and harmony, allowing the power of the universe to flow freely, so as to bring good fortune to those involved. The main idea is to establish the Commanding Position in the room, and there to place either the desk or the bed, or whatever is the main item of furniture."

"Pure superstition," I said, dismissively.

"Perhaps," said Father Brown. "Whatever efficacy there may or may not be in those principles, the fact is that many people in the East, and also some in the West, believe it to have considerable value. And a highly superstitious man, such as Major Edmundswell, might be prepared to put great faith in those ideas. Faith alone, however it is used, can have intense power in a person's life."

"The arrangement as we see it now is bad *Feng Shui*," said Holmes. "As was the positioning of certain items in the bedroom itself."

"You are suggesting that the furniture was originally rearranged in a more propitious way," I concluded.

"That is quite clear," continued Father Brown. "And as a result of this arrangement, the old man was content with life. But when somebody moved the objects in the room into a different order, then his own personal harmony was destroyed."

"Adding to his sense of doom," concluded Holmes.

Father Brown nodded.

We thanked Miss Edmundswell for her assistance and made our way back downstairs and outside. The summer breeze felt refreshing after the stuffiness of those rooms.

"It all sounds rather dark to me," I told my companions. "The conclusion has to be that somebody had been plotting this poor man's death."

"And yet we cannot prove anything," said Father Brown.

"Perhaps not," said Holmes as he reached into his pocket and took out a slip of paper. "But I took the liberty of removing this from the pocket of his tweed jacket. The one I found hanging up in the wardrobe."

"Holmes!" I rebuked him. "I hope you haven't lowered yourself now to becoming a common pick-pocket."

"Hardly," he replied. "The man who owned that jacket, and therefore this paper, was in no position to object."

"Is the paper relevant to our case?"

"Possibly not. But then again, it is accompanied by a receipt for cleaning the jacket, dated only two months ago. And anyway, it is the only lead we have at the moment."

"What does it say?" asked Father Brown.

Holmes opened the slip. "It appears to be one-quarter of a newspaper advertisement."

"Why would he tear it up?" I asked.

"Or more to the point," added Father Brown, "why would he retain a portion of it?"

"It has frustratingly little to tell us," said Holmes, "except that it bears the second part of an address. *Blank, blank, den Row.*"

He handed it to the priest, who squinted down at the paper, before handing it back.

"As you say, it's an advertisement from a newspaper, judging from the quality of the paper used. The local journal perhaps. And most likely published in the Classified Advertisements."

"I think," said Holmes, "that Watson and I are going to have to investigate the newspaper, and try to discover the meaning of this advertisement and its relevance, if any, to the case in hand."

"Very well," said Father Brown. "I have other things to do this morning, so I shall leave you to find out if this is a red-herring or not. I shall no doubt catch up with you later."

Sherlock Holmes always had a nose for searching out the most notable places in any town which was new to him. As a result, we were soon at the entrance to the offices of the local newspaper.

We asked at the reception desk for the archives, and the man directed us to a small office on the upper floor. Every inch of wall-space in that office was covered in book shelving, groaning under the weight of daily newspapers, bound together according to month. These journals went back several decades – indeed to the very beginning of the newspaper's publication.

218

Holmes found the most recent publications, laid the morning editions out upon a central table, and handed the evening printings to me.

On the table between us lay the paper cutting that Holmes had taken from the pocket of our erstwhile host. We attempted to find its match.

"There is nothing quite like looking through the personal columns of the local newspaper," said Holmes, "for learning the nature and preoccupations of the local community."

"I know what you mean," I replied.

"But we have to concentrate on the advertisements."

"They too can be interesting," I agreed. "Here we have publicized some of the most amazing contraptions for making daily life just that little bit easier for the flustered housewife and the busy housemaid – advertisements for soap and ointments of various kinds, suggested treatments for eczema and hair-loss, promotions of dress fabrics, and recipes galore."

"Ah, I think I have it," exclaimed Holmes before long.

I left my perusal and joined him. Sure enough, the corner of the preserved fragment matched exactly the corner of an advertisement in the bottom right hand corner of a newspaper dated some three months previously.

"Make a note of this, Watson: The address on the advertisement turns out to be Ogden Row, here in Peterborough. And it appears to recommend the services of a clairvoyant – a lady who calls herself 'Sister Adeline' who promises to consult the stars, her crystal ball, and the cards, on behalf of any honest inquirer."

"And one who is no doubt willing to pay her a consultation fee," I added.

"Much like any physician of body or mind," added Holmes.

"*Touché*," I returned. "Although I hope I'm not half the charlatan that many of these people often turn out to be."

We returned the newspapers to their place and asked the person at the front desk for directions to the address we had discovered: Ogden Row. The man was very helpful. He even drew us a simple map to help us find it.

We hurried out into the fresh morning air.

I followed Holmes through the streets of the city and was surprised when we quickly reached a narrow street with a sign declaring it to be the place we sought.

"Ah, there you are," said the now familiar voice of Father Brown. "I was confident that you would find your way to this part of the city eventually."

The little priest generally preferred to remain silent, except when spoken to. But when he did have something to say, it was always worth paying attention.

"But how did you know to come here?" asked Holmes.

Father Brown gave his enigmatic smile. "A priest who hears the confessions of others learns a great many facts about the most amazing places and people. Even in my own little patch of the world, the name of Sister Adeline of Ogden Row is known."

Together, we wandered down the street until we found ourselves outside the house identified in the clipping.

"Hello," I said. "This appears to be the place."

Holmes knocked on the door, and we all waited.

After a couple of minutes, the door opened, and a small soberly dressed woman stood in the entrance. She gave the impression of being the housekeeper, or one of the servants.

"Yes?" she said. "How may I help you?"

"We are looking for Sister Adeline," said Holmes.

"Oh, so you want a consultation, do you?"

"Not quite," replied Father Brown. "Just a few words with you, if you wouldn't mind."

The woman raised her eyebrows in surprise at being so readily identified.

"We are investigating a death," added Holmes.

"Oh dear. In that case, you had better all come along inside."

Sister Adeline led us into a room immediately off the main hallway. The curtains were drawn across the one window in the room, and the smell of incense hung in the still air. She was behind a desk and invited us to sit down facing her.

"Now, gentlemen," she began. "How may I help you?"

"Allow us to introduce ourselves. My name is Sherlock Holmes, and I am a retired consulting detective. This is my friend, Dr. John Watson, and the third of our trio is Father Brown."

"And, as you have already discerned, I am Sister Adeline. This visit involves a death, you say."

"Indeed," said Father Brown. "And it is very good of you to agree to see us at such short notice."

"Having a priest on my doorstep isn't an everyday occurrence," she replied, "though not entirely unknown."

Holmes stepped in. "Have you ever met a man called Edmundswell?"

The lady's face gave a brief sign that the name did indeed mean something to her. "The name does ring a bell, Mr. Holmes. I believe he is a local businessman."

"We understand that he might have come to visit you here in recent months."

The woman frowned. "Could you please refresh my memory about which occasion you're talking about?"

"He visited you in late June or early July."

The occultist looked through her diary.

"Ah. Yes. Major Edmundswell visited me one evening toward the end of June this year. He came in the company of another man."

"Did this other man give you his name?"

"If he did, then I have no record of it."

Holmes put his hand into his pocket, and drew out the scarf which had been found with Edmundswell at his death.

"Sister Adeline," he said gravely. "Do you recognize this scarf?"

The small woman picked it up and examined it carefully. Then she turned her gaze upon Holmes.

"Is this part of a police investigation?" she asked. "Because if so, then I might refuse to answer any more of your questions."

"The police have nothing to do with this," said Father Brown.

"Not yet, anyway," added Holmes.

"And not likely to have," added the priest.

The occultist drew in a deep breath.

"Before our meeting that night, the man who accompanied the Major on his visit here took me to one side and gave me some money – a couple of twenty pound notes, to be exact, on top of my normal consultation fee. The man handed me this scarf and instructed me say that the Dog Days would die along with the owner of the scarf."

"And you said that to the old man?" I asked.

"Indeed. Why ever should I not? I passed on those words, although I had no idea of their significance. And I had no idea to whom the scarf actually belonged. People visit me for consultation, Dr. Watson. I don't consider myself responsible for whatever anybody believes as a result. It was his own choice to believe and make sense of what I told him."

"A court of law might have other ideas about that," I replied.

She leaned forward to confront me. "But this isn't going to a court of law, is it?"

221

I said nothing.

"So," said Father Brown, "this scarf carried with it a kind of curse. Is that true?"

"Not a curse. Perhaps more a case of a bad memory."

"And this other man, the one who came with Major Edmundswell that evening. The one whose name you cannot recall. Can you tell us anything at all about him?"

"Not really," said Sister Adeline. "He was tall and thickset, but he appeared to be a decent sort of fellow. Oh, and I noticed that he had unusually large feet."

Later in the street outside, we consulted about what we had discovered during our visit to the occultist.

"What a person chooses to believe can have great power," said Father Brown. "Whether the thing they believe be true or not."

"Indeed," I replied. "I once had a patient, an elderly woman, who was troubled by deep anxiety problems. She also had a painful rash on the skin of her arms. I tried to persuade her that the rash was nothing to be alarmed about, but she demanded that I should do something about it. I tried ointments and creams, but they did nothing to alleviate the problem. In the end, I gave her a bottle of pills, telling her to take one three times a day, after meals. I told her that the tablets contained an extremely powerful drug, and I adjured her in no uncertain terms never to exceed that dose. A few days later, the old lady wrote to tell me that her anxiety was much better, and that her rash had entirely cleared up, and could she please have some more of those miracle-tablets. What I neglected to tell my elderly patient was that those pills contained nothing more powerful than sugar and glycerine."

Father Brown nodded. "And they did the trick. Good. So belief in a placebo, or in a cursed scarf, can both have a powerful effect on an individual, one way or another."

Holmes interrupted our discussion. "I think," he said, "that it is time for us to split up and go our different ways, at least for the rest of the morning. Perhaps we could meet for lunch at the little eating house on the corner of the main street. But first, I would like you, Watson, to go with Father Brown back to the Edmundswell house. I need to know what is contained in the deceased man's will. See what you can find out for me."

"And what will you be doing?" I asked him.

"I intend to delve a little more into the life and occupation of Horace Wattling, the husband of Miss Edmundswell's older sister."

222

Father Brown kept his counsel, so he and I spoke little on the walk back to the former home of Major Nahum Edmundswell. I rang the front door bell. The maid appeared, looking a little surprised to see us again so soon.

"We should like to speak to Jonathan Edmundswell," said the priest, now taking the initiative, "if that is at all possible."

"We had been hoping he would be in this morning," I explained.

"I think he probably is in," replied the maid. "Please come inside, and I'll try to find him."

Father Brown, retaining his hat and umbrella, waited with me in the front reception room until the tall fair-haired man we had met on the previous evening appeared.

"I am rather busy, I'm afraid," he said. He was clearly annoyed at having us return to the house so soon. And presumably intent on asking even more questions.

"We hope not to detain you long," said Father Brown, "but the fact is, we are still trying to make some sense of the death of your father."

"As are we all," replied Jonathan. "Are you making any progress?"

"Nothing substantial," admitted the priest.

"We're here on behalf of Mr. Holmes," I said by way of explanation. "Without asking you to reveal any details, he would like to know in general terms what is contained in your father's will."

"That is of course strictly confidential until the reading," said Father Brown, "but some general idea would be very helpful to us at the moment."

Jonathan considered the matter. "All I can tell you, gentlemen, is that the estate, all my father's possessions and wealth, will be divided equally between the three children. That is, between my sister Bella, my sister Violet, and myself. My father had strong ideas about fairness and equality within the family. He wasn't a wealthy man. In fact, he was in debt to a number of people, including the bank. However, he carried life insurance, and those high premium rates were one of the reasons for his debt. With him now dead, the insurance payment will be sufficient to settle his debts, and to leave a comfortable legacy to each of the children."

"It seems he was worth more dead than alive," concluded Father Brown.

"That is quite beside the point," said Jonathan. "Dr Hamble has determined that the cause of death was heart failure. He has made no suggestion that anybody else was involved."

"And so the burial can go ahead?"

"Indeed. The service will be held at the local Parish Church next Wednesday morning. A clerical friend of my father has agreed to conduct the service."

We again thanked him for being so helpful and made our way back into town.

The restaurant suggested by Holmes turned out to be crowded with lunchtime clientele, so we were pleased to discover that our companion had reserved a table for us. I looked around. Despite the crowd, it seemed pleasant enough, with sunlight streaming in through latticed windows, but the pastel color scheme wasn't to my taste.

Father Brown and I sat down, ordered our meals, and shared with Holmes what we had learned about the will of the deceased man.

"That is hardly surprising," he replied as our orders arrived, "but it is an important point to keep in mind."

"And what did you find out about Mr. Wattling?" I ventured to ask.

"He lives with his wife and daughter in a pleasant house not far from the home of his deceased father-in-law. He is a well-known man in the town. He owns a firm that trades in tea and coffee, importing and packaging, but his business hasn't proved as successful as it might be, or perhaps as he would wish it to be."

"So he and his wife aren't rich folk," concluded Father Brown. "I imagine they make enough to get by, but perhaps not much more."

"And on top of that," I added, "they have a sick child to care for."

We all sat quietly considering that point.

"We need to talk with Mr. Wattling," concluded Holmes.

"But perhaps we could wait until after the funeral on Wednesday," suggested Father Brown. "The family will have their minds on other things until then. It would be insensitive to distract their attention before then."

"Very well," concluded Holmes. "We can at least wait until Wednesday. But then we must have a word with him, and get this matter sorted out, once and for all."

The funeral took place on an overcast but dry midweek morning. A crowd of people had gathered, so that there was no room for everyone to join the family inside the church building itself. As a result, it seemed that even more people had thronged the surrounding churchyard than had met inside.

I stood in silence with Holmes and Father Brown, watching the mourners and waiting for the service inside to come to an end.

Eventually, the conducting clergyman led the mourners out toward the graveside, where the last resting place of Major Nahum Edmundswell lay, ready to receive his body.

As far as we could tell, everything in the service was conducted with professionalism and respect.

As the mourners stood together in the churchyard, it took only a moment for me to notice a large man, tall and thick-set. He was dressed in black, and was standing close to Violet's sister, Bella. I realized that this had to be Horace Wattling. Big Foot.

I pointed him out to Holmes, who merely nodded. He already had the man in his sights.

A few minutes later, with the service concluded, and the mourners beginning to disperse, I joined my two companions as they made their way toward this man.

"Mr. Wattling?" asked Father Brown.

The man turned in our direction. "Yes?"

"We would like to have a word with you, sir."

"Oh?" A look for deep concern crossed the man's face. "I am rather preoccupied at the moment, with the family in mourning. Perhaps if you would care to make an appointment, I might be able to see you sometime next week."

"No," said Holmes. "The sooner we have our meeting, the better it will be for all of us. This evening, by choice."

Horace Wattling looked to his wife, who took a deep breath and nodded.

"Very well," said Wattling. "Eight o'clock this evening. And I hope this is going to be an important matter."

"I am sure it will be."

"Do you know where I live?"

"Yes," said Holmes, "we know the place."

That evening, we arrived at the home of Horace and Bella Wattling and their daughter at exactly the time suggested. Eight o'clock precisely.

Horace himself answered my knock at the door. "So, you're the three men who have been asking all those questions, are you?" asked

Wattling. "You couldn't leave the family alone to grieve in peace, could you? You had to interfere, and stir up the feelings of emotional and hysterical women – my wife and her sister, in particular."

"I assure you," said Holmes, "we have no intention of causing them any further distress. But I think it would be helpful if you allowed us to come inside."

Wattling scowled, but turned and led us through the entrance hall and into the main living room of the house. There we found his wife, Bella, caring for the little girl, who appeared to be gravely ill.

The man invited us all to sit down in the easy chairs arranged around the room.

Wattling himself sat down opposite us, in such a position that we could see his feet. His boots were of an exceptionally large size, and the tread of the heel did appear to be of an unusual design. It seemed that we had found our man.

"What is your daughter's name?" asked Father Brown in his normally gentle manner.

"Her name is Hope," replied the mother, as she gently stroked the child's head.

"Very appropriate."

The woman nodded, sadly. "We would like to think so."

"With the money that you will inherit from your father," added the priest, "you should be able to afford suitable treatment for her."

"That is true, Father. Although I wish it hadn't been at the cost of my father's life. We can only hope and pray that the treatment will be effective in helping to cure our daughter's sickness."

"Mrs. Wattling," said Holmes. "We are very sorry about the death of your father, and we're trying to make sense of it."

"Sense? What do you mean? I thought it was simply a matter of heart failure."

"That is indeed what it appears to be," replied Holmes. "In which case, we're now at the conclusion of our investigations."

"We would like to finish our inquiry into his demise by telling you a story," said Father Brown.

The two parents looked at each other with expressions of concern, but said nothing. Then Horace nodded his reluctant consent.

"We will not be asking you any questions," said Father Brown, "so you don't need to say anything at all. Merely listen."

Again, Horace and his wife nodded that they understood, and appeared to relax slightly at such reassurance.

"There once was a man," said Holmes, "who had a sick daughter, but he and his wife couldn't afford to give her the treatment that she so desperately needed. Now, the man's wife had a father who was very wealthy, but the man in our story was too proud to ask him for any money to help cure his granddaughter."

"It just so happened that the rich man was also very ill," continued Father Brown, "being kept alive by strong medication every single day. Our man knew that on the rich man's death, some of his wealth would come to his wife but, not knowing how long the rich father-in-law had to live, our man decided to bring forward the moment of his demise, without incurring the wrath of the law. Now it just so happened that the sick man was highly superstitious, suggestive, and highly-strung, so our man decided to play on this flaw of his character."

"The man in our story," continued Holmes, "decided to take the sick man to visit a medium, a spiritualist. He paid this woman to declare a hex on a scarf which he handed to her. In fact, the scarf belonged to the rich sick man."

Holmes removed the ornamented scarf from his pocket, and held it out for Wattling to see.

"The scarf was exactly like this one."

Horace Wattling glared at it as though he were looking at some poisonous snake.

Holmes continued. "Our man paid the psychic to tell his sick companion that the Dog Days of Summer would die, along with the owner of the scarf. It was a simple message, but it was tantamount to laying a curse upon the sick man, and this played upon the victim's mind, making him even more anxious and neurotic."

"The man in our story decided to play on this," said Father Brown, "and, as the Dog Days continued, so our man increased his psychological pressure on the sick father-in-law, persuading his victim that he would indeed die on or before the last of the waning Dog Days: August the eleventh. It is a psychological truth that when someone is persuaded of something strongly enough, however irrational it might be, that person will alter his or her behaviour to promote the thing they believe is going to happen to them – even if it is their own death."

"Our man was perceptive, and he recognized this truth," said Holmes. "He played upon it, and persuaded the sick man to give up taking his daily tablets, and instead to hand them over to our man in the story.

227

"Toward the end of this time, the sick man eventually began to question this irrational conviction, and finally invited some friends to help him think the matter through, but by then they were too late to help him. Whilst his wife was busy at a social gathering, our man made sure that the sick man died in his bed later that same evening."

Wattling sat up at this point.

"Wait a minute," he said. "If the man you are talking about was caring for his sick daughter, how could he possibly be at the sick man's bedside at the same time?"

I remembered my visit to the kitchen on the night of the death.

"That is easily explained," I told him. "Our man had prearranged for one of the kitchen staff to take over the care of the child for a few minutes. And he paid her handsomely to do it. It would only take a few minutes for our man to then enter the garden and climb up to the bedroom window."

"Something he had done many times in the past few weeks," added Holmes.

"Of course," continued Father Brown, "this is nothing more than a story – a construct – and some of it may be entirely wrong."

"Or, on the other hand," added Holmes, with a dark look, "it could be entirely true. But indeed, we have no way of proving or disproving any of it."

Horace Wattling appeared to relax slightly at this news.

"No proof?"

"Not enough to present before a court of law."

"We know our man was physically strong," said Father Brown. "It seems that he was able to move that heavy furniture around in both the old man's study, and his bedroom, presumably without any help from anyone else. This played even more upon the sick man's superstitious mind."

"Bad *Feng Shui*," Holmes explained.

Under the withering gaze of his wife, Horace was looking even more grim as he looked around the room.

"And what became of the man in this story of yours?" asked Horace.

Holmes fixed him with his devastating stare. "That part of the story has yet to be written."

In the tense silence that followed, the child in the woman's arms groaned, and shifted her position in an attempt to find a comfortable place to lie.

Father Brown stood up.

"That is all we came to tell you, Mr. Wattling," he said. "Just a story. And now it is time for us to leave."

Holmes stood up and made his way out into the hallway, and toward the front door. Father Brown followed, with me in his wake.

Horace Wattling joined us outside, with anger showing in his face. He was evidently looking for someone to strike, and he turned his fury onto Holmes. "That was a cruel thing to do, Mr. Holmes!" he said. "Humiliating me in front of my wife and daughter. How dare you!"

"What you did was more cruel," returned Holmes. "For a man who believes in *Feng Shui*, as did your late father-in-law, being forced to lie facing the doorway was cold-hearted. It foretold his death. You knew exactly what you were doing, Mr. Wattling. And if you are thinking of raising your fists against me, I should point out to you that I have floored bigger men than you in the past."

When Wattling unclenched his fists and stood in a veritable fog of confusion, Father Brown took him by the elbow, firmly but gently leading him away from the house and into the depths of the garden, where they began to talk quietly together.

Holmes and I left them to it.

A couple of weeks later, I received a telephone call from Sherlock Holmes, inviting me to visit him as soon as convenient. He had received further information about the Edmundswell case.

As I sat down, he lounged back in his armchair with his long legs stretched out, puffing on his pipe, and gazing into infinity.

"I have received a communication from Father Brown," said Holmes. "He informs me that the little girl, Hope Wattling, was indeed sent to the sanatorium suggested by the family's doctor, and is now back home again, considerably better in health than she had been."

"That is very good news," I replied.

"But there is sad news as well. Her father, Horace Wattling, having made sure that his family was well provided for, has now taken his own life: An overdose of digitalis."

"The tablets he had taken from Edmundswell."

"Indeed. Enough that he was able to ingest more-than-sufficient to end his own life."

"That has to be an admission of guilt," I concluded.

"I would agree."

I considered the matter further.

"So instead of leaving the tablets each day to dissolve in the glass of water by the sick man's bedside, he stole them and kept them with a view to using them later. That sounds extremely cold and calculating."

"But I imagine he was filled with remorse in the end, and could think of no better way out of the situation. He was unable to live with himself and his guilt. If he admitted his crimes to the police, he would have been hanged and his family would have been disgraced. This way seemed to him the better way out."

"So what was the tablet you saw at the bottom of that glass of water by his bedside? What was it that killed Nahum Edmundswell that night?"

Holmes gave an enigmatic smile. "The rest of the digitalis, of course. An analysis of the glass of water showed that it contained sufficient to kill a dozen men. Half a glass would have been fatal. But any evidence that this might have been a murder has gone with Wattling to his own grave. The new science of fingerprint identification might have pointed to him, but they revealed only those of the dead man himself. We put all of this to the Insurance Company, but, after consulting with Scotland Yard, they have decided not to take the matter any further. If we were to exhume the body of Edmundswell, and a forensic *post mortem* examination, whatever the result, would cause even more hurt to the family. After all, the man who might have murdered him is himself now dead. I suggest, Watson, that we leave the matter alone now."

I left Holmes to care for his bees and I returned to my own care of the sick, in my traditional and well-tried methods, as a medical practitioner. The human mind is a notoriously difficult area to study, so I think I shall leave that subject to those who understand the matter best of all. And, one day, perhaps, I might read up further upon the subject. I might even pay a visit to Vienna. Who knows?

The Inside Man
by Mike Adamson

I have made no secret of the degree to which I have missed my friend, Mr. Sherlock Holmes, since his retirement in 1903. Some might say that to step back from one's life's labours at the age of just forty-nine years is premature. I struggled with the thought that the Prince of Detectives no longer watched over the city of London, but I knew Holmes had his reasons, and that they had nothing to do with notions of belonging to a bygone era. After a quarter-century of unremitting effort, he deserved his rest and diversion, and I had been glad to see him settle into his villa at Hodcombe Farm, near Beachy Head on the Sussex coast, to write the definitive work on the art and science of criminal detection.

For myself, I was long comfortable with the usual rounds of a London doctor, and the balm and comfort of my marriage. Nevertheless, I would often look back nostalgically at my crammed notebooks and piles of manuscript, the tangible record of those years when it was Holmes and Watson against the world. My stories of villains and dangers, of the unforgiving streets of the metropolis and our expeditions elsewhere, were still good for dinner invitations. My intimate experience of the cases dramatised in *The Strand* sometimes held fellow diners rapt until late hours.

But Holmes and I kept up a lively correspondence, and had made the journey in one direction or the other countless times. There had been occasions when cases raised their head that no degree of retirement could keep Holmes from investigating. Thus, when a letter arrived in the May of 1910, inviting me at once to the coast, I sensed something of the breath of adventure we had shared long ago and was only too happy to oblige.

The salt tang of the sea filled my nose when I departed on the express from Victoria Station to the Channel city of Eastbourne. Clouds chased before the sun on a brisk west wind. *Quite the glorious day,* I thought as I hailed a cab and loaded my case aboard. The automobile had become a familiar sight on British roads, and I enjoyed the drive. The French Renault made its way westward into the green countryside above the Channel coast, and at last deposited me at my destination, the village of East Dean, where Holmes had specified we meet. I paid off the cabby and the vehicle departed with a honk from its horn and a swirl of exhaust vapours, and when I turned about, there he was.

At fifty-six, Holmes was a study in rude good health. His hair had thinned and greyed, and he had picked up the pleats that attend maturity, but the sparkle in his eyes was unchanged and his spare frame and straight back were much as I recalled. A hand was thrust toward me, which I took with pleasure. "Holmes, it's so good to see you."

"Likewise. It has indeed been too long since we last sallied forth."

"It's a case, then?"

"You know me too well. Though I have adamantly maintained the sanctity of my retirement, there are times a matter presents itself that will not permit of its overlooking." He took my case from me and escorted me along toward the sixteenth-century frontage of the Tiger Inn. "You're just in time. I received a letter two days ago, promising another visitor with matters intriguing, even troubling to me at a professional level, and I knew you would never forgive me should you not be part of the deliberations. You brought the 1898 notes?"

"As requested." I patted the case in his hand. "Whatever is it about?"

"I'll allow our guest to expand upon that." He stepped up to the portico of the inn and ushered me into the comfortable and homely interior. "Watson, say hello to Father Paul Brown."

Father Brown was one of the more unusual fellows we had encountered in our adventures – if for no other reason than that there was absolutely nothing remarkable about his appearance. He was of middling stature, with mouse-brown hair and a round and largely forgettable countenance, though his eyes held depths I had always found at once intriguing. Holmes and I had last crossed paths with Father Brown in the case of a Mother Superior accused of embezzlement. He always had the air about him of one who has seen enough, and thought enough, to have a profound grasp upon the world – or at least upon human nature. He wore the cassock of the Catholic faith, with dog collar and rosary, and a *capello romano* hung upon the inn's coat rack.

Holmes had ordered morning tea, and we took sandwiches and scones in the quiet, airy dining room. Clearly, I saw he had been up in his attic to ferret out the file in question, a manila folder that lay on the table, marked up in my own hand: *Cranleigh Conviction,*

232

September, 1898. I wrinkled my brow and tried to recall, but after a dozen years the name meant nothing without a jog of the memory. With a plate before each of us and steaming tea in hand, Holmes introduced the matter.

"I recently received a letter from Father Brown with a most concerning proposal – that you and I, Watson, though obviously more me than you, failed in some rather significant measure back in '98. Now, it is self-evident that not every case can be tied off with the proverbial bow of ribbon and set upon the display shelf as a perfect, complete example of the deductive art. From time to time cases are unsatisfactorily concluded, or the solution is in some way imperfect. It is such an eventuality Father Brown has drawn to my attention. Father, do tell Dr. Watson what you told me."

With a frank expression, as of one who frequently considers mysteries more mundane than esoteric, he began. "Last week, I was called to give last rights to a gentleman by the name of Hubert Mundy. He was an ex-railwayman – a stationmaster in Chelmsford before his retirement in 1902. He made a deathbed confession." He raised a hand at once to forestall any consternation. "I'm in no way contravening the sanctity of confession, my friends. Mrs. Mundy was present, as was the family doctor, and Mr. Mundy's remarks were addressed to us all. Indeed, he was able to stress that it was his wish that some use be made of the information he was at last able to divulge." He took a sip of tea and went on quietly. "I've heard very few such confessions in my career, but they typically reveal something dire of which the one nearing his judgement is desperate to unburden himself.

"In this case, Mr. Mundy told us that he had lied egregiously – specifically, to the law – to provide an alibi to a man who had threatened his family. He did as he was asked, thus falsely directing the case, took his remuneration, and said not a syllable until the last minutes of his life. The party in question was one Jerrod Cranleigh, Esquire. Mr. Mundy told me he had helped steer Sherlock Holmes wrong – and upon that note I determined to write at once. If a wrong remains to be righted, or some justice can yet be served, then the mystery lies unsolved."

I set down my cup, took out my notebook, and, with an expression between amusement and intrigue, began to write.

"I, of course, located the Cranleigh file and reviewed the case," Holmes went on, "and there were elements which today strike me as unsatisfactory. I recall being unhappy with them at the time, but letting them go for want of any further connection, especially as the case secured a conviction anyway."

"This Jerrod Cranleigh was alibied," I asked, "so who was convicted?"

"His brother," Holmes returned with a quirk of the brows as he opened the file, and cleared his throat. "Let me take us back to the latter days of the nineteenth century. Before the motorcar was more than a curiosity, before Marconi sent his first wireless signal. When Verne, Wells, and Machen were the most *avant garde* writers, and it seemed Her Majesty would last forever. In the September of the year, we journeyed to Harpenden, near St. Albans in Hertfordshire, to investigate a case of apparent highway robbery – unusual in the modern age, to be sure, but no less real. The chief protagonists were the Cranleigh brothers, Horace and Jerrod. They were of an embittered family, having been of good income and social standing in years gone by, but fallen on financial hard times that saw them turned out of their genteel home and consigned to labour.

"Horace took a position as coachman to the Harrington family, whose estate lies a couple of miles east of Harpenden. He was employed for several months before an unhappy adventure befell all concerned. Sir Basil Harrington, his wife, and son set out upon a journey to London as they had many times, first by coach to the town, thence by rail to the metropolis. On this occasion they were conveying the family jewels, a collection worth at least thirty-thousand pounds, to their jeweller for cleaning and resetting. None but the family knew of this valuable cargo, or that the appointment with the jeweller had even been made. Nevertheless, the coach was attacked by ruffians as it passed through Lower Gustard Wood, less than a mile from home. The jewel case was taken, and all were assaulted to one degree or another. Sir Basil was armed, and discharged several rounds from a pistol, to no effect, before he was struck by a flung stone and knocked unconscious. Cranleigh also was assaulted, but recovered sufficiently to get them into town and seek both medical and police attention."

"Clear enough so far," I said cautiously. "The servant driving the master into a trap is as old a trick as highway robbery itself."

"That was my conclusion," Holmes returned with a thoughtful look. "The coachman was close enough to the family to learn of the appointment, with time to alert others to the rich rewards on offer. That he was the inside man was obvious. What was never clear was how the gang was organised. But it seems matters were more complicated. The jewels, for instance, never turned up in the London underworld: They seemed to vanish utterly. They must have been sold and then reworked with consummate care. Sir Basil never recovered any part of the treasure, and was consoled with only an insurance settlement – smaller than he would have preferred, as the underwriters found fault with his precautions."

"What precautions?" I asked wryly. "He seemed to be begging to be robbed."

"He relied on secrecy alone – often enough an effective tactic. Had Cranleigh not been connected with a criminal fraternity, there would have been no issue." Holmes shrugged his thin shoulders. "Yet the fact remains, there must have been an outside agent involved: The one who recruited the thugs to begin with, and supervised the disposal of the goods, however long that took. This person was never identified. Horace Cranleigh could not be coaxed to betray that party. He went to prison protesting his innocence in total."

I flexed my hand over the notepad and helped myself to another sandwich. "I haven't reviewed my old notes yet, but I seem to recall you had a candidate for that outside agent."

"Logic suggested Cranleigh's somewhat sinister brother, Jerrod. A ne'er-do-well of all trades, fully as embittered as Horace, and just the sort to be in on such a caper. He worked as a farrier in a nearby village. The problem was that he was positively alibied far away in Chelmsford that day – by Mr. Mundy, who has in effect now withdrawn that testimony."

I glanced between Holmes and the clergyman. "He committed perjury to protect his family, yes? My first thought is to wonder if they are still at risk. The words of a dying man may not be the most objective."

"I doubt they are in any immediate jeopardy," Holmes replied in a musing tone. "For reprisal to be taken against them now can hardly serve the purpose of keeping secrets. It would be merely punitive, and as good as an admission of guilt on the part of those freshly implicated."

"How did the case stand regarding those other parties?" Father Brown asked, peering owlishly from behind his spectacles.

"I identified a network of affiliates – low-life and scoundrels – but they were small fry. Individually they knew too little to make a difference. A witness saw the offenders together, a shopkeeper likewise, but of the thugs who performed the robbery only one was ever arrested. The rest are thought to have scattered back to other counties and were untraceable – not that too great an effort was made, when the evidence began to point toward Horace.

"The case petered out with only him to take the fall on behalf of them all." Holmes sighed and finished his tea. "More of the evidence was circumstantial than I was comfortable with – a person seen here, a word overheard there. *He-say, she-say.* I *knew* Horace was protecting someone, probably his brother. But the case was actually a minor one, and I was satisfied at the time that we had the right man. Horace was unable to answer key questions about his movements and associates – such as why he chose to drive on to Harpenden instead of seeking help from the church right there in Gustard Wood, thus contriving to take long enough to raise the alarm for the thugs to make a clean getaway. He also escaped suspiciously free from serious injury." He raised a brow with a smile. "The old, old story, gentlemen, from the days of Dick Turpin himself."

"So why look further, eh?" Father Brown nodded, his expression introspective. "And the thug who came under arrest?"

"A carter by the name of Saul Olds, according to the file here. The dragnet picked him up hiding in a forester's hut in Gustard Wood proper, a mile north of the event. He was identified as one of the assailants by Lady Harrington, as his hessian mask slipped during the affray. There wasn't much he could tell us, and after some pressure was brought to bear he dealt to bring his sentence down to two years' hard labour, plus a flogging. The information he provided was patently useless, but he cooperated insomuch as he was able."

"What did he say?" I asked softly.

"That he had been hired by a go-between – an ex-con known only as 'Scar', for the knife slash on his face, who organised the job on behalf of someone else. He was described as hard as nails, tallish, with an accent from Leeds or Bradford. He had unkempt hair, was bearded, and had a puckered knife wound down the left side of his face." He rolled his eyes. "I ask you! The scar, the accent – all too melodramatic to be real. I doubt such a person ever existed. However, some very real person posing as this 'Scar' is another matter. Had Jerrod Cranleigh not been placed unequivocally forty miles away on that day, I would have been inclined to say it was he."

"And now?" Father Brown asked, a pale brow uplifted.

"My instincts are as they were then. The police picked up Jerrod Cranleigh the next day at his work, searched both his work and his place of residence, and found nothing incriminating. He claimed to have been visiting the family in Essex and produced Mr. Mundy as a witness. I confess, the stationmaster's certainty threw me off the scent. Also, I failed to pursue that dimension to these events because a second witness came forward: A young woman working on a nearby farm.

"She claimed to have seen Horace Cranleigh in a pub a few nights earlier, in company with rough-looking characters, one of whom was definitely Olds. Circumstantial yet again, you'll note. Cranleigh and Olds claimed not to know each other, but given Horace's humble status and superficial corruptibility – no marriage, no children, fond of cards and racetracks – he was a good enough candidate for a jury to find him guilty."

For a long moment Holmes stared into some middle distance, then sighed. "Now I must of course wonder if the second witness was paid as surely as Mr. Mundy – one to alibi Jerrod, the other to condemn Horace. If so, their testimony dovetailed to conclude the case, after which it was thought of no more."

"Which abruptly sounds as if it was the desired outcome," I mused.

Holmes poured a second round of tea from a large earthenware pot, and when we had fresh brew before us he resumed his seat and gestured to the priest. "What are your impressions, Father?"

"Hmm?" Brown murmured, as if he had been far away in thought. "Oh, Jerrod is guilty. Horace merely took the fall for the family."

"Would you care to expand upon that?" Holmes invited, and the priest sipped his tea as he marshalled his thoughts.

"Remember, Mr. Mundy was a parishioner, so events took place rather on my own doorstep. The Cranleigh family, while by no means devout, are far from unknown in the Essex countryside. They were respectable folk in their parents' day, but financial mismanagement rather precipitated them upon the kerb of life. Understandably, the younger generation railed against fate ever after. Their parents have entered early graves – no foul play was suspected, and I presume shame and regret to have provided all the impetus needed to greet the hereafter rather ahead of schedule. Notably, the family have recovered their landed ways, securing an estate somewhere out toward Tiptree, if I recall. They moved in around 1903, if memory serves. No fanfares from the society papers. The stigma of having a brother still serving time rather kept attention elsewhere. They claimed success in trade, a rebuilding of old traditions, that sort of thing, and have lived very quietly ever since."

"So," I mused, "when Horace came out of prison, he went home to a mansion?"

"Worth a tough young man sacrificing his twenties, would you say? To return his family to luxury and position, and no doubt receive a hero's welcome?"

Holmes nodded assertively. "It certainly is. A dire way to mend fortunes, admittedly – a drastic plan, but desperation drives the bitter to all manner of deeds. It sounds as if they successfully realised the value of the Harrington diamonds, and stories of successful deals are but a smokescreen. If so, Jerrod Cranleigh got away with something that should have rightly seen him do ten years at his brother's side. Horace, of course, cannot be convicted twice for the same crime, nor for declining to speak."

He sat forward with a gleam in his eye, such as I used to see long ago. "Gentlemen, a criminal is out there playing the Lord of the Manor when he has a considerable debt to society still against his name. It may or may not be possible to uncover what happened to the gems, and thus stand any chance of returning their value to the Harrington family, but at bare minimum we may yet connect the perpetrator to the deed. Are you up for the hunt?"

Both Father Brown and I replied very much in the positive. "Excellent! Then our goal is something to tie Jerrod to the theft. The stationmaster's confession creates clear doubt, but is not enough. Tangible proof that Jerrod Cranleigh was in fact 'Scar' on that morning in 1898 should be our grail. There is no statute of limitations in British justice, so we may bring our evidence to the attention of the law in full expectation it will be acted upon."

We determined at once to put best foot forward, to which effect Holmes walked along to the village post office. There he sent a telegram securing rooms at The Ship, a public house in Chelmsford, which would be our first port of call, to interview the widow Mundy. Then he telephoned into Eastbourne for a cab, and the vehicle was at the Tiger Inn twenty minutes later. It seemed Holmes had fully anticipated our expedition, for he had thrown a few amenities into a suitcase, which he produced from under the dining table.

We three stepped out, loaded our luggage, and were at once speeding east through the countryside in good time to take lunch at the station cafe and board the five-minutes-to-one train to Victoria. Holmes wore his signature deerstalker, and I knew his revolver would be in his case. He was treating this matter like our adventures of old.

The train put us off in London at twenty-past-two, and we engaged a cab to whisk us through the City to Liverpool Street

Station. I found I missed the more sedate pace of olden times, when the only sound was the rhythmic clop of hooves. I did *not,* however, miss the horse droppings which had been the characteristic of every London street since time immemorial. Yet the odour of vehicle exhaust also served to remind one that all progress comes at a cost.

We took tea at the station cafe, and were on our way to Chelmsford at half-past-three for a sixty-five minute commute, arriving at the country centre in mild air and sunshine. The Ship was just a few hundred yards up Rainsford Road from the station, and we were soon signed in. I had cause to wonder at the way things had changed over the years. In the old days, the journey would likely have taken much of the day, but with the benefits of telephone and motor transport we covered the distance from Sussex to our lodgings in Chelmsford in just four hours, including idle time.

Father Brown excused himself to visit Mrs. Mundy and arrange for us to call, assuming she was willing to speak of the matters in hand, and returned within the hour to assure us she was quite ready to receive guests. We walked out in the pleasant afternoon, a stroll up toward Admirals Park, and were shown to a neat house in a street close by.

Mrs. Mundy was a small, silver-haired woman, perhaps fifteen years our senior, in the traditional black of mourning wear, though since the passing of Her Majesty the convention had rather waned. She wore spectacles and her hair was drawn back quite severely under a black bonnet, which seemed very much out of style. She welcomed Father Brown with obvious affection and served tea and cake in a sunny parlour.

"Father Brown tells me you gentlemen are interested in what my Hubert might have meant with those last words he spoke." I saw a reserve in her demeanour, which told me under what control she held herself. Her husband was not yet in the ground, and her grief was fresh.

Holmes was at his most tactful. "Madam, we believe multiple injustices occurred in 1898, of which only some were counterbalanced by prosecution. Your husband told the police that he saw a Mr. Jerrod Cranleigh on the platform of his station on the day in question. This placed Cranleigh beyond the scope of the investigation of events in a wood near Harpenden. Your husband's last words retracted that statement, and expressed the thought that he had protected his family with the lie."

"Every word is true, Mr. Holmes. And he regretted, every day of his life, that he set you awry from your case. But can a man be

239

faulted for taking the path of least resistance when his family's well-being, their very lives, have been made the price of any other course of action?"

"Not by me," Holmes said softly, with a sip of tea. "What's done is done. We are hoping, however, that justice might yet be more fully served. Could you tell us all you recall of the events surrounding his testimony?"

"I'll do my best." The lady composed herself, the afternoon sun making her room a warm and peaceful sanctum. "Hubert confided in me, but not in our children. They have never known anything was amiss, and I want it to remain so." She received our assurances to that effect by a smile and nod.

"Hubert was approached a couple of days earlier, as he was closing the station after the last train through. He was menaced by masked men who threatened all our lives unless he cooperated. They gave him a few body blows to underline their point, then put a sovereign into his hand as the first instalment. They were quite willing to pay, because payment incriminated Hubert, it 'made him a conspirator', as they put it.

"Well, Mr. Holmes, we never touched their money! There's twenty pounds, paid five at a time over a year, put away in a bag in the attic. We never benefited from their blood money, but didn't dare give it away either, lest it draw attention." She shook her head, a far-away look in her eyes. "It was easier to forget it ever existed."

"These men," Holmes prompted. "How did they organise the giving of testimony?"

"Oh, they contrived an incident on the platform, a fall over some luggage near the ticket office which prompted the stationmaster's attention. That made certain Hubert came face-to-face with the person for whom he was to speak up. Except the one who made the fall was someone else entirely." She smiled faintly. "I can't tell you how good it is to finally speak these words. Secrets kept too long seem to fester, like old wounds."

Father Brown patted her arm. "There, now, Elspeth. All will be well in the end."

"Then, the next day, the police came by to show a photograph of a gentleman and ask if he had been seen – that's when the lie was told. We knew that man was up to no good, but what could we do?" She savoured her tea and shook her head slowly.

"How was the money received?" Holmes asked.

"Usually, late in the evening, when Hubert was closing up, a last passenger would have a near-collision with him, whisper a reminder in his ear, and a five pound note would appear in his hand or pocket. Very carefully done, but they never let him forget."

"Did your husband ever get a good look at those passing the money?"

Mrs. Mundy made a displeased face. "Once or twice. A little man with a face like a rat is how Hubert described him. That's as good a description as any. Nasty piece of work, that Tom Savage."

"You *knew* him?" Father Brown interjected.

"Not at first, but many years later. It would be two years ago, we went to the county fair down at Hylands House, and who should be there but a group from that estate near Tiptree, with their produce. Well, the rat-faced chap was with them, and Hubert knew him right away. He said, 'Makes a change, him not handing out fivers with menaces.' Well, they were back-to-back with us in the tea garden and I overheard his name mentioned. Little *swine* of a man."

I wrote it all down as fast as my pencil could fly. I could almost sense the gears of Holmes's mind meshed and turning as they always had, and smiled tightly to myself. I would be surprised if this ended up as a wasted trip.

There was little more Mrs. Mundy could tell us. After a convivial period, we bade her good evening and took a stroll in Admirals Park as the sun declined over the trees.

"It seems no matter how quietly the Cranleighs have lived, they cannot or will not disassociate themselves from their criminal connections," Holmes mused, indulging in a small cigar, the first tobacco I had seen him use. I was frankly glad. The amount he used in the old days could hardly have been good for him, or myself. "I would give fair odds this Savage was involved in the jewel theft in some capacity. His physical stature rules out his having posed as 'Scar', but there are many tasks for extra pairs of hands in any criminal enterprise."

"They share a secret," Father Brown said simply, as if it were the most obvious thing in the world. "They hold each other's safety from the consequences of their actions in the palms of their hands, and cannot afford any falling out among the conspirators. One word of betrayal, and those consequences become very real. The thought that all members of their grubby little club would likely go down together would compel cooperation. But such a situation begs its own abuse."

I smiled as the penny dropped. "You mean any one of them could exploit the others for some personal gain by holding the general peril over their heads?"

"Exactly. It is rare for any criminal group to maintain the loyalty and fraternity found among those of nobler association. Perhaps only family ties have provided them their compass in this, yet there are obviously also members outside those affiliations."

"This creates an inherent weakness in their fellowship," Holmes mused. "That it has survived twelve years intact speaks of a firm hand in charge."

"Jerrod or Horace?" I asked.

"Jerrod may have been the mastermind behind the theft, perhaps behind placing Horace with the Harrington family in the first place. But Horace did his years and survived them, and prison hardens a man. I would not be surprised if he had assumed leadership of their band, both for his toughness and as a matter of tribute for his sacrifice."

"What's the next step, Holmes?" I prompted.

"Information. I shall draft a telegram to go first thing in the morning, seeking a little background. Then we must roam farther afield." He sent me a quizzical look. "You learned to drive a motorcar, didn't you?"

"As well you remember," I replied with a smile, casting my mind back on that particular affair, now many years in the past. "I haven't had a great deal of practice, but the skills come readily enough to hand. Are you considering hiring private transport?"

"It offers unparalleled flexibility. It isn't bound to destinations, like rail, and avoids the presence of an outside party, unavoidable when using cabs."

"I'm your man!" Abruptly I found myself quite looking forward to tomorrow's sortie.

We took a late breakfast around nine, when Holmes returned from the post office, and then made inquiries and found our way to a small automotive agency to secure the hire of a vehicle suitable for our purposes. By midmorning I had purchased a touring map of Essex, and a sporty 1905 Spyker, in green with yellow trim, was parked outside The Ship. The great Dutch make was renowned for its nimbleness and performance, and I was sure it would provide us all the mobility the case demanded.

During brunch, a telegram was delivered for Holmes, and he smiled over the contents. "I called in a favour for old times' sake. It's from Chief Inspector Hopkins at Scotland Yard, advancing me the authority of the Metropolitan Police to request assistance from the Essex Constabulary. Our first stop of the day: To seek background on this Mr. Tom Savage."

Chelmsford was the county town for Essex, and therefore its police held a range of records for the county as a whole. We drove the quarter-mile to the tall building on New Street and had the pleasure of seeing Holmes invoke the goodwill of the Yard, which set wheels in motion to pull any records on file regarding the Cranleigh brothers' retainer. We arranged to return later that afternoon. Then, with an air of adventure, I headed us west.

Chelmsford to Harpenden was around forty miles as the crow flies, half as much again on country roads, and our journey took a couple of hours, passing through such centres as Roxwell, Harlow, Hertford, and Welwyn Garden City. Driving was a much more labour-intensive form of travel than relaxing in a fine coach with a newspaper, but the sense of freedom was remarkable. We took a sandwich and ale at a public house in the latter-mentioned township before pressing on, and at one in the afternoon I pulled off the road and switched off the engine in the cool shade of Lower Gustard Wood.

"Lamer Lane. The *locus in quo*," Holmes remarked as we disembarked. "The road passes south, then west toward the town, and it was on this stretch that several masked men bailed up Sir Basil Harrington's coach, assaulted the occupants, and divested them of goods to the value of thirty-thousand pounds." He stalked a few yards, looked around the green and quiet countryside where cows drowsed in green pasture, and set fists on hips. "Let us reconstruct the event."

Father Brown put up his always-carried umbrella against the May sun and looked each way along the quiet stretch. "The woods are fairly dense, still, though they have been cut from their former extent. Even in daylight men could hide, unseen until they moved." He shook his head in a certain puzzlement. "How did they convince the coach to stop? There is no mention of them bearing firearms in the report."

"Horace Cranleigh claims they stepped into the road and he reined-in to avoid running them over. He was fairly credible on this point: Highway robbery is long enough in the past that one might indeed be more inclined to avoid a pedestrian than automatically define him as some enemy and whip-up the horses instead. Yet the witnesses were unanimous that their attackers wore masks made from hessian sackcloth, and that mitigates against the driver not drawing the conclusion that they were being assaulted *before* he

243

could draw the coach to a halt. This was another factor which the jury easily attributed to complicity."

I walked a little way and turned. "All right. We have a coach and pair, brought to a halt in this lane, several masked men about it. The driver is pulled down and given a few taps to support his claim of innocence. Sir Basil produces his pistol and fires several shots, though his aim is spoiled by either the shaking hands of shock, or a natural lack of marksmanship. The assailants gain access to the coach, drag out the knight, his good lady, and their son, deal them some sharp attention, though nothing too severe according to the records, and disappear with the gem case into the woods." I gestured with a driving glove into the greenery surrounding us. "They scatter, Olds being arrested a mile north, having gone to ground. The gems are never seen again."

"Excellent summary, Watson," Holmes said with a nod. "From this, we may assume that the one to whom the goods were entrusted either secreted them in the immediate area, some hiding place to which he could return later and retrieve them, or he had a fast horse – or even a bicycle – waiting. Yet neither the farmers 'round about nor the vicar just along at the church recalled a rider going through hell-for-leather. I'm more inclined to think the gems were hidden nearby, and recovered when the dust settled."

"It must have been an exceedingly secure hiding place" I remarked, brows up. "I wouldn't like to entrust thirty-thousand pounds to a hole in the ground and hope for the best."

Holmes's eyes sparkled. "Another accomplice, then? Someone who could casually take possession without attracting attention?"

The wind stirred the trees in fresh rustling for long moments. Then Father Brown cleared his throat. "What do we know about the younger Harrington?"

From the file, very little. Nineteen years of age, he was on holiday at the time, home from college – Oxbridge Academy. He was a sporting type and thought "very proper". The account faded out there. More attention had been paid to his mother's shock, she having taken to her bed for a month after the event while Sir Basil railed for a conviction. Holmes had met the family just once, promised them justice, and assisted the Essex Constabulary to conclude a successful case before the Chelmsford Crown Court, which sent Horace Cranleigh to Springfield Prison. Holmes had given no further thought to the boy since that day.

There was no public library in Harpenden, but in ten minutes we were in St. Albans, and a swift consultation of the various current volumes of society figures was undertaken. The Harringtons were, of course, listed alongside the minor peerage, and brief biographies were revealing. Young Archie Harrington, now thirty-one, had avoided both military service and a business career in a most surprising way – a string of lucrative wins at various race meetings. Between 1900 and 1906, it seemed he had developed the devil's own luck, making some fourteen-thousand pounds at the tracks. He had subsequently invested in the family estate, becoming a horse breeder.

"Oh, yes," the barkeep, a balding chap with a broad girth and a florid face, said as he pulled pints in the afternoon at The Peahen in London Road, "'Lord Archie', as we call him, has made a name throughout the whole area. He saw the way the motorcar was going to send horses obsolete and wanted to keep something of the grand old way, so he breeds for the racetrack." He passed over foam-topped glasses and we sipped with pleasure. "His luck was good for the rest of us, too. He employs a fair army of grooms, farriers, and saddlers. If old Sir Basil had had his way, none of it would have happened."

"He is opposed to his son's success?" Father Brown asked, with the most innocent expression I had ever seen.

"Not as such, but the old man wanted his son to be Army, had his heart set on a colonel in the family one day. *Colonel Sir Archibald Harrington* was how he'd introduce the lad when he was a nipper. But after the disaster with the family fortune, then Archie falling on his feet, the old gaffer has sort of taken a backseat. Running down the clock, I suppose, until his title goes to the lad. It's an old one. He's a baronet." Polishing a glass, he nodded along the bar to framed photographs. "There's the family in happier times. They were often down this way for one event or another. Even stayed in this hotel once."

I studied the grouping – knight, lady, son. An only child, it would seem. They appeared in all ways a normal family in the minor aristocracy. "Old money, are they?" I asked with a bluff sort of interest.

"Not terribly well-off as the peerage goes," the barman replied with a shrug. "They only have a dozen servants to look after the hall, not forty. Investments in gutta-percha and other Indian commodities, as I recall. Enough to keep them solvent, I daresay, but not to support

245

the kind of ventures the lad had in mind. Still, luck smiled on him and the whole world's rosy."

He went on to serve other customers and we settled into a corner table. "Luck?" I asked with an ironic tone.

"A consistent winning streak over seven years?" Holmes shook his head. "Beyond the bounds of statistical probability. Even allowing for a thorough knowledge of his field, as would seem to be the case, it is too remarkable an eventuality. The odds now favour Archie Harrington as the architect of the theft. For his run of luck to commence some two years after the robbery suggests the gems had been sold on in that time, and the rewards were reaped slowly and carefully, a few hundred pounds here and there, no doubt simply through faked betting slips. He was in effect paying out himself, a way to explain coming into such sums."

"A bookmaker would have to be in on the scheme," I observed.

"Supplied by the Cranleigh brothers, probably. I would not be surprised if it was our Tom Savage. And of course, young Archie would surreptitiously pay out Horace and Jerrod, which they then passed off as the fruits of business."

Father Brown set his glass down and nodded gravely. "So the inside man had an inside man. Perhaps it was Archie Harrington who approached the Cranleighs – certainly advised them of the journey to London. He took a beating to reinforce his innocence, and they passed the stones off to him, directly or indirectly. His underworld contacts? At this point we can only surmise, but a public school education is nothing if not complete."

Holmes shook his head gravely. "How could I have been so blind? Twelve years ago, I was fixed upon the robbery itself and the way Horace set it up. I assigned his failure to establish his innocence to simple ineptitude, and if that was my intellectual condescension, then I am duly ashamed. I helped deliver a conviction as Sir Basil needed, and there is no doubt that a guilty man went to prison. What I did not see at the time was that it was his intention to do so."

I sighed into my glass. "None of this connects Jerrod with 'Scar'. And demonstrating that the Harringtons were robbed by one of their own will be a fierce task."

To be thorough, we returned to Harpenden and visited the Old Cock Inn, in the High Street, listed in the file as the place the second witness saw Horace Cranleigh with the toughs, one of them being positively identified as Olds. We refrained from further beverages –

my equilibrium informed me I needed my balance for the long drive back to Chelmsford.

Holmes was in an officious mood by this point. He opened the file in a corner of the bar, more interested in the facts than the place, I thought. "And here we come to the second eyewitness: Claire Portman, twenty-one, a kitchen hand at the local Wilson farm, came forward to positively identify the parties as having met in this very bar, two nights before the theft. We are now assuming she was paid to do so. The file records very little about her, though it gives a home contact address as '*Holy Family and All Saints, Witham*', with the notation that her nearest relatives were not literate and their priest read and wrote letters for them."

Father Brown cleared his throat. "Holy Family is an Essex parish, my friends. Given that Witham is just a few miles from Tiptree, I think a visit to All Saints to beg a consultation of their registers might bear fruit."

Holmes and I shared a glance filled with ideas. "The witness just happened to be from the same county as the offender?" I said. "Not beyond the bounds of coincidence, of course, but allowing for the supposition that she was employed to testify, the connection becomes especially clear."

"Back to Essex, then?" Father Brown wore a pensive look.

Holmes nodded assertively and we were soon on the road, after locating a chemist from whom we purchased a couple of gallons of petroleum spirit for the journey. The afternoon was filled with glorious sunshine, and we were glad of the Spyker's open top, its rain cover folded and lashed at the rear. Witham is some six miles east of Chelmsford, and we delivered Father Brown to the rectory, where he was admitted with *bonhomie*. While he was engaged in his perusal of the records, Holmes and I returned to Chelmsford to check the progress of the police file clerks. We would make mutual reports over dinner, after retrieving our friend.

The long evening as summer approached found us taking our repast by windows overlooking the high street, and we could each tell the other had something important to offer. "Please," Father Brown offered as our meals arrived. "You go first."

Holmes cleared his throat and took a sip of cider. "We assumed correctly that this chap Savage would have a record. Petty stuff – a drunken arrest or two, public affrays more than once over the years. Suspected of handling stolen goods, but unproven. Apparently he is a common sight at race meetings – worked as a bookie's runner when he was a boy, and held a license as a turf accountant earlier in the decade."

"I'll give short odds he was Archie Harrington's bookie," I said with a smile, sampling the roast and vegetables before me. "Harrington would give him a wedge of illicit cash before they ever reached the track. They would fiddle the slips and it would be handed back as winnings, all aboveboard."

"And thus, the new Harrington largess resides in the hands of the next generation, after diversion from the control of the previous, as well as the strings and assumptions thereof. Presumably, Harrington split the value evenly with the Cranleigh brothers – even fifteen-thousand pounds is enough to tempt the embittered to give up their liberty." Holmes gestured to the priest. "And your discoveries, Father?"

The mousy man blinked through his glasses with a quiet smile. "Miss Portland was born near Witham in 1877. She was christened in that very church. She travelled the district for work on farms and the occasional factory. She seems to have gone far from home just the once – in 1898 – for a month or two, which put her in the right place to witness that meeting. Then she returned to Essex, where she remained to the end of her days."

"She's – *departed*?" I asked softly.

"Died in childbed in 1903, I'm afraid." He crossed himself with a silent prayer for her soul. "But the story is not yet complete. The Portman family evidently crossed paths with the Cranleighs at an early date, as Claire's brother, William, is recorded as marrying Emma Cranleigh, sister of Horace and Jerrod, in 1900, once again in the same church."

"She was almost a Cranleigh by association," I breathed. "Taken together, I can't see a magistrate or jury failing to see this as evidence of the pointed manipulation of the old case."

Holmes nodded in agreement. "I think we have enough in hand to convincingly demonstrate conspiracy – that the court was skilfully directed to the conclusion it reached, and that Jerrod's whereabouts on the day in question are *not* established." He glanced at Father Brown and me over his glass. "Yet again, however, the mere fact that new fortunes have come to the Cranleighs and to Archie Harrington since the theft is entirely circumstantial. The pattern fits beautifully, but unless we can unequivocally place Jerrod Cranleigh in time and space, connecting him with the event, our evidence remains *soft.*"

248

He breathed a sigh of frustration. "I blame my own impatience at the time. I placed too little importance on what appeared an open-and-shut case, and to my chagrin have permitted a rank injustice." He smiled, took a sip of cider, and continued. "My friends, I have never claimed perfection, merely the ongoing fine-tuning of a system of investigation, and I am not entirely surprised to learn that in some instances I was incomplete in my cogitations. But I am glad to say that the challenge is accepted, and the remaining pieces of this puzzle *will* be dropped into place."

With Holmes's promise to that effect, our fellowship parted company for some days. Father Brown returned to his parish, and I to my patients in London, but I held myself ready to travel and, sure enough, a telegram arrived, inviting me to attend a meeting at the Shire Hall on Tindal Square, Chelmsford, and to bring my notebook. I caught the train on a breezy morning and walked up the four-hundred yards from the station, taking in the beautiful old cathedral behind the Hall.

I found Holmes in the downstairs hallway, Father Brown already in attendance, and was introduced to Inspector Robeson of the Essex CID. I made warm reacquaintance with the now-senior Stanley Hopkins, a Chief Inspector at the Yard and an enthusiastic devotee of the Holmesian method from the 1890's. A moment later I felt a hand on my collar, and turned to find the familiar but now silver-framed features of our old friend, Lestrade.

Hopkins hooked thumbs in his waistcoat pockets and beamed a smile. "I got in touch with ex-Superintendent Lestrade when I knew the case was back on. I knew he would want to be here."

We shook hands, and the long-retired Detective Superintendent assured us with a smile he would not have missed this for the world.

An usher showed us upstairs to the Assembly Room, where the Assizes Court had met since the later eighteenth century. Here we found seating arranged for a group, and several of the people we had come to know about were already in attendance. Horace and Jerrod Cranleigh, Archibald Harrington, Saul Olds, and Tom Savage were arranged across the front row, and I sat with Lestrade, Hopkins, and Father Brown at the back as Robeson and Holmes went to the desk at the head of the room. The latter perched on its corner, extracting a folder of papers from a briefcase as Inspector Robeson cleared his throat.

"Gentlemen, thank you for coming. I admit my approach was rather ambiguous, but I certainly did not mislead when I said your

249

attendance was very important. I see you're rather surprised to see each other, all in the same place at the same time. I would stress that at this point no one is accused of anything. You are, in fact, entirely at liberty to leave if you so wish. You may walk out at any point. However, proceedings will continue in your absence and you may be sought out once again if reason emerges." His words had a sobering effect, and the five glanced back and forth, abruptly tight-lipped.

Horace, sandy-haired, square-jawed, was the steady, solid-as-rock sort now. Despite his good suit, and the trappings of a gentleman, he had the bearing of a man who has survived the worst life could send his way, and he sat with eyes narrowed, an observer rather than a participant in the moment. To my doctor's eye, Olds was well into alcoholism. I doubted he would see another year. His prematurely aged features were set in a mask of apprehension, as though he feared the penalties he had paid were somehow insufficient, that his past offences would come back to haunt him once more.

The younger Harrington, immaculately suited, dark hair in the new undercut style, wore a profoundly annoyed expression, his hauteur striking me as pure defiance. He was a son of privilege who was raised to believe his very social status made him immune to little things like the process of law. Tom Savage was rat-faced. Not even a bath and his Sunday best could make of him more than he was: A horsefly of the racetracks. Jerrod, darker than his brother and hard as nails, was the man at the most profound unease, however, as if he remembered Sherlock Holmes only too well, a face he had hoped never to see again.

"Now, I'm going to hand you over to Mr. Sherlock Holmes, who has been making some discreet inquiries concerning a case with which he helped the Essex Constabulary many years ago. I'm sure you all recall it well."

Holmes rose from the desk and put his hands behind his back, studying the five faces before him for a long, silent moment. "Twelve years ago, I was called in by Sir Basil Harrington to assist concerning the theft of the Harrington diamonds, which occurred in Lower Gustard Wood, near Harpenden. The diamonds were never recovered, and two of the men in this room were convicted – Saul Olds for participating in the theft, for which he served two years, and Horace Cranleigh, as the principal force behind the crime, who served seven years of a ten year sentence, the balance being remitted for model behaviour. Let me remind us all at once that neither Mr.

Cranleigh nor Mr. Olds can be brought to account a second time for those events. They were asked here merely as a courtesy. Today, I would like to address aspects of the case which have so far remained shrouded in mystery, with an eye to a potential committal hearing, should Inspector Robeson feel the evidence sufficient."

Jerrod Cranleigh and Archie Harrington exchanged a sharp glance but remained silent, as composed as they might hope to be when a sudden question hung over their liberty. Indeed, I thought I saw some communication in that look: *Stay quiet, say nothing!*

Holmes paced a little as he spoke. "In 1898, in the courtrooms not far from here, Mr. Jerrod Cranleigh was not a participant in his brother's trial. This is because, though he was arrested and his abode searched meticulously, no incriminating evidence could be located. In addition, Mr. Hubert Mundy, the old stationmaster here in Chelmsford, provided a statement to the police that Mr. Cranleigh had been in *this* town when the offence occurred." He took a few seconds' dramatic pause. "Mr. Mundy passed away recently, and made a dying confession to the lie of that statement." His eyes went to Jerrod, hard and direct. "He also spoke of threats and inducements, bribes – which are in material evidence. His candour, long delayed, has set in motion a fresh investigation.

"In the original case, Mr. Olds was linked with Mr. Horace Cranleigh by the now-deceased Miss Claire Portman. When apprehended, he could only tell us that he had been recruited by a character he named 'Scar', on account of a facial disfigurement – a person who could not be located, then or ever since. It is my intention to demonstrate that no such person ever existed – merely the impression of him in the minds of a handful of men brought together to rob the Harrington coach.

"The original crime was not a difficult deduction: That Mr. Horace Cranleigh drove his master and family into an ambush. Despite his protestations of innocence, there are no doubts that he was guilty, and has duly paid society's price. However, I knew then that he was protecting someone. I just couldn't identify whom. I believe I can do better now."

He took a sip from a glass. The room was so silent that we heard passers-by in Tindal Square below, and I knew heart rates would be elevated in the front row. Only Horace and Olds could actually relax.

"The problem – and clue – were inherent in the boldness of the assault. The gem case was taken by force, during which the occupants of the coach were injured, but *mildly*, as if the ultimate sponsor of the venture did not in fact *want* them hurt. Though fired

251

upon, the thieves did not respond with similar force. One might wonder if the gun was loaded – by someone – with blank ammunition, both to render Sir Basil's defiance ineffective and to ensure no serious injury could occur. When inspected, the weapon contained four spent cases and two unfired, normal rounds." Holmes waved a hand in dismissal of his conjecture. "The gem case, once wrested from the family, was carried into the woods and vanished from all human ken." He smiled. "Mr. Horace Cranleigh played out his charade by driving the family into Harpenden – not to the vicarage nearby where the shots had indeed been heard – to raise the alarm. The police dragged the area within two hours, apprehending Mr. Olds, and the rest is a matter of record. There is no need to rehash those affairs. Let me instead tell you where my fresh endeavours have taken us."

Now we came to the meat of the affair, and I was all ears, experiencing a great sense of nostalgia to see Holmes in his element once more. I wrote quickly, my hand cramping a little, and had thoughts of showing *The Strand* a new story in the months ahead.

After a pause, Holmes looked up with a pent smile. "Mr. Harrington: You may be unaware, but I once performed a small service for Oxbridge Academy, many years before you attended there, and I was able to visit the school without issue. They cadged a guest address from me, but that is quite beside the point. My object in visiting was to beg a look at the old registers – ostensibly to check your academic performance, and incidentally, also your aptitudes.

"I was not especially surprised to find you showed a keen interest in drama. I can fully imagine how stifled you must have felt when your father disapproved of a career in the arts and required you to enter military college upon leaving school." He let a few moments go by. "But I was surprised to find that Jerrod Cranleigh was a classmate in 1896." That bombshell brought my eyes up and I glanced at Father Brown. "This was immediately prior to the financial ruination of the Cranleigh family. You were both keen about the stage, and your old drama teacher, Professor Maturin, remembers you taking part in that year's student production of *Dr. Jekyll and Mr. Hyde*. Your dramatic makeup was well praised, then and now. It was a great shame matters intervened – insolvency for one, familial duty for the other – as it seems the stage was robbed of talent it could sore do without.

"Two years later all was tragedy, of course. But Professor Maturin recalled receiving a letter from you, inquiring about a theatrical supplier in London." He drew a paper from the folder.

"This is it. He kept it as a memento of a brilliant student. I believe that is your hand, Mr. Harrington. It's easily enough verified."

Harrington and Jerrod Cranleigh had developed a film of perspiration, though neither was careless enough to speak, knowing Inspector Robeson would take especial interest in any comment. They seemed to be fuming inwardly, bottling up anger, fear, and dread, hiding it all behind a mask of granite composure. Holmes paused, my hand catching up.

"The supplier is still in business. I've used them myself in pursuit of my various aliases in years gone by. They were delighted to receive a visit from one of their most prized customers. Once again, I was able to beg a look at their old ledgers, and there is an entry recording your order in August 1898 for wigging, a false beard, greasepaint and tints, and latex – the sort of natural rubber solution used to construct disfigurements, such as scars. Payment is recorded as by banker's draft, and I'm sure there will be a record thereof as well. They also recorded the address to which the package was sent: Wilson Farm, outside Harpenden, consigned to Miss Claire Portman."

Now one might have heard a pin drop, and the inspector looked at the men in the front row with a very stern set to his brows. I read in the way they carried themselves a great tension, a clear admission of *something*.

"Then I moved on to the matter of the diamonds. We may comfortably assume they were recut, reset, and modified so as to be unrecognisable and beyond any reclamation. The stones, though excellent, were far from unique. One, however, was quite remarkable: A lozenge-shaped clear diamond of some sixteen carats and sixty-eight facets. This was the centre-piece of the collection, the real value. Some comparative cross-checking revealed a stone almost answering that description, of fifteen carats and eighty-four facets, which appeared on the market in 1902 with a provenance of importation from South Africa, after preparation in Amsterdam. The difference in weight is small enough to be the result of the introduction of the additional facets, a simple enough task for a good cutter." The implications were plain enough, and he pressed on. "I traced it back through its bill of sale, and the originating dealer is no longer in business, having retired years ago. He passed away recently, leaving only the documents of authentication – likely forgeries, which may also be demonstrated."

I saw Jerrod Cranleigh swallow hard, the perspiration at his brow a bright patina. I felt he was holding back some dreadful outburst by a feat of will.

Holmes opened the folder. "Documents from the school, from the supplier, and the diamond exchange – all dated and verified. These are the tangible evidence, and I am the first to admit they are less than I would have desired to build a case upon. Nevertheless, here is my reasoning." He paced a little, then turned on his heel to face the group.

"Mr. Harrington: Unwilling to fall in with your father's wishes as per the arrangements of your life, you determined to take from the family the wealth which constituted their main claim to privilege – the very collateral of prestige. You approached your friend, Jerrod Cranleigh, knowing he and his family were recently dispossessed and bitter about it. You offered them a chance at a good measure of the value of the Harrington fortune if they would help you with the theft. You obtained the means to change Mr. Cranleigh's appearance, making him the chimerical 'Scar' who brought together the ruffians to actually do the job. You probably changed the bullets in your father's revolver for blanks, and in the confusion after the assault substituted normal cartridges for the two unfired blank rounds, though this is merely my supposition. The men 'Scar' hired were under strict orders not to get *too* rough. You had no wish to hurt your parents physically – merely to rob them blind."

His words had taken on a steely edge, and Harrington shifted in his seat with a toss of his head, as if dismissing the argument as nonsense. But he still remained absolutely silent.

"The gems were taken, and you suffered some minor mistreatment in the process, as did Horace Cranleigh, but not long after you were able to return, unnoticed, to that lane through the woods and retrieve the gems from their hiding place. You delivered them, at a later date and with great care, to an underworld receiver who reworked them and sold them on under forged provenance over the following years. Horace Cranleigh agreed to take the blame, going to prison to pay for everyone's ambition, thereby distracting the law from even noticing the wider conspiracy. Only Saul Olds did not get away cleanly, and paid for his part in blood and sweat.

"Enter Tom Savage, turf accountant, who was expertly placed to engineer your remarkable run of luck at the tracks over so many years, winnings commonly held to equal at least fourteen-thousand pounds – easily checked by *subpoena duces tecum* upon your bank accounts. You went to considerable lengths to cleanse the money you received from the fence and disguise its origins from your parents." Holmes smiled with a steely edge. "Yesterday I paid a visit to Sir Basil and Lady Harrington to let them know the old case had come once again under my scrutiny. We spoke at length. I congratulated them on their son's remarkable run of luck, and they recalled you proudly flaunting your betting slips to them after each track-side triumph." His pause was filled with meaning, and Archie's features seemed set in a mask of self-control. "Hubris? Gloating? Or the need to iron-clad in their minds a very specific idea of the money's origins? No matter. Your patience and single-mindedness of purpose were remarkable.

"However, Tom Savage was already known to another party peripheral to this affair – the stationmaster here in Chelmsford who was pressured to alibi Jerrod Cranleigh. It was, after all, Mr. Savage who delivered his payoffs over the following year." The small man abruptly seemed like a caged animal, primed for flight. The whites of his eyes showed and he panted softly.

"But, you might point out, Horace Cranleigh and Saul Olds were seen conspiring in a pub in Harpenden two nights before the theft. Indeed they were, as the court was made keenly aware, by the testimony of the late Miss Portman. But when parish and county records are consulted, we find her brother is married to the sister of Horace and Jerrod. They practically kept it in the family, sending a trusted member, rather than inviting a loose end by running the risk of recruiting a stranger, to make that vital connection and point the court in the direction desired.

"And it was vital that the court believe Horace behind the theft. He had accepted the loss of his twenties as the price of rebuilding the fortunes of which his family had been deprived. Such testimony, in parallel with Mr. Mundy's statement of alibi, ensured that no one was even looking at Jerrod Cranleigh after that point. When the payout started to arrive from Mr. Harrington, he was in a position to return the family to the standard to which they used to be accustomed. When Horace was released, he came home to a country estate and the respect of his kin – all of whom, incidentally, it could be argued, are accessories to the theft of the Harrington diamonds."

Two constables had appeared by the doors of the hall and advanced at Inspector Robeson's nod. They stayed back far enough not to intrude, but their presence forestalled any attempt to leave.

Holmes spread his hands with a steely smile. "There we are. Inspector Robeson has my report, and the evidence, such as it is. A jury may or may not find these arguments compelling, and the evidence is broadly circumstantial. But after all, so was that on which the original conviction was based." He turned to the silent police officer. "You have the floor, Inspector."

Robeson rose with ponderous dignity and beckoned the constables. "Mr. Jerrod Cranleigh, Mr. Archibald Harrington, Mr. Thomas Savage, I'm placing you all under arrest on suspicion of your various roles in the theft of the Harrington diamonds, twelve years ago."

The constables closed up, with expressions that brooked no nonsense, and Harrington was the only one to speak. "Mr. Cranleigh and I can both afford the finest lawyers in the land, Mr. Holmes. And should The Crown not succeed in making your case, you may expect a countersuit for slander."

The morning sun was warm on our faces when we walked out into Tindal Square. Hopkins suggested lunch, his treat.

"I would have paid money to see that, Mr. Holmes," Lestrade said with pleasure. "That was vintage Sherlock Holmes! It's just a pity so many years have elapsed that no more secure a connection could be made."

"The price of my own carelessness at the time, Lestrade. I am happily retired, but it does smart, professionally, to know those of equal or greater guilt wriggled off the hook. Horace Cranleigh would likely have received a much lighter sentence, had it been known he was *not* the ringleader, while Mr. Harrington would have likely received a heavy one for betraying his family and social stratum."

"No matter," Lestrade returned with a small shrug. "Unlike your lofty mental gymnastics, Mr. Holmes, this is the kind of territory where most detectives live. My life, and Stanley's, have certainly been spent there. We do our very best, then leave it up to the courts. That's all we can do. We'll hear what they make of it in due course."

Holmes turned to the mousy priest who walked with us, his umbrella raised against the sun. "Father Brown, you have my inestimable thanks for spotting the connection. I would doubtless have wasted time and precious thought exhausting other options before arriving at that which was, ultimately, the most logical conclusion."

"My pleasure, Mr. Holmes. I'm glad this matter could be concluded satisfactorily. *Are* you in any jeopardy from that threat of legal action?"

"I doubt it. That was the predictable defiance of the offender discovered, and such rarely amounts to more than bluster."

"To lunch?" Hopkins suggested, with a gesture along the way. We ambled forth, agreeing to remain in touch, for we all had a vested interest in the outcome of the case.

For myself, I was simply delighted to have had the chance to accompany Holmes on one more case – to relive something of the spirit, the vibrancy, of those long-ago days when the name of Sherlock Holmes made villains tremble.

Post Scriptum

I had not given the case thought in a long while when I happened upon a most satisfactory reminder. In the glorious July of 1911, Mrs. Watson and I holidayed on the Sussex coast with Holmes, and as we took breakfast in his airy kitchen, I turned the page of his London newspaper to find a whole column devoted to the reopening of the Harrington diamonds affair.

According to the journalist, the sharp lawyer, Mr. Peter Culver, had argued for the defence, maintaining that the circumstantial nature of the evidence was preposterous and Holmes must be quite senile to occupy a court's time with such balderdash. However, the Chelmsford Crown Court found Holmes's logic compelling, and Harrington, Cranleigh, and Savage received ten, eight and three years respectively. Sir Basil Harrington was reportedly considering a punitive damages case against both his son's estate and the Cranleigh family, and word was that the knight's heir was disinherited in total.

A pull at the bell, and a telegram envelope came through the slot. Holmes thumbed it up, tore it open and read for a moment, then gave a bark of satisfied laughter:

Congratulations Holmes and Brown STOP Case closed STOP Hopkins STOP.

I raised my teacup, and my dear lady joined in the toast. "Here's to the successful conclusion of Sherlock Holmes's last case!" I was, of course, joking.

"Last?" he replied with the look of a laugh kept under control. "Beekeeping may occupy my days now, but let's not be hasty!"

257

The Keepers of Secrets
by Naching T. Kassa

December of 1910 was a momentous month for me. Not only did I see Holmes's case involving Dr. Leon Sterndale published, but I was also involved in one of the most interesting affairs in our long association – a case which would challenge not only his faculties but those of a certain humble priest.

Holmes had telephoned with an invitation to visit his cottage in Sussex, and as my wife had gone away to visit relatives, I happily agreed. I took the train and, by evening, had reached his front door. He, himself, greeted my knock.

"Good afternoon, old fellow," said he. "Come out of the cold and sit by the fire. You'll find my other guest has already taken your usual chair. You'll have to take mine."

"Other guest?"

Holmes nodded toward the umbrella stand near the door, where a rather bedraggled specimen had been placed. I knew it at once.

"Father Brown!" I said as I entered the sitting room. The bespectacled priest rose from his chair and shook my hand.

"It is good to see you, Doctor," he said, blinking. A smile brightened his rotund face.

"Whatever brings you here?" I asked.

"I was invited to dine at the manor house of Sir Roger Alcott and thought I might pay my respects to Holmes. It seems I could have waited, for we have been invited to the same affair."

"Your company is most welcome," Holmes said. "I haven't had news from London for some time. Watson's visits have been few since the addition of his new patient. A rather illustrious gentleman, all told."

"How on earth did you deduce that?" I cried.

"The stub of the first-class ticket, which protrudes from the pocket of your coat. Just two months ago, you lamented the fact that you couldn't travel in such a manner. Your suit is new and of a fashionable cut. It's obvious your fortunes have improved since last we met."

"That is quite true," I replied. "But how did you know my patient is a man?"

258

"The stick pin," Father Brown murmured. He stared at me, his face somewhat blank and a trifle unnerving. "A ruby isn't the sort of thing a lady would bestow upon her doctor. And you were never one to purchase such for yourself. The fact that you wear it proudly proclaims it as a gift."

"The Duke of Winchester is a great admirer of rubies," Holmes added.

"I thought it might be he," the little priest said. "His physical condition seems to have improved of late. Though his spiritual one leaves something to be desired."

I looked from one man to the other. The shock must've been apparent upon my face, for Holmes threw back his head and laughed.

"Come now, Watson, take your seat before the fire. Sir Roger Alcott, our host, has encouraged me to bring a guest of my own to this dinner. I trust you will accompany us?"

"I should be delighted. Though, I must say, I have never heard of Sir Roger before this moment."

"I have met him but once. He invited me to tea at the manor last year." Holmes turned to the priest. "Do you know him, Father Brown?"

"I know of him, but I have never met the man. To be frank, I was surprised by his invitation."

"Perhaps he needs spiritual guidance," I suggested.

"It may be. Otherwise, I will make a poor companion for conversation."

"I suppose we shall know soon enough," Holmes said. "Sir Roger has offered to send a motorcar, and I have accepted. Come, we've just enough time to sample some of this excellent claret before venturing into the chill country air."

We arrived at the large manor house of Sir Roger at the stroke of seven and were led to the drawing room by his butler, a dour man that Holmes called Travers. Father Brown followed, his gaze on the many paintings which adorned the walls. He muttered something, and I dropped back so that I might hear him better.

"It seems our host enjoys the exploits of Teutonic Knights," he said, gesturing to the canvases. "Many of these depict the Order of Brothers of the German House of Saint Mary in Jerusalem. They were known for their protection of pilgrims on the road to the Holy Land. The armor standing there was worn by such knights."

"It appears you shall have a subject to discuss after all."

The little priest smiled, and we continued on.

Our host's affection for all things knightly became more apparent once we entered the drawing room. Tapestries, portraying the story of King Arthur, hung from the northern wall, while various swords, including a handsome pair of rapiers, decorated two of the others. A portrait of a beautiful woman hung above the fireplace.

"Guinevere?" I posited to Holmes and the priest.

Father Brown shook his head. "Rebecca, Isaac of York's daughter. A woman known for her devotion and faith."

"Ah," I said with a nod. "I know the story. It is *Ivanhoe.*"

Holmes stared at me, and I quickly elucidated.

"*Ivanhoe* is a work of fiction by Sir Walter Scott. It's an adventure story, one of knights, and kings, and Robin Hood. The story centers around Ivanhoe, a knight, who must act as champion to Rebecca of York, a woman of the Jewish faith. She has been taken captive by a member of the Knights Templar, a man desperately in love with her. When she is accused of witchcraft by the Templars, this man hopes to be her champion. Instead, he is forced to fight Ivanhoe. The knight's name escapes me at the moment. I believe it is something French."

A troubled expression replaced the blank one which Father Brown usually wore. "The story is a sad one, where Rebecca is concerned. She is in love with Ivanhoe, but because of her faith and his love of another, she cannot marry him." He shook his head. "I fear there is some similarity here. And that we have been brought to this manor for a dark purpose."

Holmes glanced up sharply. I saw the eager gleam in his eyes, but before I could speak, our host had joined us.

Sir Roger Alcott was a tall, handsome fellow, much like the knights he so admired. Teutonic in feature, with his blonde mane and mustache, he stood just an inch over Holmes and towered over Father Brown. He gazed at us with piercing blue eyes and his grip wasn't unlike iron when he shook my hand.

"I am pleased you could come. And I pray you will forgive me. Dinner will not begin until eight when my other guests arrive." He paused, then said, "I am in dire need of your services, gentlemen. There has been a murder, and only you two can solve it."

"You must realize," Holmes said. "I have been retired for some time. I no longer accept cases."

"Ah, but this is no mere murder, sir. It is a puzzle, yet to be solved. And, your deductive skills are legendary, Mr. Holmes. Pray, hear me out before you decide."

Holmes nodded. "Very well."

"And you, Father Brown," Sir Roger said, turning. "I have it on good authority that your mind is sharper than most and that your reasoning is tempered by intuition. I have, of course, spoken with your friend, Flambeau."

The little priest said nothing, but the flush which rose in his cheek spoke of his embarrassment. "You haven't called the police?" he asked.

"The police were called and justice, I'm afraid, didn't prevail. The murder I speak of occurred more than eight years ago, in this very house."

"Then there has already been a trial," Holmes said.

"There has. And an innocent man was sent to the gallows. A witness recanted his testimony after the deed was done."

"The murder of which you speak. Was it of a woman?"

"She was more than a simple woman. She was Rebecca Malkin, the American adventuress."

Holmes nodded. "Your wife."

Sir Roger's eyes widened, and his face grew pale. For a moment, I thought the brave knight might stumble and fall upon the carpet. "How could you know that?"

"The painting above the fireplace. She wears a smaller, daintier version of your own ring upon her left index finger."

Sir Roger glanced down at the ring upon his left hand, then covered it with his right. "She was my wife. We kept the marriage a secret."

"For the sake of your family?" Father Brown said gently. "Or hers?"

"For mine. She was an orphan, raised by an aunt in New York. She wasn't of my faith, and I would have been excommunicated. My father would have disowned me. I loved her and would have done anything for her, but she wouldn't allow it. She knew I loved my church. If only we'd had more time. Perhaps a solution might have presented itself."

"The marriage was secret. And yet, you exchanged rings?" Father Brown asked.

"I wanted to shower her with gifts, but she would have none of it. It was the only token of love she would allow me and the only worldly thing she valued."

"I have read of the circumstances involving the lady," Holmes said. "Unfortunately, the local constabulary believed the case a simple one and didn't invite me to investigate."

"If only they had. Poor Tom Forrest wouldn't have hanged."

"I know nothing of the case," Father Brown said softly. "Would you mind very much repeating the facts?"

"Of course," Sir Roger replied. "My wife had been invited to dine here, as we lived apart, and, during dinner, she became ill. She retired to a room and remained at the house during the night."

"Was a doctor called?" Father Brown asked.

Sir Roger's face colored at the question. "She wasn't really ill. She often feigned illness to stay under the same roof as me. I left her in her room at midnight. When I visited her the following morning, she didn't answer her door, and I didn't find her inside. I went looking for her and found her . . . ." Again, great emotion overcame him, and he was forced to compose himself. "I found her in the stables, dressed in her riding clothes. She had been strangled.

"I remember little of the investigation, so aggrieved was I. A constable spoke with me and an inspector from London – I believe his name was Gregson – but I was oblivious to what they said. My world had ended.

"I woke from my stupor when Tom Forrest was placed under arrest. He had been my stable lad before the South African War and had returned a rather broken man that July. I had taken pity on the poor fellow and had given him employment. I was horrified when I learned a witness, another man in my employ, had followed him into the stables and found him bent over the body of my dear wife, his hands at her throat.

"I am ashamed to say it, gentlemen, but a thirst for vengeance overcame me. If Tom Forrest had been within my reach, I would've killed him on the spot. It mattered little that Frank Mudwillow, witness to the murder, was a spiteful man. Nor was it relevant that he bore Tom an intense and villainous grudge. The constabulary said it was so, and Frank said it was so. I believed them utterly. On the day of Tom's hanging, I gave a party and drowned myself in my cups, cursing the day the traitorous murderer had been born."

These words seemed to drain the life from Sir Roger. He fell into a nearby chair and covered his eyes with one hand.

"And then, the worst of it came to light. The witness, having grown of an advanced age and having long since left my service, lay dying in his hovel. Terrified of what lay ahead, he confessed all. He had borne false witness against Tom. He had never seen the murder, had never even seen my wife that day. He had simply feared that Tom, having returned after so long an absence, would take his place.

"Can you imagine my remorse, gentlemen? No, I'll wager you cannot. Not only had the man who murdered my Rebecca gone free, he had left an innocent to die in his place! I knew I must find the killer, even if it meant losing my fortune, my life, and my very soul."

Father Brown stood frozen at these words, as though they had turned him to stone. Holmes, on the other hand, seemed to quiver with energy. The two men struck me as such opposites. I couldn't possibly imagine them working together to solve this particular crime. But such had happened before.

"For weeks," Sir Roger said, "I have wracked my brain and memory to think of something – *Anything!* – which might bring the murderer to light. Rebecca's bedroom has been closed these eight years. I couldn't bring myself to enter it, nor to have a thing in it touched. Only last week did I find the courage to go in and search for a sign which might guide me to the one who killed her."

"You have found a clue," Holmes said.

Sir Roger rose to his feet with renewed vigor. "I found this," he said, reaching into the pocket of his coat and withdrawing his pocketbook. Upon opening it, he displayed a folded sheet of paper, one which showed signs of crumpling. "It was in the waste basket."

Holmes took the sheet and spread it out upon the table. A note, written in large, neat letters, read: "*Must speak with you. Come to the chapel at seven.*" It was unsigned.

"The chapel?" I said.

"There is an old, ruined one about a mile west of the house," Sir Roger said.

"What time did you find the body of your wife?"

"It must've been half-past-seven."

"Was there any indication she had visited the chapel?"

"Indication?"

"Did you notice anything? Anything which might have led you to believe she had been there? A weed in the crease of her pantleg? Earth or mud on her boots?"

Sir Roger shook his head. "I could not say. I cannot remember if there was or not. No investigation was made after Frank Mudwillow came forward."

"The only evidence was the word of this man Mudwillow?" I said, somewhat taken aback. "There was nothing else?"

"My wife's bracelet and wedding ring were missing when I found her. Later, when Tom was arrested, the bracelet was found in his pocket. He claimed he had found it in the yard, but it was assumed he had taken it after killing her. The wedding ring was never found."

"A motive for the murder," Holmes said.

263

"Were there no other witnesses?" Father Brown asked. "Did anyone else see your wife alive?"

"No one."

Holmes paced the floor. "You have set us on a cold trail, Sir Roger, but there is some hope."

"You will take the case then?"

Holmes nodded. "Though I would appreciate any help you could give, Father Brown."

The little priest nodded as well.

"It is likely your wife kept her appointment," Holmes said, "and was killed at the chapel or upon her return. If we could find the author of the note, it might explain much. Do you recognize the handwriting?"

"I do, Mr. Holmes. It is in the hand of our parish priest, Father Michael Middleton. I brought the paper before him yesterday, and though he blanched with fear, he denied all knowledge of it. He implied it was a forgery."

"We are the keepers of secrets," Father Brown said blandly, "but we aren't permitted to share them. Was Father Michael present at the party?"

"He was. Though he left soon after dinner."

"Perhaps he passed the note to her before he took his leave," Holmes said. "Who else attended the party?"

"It was a small gathering. Jasper Croix and Dr. Horace Prescott, two of my old school chums, were the only others present. We were playing bridge, you see. Both men left after my wife went to her room."

"Were any of these men aware that you had married Miss Malkin?"

"We shared the secret with no one. My wife concealed her ring. I didn't wear my ring until . . . after she had passed."

"And who married you?" Father Brown asked.

"A clerk in London. Ours was a civil marriage."

"I should like to speak with Croix and Prescott," Holmes said. "And, perhaps, Father Brown would have a chat with Father Michael?"

Father Brown stared blankly at Holmes, as though he had heard only the last words my friend had spoken. He opened his mouth as if to speak, then clamped it shut and nodded.

"And so you shall," Sir Roger said. "I've invited all of them here for dinner. They should arrive in – " He consulted his watch. "Fifteen minutes."

After this exchange, our host took his leave that he might make the proper preparations for the coming dinner. He left us alone.

Silence pervaded as Holmes withdrew his cigarette case and set to smoking. Father Brown stared at the note upon the table. He cleared his throat and turned to us.

"Do you not find it strange," said he, "that our host should duplicate the dinner party he gave the night before his wife's death?"

"It is suggestive indeed," Holmes said, tossing a match into the fire. "It seems he suspects one of the guests."

"And he wishes us to discover which one."

"To what end?" I asked.

"Justice," Holmes replied.

Father Brown shook his head. "That may be the case, but I believe there is more to it. He still thirsts for vengeance."

The door opened then, and Travers reappeared.

"Father Michael Middleton," the butler intoned. A young man nearing thirty and dressed in a cassock, entered the room. Travers took his leave.

The priest looked from one to the other of us, his gaze lingering on Father Brown the longest.

"Are you Father Brown?" he asked, his tone traced with awe.

"I am," the little priest said.

"Sir Roger said you might come." He took the little priest by the hand. "I have so much to ask you." And with nary a word for Holmes or myself, he and Father Brown withdrew to a quiet corner of the room.

"I wondered how Sir Roger might induce him to come," Holmes said, snatching up the paper from the table. "It didn't seem he would be willing after having seen this crumpled note."

The door opened and Travers entered once more. This time he was accompanied by two men who he introduced as Jasper Croix and Dr. Horace Prescott.

Jasper Croix was tall, with a large ginger mustache. He wore the garb of a country squire and spoke in a booming voice. He greeted Holmes and me with a hearty handshake the moment he learned our names.

"Did you hear that, Horace?" he boomed. "We have Sherlock Holmes and his colleague, Dr. Watson, in our midst."

The mention of our names elicited a nervous glance from Father Michael. But Father Brown soon drew him back into conversation.

Dr. Horace Prescott was quite different from his companion. His expression was solemn and somewhat ascetic for a country doctor. He possessed an extensive knowledge of medicine, far more than most in his profession, and by the end of our conversation, I had seen him for the enlightened man he was. I told him he would make a fine surgeon in London.

"My work is here," he said with a modest smile. "London holds little for me. There, I am one among many. I was born and bred here. I have no wish to leave."

"Then the village is lucky to have you."

"Thank you, Doctor."

"This is indeed a momentous occasion," Croix said as he and Holmes joined us. "You should have brought your camera, Horace. I'll have you know, Dr. Watson, that Horace is one of the finest photographers I've ever had the pleasure to meet."

"It's only a hobby," Prescott said, shaking his head.

Father Michael approached then, and Croix shook him by the hand. The young priest winced when Croix released him.

"What is it, Father?" Croix asked.

"A cut," the young priest said a trifle sheepishly, displaying the plaster which covered the base of his thumb. "I thought I could make a better sandwich than my housekeeper. She has forbidden me from entering the kitchen for the foreseeable future."

"Dinner is served, gentlemen," Travers announced from the doorway.

We followed him down another hall and into a large mahogany-paneled room, one which could be counted among the most sumptuous I had ever seen. A large, ornate table stood at the center, set with golden goblets and gleaming silver. I found my place to the right of our host, along with Mr. Croix and Father Brown. Holmes, Dr. Prescott and Father Michael sat to his left.

The dinner was a delicious one, with roast pheasant as the main course. To my surprise, none of the conversation touched on Sir Roger's wife or the murder. Instead, it centered on country life and the weather.

Following a fine dessert and wine to match, Sir Roger suggested we retire to the drawing room for a cigar and glass of brandy. Father Michael begged off, saying he must return home.

"I should like to speak with you again," Father Brown said to the young priest. "Will you give me your address? Perhaps I could visit tomorrow before I take the train to London."

Father Michael smiled and quickly jotted down the address in his notebook. He tore out the page and handed it to Father Brown. "I look forward to your visit."

He shook hands with each of us, wincing a little when he reached Dr. Prescott, and then disappeared from the room.

"I will stay," Croix said. He had consumed more wine than the rest of us, and his already sonorous voice had gained volume with every sip. "I cannot pass a good brandy by."

Dr. Prescott grinned. It was the first time I had seen him do so. "I shall stay."

"Very good then."

Holmes dropped back beside Father Brown, who handed him the small sheet Father Michael had given him. He gave it a cursory glance, then tucked it in his pocket as we entered the drawing room.

Sir Roger charged our glasses with a brandy of superior quality, and we seated ourselves before the fire.

"To what shall we drink?" Sir Roger asked.

Croix lifted his glass to the portrait of the beautiful woman above the fireplace, and in a voice surprisingly subdued, said, "To Rebecca."

"Rebecca," we responded.

"Do you remember the day you met her, Croix?" Sir Roger said softly.

The ginger-haired fellow nodded, his cheeks ruddy with drink. "I'll never forget it. It was a day much like this one, a day of chilling sunshine over new snow. She smiled when she saw me and seemed genuinely interested in what I had to say. When she asked about my profession, I feared she might lose interest. Not many women actually understand electroplating, let alone ask questions about the process, but she did. I suppose I fell in love with her then."

He paused and with a soft laugh said, "But who among us did not? I'll warrant that even Father Michael might have spared her a thought. A chaste one, of course."

Sir Roger nodded.

"Prescott knew her first. He met her at Oxford. Why she attended school when she couldn't earn a degree, I'll never know. But she was like that. Proud and intelligent. I don't believe anyone could force her to do something she didn't wish to do."

"It's true," the doctor said, toying with a link in his watch chain. "Her character was beyond reproach. If only . . . ." he trailed off.

"A shame," Croix said, and took another sip of brandy.

"Come now," Sir Roger said, affecting a smile. "She wouldn't wish us to speak of her so. We are here, albeit a trifle late, to celebrate her life, not mourn her death."

A knock sounded upon the door and Travers appeared in the doorway, pale and drawn. He glanced at Sir Roger and then at Dr. Prescott. "I apologize for interrupting you, sir," he said. "But the presence of Dr. Prescott is needed at once. Father Michael has taken ill. He . . . he cannot seem to catch his breath."

I rose from my seat and hurried after Dr. Prescott, who had rushed from his. Travers and Sir Roger led us to the foyer, where Father Michael lay gasping upon the floor. I was dimly aware of Holmes behind me and the presence of Father Brown, who knelt on the other side of the young priest.

"He didn't seem quite right when he wished me goodnight," Travers said. "And then, quite suddenly, he collapsed."

"*Bwaa!*" the young priest moaned.

Father Brown looked to Dr. Prescott, who shook his head. The little priest began the Last Rites.

Father Michael reached up and took hold of Father Brown's cassock, clutching at it with his fingers. "*Bwaa gil bear . . . murdered . . . .*"

A seizure followed these words and the poor priest lapsed into unconsciousness. Within moments, he had passed from the earth.

"Dear God," Sir Roger whispered. "What has happened?"

"I don't understand it," Dr. Prescott said. "I just don't understand it."

I glanced up at Holmes, who gave an almost imperceptible shake of the head.

Dr. Prescott rose to his feet. "Shall I make arrangements, Sir Roger?"

The knight gave a curt nod. "The telephone is in the hall."

Dr. Prescott hurried off.

Holmes leapt into action the minute the doctor had gone. He examined Father Michael's hand, paying close attention to the plaster around the thumb.

"What do you make of this, Watson?" he asked.

I peered at the spot he indicated. It appeared as though something had pierced a small hole in the plaster. I removed it, and upon inspecting the wound beneath, nodded.

"It is the point of introduction. There is no doubt of it."

"What are you saying?" the knight asked.

"This is nothing short of murder, Sir Roger," Holmes replied. "Father Michael was poisoned."

"The disorientation, his struggle to breathe, and the lapse into unconsciousness are all symptoms of sodium cyanide poisoning," I added. "There is a fresh pinprick – just here – in his wound. The poison was introduced here."

"And it appears you have supplied the weapon," Father Brown said, staring at my lapel with his strangely blank expression. I glanced down and found that my ruby stickpin had gone missing.

"Only one man was missing when we came to Father Michael's aid," Father Brown continued.

"Croix!" I cried.

"Come," Holmes said. "We must make haste."

Even in middle age, Holmes still showed the speed of an athlete. He sprinted toward the hall which led to the drawing room, leaving all but Sir Roger behind.

Croix's shout sounded from the room just as Father Brown and I reached it. What we beheld, as we entered, chilled my blood.

Croix and Dr. Prescott were locked together in what seemed to be a struggle to the death, and Holmes was attempting to insert himself between them as they wrestled. All three of them seemed to be clutching at something.

It was my stickpin.

I rushed to Holmes's aid, throwing myself against Croix and separating him from Holmes and Prescott. We fell to the carpet as Holmes wrenched the pin from the doctor's hand.

"Water and soap," Holmes commanded, mastering the situation as only he could. "And be quick about it!"

I struggled to my feet as Travers hurried from the room. I followed him to the kitchen, where basins of water and cakes of soap were provided. We took them back to the drawing room, where the men quickly washed their hands.

I examined each man, beginning with Holmes, and observed no signs of wounding or rashes. It seemed the danger had passed.

"He tried to kill me," Croix said, a trifle sulkily. His gaze smoldered as he stared at Prescott. "Due to my rather delicate condition, I fell asleep on the settee. When I awoke, you were hovering over me – with *that*!" He pointed to my stickpin, which Holmes had set upon a folded handkerchief and laid upon the table.

"You tried to kill yourself!" Prescott retorted. "I merely stopped you."

"The deception is at an end," Holmes said, silencing them both. "Father Michael has named his killer."

Both men stared at Holmes with wide eyes.

"Father Michael mentioned no one," Prescott said.

"On the contrary," Father Brown spoke up. "We may have thought the words simple gibberish from a disoriented and dying man, but they still made sense. And, God rest him, even in death, he didn't betray the trust he was given, nor the secret of the confession made to him. He gave us a clue as to the name of the man who poisoned him – the same man who used the father's good name to entice a virtuous woman to her death."

Sir Roger, who had remained downcast since our return to the room, suddenly raised his head. He stared at the two men, his gaze feverish.

"He named Bois Guilbert," Holmes said.

The strange words Father Michael had spoken did make sense, and I cursed myself a dunderhead for not understanding them sooner. I glanced up at the portrait above the fireplace.

"Bois Guilbert," I said. "The Knight Templar who coveted Rebecca of York."

"No, Prescott!" Holmes cried, leaping upon the doctor. He pulled the man's hand from the pocket of his coat and shook the object he had withdrawn from his fingers. A packet fell to the floor.

"Do not touch it!" Holmes warned. "It is undoubtedly sodium cyanide."

Prescott fell back on the settee, his face ashen.

Holmes withdrew the two sheets from his pocket and held them before Prescott. "The crumpled sheet is the one you convinced Father Michael to pass to Miss Rebecca Malkin, forging it in his hand. She came to meet him, thinking he had somehow learned of her marriage to Sir Roger. It is a passable forgery, but by no means identical. I compared the address he gave Father Brown to this one and noticed ten differences between the two notes.

"When she came to the chapel and found you there, you begged her to marry you. She refused and when you persisted, she revealed the fact that she was already married. In a fit of rage, you strangled her. You returned her body to the stables, knowing that her death couldn't be tied to you, and left her there.

"It is no secret that you loved her," Holmes said. "You knew her first, long before Croix or even Sir Roger. In your own twisted way, you believed you had claim to her. That's why you took the wedding ring from off her hand. Why you had it refitted and molded into a link for your watch chain. You are wearing it even now."

Dr. Prescott glanced down at the link. "I didn't believe her when she said she'd married Sir Roger. Then she showed me the ring – *his* ring – and a red mist rose before my eyes. I did not mean to kill her. Were I in my right mind, I never would have. I swear it."

"And yet, you allowed another man to die in your stead," replied Father Brown. "Was the guilt too much? When Tom Forrest was blamed and hung for your misdeeds, did it become too much to bear? Is that why you confessed your sins to Father Michael?"

"How could you know this?" Prescott cried hoarsely.

"Father Michael asked for my guidance. He did not mention you or what you had done by name. But his questions raised . . . concerns."

"You feared Father Michael might betray your secret," Holmes said, "and so you plotted to kill him."

"Not just that," Prescott retorted. "He blackmailed me."

"I find that hard to believe," Father Brown muttered.

"He called it *penance*, but it was blackmail all the same. He said I must atone for my sin, and that Tom had died for me just as Christ had died for the world. He forced me to perform my duties for a lower fee, giving me but a pittance to live upon. I was his slave, forever at his beck and call, and when I tried to defy him, he threatened to reveal my crimes to the bishop."

"Last month, a friend offered to sell me his London practice and Father Michael would not allow it. He said I must stay in the village and serve the people that I had wronged. After eight years – *Eight long years!* – I could take no more. My hobby of photography put the sodium cyanide within my grasp, and I bided my time, waiting for just the right moment."

"Which came when you noticed the plaster upon Father Michael's thumb," Holmes said. "Or was it when he winced at the shaking of Croix's hand? The former? I thought as much. And then, a quick brush by Watson, relieving him of his stickpin, adding thievery to the crime of murder. You dipped the pin and concealed it in your hand when you shook Father Michael's. You didn't fear capture. You knew, as a doctor, you would be called to his side first. If he wasn't far gone, you would have finished him.

"Your plan proved unnecessary, and so you moved on to the next. One man had already died in your stead. Why not blame another? Croix was the logical choice. His profession in electroplating gave him access to sodium cyanide, and he was a

271

known admirer of Miss Malkin. You would have murdered him as he slept. Only he awoke and spoiled your plan."

Sir Roger shook his head as though in disbelief. "You did all of this to cover the death of my beloved?"

"It was like quicksand," Prescott whispered. "I just couldn't seem to pull myself free of it."

Sir Roger turned. He crossed the room, reached for the rapiers on the wall, and pulled them down.

"You cannot do this!" Father Brown cried, stepping before him. "I feared this might be your aim – that the failure of British justice might force you to consider other means of dealing with the man who killed your wife. You have brought us here to name him guilty so you might kill him!"

Sir Roger hefted the blade. "It isn't quite that simple, Father, but you are correct. I do seek other means. I seek God's justice and offer Prescott trial by combat. If he defeats me, he shall go free. If I defeat him, then he will die."

"And you expect us to stand by and watch?"

"You believe in redemption, don't you, Father? What of Flambeau and the life he led before you entered it? Do you not believe the same for Prescott? And you, Mr. Holmes – I read Dr. Watson's story concerning the Cornish Horror. You allowed Dr. Leon Sterndale to leave for Africa after his fiancée had been murdered by her treacherous brother. Can you not extend the same courtesy to me? British justice has already caused a tragedy. I seek only to right that wrong."

"You seek revenge," Holmes replied. "Not justice." He too stepped before Sir Roger. "And if you intend to take his life, you will have to face me for it."

"You would be his champion?"

Holmes nodded. "His trial must be a fair one."

"And there is nothing fair about this!" Father Brown said softly. "He has already ruined himself. Must you allow him to ruin you too? I did not know your wife, but she must've been a lady of great courage, even until the end. She cared a great deal about your soul. To have it stained with blood . . . this is the last thing she would want for you."

The knight faltered, his face a mirror to the emotions which roiled within him. He glanced up at the portrait, threw down the blades, and crossed to Prescott. I thought he might strike the man, but instead, he held out his hand, palm up.

"I shall not allow you to defile all that she held dear. The ring. Give it to me."

Prescott, who had seemed the very picture of remorse, scowled. He fumbled at the chain, broke off a piece, and handed it to Sir Roger.

Holmes clapped a hand upon the knight's shoulder. "I will do all I can to see justice – *true* justice – done," he said. "You have my word."

Father Brown leaned in toward me and whispered, "Your friend is a great man."

"I believe he would say the same of you. What you said to Sir Roger – it wasn't just kind. It was clever too."

The little priest smiled. "I'm just relieved, really. It seems Sir Roger and I found something to speak of, after all."

A Meeting at the Café Lyons

by David Marcum

"I'm getting too old for this," the man thought to himself, leaning back in his chair and stretching his long legs before him, aware that he was being watched, and carefully staying in character as he'd learned so long ago when, as a young man, he'd trod the boards for a year or so. He'd learned that even when he wasn't stage front, reciting his part, he was still expected to *be* the character, behaving as that character would, in every motion or pause, every turn or glance or scratching of his nose.

He really *wasn't* too old for this, and he mentally shook his head at the use of the cliché, even if it was only in the privacy of his own thoughts. Just a few weeks shy of his fifty-ninth birthday, he still felt that he was in his prime. His health was better than that of many others his own age, despite all the abuses he'd heaped upon himself as a younger man. He was very glad that he'd finally understood that his dark moods and restlessness could be distracted and eventually defeated by turning his mind in different directions – for if there were no problems to distract him along one line, he could do research down another, keeping himself occupied until the emptiness inside closed back up.

The café wasn't too crowded, as would be expected on a rainy Sunday night. The temperature was dropping, but he didn't think it would get cold enough to snow. Rather, the night would be miserable with that peculiar seaside dampness that slid under the collar and chilled the skin, and yet having the peculiar feeling that one's clothing was soaked with cold perspiration. In defense against it, he took a sip of whisky – *whiskey*, that is, he thought, smiling inward at the difference between the Scottish and Irish spellings of the word. After all, he was Irish – or had been for nearly a year now – and such little matters of pride and identity should now come natural. But they didn't, and it worried him, because he couldn't afford to slip. Not now that things were finally starting to get interesting. And dangerous.

"I really am getting too old for this," he thought to himself.

The patrons were what one would expect for that part of the city. He'd been to Liverpool many times before, but he'd never cared for it. He'd visited the rich houses, and the government buildings, and the port, but he'd never been here, Toxteth, just a couple-thousand feet east of the Royal Albert Docks. In truth, he'd never heard this place mentioned before until he was directed here to introduce himself to someone. He'd made his way to the Café Lyons, not far from the small boarding house in Mathew Street where he'd stayed since his arrival the previous night, directed by the little Irish widow, Mrs. O'Healy, who owned the place.

She'd been anxious for news from America, somehow assuming that he would have certainly encountered at least one of her cousins who had emigrated there long-ago. Using tricks he'd learned long before from exposing fraudulent mediums – listening to her questions, seeing her reactions to his answers, and adjusting his next comment accordingly – had helped him to construct a series of vague-enough responses that she was pleased with what he told her, though thoroughly and completely fabricated, and anything that seemed a bit off in his answers was simply attributed to the fact that he was an Irish-American – or so he claimed – and she would expect such small differences from the statements of a true Irishman.

He shifted in his chair and wondered how long he'd need to wait before being able to converse with the man he'd come here to meet. He found that he was playing with his beard, even though he hadn't been aware of doing so, and, while he didn't abruptly stop, he frowned inwardly at himself. He hated the thing – it looked like a goat's tail on his otherwise clean-shaven face – but he'd begun growing it a full year before, in late 1911, on the very day that the Prime Minister had personally asked that he undertake this ill-defined but important mission.

The beard was a useful thing, a distraction on his lean face that helped prevent the need for more elaborate disguises, but he hated it nonetheless. Yet he realized that he was becoming a little too accustomed to it. Common sense told him that was a good thing – that he was sinking deeper into the safety of his role – but he didn't want to be too deep. After all, one day the beard would come off and he would return to his real life, and he didn't want to spend the next year after that reaching up to stroke his bare chin.

He tried to remember if he'd become someone else so deeply the last time he'd tried this, from 1891 to 1894, but he knew that he hadn't. Not really. He'd played so many roles during those three desperate years that when he'd returned to London in April of '94, settling back into his real life had been no worse than taking a long long-overdue bath to wash off too much accumulated grime.

There was some sort of commotion rising in the back room, whose plain closed door was straight across the café from where he sat, as if he were on the front row of a play as the performance begins. He heard a woman's strident tones and, even though the words were unknowable, he knew that someone on the other side of the door was catching hell. He suspected that it was the man he was here to see – a man named Alois.

He'd followed a long trail over the past year to this, the Café Lyons, in order to somehow convince Alois to introduce him to the German spy master. He'd started his pilgrimage in Chicago, graduated from an Irish secret society in Buffalo, and then crossed an ocean to give serious trouble to the constabulary at Skibbereen – all while making occasional hurried visits back to London to strategize with his brother, and then to Sussex in order to make appearances as himself before speedily returning to this, his other identity. It had taken a great deal of effort, and a bit of the luck that he'd always been able to generate for himself, to create a completely new character and ease him into an existing society so that, just months after his initial appearance, it was hard to remember when he wasn't there.

When the Prime Minister had come to his Sussex home a year earlier to personally request his help, he'd agreed immediately, but it had taken a few more days to figure out exactly how he wanted to do it. There was a war coming, the Prime Minister had said, as if he were relating startling news that hadn't been considered before, which was ludicrous. The signs had been there since before the century's turn, and he and his brother, along with his best friend, had been working for years to prepare for, and also to delay, the inevitable for as long as possible. This had been done both in England and on the Continent, with a move here, a countermove there, the danger always ever-escalating. But now he was in much deeper than he'd ever anticipated, eleven months into a mission that could conceivably go on for many more years. As important as it was to delay the war, and get Britain on the best footing possible, he hoped that it wouldn't be for that long. "Christ," he muttered aloud to himself, his Irish-American accent flawless. He dropped his hand from his goat-tail beard, retrieved his *whiskey* (and not *whisky*) and took a sip as the plain door slammed open.

First out was Alois, the man he was here to meet. Alois was a German who had moved to England two or three years earlier, first settling in London, and then relocating to Liverpool. There was an angry frown on his pinched dark face. He was about thirty, had black hair – or so it appeared in the dim light of the café – oily-looking and brushed straight back, and a dark mustache. His lower lip was pulled up tight and thrust forward in what one might think was irritation, But he had also looked that way a few minutes earlier when he'd walked over to take the order for whiskey and a bowl of stew.

The plain door, which had drifted shut, opened again to reveal a dark-haired young woman of just twenty or so. It was to be assumed that she had been responsible for the rather shrill voice of a moment before. Her eyes went to Alois, who pointedly ignored her. Instead, he went to the small window leading back to the kitchen, where a couple of plates sat ready for delivery. He picked them up and carried them quickly – the long way around to avoid the woman – to a table along the back wall, near the plain door, where he set them before a fat old man and his lady before pausing to converse with them for a moment.

The woman must have already been in the back room, because when the *faux* Irish-American had arrived a few minutes earlier, there had been no sign of her. Instead, he'd found his seat, placed his order with Alois, and within minutes received his food and drink. Then, seeing that everyone was taken care of for the moment, Alois had vanished through the plain door. It was only a minute or two later that the woman's voice had been raised, apparently causing Alois to flee back to his employment and responsibilities while the woman followed, now watching him plaintively from the doorway.

The stew was good enough, and at least hot, and a couple more spoonfuls had been taken aboard when the plain door was pushed wider and another figure moved past the woman. He was a dark-haired fellow, his rather long hair parted on the right, and combed over his rather high forehead. He appeared to be around twenty-two, and he somewhat resembled Alois, although a bit shorter and heavier. His clothes were shabby, and his shirt, underneath his limp thin coat, had several colorful daubs, as if he had been painting – and not the walls of a room. No, the colors were more the shades one would find in amateur watercolors. A bit of closer observation showed that the backs of his fingers and knuckles had the same matching shades. Yes, definitely a painter, probably an amateur. There was something about his expression, however, already quite bitter for one so young, that indicated he would never be a true artist. He wouldn't have the soul for it. The *faux* Irish-American smiled to himself – That sounded like a description that his best friend might make, whereupon he would snap back to "Cut the poetry!"

Curiously, the younger man, who had been looking toward Alois, suddenly cut his eyes across the room, focusing with a dead contempt on the Irish-American, as if he'd heard his judgmental thoughts and was angered by them. It was unnerving, jarring – like looking into a dark hole in the ground that has suddenly opened at one's feet, the cold breath of the deep earth and an accidental fall to terrifying death avoided by mere inches – but no outward response was given, other than to set down the spoon and take a sip of whiskey. And then the younger man looked away.

For just then, the woman made a small surprised jump and a tiny noise, and then turned to look behind her as yet one more person came through the plain door.

Alois, the younger man, and the woman, were all strangers. But not so the next to emerge from that back room. A familiar face – and one so unexpected in this grim place, and just at this moment, that the whiskey caused a coughing fit as it went down the wrong way. It burned his throat while tears occluded his view of the newcomer.

The man was short – shorter than both the young man and the woman – but quite round. He had a round head as well, and he might have looked like a snowman if not for the black priest garb that adorned him. He carried a *cappello romano* in one hand, which when placed on his head out of doors would further ruin the snowman effect. In the other was a bundled black umbrella, never far from his grip. It had come in handy before on a number of occasions – and not just for protection from the rain.

The coughing caused by the whiskey's burn drew their attention, but Alois, the woman, and the younger man all looked right back at one another in some sort of *tableau*, a moment frozen in time that could go in any direction, any possibility. Then the woman threw back her shoulders and marched to the front door, throwing it open and stepping outside into the night. The younger man went to Alois and began to whisper harshly, his conversation punctuated with stabbing gestures. Meanwhile the priest, for that is what he was, glanced across the room and, seeing a subtle welcoming gesture of a couple of slightly moved fingers, crossed over and sat down.

"Mr. . . . ah . . . ?" asked the priest, looking at the man who was much changed from the last time they had met.

278

"Altamont," said the *faux* Irish-American in a flat mid-Western accent, with just a tinge of Irish lilt. He finished wiping his eyes. "From Chicago. You might recall when we met a few years ago."

The priest nodded. "I do. We've both traveled a bit since then."

"Would you care for something to drink?" asked Altamont, pushing back the remains of his stew. It had been more than decent, but he'd never been one to over-eat, and enough was enough.

"No, thank you," said the priest. He looked Altamont up and down and said very softly, "You are much changed, sir. This is no short-term disguise. That beard – well, it's been cultivated for a while."

"A year," said Altamont slowly, his voice just as low. He glanced from side to side, making sure that there was no one nearby who could overhear them. He'd been careful to choose this seat when he arrived, with his back to the wall facing the doorways in much the same way that an American gunfighter or Italian mobsman seats himself when in a public place so as to see approaching enemies. He'd also checked the table when he'd arrived for one of Edison's carbon-button microphones – there wasn't one, and he and the priest could converse freely – although this café could not be considered a safe space. Alois might simply work here as a waiter, or it could be the front for the German spy network working actively in Liverpool.

"I thought you were in Sussex," said the priest. "Clearly you have a different agenda."

Altamont nodded. "A year ago," he said, his voice very low and very un-Irish, "the Government asked me to help root out the German spies in England. The war we've feared for so long is now considered to be inevitable – it's not *if*, but *when*. I think that they pictured me moving back to London and setting up a room in some great stone ministry building, slowly filling it with cabinets of reports and diagrams pinned to the walls, and clerks running in and out with dispatches. That's what my brother went ahead and established. But I decided that the best plan would be to come at the situation from an oblique angle – to worm my way into their organization with established credentials that they can respect, and then stay embedded for as long as needed, gathering names and intelligence while feeding them crumbs to gain their trust before giving them a big lie at the very end, to choke them at just the right moment."

"And how does that get you here, in a dingy Liverpool café on a cold and rainy December night?"

"I considered the best way to approach the problem, and quite frankly, I didn't want to pretend to be German for as long as this might take. Then the idea of being Irish occurred to me. Quite frankly, I've borrowed a good bit of my plan from a brave American I met back in '88 – John Douglas, as I knew him then. He had gone by several other names before that. His real name was Birdie Edwards – a Pinkerton man – who had infiltrated a hive of Pennsylvania murderers called 'The Scowrers' under the name of 'John McMurdo' – a pleasant and winning Irishman from Chicago. He lived among the thieves and murderers for months, participating in their rituals, joining the crimes that couldn't be avoided and preventing those that he could, and gathering evidence until the lot of them – or at least almost all of them– were caught up in one great bag and brought to trial."

The priest nodded. "I understand. You went to Chicago and took on this new identity – *Altamont* – and you've been progressing since then."

Altamont nodded. "And gaining credibility as I went. I'm trying to attract the attention of the German spymaster, and I learned that one of his top agents is here – the waiter." He cut his eyes toward Alois. "I've arranged a meeting – but it seems that you were already here to meet with him first." He took a sip of whiskey, keeping his eyes locked across the glass upon the little priest. "Considering the importance of my mission, might I ask why?"

The smaller man smiled. "You may, and perhaps something I say may help you. Nothing that I've heard is secret under the sacred seal of confession." He glanced toward the counter, where the younger man was now standing while Alois walked over to another of the tables, speaking with a man about something on his plate.

"A couple of years ago – in mid-1910, it was – I met Bridget – it was she whom you just saw leave. She is a good Catholic, but she'd had a falling out with her father over Alois. The two of them had met a few months earlier at a Dublin horse show and, in spite of the vociferous objections from her father, eloped to London, where they were married at the Marylebone Registry Office. Soon after, now feeling quite guilty for the events that led to her marriage, she came to the church where I was serving and spoke to me about it. As I said, this wasn't under the seal of confession, so sharing it with you is no violation.

"I counseled her and provided, I believe, some peace. Besides feeling guilt about her non-Catholic marriage, she was upset because her father disliked Alois so much – her husband is German, after all, and ten years older than Bridget. Soon after, the couple decided to move to Liverpool. I had no further thought of them until today, when I happened to be here on other business and ran into her. I'm on my way to Dublin with instructions regarding the planned response when the third Irish Home Rule Bill comes up in a few months. It's expected to fail, and it's uncertain what the reaction will be.

"I encountered Bridget in passing on the street, and she begged me to stop by their small apartment in Upper Stanhope Street. There, she told me what had happened in her life since her move to Liverpool, confiding that their marriage has been an unhappy one. She and her husband have a small son, born last year, and sadly Alois beats her when he drinks – which is far too often. She fears for their safety, and also that he will leave her and return to Germany, and she asked for me to speak with him – for all the good that it will do.

"Bridget asked a neighbor to watch her child, and then we set out for this café – a walk of about half-a-mile, I suppose. Not long after we left their apartment, we ran across Alois's half-brother, Adolf, who has been staying with them for the last month or so. He is . . . well, perhaps I should keep that opinion to myself. But I gather that his presence is a further strain on both their marriage and their finances, as he refuses to find a job, instead, practicing to be a painter – an artist. If his works lying around their apartment are any indication, he will not achieve his goal. They are dark things, and odd – the shadows, for instance, fall the wrong direction – *toward* the light source which causes them, instead of away.

"But in spite of the added strain that Adolf causes on the household, and the fact that the two brothers don't get along at all, Bridget felt that Adolf should come along with us and help to talk some sense into her husband – that he should ease his drinking, and perhaps start attending church. We arrived at the café and she wheedled Alois into the back room. Between you and me, I knew it was a wasted effort – and it was – because he didn't have the time to talk with us now, and his heart is that of a hardened sinner, but I was compelled to try. Miracles do happen, after all. I have seen them – and so have you, although you might not name them as such."

Altamont nodded. "With age comes wisdom – and I'll admit that includes a realization that man's understanding of the overall world – nay, the entire universe – around us, is really nothing at all. We understand the greater picture as well as an ant would if he were placed in the British Library and told to read and understand every

281

book. You're right, Father – I have seen miracles, and I would not gainsay them, although man's power of reason, limited as it is – "

His thought was to remain unuttered, however. The front door suddenly opened and a plump well-dressed man in his fifties entered, paused, glanced around the room, and then walked with confidence toward and then behind the counter. The younger brother, Adolf, had by then slipped over to one side, now standing once more at the plain door. Alois glanced toward the counter, and then continued his conversation with the customer.

The well-dressed man moved as if he owned the place – and in fact, it would soon be known that he did. This was Mr. Herbert Creighton Vines, a fellow of great importance in his own mind, and in actuality, he did have some little influence in that immediate neighborhood, owning several other cafés, a number of downtrodden lodging houses, and a couple of brothels that catered to the sea trade. It was a rough neighborhood, quite close to the Mersey, but he had influence there.

He went to the till, pulling it open to retrieve the day's takings – although from the viewpoint of Altamont and the priest, it simply seemed as if he were opening a drawer. But it wasn't simple for very long, as he slammed it shut and cried, "Alois! Today's money – *It is gone!*"

The room, which had carried a low buzz of conversation throughout the last few minutes, fell silent as Lyons immediately became the center of attention.

Alois left the customer to whom he'd been talking and hurried over to Vines, where they began to carry on a fierce but whispered conversation, with much gesturing – first upon Vines' part, and then the German's. At one point, Alois raised his voice, saying in a thick German accent, "But Mr. Vines – !" Meanwhile, Altamont tapped a finger upon the table, thinking quickly.

"The half-brother stole the money," he said quietly.

"How do you know?" asked the priest.

"While we've been talking, I watched him slip open the drawer and load his pockets. I was trying to decide what to do about it – to ignore it, or inform Alois to somehow win his favor – when the door opened and that man came in – presumably the owner."

The priest glanced from the rising tensions between Vines and the waiter and back to Altamont, whose expression had grown quite dark.

"What is the difficulty?" he asked. "Surely it will be quickly sorted."

"But in what way?" hissed Altamont. "Up to this minute, the variables of the situation were only somewhat known to me. Now, regardless of whether Alois is accused, or his half-brother Adolf is exposed as the true thief, the situation will be turned upside down – at least for a while, and what I know may not matter. I need an introduction from Alois to the next spy up the chain, and I don't know enough about him to know how being fired from this job might affect him."

Before the priest could reply, Altamont continued. "I must do something bold – but I'll need your help. Can you distract Adolf – talk with him while I speak to Alois and the owner? I very much doubt if he would step forward and confess what he's done, but you must keep him from doing so."

The priest smiled. "It's an ethical dilemma, and that's for sure: Convince a thief to hold his tongue and hold onto his guilt, versus the greater good – "

"I assure you that it's for the greater good."

The priest nodded. "I'll worry about Adolf's soul in a few minutes, after your task is complete. But for now, what are you planning?"

"I recall that Birdie Edwards gained the trust of his foes by confronting the authorities. I'll do the same."

And by now the authorities were present – in the form of a weary-looking constable who had been summoned by the café owner regarding the emptying of his cash drawer. Altamont looked at the priest and nodded. "It was good to see you again, my friend. I look forward to doing so again in the future."

"As they say across the Irish Sea," answered the priest, 'May the road rise to meet you.'"

They glanced toward the counter, where the owner was outlining for the policeman how he'd found the drawer empty and, with vicious jabs of an extended forefinger toward his waiter, how Alois must be the guilty party.

With a nod to the priest and a sighed comment – "I'm getting too old for this!" – Altamont rose and then began to move toward the door. When his movement caught the attention of the policeman, he broke into a run, seemingly slipping awkwardly on a slick spot as he reached the door, delaying him just enough to allow the constable to lurch into motion behind him and follow outside. Meanwhile, the priest rose and walked slowly to the younger brother, Adolf, by the plain door, moving as one would toward a skittish wild animal. He

283

was soon beside the man and, looking up into his face, he began to speak, rather amazed at what he saw, but forcing himself to continue.

The constable returned with Altamont in tow, dragging him beside the owner and the waiter. With a rather vicious shake of his arm, Altamont explained how, just a few minutes earlier, he had seen that the waiter was in the back room and, when no one was paying any attention, he'd risen and crossed to the counter, where he'd opened the drawer and pulled out the daily takings. He then reached into his pocket, pulling out a roll of bills, which he handed to the owner.

Altamont suspected that his own funds, being used to pay for this lie, were more than the owner was used to seeing on a typical day, let alone a rainy Sunday night, but he counted it and declared that he was satisfied and wouldn't press charges. It was likely that he didn't want any more association with the police than was necessary. The constable seemed relieved, but provided the typical warning that he'd best not see Altamont back in that neighborhood any more. Then he spun him toward the door and released him, causing the older man to stumble on his way outside. As he looked back before leaving, he observed Alois giving him a speculative glance. He knew that the German would now be willing to talk with him, if only because he was curious about Altamont's actions. And when Altamont explained it to him correctly, invoking the names of their common acquaintances, there would be enough of a connection for Alois to pass him upwards toward the German spymaster.

Finding a nearby alley, Altamont chose to wait for the priest. He was contemplating how best to re-approach Alois when he found that he was playing with the goat-tail beard – all without conscious thought. *This is intolerable!* he growled to himself, vowing to be more mindful of his every action. Someday he would leave Altamont behind, and he didn't want – at any time when that day came – to find himself still in any part of Altamont's skin.

The priest came out of the café and paused, looking at the ground. He stood there for almost a minute, a long and awkward time while Altamont waited to raise a hand and attract his attention. Finally, the priest gave what looked like a shudder, and then he threw back his shoulders as if tossing off something that was trying to climb upon him from behind.

Then he looked up and noticed Altamont in the shadows across the street. It almost looked as if he were deciding whether to cross over and speak one more time, or if he might turn and go in the other

284

direction. Then, his decision made, he stepped forward toward the alley.

Altamont was shocked at his appearance. It was as if the little priest had aged ten years in ten minutes. Underneath his flat black hat, his face was pale and sunken, and his fingers clutched his umbrella so tightly that his knuckles were white. His lips were working as if repeating a catechism, and they were wet, as if he'd forgotten to swallow.

"Good God, man!" cried Altamont in a low voice when they were back in the alley, away from the street. "What has happened?"

The priest swallowed, and again. "I . . . barely know how to describe it. When . . . when we encountered Adolf on the street, while walking here, I gave him very little notice. The same when we spoke to Alois in the back room. But just now . . . when he turned his full attention onto me, curious as to why I seemed to know about his theft and what my motive might be in keeping him from becoming involved in your intervention, he . . . he . . . ." He fell silent, searching for the words. Then he looked up. "When he turned his full gaze upon me . . . and I saw directly into his eyes, it . . . he . . . it . . . *It was as if I was seeing the fires of Hell!* I . . . ." His voice faded. There were no more words to explain.

The priest searched Altamont's face, determining if he had conveyed what he had felt and seen, knowing that his words were inadequate – they could never explain what he'd perceived – and that he was talking to a man who prided himself on rational logical thought. "No ghosts need apply," Altamont had once said in another life, and surely that applied to . . . whatever it was that the priest had tried to express. His despair grew, and the idea he'd never be able to adequately share what he'd observed, or how he could warn anyone. But then, the other man gripped his shoulder, forcing his attention back to the present.

"Father Brown," said Sherlock Holmes, all pretense of the Irish-American criminal Altamont gone for just that moment. "As I said, I have seen miracles – and as that word is defined, those are not just the product of the intervention of Divine Goodness. A miracle is, by definition, a surprising and inexplicable event, usually considered to be the work of a divine agency – and sometimes these interventions are terrible. The Bible tells of a flood that killed everyone on earth, save for one family. Entire cities were wiped from the earth for sinning against the Divine. The Egyptian army died while pursuing the Israelites across the Red Sea during a

285

miracle that only benefited them. The miraculous can also have a sinister side.

"I don't know what you have seen, but now that you have seen it, you can be an agent to oppose it. You have seen this for a reason, and there is no man I'd rather have on our side in the coming months and years."

"But – " said Father Brown, still shaken, but rediscovering his usual resolve and moral certainty once again.

"You have been surprised," said Holmes. "Shocked by something beyond your immediate understanding. But you *will* understand. I am certain of it. And consider – now you *know*, and knowing is better than not knowing."

The priest nodded, at first hesitantly, and then more sure. He raised his hand to Holmes's, still gripping his shoulder, and squeezed in return.

Then, stepping apart, he said, "What is your plan now?"

Holmes – now Altamont once more – stroked his beard, saying, "Tomorrow I'll arrange an encounter with Alois Hitler and introduce myself, explaining that my own masters wouldn't have wanted to see him arrested. Then I expect things will move along as planned."

"And the half-brother?" asked Father Brown. "Adolf Hitler? Will you also – ?"

Altamont shook his head. "I think not. I am, of course, most curious whether I would also see what you observed, but I can think of no reason to involve him in my business with Alois. Perhaps I'll run across him another time." He started to add that for now, he would leave that to the priest, but he could see just how shaken the little man was at whatever he'd seen, and instead decided to end their renewed acquaintance then.

"Farewell, Father," said Sherlock Holmes, offering his hand. "Until we meet again."

"Go with God, Mr. Holmes," said Father Brown, making the sign of the cross.

They shook hands and then stepped back onto the rain-slicked pavement, lit only by the light from the café window across the street. Altamont turned north and the priest south, and then both were lost in the murky darkness.

NOTES

The question of whether Adolf Hitler, the most evil man to walk the earth until recently, lived in Liverpool from November 1912 to April 1913, has been debated for years. According to a manuscript written in 1930 by his sister-in-law, Bridget "Cissie" Dowling Hitler, Adolf moved there to avoid conscription in Austria-Hungary. She wrote that he spoke very little English, never obtained a job, and spent his time wandering the streets and drinking at a few local pubs.

Bridget Dowling had met Alois Hitler, Jr. in 1909 – some sources say at the Dublin Horse Show, and others at Dublin's Shelborne Hotel. For a time, Alois convinced both Bridget and her father that he was a wealthy hotelier touring Europe. Bridget's father did not like the non-Catholic Alois, who was nine years older than his daughter, then just seventeen and fresh out of Convent School. In spite of the elder Dowling's feelings, Bridget and Alois traveled to London in June 1910 and eloped, moving back to Liverpool. Their son, William Hitler, was born nine months later in March 1911.

In Liverpool, Alois and Bridget lived at 102 Upper Stanhope Street, later destroyed by German bombings during World War II. During this time, Alois was employed at a cafe in Toxteth, a rough neighborhood to the east of the docks along the Mersey. Their uneasy relationship continued until May 1914, when Alois abandoned his wife and child, returning to Germany, where he bigamously married another wife.

In her 1930's manuscript, Bridget indicated that not only did Adolf Hitler stay with his half-brother's family for a while, but it was during that time she awakened his interest in astrology, and she also convinced him to shave the sides of his mustache, giving him that idiotic look that marks him as an irredeemable moron, along with being one of history's most evil pieces of filth.

Alois and Bridget's son, William, lived in Germany for much of the 1930's, working in a position that had been obtained for him by his half-uncle Adolf, but in 1938 he fled, not liking what he was seeing, and he and his mother ended up in the United States. At the start of the war, William was drafted into the US Navy, curiously retaining his name, "William Hitler". He was wounded, received the Purple Heart, and was discharged in 1947. Only at that point did he – and his mother – change their last names to "Stuart-Houston". They are buried side-by-side in Coram, New York.

Most historians discount the story of Adolf Hitler's visit to Liverpool as an urban legend. The only source is Bridget's manuscript, probably written in 1940-1941 during the early years of the war when there might have been an interest in its publication. In the 1970's, historian Robert Payne, writing his own biography of Hitler, found the manuscript, and a number of excerpts were published in newspapers. While historians general treat the idea as false, there is also no firm evidence that Adolf Hitler *wasn't* in England during those months.

287

I personally think that Hitler was in England. To paraphrase "The Second Stain":

"How did you know [Hitler] was there?"
"Because I knew [he] was nowhere else."

More about the topic can be found at the BBC Website "Your Story: Adolf Hitler - Did He Visit Liverpool During 1912-13?"

https://www.bbc.co.uk/legacies/myths_legends/england/liverpool/user_1_article_1.shtml

The Sins of
Sherlock Holmes
by Joseph S. Walker

The brutally cold weather gripping London throughout January of 1914 provided, in the view of many in the capital, an appropriately foreboding backdrop for the unrelenting stream of sobering news from the Continent. The peoples of Europe were, in ever greater numbers, angry and restless, and every day brought bulletins of some ancient grudge between nations abruptly rekindled, some desperate group of refugees seeking asylum, some border bristling with armaments. Diplomats shuttled ceaselessly across the Continent, pursuing ever more desperate plans for compromise, as generals drew their lines and hatched their plots. War loomed, and it appeared less likely with every passing week that England would be able to hold herself aloof from conflict.

In brief, whatever cheer the recent holidays provided had already faded into memory as two figures, advancing from the direction of the nearest train station, walked along a quiet lane in the northern reaches of the metropolis, treading carefully through several inches of snow in the darkness of the winter evening. One of the figures was a tall, solidly built man in stylish evening attire, beneath a topcoat which almost swept the chilled pavement. His companion, conventionally dressed aside from a clerical collar, was so short that someone glancing from a distance might easily have taken him to be the taller figure's son. A nearer observer would recognize him as being, in fact, likely the older of the two men, though his face radiated a kindly innocence that rendered him still a little childlike. Clinging tightly to a black umbrella, he walked briskly to keep pace with the longer step of the other, sometimes humming a little under his breath.

The road had perhaps cut through farmland a generation prior. Now it made its way between estates of an acre or more, with large homes set well back from the street and some distance from their neighbors. Each time the men came to a post at the head of the walkway to one of these homes, the taller man struck a match to check the address in its flickering glow. At the fourth post, the name, engraved ornately on a square of bronze, read simply *Tyndale*.

289

"Ah!" cried Flambeau, for the taller man was indeed that famous adventurer, once the most daring thief in Europe, now, reformed, a private detective already known for his interventions in several bizarre crimes. He shook out the match before it could singe his fingers. "Our destination at last, Father Brown."

"Tyndale," Father Brown said. "Is this the home of the industrialist, Janus Tyndale?"

"It is."

"Why did you not tell me it was he who summoned you?"

Flambeau shrugged. Whatever nation he now called home, there could be no doubt that his eloquent shrug was the gesture of a Frenchman. "I admit, *mon ami*, that I feared you would decline to accompany me, preferring to avoid the company of a man who profits from the production of the machines of war."

"What would that avoidance gain me, my dear fellow, or him? Did Christ not regularly keep company with the most wretched? Remember my station, Flambeau. I am tasked to seek out even the most barren of ground." The little priest smiled. "Surely you remember the circumstances of our first meeting."

"As though I could forget! Very well, Father. In that case, we proceed." Flambeau led his friend up the walkway, noting, to their left, the broader path that would lead carriages or automobiles around the side. The house in front of them was large, some twenty rooms at a guess, with a handful of lit windows testifying to the life within. It offered clear evidence of affluence, but Flambeau thought he had never seen a house so blandly designed, so bereft of interesting or distinctive features. He pointed this out, using his ornately carved walking-stick to gesture at the unadorned, virtually colorless face of the structure.

"Yes," Father Brown said. "There is something disconcerting about such determined anonymity."

Flambeau's response was cut off by a piercing noise from the house – a high, anguished scream that cut through the night, briefly freezing the men in place and stilling their blood more effectively than the frigid air. "What horror is this?" Flambeau hissed, reaching for his companion's shoulder.

"We must see," Father Brown said. Before they could rush to the doorway before them, however, more sounds were heard, this time wild, indecipherable shouts coming from around the corner of the house, and then, unmistakable to them both, a handgun firing twice in quick succession.

"That was not inside," Flambeau said, his voice equal parts anxiety and excitement. "Perhaps you should return to the road while I investigate the back of the house, little father."

"I'll go with you." Father Brown's voice remained calm and simple. Flambeau knew better than to protest, but he made sure to stay in front of his friend as the two men struck out into the unmarked snow and made their way around the building. They skirted the drive, with its confused jumble of wheeled tracks leading to another structure behind and to the side of the house – clearly, by the placement, originally stables, now likely a garage. There was nothing else of note at the side of the home. Continuing around to the rear, they found themselves plunged more deeply into darkness. They had the impression of a wide expanse of lawn stretching away, but the only real illumination, emanating from an open doorway near the middle of Tyndale's home, was a long rectangle of yellow light reaching across a swept flagstone veranda, almost touching the snow beyond.

A young man in the livery of a butler stood in the opening, his arms crossed against his chest in a vain effort to still his trembling. He was staring so intently into the dark grounds that Flambeau's hail caught him completely by surprise, making him jump and squeak. "Hello the house!" the Frenchman cried. "What's the trouble here?"

The servant shrank back into the doorway, peering around the jamb in their direction. "Who's there?" he demanded. "Mr. Naylor's out here, and he's armed, as you'll have heard. Stand where you are, if you don't want a bullet to find you."

Flambeau and Father Brown stopped, some ten feet from the door. "We mean no threat to this home or its occupants," Flambeau said. "I was summoned here by Mr. Janus Tyndale. My name is Flambeau."

"Stand there, whatever your name is!" the young man said. "You've picked a bad night for your visit, a d----d terrible night! Stand there until Mr. Naylor comes."

"I'm here," came a new voice from the darkness. The form of the speaker it belonged to became steadily more distinct as he approached. He was a tall man, at least as tall as Flambeau. He wore no coat or hat, seemingly having rushed out into the cold at some unanticipated event. He carried, in his right hand, a revolver. The fiercely bristling beard and thick head of hair he bore, both a brilliant red, were streaked with gray, and Flambeau judged him to be in his late fifties. He moved with vigor and strength, though his gait was a clumsy shuffle, and he dragged his left leg a bit. "Who are the strangers? You, there – What's your business?"

"Mr. Naylor, sir," the butler said. "I've called for the police. Are you injured?"

"Nothing serious," Naylor said, continuing to approach. His accent was American, his voice rough and uneven. "I tried to follow him into the woods and fell over a branch. Twisted my knee. He's long gone." Naylor grunted and stooped. His hand came out of the snow holding a long knife with red stains along the blade. "The villain dropped this, though." He was close enough now to see Flambeau and Brown, and he regarded them with a cold glare. "More unexpected guests. Accomplices, is it?" He held up his firearm, not quite pointing it at them. "Get inside, both of you. We'll let the coppers have a look at you."

"I am not accustomed to following orders," Flambeau said rather stiffly, "whatever force may accompany them."

"I don't care what you're used to." Naylor's voice sounded like he was pushing it through a handful of gravel lodged in his throat. "We're all going inside to wait for the police. They won't be long answering a murder call."

"Murder!" Father Brown said. "It's as I feared, Flambeau. I beg you not to stand on pride. Clearly we must go inside. Say we do so to escape the cold, if you cannot bear being compelled to enter."

Flambeau sighed heavily, but began moving toward the door. "As you wish, my friend."

Naylor was close behind them as they crossed the threshold, finding themselves in a large, elaborate kitchen. "Bracken," he said to the butler, "get everyone into the office. We'll all wait there together."

Bracken hesitated. "Mr. Ernest is with – with his father, sir. He is quite distraught."

"No doubt," Naylor said, "but there will be time for that later. Get him to the office, and close up Mr. Tyndale's bedroom. And bring Anders and Woodson." He gestured to a passage at the far end of the room. "Through there, gentlemen. The second door on the right."

Following his directions, Flambeau and Father Brown found themselves in a large room at the front of the house, lined with bookshelves and outfitted as an office. The space was dominated by a rather utilitarian desk covered with mounds of papers and files. There were two couches and a scattering of other chairs. They stopped in the middle of the room and turned to face Naylor, who was standing in the doorway, the gun now quite definitely pointed at Flambeau.

"Pray lower that weapon," Flambeau said. "Whatever has happened here, I assure you we played no part in it."

Naylor grunted. "I'll not be killed because I trusted the word of a stranger. You're carrying a gun yourself, in the right-hand pocket of your coat."

Flambeau pursed his lips. "What of it?"

"Turn to face the far corner," Naylor said. "Take it out slowly and let me see you unload it. Then you may pocket it again."

Flambeau stiffened and pulled himself to his full height. Father Brown rested a hand, lightly, on his friend's arm. Flambeau looked down at him, shook his head in resignation, and turned away from Naylor to follow his directions. Holding his revolver by the barrel, he opened the cylinder and shook the bullets into his left hand. He displayed them, rather contemptuously, to Naylor, and put them in his left-hand pocket, restoring the revolver to the other. Naylor nodded and lowered his own weapon, but continued to hold it.

Bracken came into the room from the hallway, followed by two women. The younger, generously built and blond, was attired in a simple gray shift. Her companion, a lean older woman whose bitter face spoke of a difficult life, wore a stained apron over similarly plain garb. Once inside the room, she stood perfectly still, staring at the far wall with a dull expression, as though trying to make out the titles of the books from a distance. The younger woman glanced at the strangers and shied to the side of Naylor, who had positioned himself in a corner of the room. "Mr. Naylor, sir," she said. Her voice was high-pitched and fluttery. "Is it true? Mr. Tyndale is dead?"

"We're waiting for the police," Naylor said. "You'd best sit and be quiet until they get here, Woodson."

A door at the side of the room opened and a young man came in. He wore a quilted dressing gown and had plush slippers on his feet. A neat, thin black mustache sat in the middle of his round, rather pink face. He swayed on his feet a bit as he surveyed the room: Flambeau, his arms crossed, leaning casually against the mantel. Father Brown, drifting between the desk and shelves, his hands clasped behind his back. The old cook, still standing just inside the door, staring at him balefully. Bracken, in the center of the room, his face a mask of confusion. Finally, Naylor, in the corner with his gun, Woodson standing close by.

293

"He's really dead," the young man said, directing his comment to the armed man.

"I know," Naylor said.

"What are we to do?"

"We're waiting for the police," Naylor said.

The young man gestured vaguely at Flambeau and Father Brown. "Who are they?"

"Found them in the yard," Naylor said. "Holding them to be questioned."

Flambeau stiffened. "Don't be absurd. I most certainly am not being *held*." Before he could go on, a vigorous pounding sounded from the front of the house.

"That'll be the police," Naylor said. He put his gun in his pocket. "Bracken, let them in."

A moment later, Bracken led two uniformed officers into the room. They were followed by a bluff, stout man with a heavy walrus mustache who brushed at patches of snow and leaves clinging to the front of his suit. He came up short at the sight of all the people in the room. "Fell on your doorstep," he said. His face flushed. "Damn nuisance. Pardon the appearance. I'm Inspector Mallard. Who's in charge here?"

Naylor stepped forward quickly. "Inspector, this is one of the homes of Janus Tyndale. I'm sure you recognize the name."

"Certainly. Most important man."

"Very important." Naylor pointed to the side door. "His bedroom is on the other side of that door. You'll find him dead on the floor."

Mallard gave a grunt. "Murdered?"

"His throat has been cut."

"Huggins, Welsh, check on that, will you?"

The two uniformed policemen went into the next room. In a moment one came back to the doorway. "Right enough, Inspector. Very deep wound."

"Have a look in a moment. Must know who's who first. Quite a crowd to find in a home in the middle of a cold night." Mallard produced a notebook, flipped it open, and looked at Naylor through narrowed eyes. "Who would you be, sir?"

"My name is Crandell Naylor. I'm Mr. Tyndale's personal assistant."

"You're American?"

"Yes." Naylor gestured at the young man with the thin mustache who had sunk onto one of the couches and held his head in his hands. "This is Ernest Tyndale, Janus Tyndale's son."

Mallard's eyes flicked up from the pad. "Sympathies for your loss, sir," he rumbled. Ernest Tyndale gave no sign of having heard.

Naylor went on, pointing to each of the servants in turn. "Bracken, the butler. Anders, the cook. Woodson, the maid." Woodson was still standing as close to Naylor as she could, looking at the policeman bashfully. Anders sat erect in a chair near the window, staring into space and rubbing her hands together. Bracken stood at attention in the center of the room, nodding when his name was spoken. His face was very pale.

"I'm afraid I can't introduce these last two," Naylor said. "We found them on the grounds when I gave pursuit to the killer."

Mallard grunted again. "Pursuit, is it? One step at a time, if you please. Would you gentlemen identify yourselves and your business?"

Flambeau had been restraining himself heroically. He gave a quick bow. "My name is Flambeau. I am a detective. This is my companion and associate, Father Brown." He stepped forward, fished in his breast pocket, and produced a telegraph sheet, which he handed to Mallard. "And this is my business."

Mallard scanned the page. "'*Urgent need of your unique qualifications. Please call on my home tonight.*'" He looked at Flambeau. "You don't know what it was about?"

"No."

"Had you ever met Mr. Tyndale?"

"No. I have seen his picture, of course."

Mallard put the telegram in his pocket. "You always bring a priest on business calls, Mr. Flambeau?"

"Father Brown frequently has the kindness to offer me his insights," Flambeau said stiffly.

"No doubt," the policeman muttered. "All right, let's have it. What happened here?"

Once again it was Naylor who spoke. "We dine early in this household, Inspector, in accordance with Mr. Tyndale's preferences and habits. It was about seven o'clock when the three of us – myself and the Tyndales, senior and junior – finished eating. We brought coffee and brandy into this office and attended to business for some hour-and-a-half."

"What sort of business?"

Naylor opened his hands. "The endless business of preparing for war. As you must know, Mr. Tyndale was one of the main suppliers of arms to His Majesty's forces."

"Not a pleasant occupation," Mallard said.

"But a necessary one." Naylor gestured at the desk with its mounds and drifts of paperwork. "And complex. Ernest left us shortly after eight. He said he had a headache."

"I did," the young man said, still holding his head between his palms. "I still do. I went upstairs and was dozing until I heard the commotion."

Naylor picked up the story. "It was about a quarter-to-nine when Mr. Tyndale said he wanted to work alone for the remainder of the evening. He bid me good night."

"Was this his usual practice?"

"Far from it," Naylor said. "I can't, in fact, recall another instance of his dismissing me before he was ready to retire for the night."

"Your pardon, sir," Bracken said. "I can perhaps explain. Mr. Tyndale told me earlier in the day that he would be receiving a guest at nine, and wished to confer with him privately. He impressed upon me with some force that neither his son nor Mr. Naylor was to know."

"There you are," Flambeau said. "The guest, of course, was to be me."

"Get to you soon enough," Mallard said. "Go on, Mr. Naylor."

"I had just reached my own room, upstairs, when I remembered a file I wanted to read which I had left here. I came back downstairs and knocked, but received no reply. I entered the room and found it empty, but I believe I could hear Mr. Tyndale moving around in his quarters."

"Why is his bedroom on this floor?" Mallard interjected.

"Father was in poor health," Ernest Tyndale said. For the first time, he looked directly at the policeman. "Stairs were a trial for him. He also suffered frequent insomnia, and found it convenient to be near his office in case he wanted to work in the middle of the night."

"I see," Mallard said. "Then what happened?"

Naylor again pointed at the desk. "I had just picked up the file I needed – you can see I dropped it there on the floor – when I heard a piercing scream coming from Mr. Tyndale's room."

"We heard it as well," Flambeau said. "We were just coming up the walk. It must have been two or three minutes before nine."

296

"Of course I ran to the door and opened it as quickly as possible," Naylor said. He closed his eyes, took a deep breath, and went on in his constricted voice. "Mr. Tyndale was stretched out on the floor, with a horrible gash pumping blood from his throat. A man I had never seen before was standing over him, holding a knife stained red."

"Describe the blighter," Mallard said, his eyes sharpening.

Naylor ran a hand over his heavy beard and thought. "Average height and build. Dressed all in black. He had dark hair and a heavy mustache which ran down to his jawline. I think the word I want is *swarthy*. He reminded me of Italians I used to work with in New York."

Mallard seemed to find this significant. "In what way?"

Naylor shrugged. "The way he carried himself, I suppose. I don't know how to express it, exactly."

"What did he do?"

"As soon as he saw me, he leapt for the door to the hallway and ran for the back of the house. I confess surprise slowed me, Inspector. Or perhaps I'm getting old. Twenty years ago I would have had him before he left the room." Naylor sighed. "I wasted time trying to get my gun from my pocket. It snagged on the fabric."

Mallard looked up sharply from his notebook. "Are you in the habit of going armed, Mr. Naylor?"

"Always," the American said. "One of my duties was to serve as Mr. Tyndale's security."

"You've done a marvelous job," Ernest Tyndale muttered from the couch. He was once again holding his head between his palms.

Naylor stiffened but did not reply. "By the time I went after him, he'd reached the back door and was running away from the house. I called out after him, and shot at him twice, but I don't believe I hit him."

"Father Brown and I heard the cries and the shots," Flambeau put in. "We came around the house and met Bracken, here, looking out into the darkness."

"I went after him, but it was hopeless," Naylor said. "There's a stand of woods, some hundred yards from this building. His tracks went straight to it and disappeared in the underbrush. Looking for any sign of him, I fell over a branch and twisted my knee. I decided continuing the chase was hopeless. When I made my way back, I found these two."

"At which point you held us at gunpoint and compelled us into this room," Flambeau said bitterly.

297

"You'll get no apologies from me," Naylor said. "I didn't know you weren't part of it. For that matter, I still don't." He produced the knife from his pocket. "I did find this in the snow."

"I'll have that," Mallard said. He took the blade and put it carefully in an inner pocket. "All right," he said. "Does anyone recognize Mr. Naylor's description of the killer?"

Most of the people in the room looked at each other. Ernest Tyndale didn't move from his posture of misery. The cook, Anders, was still staring at the opposite wall, seeming not to hear or understand anything happening. Father Brown stood at the desk, looking at some of the papers scattered across the surface. None of them said anything.

"Right," Mallard said. "What about a motive? Can anyone suggest a reason why Janus Tyndale might have been marked for murder?"

"For God's sake, isn't it obvious?" Ernest Tyndale's voice was choked with anger. He stood and glared at the policeman. "You heard Naylor. You know it yourself. Without my father's weapons, the British Army will be utterly unprepared for what is coming. Clearly some enemy power is aiming to hobble us, Inspector. You can write in your little notebook there that this is a war crime." He rubbed his temples. "My father is the first casualty of the new war. There will be many others. The Prime Minister must be informed immediately."

Naylor cleared his throat, though his voice still came out roughly. "I'm afraid Ernest is most likely right, Inspector. It's likely this will end up being more than a case for the police."

"That's as may be," Mallard said, "but for the moment, it is my case. I'm sending for more men. I know those woods, Mr. Tyndale. There are a hundred places he could come out and have a car or horse waiting for him. We'll try to cover what we can, given the darkness. In the morning, perhaps dogs. We can at least find out what direction he goes."

Ernest Tyndale groaned and sank down on the couch again. "By the morning, your superiors will have taken over the case. By the morning the nation will be in an uproar."

"No doubt," Mallard said. "But again I say, it's mine now. I'm going to inspect the victim and the scene. I will require you all to stay here for the moment. When I'm done with my inspection, I'll interview each of you individually."

"Do you mean I must stay in this wretched room, with the body of my father only feet away?" Ernest stood and scoffed. "I deny your authority to require it. I'm going back to my room. This headache is maddening, and I have a thousand details to attend to." He looked around the room. "I suppose it's occurred to all of you that I am Tyndale Arms now."

"Of course," Mallard said. "No disrespect. I only ask that everyone remain in this home, not in this room specifically." He tucked his notebook into his pocket. "I'll attend to you as soon as possible, sir."

He gave the young man a deferential nod, which Ernest Tyndale, already halfway out of the room, did not see. Mallard looked around quickly at the others in the room, squared his shoulders, and went through the side door. From where they stood, now side-by-side near the fireplace, Flambeau and Father Brown had a brief glimpse of the scene of the horror. The body was splayed across the floor, the famous face turned away from them, the angry red wound standing out vividly against the late man's white skin and dark business attire. Then the door was closed.

The maid, Woodson, put a hand on Naylor's arm. "It's all so terrible, sir. I fear I'm going to faint dead away. How brave of you to chase that horrible man."

Naylor's mouth twitched. "Anyone would do the same." He delicately removed the woman's hand from his sleeve. "Bracken, please see Woodson to her quarters. She might benefit from a dose of brandy. I'll be in my room when the police want me." He went out into the hallway, Woodson's eyes following his every step.

Bracken took her arm. "Come, Woodson." He looked at Flambeau and Father Brown. "Your pardon, gentlemen. I'll return to see to any needs you may have."

Of the inhabitants of the house, only Anders, the old cook, remained. She looked around slowly, rose, and left the room without a word, leaving the priest and his friend alone in the room.

Flambeau immediately began pacing restlessly. "We are useless here," he said. "When Mallard's reinforcements arrive, I will ask his permission to join them in searching the woods. Surely this rash assassin left some clue as to his direction."

"I do not advise it," Father Brown said, "unless you feel you need the exercise."

Flambeau stopped and looked at his friend, who was examining the titles of the books on the shelves. "You think his escape is already assured?"

"In a matter of speaking," the priest said. "I am comfortably certain that no man will be arrested for Janus Tyndale's murder." He

299

sighed. "This is a sad household, my friend. A tragic household. Perhaps an evil one."

"We might say the same of any home touched by murder. But you seem very sure of yourself! What have you seen that I have not?"

"Footprints in the snow," Father Brown said, his voice almost dreamy. "And the terrible power of parental love."

Flambeau frowned, but before he could say anything, Bracken returned to the room. "It appears you are to be our guests for the moment, gentlemen. May I be of any service?"

"Yes," Father Brown said, turning from the shelves. "Thank you, Bracken. We would like coffee."

"Certainly, sir." The butler began to turn.

"We would like the cook to bring it to us," the priest continued.

Bracken turned back to him. "Excuse me, sir?"

"The cook," Father Brown said, his tone casual. "I believe her name is Anders."

"It is, sir. I believe she has gone to her quarters."

"It won't be the first time she's been summoned from them. I think you must be on hand to assist Inspector Mallard immediately if called, Bracken. It will be best for everyone if Anders brings us what we require."

Bracken's expression was dubious, but he nodded. "As you wish, sir."

Again, Father Brown spoke before he could leave. "Have her bring it to Mr. Naylor's room. And could you kindly tell us the way there?"

Bracken's brow creased, but he seemed to have given up trying to understand the little clergyman. "Mr. Naylor's quarters are upstairs, sir. Turn right at the end of the staircase and go to the end of the hall."

"Thank you, Bracken. Flambeau, if you will accompany me?"

Flambeau held his tongue until the two men reached the top of the house's central staircase and nobody else was in earshot. "Will you tell me what's going on?" he whispered.

"Dark business," Father Brown said, as they started down the hall. "I cannot tell you everything, my friend. I do not see it yet in full. Be patient, I beg you."

"Remember I was a criminal for many years, Father. Patience does not come easily to men accustomed to taking what they want."

Father Brown smiled at this, then lifted his umbrella and tapped its handle firmly on the door at the end of the hall. After a moment it was opened, and Crandell Naylor looked at them with something close to active hostility. He was holding a pen. "My apologies, gentlemen, but your business, whatever it may have been, was with my late employer, not me. I have no time. Ernest was right. Whatever happens with this murder case, there are a thousand things to attend to as soon as possible."

"We will take as little of your time as we can," Father Brown said. "We have asked to have coffee brought here."

"Have you? That's making very free with the hospitality of a dead man, I'd say."

"We asked to have Anders bring it."

Naylor's gaze sharpened. "Indeed."

"May we come in? Surely it strains you to stand so long on your injured leg. Though I must say it seems to be improving quickly."

Naylor's jaw tightened. "The infamous Flambeau's little priest friend," he said in his American-inflected rasp. "I begin to recall hearing some things about you." He stood back from the doorway and gestured them inside. "Very well. We'll talk."

It was a small sitting room, somewhat cramped with a writing-desk, a divan, and several chairs. The door in the opposite wall no doubt led to Naylor's sleeping chamber. Naylor threw himself into the chair behind the desk, stretching out his legs and lacing his fingers across his stomach. "I'm surprised to find I'm looking forward to this interview," he said. "I don't often find myself in a position of this precise nature."

"I would think not," Father Brown said. He sat in a chair to the side of the desk. Flambeau, shaking his head, took a seat in the corner of the room. Something was happening here he could not wholly comprehend, something in the way the piercing gaze of the American met the gentle eyes of the priest. He felt he could do nothing but observe.

"Shall we speak openly, then?" Naylor asked. "Or do you prefer to wait until we have been joined?"

"I suspect that would be simpler," Father Brown said. "Unless you'd like to tell us everything now."

A smile tugged at the corners of Naylor's lips. "I am not a man given to confessions, Father, though I've been present for many."

A light tapping sounded at the door. Flambeau sprang to his feet and opened it. Anders stood there, holding a tray with a pot of coffee, three cups, and the necessary implements. The look on her face suggested she would sooner be walking to the gallows, but she came into the room, put the tray on a low coffee table, and turned to depart.

301

Father Brown stood and took her arm. "If we may have a moment of your time, Anders." He steered her to a chair across the desk from Naylor and resumed his own, leaning forward to look closely into her face. "May I know your Christian name?"

The woman looked fearfully at Naylor, who nodded at her. "I think you can be honest with these men," he said. "Entirely so."

The woman looked back at Father Brown, licked her lips nervously, and, for the first time since they saw her, spoke, her voice low and trembling. "Catherine," she said.

"Catherine. As you have heard, I am a priest. I will do nothing to harm you, my child. I simply wish the truth." He reached forward and gently took her hand. "Is it not the truth that Ernest Tyndale is your son?"

Flambeau, who had resumed his chair, leapt to his feet as Catherine Anders recoiled from Father Brown, clutched briefly at the arms of her chair, and burst into tears. Naylor calmly produced a handkerchief and handed it to the priest, who in turn pressed it upon the distraught woman. Once having given vent to her emotions, the woman surrendered to them entirely, her sobs coming in great heaving bursts as Father Brown patted her arms and made meaningless sounds of comfort. It was some ten minutes before she had regained sufficient control of herself to speak.

"You have guessed right, Father," she finally said. "Though I'm at a loss to know how you have seen through a secret so long held."

"Often secrets stay hidden simply because people refuse to see them," Father Brown said. "No doubt for many years, most of the people you have met have seen you simply as a servant, and allowed their gaze to move right past you. You may as well have been a blank piece of paper with the word '*Cook*' written upon it. They did not see how the line of your neck, the structure of your hands, the delicate structure of your nose, accorded with those of your young master. They did not see the way you looked upon him tonight, when everyone was concentrating on Mr. Naylor and the inspector."

Flambeau had resumed his seat. "I am well compensated for fetching a priest along on my business calls," he said, "but Father, what does this have to do with the terrible events of tonight?"

"Everything," Father Brown said. "Won't you tell us your story, Catherine? How did you come to be in the guise of a servant in the home of your own son?"

For long moments, the unfortunate woman looked down at the damp cloth she worked between her fingers. When she finally looked back up at the priest, her eyes were more alert, her bearing

302

more erect. Flambeau found that he could see in her, still, something of the attractive, vivacious young woman she had been. He glanced at Naylor. The American was leaning back in his chair, his fingers steepled, watching the scene through eyes almost closed.

"I will be as brief as possible, sir. My father was Edwin Anders. It is possible you know the name, though it is many years now since his death." She paused and collected her thoughts. "My father was the chief business rival of Janus Tyndale. How they hated each other, sir! I was raised to hate the name of Tyndale as I would hate the name of Lucifer himself. They were always at odds over some government contract, or new patents, or anything at all. Each pursued the destruction of the other through every means possible."

A tear rolled down Catherine Anders's cheek, but she went on, her voice brittle.

"In 1888, Janus Tyndale was newly married to a woman whose family connections enabled him to expand his business tremendously and finally gain an undeniable, unchallenged superiority in their battles. He was able to put himself in a position where he owned tremendous debts that my father had rashly taken on in an effort to match his growth. He could have called them in at any moment and seen the Anders family reduced to abject poverty. But his victory was bittersweet, because he learned that his new wife could not give him the one thing that would make his triumph complete: A child."

Flambeau felt something cold grip his heart.

"He went to my father." Catherine's voice almost broke, but she steadied herself. "They made a bargain, sir. My father was given forgiveness of his debts. And Janus Tyndale was given me."

In the heavy silence of the next few minutes, Father Brown once again took Catherine's hand. She gripped it tightly before she was able to resume.

"It was a simple matter for him to bribe the authorities so that his wife's name appeared in the records of Ernest's birth. I begged to be allowed to stay with my child. The only way Mr. Tyndale would allow it was if I agreed to become a servant in his household. I was never to tell the child, or anyone else, the truth. I was never to seek favor with the boy or make any kind of connection with him." Catherine's mouth tightened. "It was his continuing wrath against my family. He delighted in seeing the pain it caused me, watching my son grow up and never being able to even touch him."

"My God," Flambeau said.

"No," Father Brown said simply. "Not God."

"What of your father?" Flambeau asked.

Catherine bit her lip. "He continued being overly ambitious. I think, perhaps, he regretted what he had done, and took desperate chances in an effort to reverse it, but I will never know for certain. Janus Tyndale permitted no contact between us. My father soon found himself even more deeply in debt than before. I begged Mr. Tyndale to help him, but he only laughed. Four years after Ernest was born, my father killed himself." She shrugged. "A few years after that, Mrs. Tyndale died. She was never in good health. So the only people in the world who knew were me and him."

"You have been subjected to unimaginable torment," Father Brown said. "I am deeply sorry for you, my child." He patted her hand. "Now I'm afraid you must bring your story up to tonight."

Catherine took a deep breath. "It's so strange to be speaking of things I've been quiet about for so long."

"We are honored by your honesty, my dear, and your courage," Flambeau said.

Catherine nodded, though she did not look at him. "Janus Tyndale changed after his wife's death. He was always ruthless, but he became cold, calculating, interested only in improving his own lot. He seemed to perceive the entire world as he once viewed my father: As an enemy to be vanquished." Her voice broke. "I've had to watch my son – *My son!* – become more and more like him with every passing year. That dear, sweet child has himself become the shadow of his father, black-hearted and grim. I could do nothing to stop it. But tonight – " She shifted her gaze to Naylor. "I overheard you, sir – the talk you had with him."

"I surmised as much," Naylor murmured.

"I didn't mean to. I was in the closet when the two of you came into the bedroom. I was helping Woodson, putting away clothes she had laundered. You were arguing." She stopped. "I can't pretend I understood it all."

"We were discussing some rather risky ventures Mr. Tyndale had undertaken," Naylor said. "There's no need to get into details. I told him that, if things went badly, he could well end up in prison. I'm afraid he laughed. Then he explained how he had arranged the matter so that, if the authorities did get wind of his activities, they would be traced back not to him, but to his son. To Ernest."

Flambeau made a disgusted noise. "The scoundrel."

"It made me cold all over," Catherine said. "Everything he went through, everything he put me through, to have a son, and he was ready to sacrifice Ernest for his own safety." She set her jaw. "Mr.

Tyndale kept a collection of weapons, all the models made by his company. The knives are kept in his closet. I remember seizing one. When I heard Mr. Naylor leave, everything turned red. I think I screamed. The next thing I knew, Mr. Tyndale was on the floor, bleeding. Mr. Naylor was there." She turned her gaze to him again. "You took the knife from me and told me to run to my room and stay there. I did. I sat on my bed, shaking, expecting at any moment for the police to come and put me in chains. But they didn't. Instead Bracken came and brought me to the office, and I heard you tell that story."

"Yes," Naylor said. "I feared that at any moment you would break and shout out the truth. You bore it very well."

"I don't know how much longer I can," she said. "I've killed my son's father." She looked to the priest. "Am I not damned?"

Father Brown smiled gently. "You have been most cruelly used, Catherine, for a quarter-of-a-century. You are human, as are we all. I believe any human can be driven to a point where murder becomes not only possible, but inevitable. We can be driven there through suffering, through anguish, through rage. You have sinned, child, but sin can be forgiven."

"Inspector Mallard may not agree with that particular theology," Flambeau said.

"I don't propose to put the question to him," Father Brown said. "I see no reason for the police not to continue searching for their mustached anarchist. I'm sure they'll benefit from the good, healthy exercise of walking through the woods." He smiled. "The dogs will enjoy it."

Catherine looked hesitatingly at each of the three faces watching her. "You aren't turning me in?"

"Certainly not," Flambeau said. "You have already endured more suffering than any court could impose. Mr. Naylor, you concur?"

Naylor spread his fingers. "Surely my position is obvious from the actions I have taken."

A new expression spread across Catherine's face. "Then I can finally tell Ernest the truth."

"Not immediately," Naylor said quickly.

"I agree," Father Brown said. "It would cause too many questions, coming on the heels of the murder. It would be asking too much of the boy to deal with the acquisition of a mother and the loss of a father simultaneously. Wait, Catherine. Choose your moment."

He stood. "And now I think you should return to your room. You may be summoned by the inspector at any time."

Catherine rose. She seemed somewhat unsteady, but her face was more open than before, the lines less deeply etched. "Bless you, sir." She looked around. "Bless all of you."

"And you, my child," Father Brown said. "If I may, I will call upon you in a week or so to see how you get on."

She clasped his hand. "I would be most happy to see you," she said.

As soon as she had left the room, Flambeau stood. He held out his hand to Father Brown, who shook it. "Perhaps someday, little father, I will cease being amazed by you. Even once you had perceived the relationship between the wealthy young man and the cook, I cannot understand how you made out the reality of tonight's events."

"I believe I can," Naylor said. He opened his eyes fully and leaned forward, looking keenly at the mismatched pair before him. "I believe your friend heard not just a scream, as everyone else did, but a *woman's* scream, which could not be accounted for by my narrative. I believe he noted that my clumsy progression across the yard served to effectively obscure the fact that there was only a single set of footprints in the snow. I believe he noted that the knife I plucked from the ground could just as easily have been up my sleeve. I believe he wondered why my clothes were not marred by snow and other debris, as the inspector's suit was after his own fall. Do I come close to the mark?"

"Of course," Father Brown said. "It was obvious your story was false, though I believe it clever enough to continue blinding Inspector Mallard to the truth."

"I count that no great accomplishment," Naylor said. "I am familiar with Mallard's work. A child could put him on the wrong track."

"But why?" Flambeau asked. "Why take such a risk for this woman? And how could you possibly have conceived a plan and acted upon it so quickly?"

Naylor indicated Father Brown. "I believe your friend can tell you."

Father Brown raised his eyebrows. "Shall I?"

Naylor simply nodded.

"All right," the priest said. "Flambeau, I have the honor to introduce you to a man I know has inspired you. I have been fortunate enough to make his acquaintance before. This is Mr. Sherlock Holmes."

Flambeau's mouth fell open. He looked at the man behind the desk, whose eyebrow was raised in amusement. He staggered back a step and fell into a chair. "Impossible," he said. "I don't believe it."

"I'd remove my disguise, but I fear it would be an involved process," Sherlock Holmes said. The gravelly American voice had disappeared entirely, replaced by a crisp London accent. "The beard is real, to my considerable discomfort, though the color of course is not. Perhaps you will be convinced if I tell you that we came very near to meeting once before, on the docks in Marseilles, after that very neat bit of business with the Countess's necklace. Had my driver been twenty minutes faster that day, you would, I think, still be in a French prison."

Flambeau smiled. "I am gratified by his incompetence," he said. "It has given me the opportunity to redeem myself, thanks to this excellent priest."

"Indeed," Holmes said. "For a moment, downstairs, I hoped that my American veneer had held up, even against one I have encountered previously. I should have known better." He looked to the priest. "Were you fooled for an instant?"

"It is a superb mask you have constructed," Father Brown said. "I was not certain until I saw you in the full light of the office."

"It is no slight to your performance, sir," Flambeau said. "Our clerical friend here has a most enviable ability to see what is before him, rather than what he is told is before him. This is not the first time I have witnessed it."

"Nor I, for that matter," Holmes said, seeming only partially mollified. "Well, perhaps the occasional check to my pride is ultimately to the good. I am, at any rate, pleased to have the opportunity to meet you under my own name, Monsieur Flambeau. I've followed your second career with interest. You have quickly become quite the credit to our young profession."

Flambeau, feeling his face flush with pleasure, was gratified to hear Father Brown speak and move the discussion in a new direction. "Still, Mr. Holmes, I must say I'm somewhat disappointed in you."

"Oh?" Now both eyebrows went up.

"You have clearly been part of Mr. Tyndale's household for some time."

"Slightly less than a month. Earning his confidence was a tedious affair."

"You must have long ago perceived that Catherine Anders was the true mother of Ernest Tyndale, and how she suffered every day at his father's hand. You could have relieved that suffering. You could have revealed the truth."

Sherlock Holmes nodded, his face grave. "I considered it, many times. But there was too great a chance that the resulting chaos would prevent me from carrying out my task."

"And may we know what that is?" Flambeau asked.

Holmes folded his hands. "It is a matter of the utmost secrecy, gentlemen, but I think you can be trusted. Janus Tyndale was a traitor. Even as he provided arms to the British government, he was also financing and controlling a ring of the Kaiser's spies and saboteurs. Thanks to the work of one of my brother's agents, I was introduced to Tyndale as one worthy of his confidence, and I have been busily learning everything there is to know about his organization, save one thing: Who gives him his orders. I know that he traveled to the Continent frequently, and met his superiors there. I had come very close to accompanying him on such a voyage, at which point the entire network could have been swept up before war comes. And war is coming, gentlemen."

"And Ernest is part of this infernal plot?" Flambeau asked.

"Yes. In fact, his father had arranged things such that it would appear that he was behind it all along, a façade which would have held up long enough, if the worse happened, to allow the father to escape to his German protectors. I protested this, part of my gambit to learn more about who was behind Tyndale. That was the argument Catherine Anders overheard, to Janus Tyndale's great misfortune."

He touched his fingers and went on. "When I saw her with his body, I understood in an instant that, if she was arrested for the crime, the secret of Ernest Tyndale's birth would be revealed. Such a scandal would be enough to drive the war news from the front pages. The practitioners of espionage are extremely averse to such publicity. They would likely abandon the son to his own devices and undo all my work."

"So you invented a mustached killer," Father Brown said.

"Indeed. There will be considerable alarm in the hidden strongholds of Germany. Has their ring of agents been discovered? It is likely that Ernest Tyndale will be summoned to a very important meeting, soon, to discuss the matter. It is likely I will accompany him. And because of that, it is a shade more likely that the coming darkness can be quickly dispelled."

"And what will happen to Ernest Tyndale?" Flambeau asked.

"Ernest is not his father," Holmes said. "Janus Tyndale was a fanatic. He truly believed that uniting all of northern Europe under the Kaiser's flag was the surest way to preserve civilization from the rise of what he called 'the mongrel races'. Ernest has no such ideology. He believes only in money. I believe he can be turned, and become an agent for The Crown." He shrugged. "It is possible that learning his true history will move him further in that direction."

Father Brown shook his head sadly. "So you propose to use Catherine Anders for your own purposes. I cannot say I fully approve of this, Mr. Holmes."

Sherlock Holmes looked at the priest, his expression softening. "I understand, Father. I can but do what I believe to be in the service of a greater good." He leaned back in his chair and closed his eyes. Catherine Anders had looked younger before she left them, but now Holmes, or Naylor, seemed older, and excessively weary. "I can but be prepared to answer for my sins."

Dawn had long since come before Flambeau and Father Brown, having been questioned by Inspector Mallard and then questioned again by his superiors, were allowed to leave the Tyndale home. They walked toward the train station under a high, cloudless blue sky, passing knots of police officers and reporters and listening to the baying of the dogs in the woods. Soon they had left it all behind and were alone on the street, each busy with his own thoughts.

After some time, Flambeau sighed. "It has been a most instructive evening," he said. "Only one thing still vexes me, Father, and I suppose it's a question we will never have answered: Why did Janus Tyndale send for me?"

Father Brown raised his eyes, which had been fixed on the snowy road. "I have an idea," he said. "The message spoke, did it not, of your unique qualifications?"

"It did."

"Forgive me, Flambeau, for you know how highly I regard you, but there are other detectives, and Tyndale was rich enough to hire any of them. When I reflect upon what makes you unique among your profession, it is this: You are reformed. You were a great criminal, and now you serve the cause of justice. Perhaps Janus Tyndale wished to emulate you. Perhaps he, too, wished for redemption."

Flambeau thought a moment, and shook his head. "I have heard nothing that would be evidence of such a wish, Father. What could lead you to believe it?"

309

"I'm surprised you must ask, my friend," the little priest said. "What answer could I give, but faith?" And so he walked on, beside his friend, swinging his umbrella and humming to himself under his breath.

The Seeds of Discord
by Adrian Middleton

The east wind swept through the brown-green treetops of the Èislek, that part of the Ardennes forest that stretched between the Grand Duchy of Luxembourg and the Walloon region of Belgium. It carried with it the sour taste of burning houses, the muffled echo of distant explosions, and the peppery scent of stale smokeless powder. The world was suddenly at war, and two travellers made their way through the rough and heavily wooded landscape that connected the two small nations. Making great haste, they pushed their way onward through the dense thickets that lay between the great trees that hid them from the world beyond.

They were a curious pair. The taller of the two, the renowned thief Hercule Flambeau, standing well above six feet tall, seemed to swagger as he walked, his long purposeful strides and sweeping cane brushed aside any obstacle, beating a noisy path guaranteed to keep the wildlife – deer, boar, rabbits, and birds – at bay. In his wake, his unassuming companion – the smaller of the pair – shuffled along behind him at an equally brisk pace. A Catholic pastor, Father Brown used a worn and shabby umbrella to bat aside stray twigs as they sprang back into place, desperate to conceal any signs of human intrusion upon the wilderness.

They had been in Saxony when the bullet of a Serb assassin took the lives of the Austrian Arch-Duke Franz-Ferdinand and his wife, and the brinksmanship between the Central Powers had dangled the threat of war over Europe like the Sword of Damocles. Desperate attempts to broker peace were being made when, in the last days of July, an anonymous telegram arrived for one of them at the Royal Court Church in Dresden. It read as follows:

> *A Friend to Pfarrer Braun*
> *Eastbourne, England*
> *28 July 1914*
> *11:55pm*
>
> *Situation grave. Dual Monarchy declaring war. Kriegsgefahr follows. Belgium mobilising. Look to Auseill. Decedo.*

311

"Evacuate," Father Brown had said, translating the last word from Latin. "It seems our time here is at an end, Flambeau. We must leave Saxony and the German Empire forthwith, or else be detained at the Kaiser's pleasure when war breaks out. It seems we are advised to travel through your home town."

"My home town? What can you mean?"

"I have known for some time that you are of Belgian, and not Gascon, extraction. I never took it upon myself to enquire further, but our anonymous friend has been quite precise in his message. This telegram is not just a carefully worded message. It summons us to the town of Auseill, and I am aware that le Comte d'Auseill is your father."

"It is true," Flambeau admitted, "but our family *is* of Gascon origin, and we are proud of the fact. I have evaded my father for many years."

"And yet he safeguards the last few dividends from your criminal endeavours."

"How can you know this? And who, exactly, is 'our friend'?"

"Someone smart enough to deduce our location. To have a telegram delivered to the Court Church at the precise time that you and I happen to be passing through Saxony would seem remarkable, unless he had the ear of the Curia."

"He is a priest?"

"A detective. As you know, I have sometimes been called upon to handle objects of ecumenical import."

"Like a certain sapphire cross?"

"Quite so. I trust that I have rarely been the first choice for such tasks, just as I trust that our friend is. I am also aware that your father is hosting the auction of a great many *objets d'art* to raise funds for his homeland. He has quite a collection, and I understand that much of it is of religious significance. It makes sense that our friend might have been asked to investigate."

"So he plans to meet us in Auseill? At the Chateau?"

"Perhaps," said Father Brown. "I can see now where you found your passion for such things, and I have an answer to the question 'Where does Flambeau keep his booty?' Where else, but among other such objects."

"You said it yourself, Paul: The wise man hides a tree in a forest. But there are only a few stolen items that have not yet been returned. It is a work in progress."

So it was that Flambeau and Father Brown agreed to travel to Auseill, and from there to seek service in the defence of their respective homelands. As a master of deception, Flambeau put in motion the complex plan that would see them get across Germany, pass through Luxembourg, and make their way into Belgium. In doing so he was pitting himself against the infamous Schlieffen Plan, by which the German Empire would invade France by passing through Luxembourg and Belgium. In preparation for this, he established new identities for the pair, his own being that of a minor Alsatian aristocrat returning to his family in Strasbourg, where he claimed that a field commission awaited him. Father Brown was to become a Trappistine, protected from discovery by his vow of silence. This unusual partnership, Flambeau had explained, was necessitated by the Monk's appointment to serve in the abbatial church at the Kloschter vum Eelabarg, a Trappist abbey in the Alsace region.

The ruse had got them a fair distance, travelling from Dresden by train for half-a-day until the service terminated at Trèves, close to the Luxembourg border. Here, Flambeau decided that the overwhelming presence of the German war machine – especially so close to a country set to be invaded – presented too many obstacles for them to continue directly to Auseill. They would arrive after his father's auction, and very possibly after war itself had been declared.

Disembarking, they switched identities for a second time, using misdirection and a stolen hat to distract the guards at the Bahnhof checkpoint before making their way across town to the market square, where they found help among Trèves' vintners who, wishing to carry on with their business undisturbed, were determined to make their own way to into the Grand Duchy.

Crossing the border on 1st August, the pair found that the Duchy of Württemberg's Fourth Army had already entered and taken control of the city of Luxembourg. As tens of thousands of German soldiers mustered for the big push into Belgium, they made a diversion, travelling to the north of the city. Parting ways with the wine sellers, they made their way up into the densely forested Oure Valley, where the Gréngewald formed part of the continuous forest that covered most of the small country. Sometimes on foot, sometimes on bicycles, and sometimes travelling in the carriages of farmers and refugees, the two men caught glimpses of enemy troop movements as they slowly passed through the towns and villages that followed the river and the railway line that covered the forty or so miles between Luxembourg and Triesvierges. These towns had only a small German presence, enough to deter dissidents, but the little news that was on offer was controlled by the Imperial Army. There was no mention of the fierce Belgian resistance, nor the emerging reprisals against the civilian population. These things would not become apparent to the travellers until they reached a town some twenty miles to the east of their destination. News reports mentioned only the advance against *"fortress Liège"*.

The Benedictine Abbaye Saint-Maurice looked down upon the small town of Clervaux from its vantage point on the hillside. A very recent construction in the neo-Romanesque style, its orange-capped towers protruded above the treetops, welcoming its visitors as they made their way along the cobbled incline that brought them to an arched gate where a small boy waited anxiously.

"Père Brun?" he called as the men approached. *"Vous êtes Père Brun?"*

Somewhat surprised, the little priest confirmed his identity and accepted the proffered paper that the boy had been holding tightly.

"Another telegram from our friend," he said, unfolding the message. "One has to admire his powers of deduction."

"It's an easy trick," said Flambeau. "There are, what? A dozen churches and abbeys across our path, surely he could send a telegram to each one."

"If he were the head of the Paris police, perhaps, but blind luck is not his method."

Flambeau shrugged.

"If you say so. I find distraction and overcomplication tie up most modern detectives, present company excepted."

Father Brown frowned, holding up the message and reading it aloud:

A Friend to Père Brun
Auseill, Belgium
4 August 1914,
8.05 a.m.

Belgium invaded. Germans here. Regards to le Comte d'Auseill. Bona fortuna tibi esto.

"We are too late, my friend," he said, passing the telegram to Flambeau. "This telegram was received yesterday. I am so sorry for your loss."

"What?" His gigantic companion examined the message. "This doesn't say that anyone has died. Why – ?"

"I'm sorry. Our friend asks that I give my regards to the Count, as if he were standing here, by my side."

"It could surely be a typographical error. The telegraph operator . . . ."

"Sherlock Holmes is not a man prone to making errors."

Hercule Flambeau lowered his head, his face a mixture of grief and regret as his friend ushered him into the abbey, just minutes before morning mass began.

After the service they met briefly with the abbot, who recognised Flambeau from his childhood. Sharing a prayer for the late count's soul, the reverend father asked what the travellers planned to do next.

"I have a duty to see my father buried," said Flambeau, "and to see the damage the Germans have done first hand."

"And as his friend, I have a duty to see the count properly interred. I expect the Germans will allow it. So long as I speak French we should be fine. They have no conflict with the church."

"Indeed," said the abbot, "and if he hasn't been detained, there should be another priest at the Chateau."

"Oh? Did he have business with the count?"

"Something to do with the recovery of church relics. He was reluctant to give me any details, but implied it was on the highest authority."

"Do you recall his name?"

"Père Damian. He said he had travelled from Saxony like yourselves. Do you know him?"

"No, I'm afraid I don't. Do you know his order?"

The abbot shrugged. "I didn't ask. Cistercian, perhaps. He accompanied three sisters of our order, but I am hoping that they will have continued their journey south and into France. I would be grateful if you could look into their well-being when you arrive."

"Of course we shall," said Father Brown. "If it's no trouble, may we rest here this evening, and we will depart after morning prayers?"

The abbot found this acceptable, excusing himself to make arrangements while Flambeau and Father Brown continued their discussion.

"There's something not quite right about this Father Damian. Why send a priest from Saxony? Especially if Sherlock Holmes has already been approached?"

"Expedience? I presume that's why Holmes contacted you."

"No, that was a courtesy because you are my friend. You may also be useful in determining the provenance of certain items. Even at his age, Sherlock Holmes needs no assistance obtaining Holy Relics."

"Will he still be there when we arrive?"

"I cannot say. Movement will be limited, and he may have been forced to hide when the Germans arrived, but if his work is not done, he will find us."

On the next afternoon, the travellers emerged from a steep woodland slope adjacent to the town of Auseill. Flambeau led his friend out onto the edge of the town, which lay among the High Fens, that part of an upland plateau which lay between the Ardennes mountains behind them and the Äifel highlands to the northwest. It was a small settlement, which Flambeau had explained was just two stops along from Triesvierges Railway Station on the Liège-Luxembourg line, lying halfway between the town of Gouvy and the fortified city of Liège. The Bahnhof was barely a railway crossing comprised of customs offices and a timber yard, while the lower half of the town was little more than a Gasthof and a smattering of homesteads. Behind them, at the top of a steep forested escarpment, were the Chateau d'Auseill, where Flambeau had been born, and a handful of buildings at the summit. These included the Parish Church of Saint Eulalia, a centuries-old cemetery, and an observation tower disguised as a *belvédère*, designed by the Dutch General Henri Alexis Brialmont, giving a direct view of the land to the northwest, and to the town of Embourg, which formed part of the Liège fortifications some forty miles away.

Despite the muffled sound of Krupp's Berthas bombarding the distant city, Auseill itself seemed supernaturally still. At first it felt abandoned. As a small settlement with a single Gasthof and scattered homes lining a single street – the Rue de Bastogne – there were few places to hide, so the absence of people and the strange yellow ash that coated the ground and surrounding buildings presented a surreal vista. Very few buildings showed any sign of damage, and there was no obvious sign that fighting had taken place, but as they moved further into the town, it became apparent that the yellow tincture covered a number of human remains, as if the bodies had been stained yellow and left where they fell. Scattered around these were the black bodies of birds, in their hundreds, as if they had simply dropped out of the sky.

"What could do this to God's creations?" the little priest asked, framed more as a statement of shock and disappointment than as a proper question. Prodding at the nearest body with his umbrella, he exerted just enough pressure to tip it over and reveal the exposed underbelly of a dead German soldier.

"Some toxic chemical, I expect," said Flambeau.

"Chemical weapons? But why would the Germans use them on themselves?"

"Not the *alboches*. My father is . . . *was* a chemist by profession. The family business has a contract delivering munitions to the Nobel Arms Company. He was also an honorary Lieutenant-Colonel of the Third Belgian Army, and that peak above us hides part of the Liège fortifications."

Father Brown considered his friend's explanation, a concerned frown on his round face. His attention, and that of his umbrella tip, moved to one of the small black carcasses that lay close by.

"Whatever it was happened at night," he said, indicating the creature. "These are bats, not birds. You had best tell me more about your father and the town of Auseill."

Before Flambeau could reply, they were disturbed by the sight of three shapeless figures, kicking up yellow ash as they approached them from the Gasthof d'Auseill which overshadowed the street, obscuring the Bahnhof and custom offices which lay beyond. What seemed at first to be hunched men in robes turned out to be the nuns they had been told about, their faces obscured by gas filters, and their demeanour more charitable than hostile. Beckoning the two men forwards, the sisters proffered a filter to each of the visitors, and ushered them towards the Inn with a promise of rest and clean air.

Leading them through a small walled courtyard whose old stone had protected the wisteria and fruit trees from the yellow ash, they entered the Gasthof proper, passing into the bar area, where boots and filters were removed, and proper introductions were made.

The three nuns were the Sisters Mary, Adalsina, and Theresa. Over a warming bowl of *Rijstpap* and a stiff glass of *jenever*, Sister Mary recounted the events of the last few days.

"We were bound from the Abbey of St. Maurice to a teaching placement in Mons. Another traveller, Père Damian, did not wish to see us travel unaccompanied. He offered to join us on our journey, and told us that he had urgent business in Auseill along the way. He was visiting the town to secure the return of certain Holy Relics to the Church. There was an auction being held up at the Chateau, and he was meeting some magnate from Eastern Europe who had offered to acquire them for the Church."

"Eastern Europe, you say? Do you know which part?"

"No, but he sounded Slavic."

"Do you know which relics?" Flambeau asked.

"There were several," said Sister Mary. "I recall that one of them was a Canticle of Saint Eulalia, and another was an illuminated copy of *The Book of Saint Cyprian*."

"In Latin?" asked Father Brown.

"Middle High German, actually," said Flambeau. "I'm afraid that was one of my, erm, *acquisitions*. Obtained it from a rather disreputable *Großbürgher* whose grandfather stole it from some Jews during the *Hep Hep* riots. Tried to convince me it was annotated by none other than Doctor Faust himself."

"A book of spells, if I recall," said Father Brown, turning to the sisters. "M. Flambeau here is the son of Le Comte d'Auseill, and in happier times he was . . . acquiring pieces for his father's collection."

"Yes. Can you tell me what happened to my father? Is he dead? Can we get to that part?"

"Of course," said Sister Mary in a more solemn tone. "The auction was meant to take place on the Tuesday, the 4th, but it was brought forward a day because the Germans were at the border. There weren't many people in attendance, but I do remember that an awful row broke out between Père Damian and the Englishman. Such accusations! Your father tried to step in and calm matters, but there were gunshots, and he was mortally wounded. The man from Eastern Europe fled, and the Englishman, who had also been shot, chased after him."

"So this East European killed my father?"

Sister Mary nodded.

"The Englishman swore that he was in some Secret Society or other. He and the Gendarme investigated the incident, but the man was never found."

"And Father Damian?" Asked Brown.

"He disappeared as well. I think he chased after his friend. It was all a little much for us, so we decided to stay another night to answer any questions. But then – "

"Go on . . . ."

"The Gardes Civique ordered an evacuation. They had news that the Germans were in Luxembourg and the Comte had given strict orders for everyone but the Gardes to leave. With war coming,

318

we knew that our placement in Mons would be suspended, so we decided to stay up at the Chateau where we felt we might best do God's work."

"And then the Germans came?"

"In great numbers. The trains carried two great siege guns and thousands of men bound for Liège. They only stayed for an hour or two, and left a company of men behind to deal with the Gardes' who were barricaded into the Observation Tower at the top of the hill, but it didn't go well."

"I take it that my father had sabotaged the mountain?" asked Flambeau.

Sister Mary nodded.

"It's so steep, and there is only a path as high as Jacob's Ladder leading up to the summit. When the Germans started to march up the hill, something happened. A great yellow cloud of dust rolled down the hillside, enveloping and burning and suffocating them. It . . . it was . . . *appalling*. Within an hour most of them were dead, and the remaining soldiers gathered for a second assault. We barricaded ourselves inside the Chateau, and waited, but nothing ever came."

"We had that strange sleep," added Sister Theresa. "Do you remember?"

"Yes, you're right," agreed Sister Mary, a little frustrated by the interruption, "but I'm sure it was nothing. None of us recalled falling asleep, and we all of us missed our Night Prayers."

"Strange," said Father Brown. Strict observances should not have been dismissed so lightly. "Perhaps the absence of church bells ringing out the hours . . . ."

"Oh no," said Sister Theresa, "Saint Eulalias has a campanile. It rang out the hours."

"Anyway," Sister Mary continued, "the next morning the Germans had all gone, their dead left behind, and we found the Englishman, just lying on the ground, staring up at the sky."

"Dead?"

"No. He is here in one of the guest rooms. Sister Adalsina has been tending to him while Sister Theresa and I have been gathering the bodies for a proper burial."

"Of course," said Father Brown. "I shall be happy to conduct a service on their behalf. In the meantime, may we see the Englishman?"

Sister Adalsina led the pair up to a first floor guest room, where she explained that the Englishman had been left sleeping. She asked that they not trouble him for too long, explaining that he appeared to have suffered a head injury, and could not remember much of what happened to him.

"Do you at least know his name?" asked Flambeau.

"I know it," said Father Brown as Sister Adalsina shook her head, "for the Englishman is our friend. The same gentleman that summoned us to assist in his investigation."

As the door opened, they were greeted by a thin-framed man who appeared to be in his late fifties, well-tucked into a single pine bed, his right arm secured by a sling and his head wrapped in a thin bandage. Flambeau gasped as they stepped into the room, and he recognised the sleeping invalid. Moving over to his bedside, Father Brown coughed politely and the man's piercing grey eyes flickered open.

"Forgive me," he said at last, "but my mind is suffering some minor disarray. I know your faces, but I cannot place your names. Nor mine, for that matter."

"You can rest assured that that is a temporary inconvenience," said the short clergyman, "for I am Father Brown, and this is my good friend Hercule Flambeau, Le Comte d'Auseill, and you are Mister Sherlock Holmes."

"I am?" The detective frowned. "Far be it from me to question the word of a man of the cloth, especially when he keeps company with a notorious criminal, but something tells me not to trust a priest at this time. Is there any way you can corroborate that statement?"

"He knows who I am," said Flambeau under his breath. "Even when he can't remember his own name, he remembers mine."

Father Brown raised a hand to stay his overexcited companion, reaching into his pocket and withdrawing the two rumpled telegrams. These he passed to the detective, who scrutinised them as the priest continued.

"I am not in possession of all of the facts, as yet, but if you will allow me to recount what little I know, perhaps it might stir some memory of your own. If not, I am sure some further investigation will make things clearer."

"Very well," said Holmes, an air of arrogance in his tone. "Impress me."

"You are supposed to be retired, and you came here incognito, so I shall presume that you are here as a favour, and not on some mission to entrap my infamous friend here. With a war in Europe looming, you were asked to conduct an investigation, or perhaps an intervention, in relation to the collection of M. Baudouin Duroc, the former Comte d'Auseill. This prompted you to send a telegram to

320

Flambeau and myself. For some reason *another* party, working with a man calling himself Father Damian, desired some part of the collection for himself. An occult piece, which suggests some unholy interest in power.

"Unfortunately, the Church is in dire financial straits, and needs money. The German Empire needs the Kingdom of Italy to join the war as an ally, and so it wants to buy some grace with his Most Holy Father, Pope Pius. The return of precious relics to the Vatican would be an ideal sweetener, and so the German Army is under orders to recover what artefacts it can, so that it may gift any symbolic treasures directly to the Vatican, and use any other spoils of war to ease the Vatican's burden of debt. In return, they hope that Papal influence can be exerted, and that His Holiness shall persuade Italy to fulfil its obligations as part of the Triple Alliance.

"Whether your favour is to The Crown or, given your connections, to the Holy Father, I have a feeling that it may also be to buy grace with Pope Pius himself. If Italy supports the Entente Powers, then the war may end sooner and with less unnecessary bloodshed.

"What I cannot yet ascertain is the connection between dead bats, bells that chime without bell-ringers, narcoleptic nuns, and what I hope shall be an episode of temporary memory loss."

Father Brown moved on to Sister Mary's story and the second telegram notifying them that the count was dead. As the short clergyman finished setting out the facts as he saw them, Holmes frowned for a second time.

"It seems logical," he said at last, "that I am indeed Sherlock Holmes. The recognition in M. Flambeau's eyes appeared genuine, and I can see from your appearance – hair growth, dirty nails, rumpled clothes, worn shoes, at least three distinct mud patterns, coal dust, and traces of that sulphurous ash from outside – that you have both travelled on foot and by other slow means for several days without rest. From Dresden via Luxembourg, I shouldn't wonder. From your faces, I can see that I should already know this. I would hope, therefore, that an examination of my own clothes might expose some further information. Would you mind?"

Father Brown recovered the pile of folded garments and shoes that rested on the bedside chair and handed them to Holmes, who laid them out on his lap. A cursory inspection was followed by a more in depth examination, during which he sniffed and stretched and ran his fingers over each item, withdrawing several objects from the pockets as he did so, sometimes accompanied with a sigh or an

321

ejaculated "A-ha!" Each time an inspection was completed, the detective threw the item aside, sometimes onto the bedside chair and sometimes onto the floor, but not in any discernible pattern. At last he was left with a handful of objects spread before him on the bed, whereupon he steepled his fingers, closed his eyes, and considered the clues. He then placed the items in order from left to right, and commenced his account. They were a receipt, a false beard, a clay pipe, a pouch of tobacco, a roll of Lucifers, two ticket stubs, a folded timetable, a wallet containing shillings and francs, a key, a shoe, a few pine needles plucked from his trousers, a brochure, a pencil, a folded handkerchief, a revolver, two spent bullets, a second receipt, a magnifying glass, a pair of tweezers, a ball of lint, and a folded sheet of violin music.

"The receipt indicates that I sent a telegram to a Cathedral in Dresden. This must have been one of my first actions upon taking this case."

Father Brown nodded.

"The false beard suggests the use of a disguise, though whether from this case or another I cannot ascertain. These clues suggest I was moving quickly, and perhaps juggling cases. The amount of tobacco used tells me that I travelled from London to Dover, where this first ticket reveals that on the morning of August third, I travelled on a ferry that left the Admiralty Pier. This second ticket confirms my journey through France and Belgium on that same day, as do my coins. This key tells me I have another room booked somewhere in this Gasthof, where my shoes were cleaned upon arrival, but have subsequently walked in woodland, and on a thin layer of soil atop both limestone and sandstone. Presumably I ascended the escarpment to visit the Chateau where, according to the brochure, I attended le Comte d'Auseill's 'Fire Sale for Victory'. It made sense to sell off his treasures before the Germans trampled across the country. I had circled a number of items, each of which would have been of interest to me for some reason.

"First we have a painting, 'Retreat to Tongeren', attributed to the artist Émile Jean-Horace Vernet. I seem to recall that I have this artist in my blood, and so I shall dismiss this as a personal interest not pertinent to the case.

"Next, the Karlmann Crystal. I believe this is a precious stone named after Carloman the First, King of the Franks, and is a precious gemstone whose theft was reported by a fake aristocrat eight years ago. I believe he could never prove that he had owned the gemstone in the first place. From the name 'Flambeau'? that I scribbled in the

322

margin, it would appear that my interest lay in the identity of the thief."

"Yes," said Flambeau sheepishly. "One of mine, although the Baron was a cad of the first water, who probably won it by cheating at cards."

Holmes raised an eyebrow and smiled thinly before he continued.

"An unredacted copy of *La princesse en Jaune* by Saint-Saëns. This corresponds to the folded sheet of music, which, according to this partial ink stamp, I purchased from a music shop in the Strand. As an opera the original, *La princesse Jaune*, not '*en Jaune*', is somewhat light and forgettable, but a piece I have enjoyed playing on the violin . . . ." He paused, acknowledging the memory. "I had never known there was an unredacted version, and I wanted to cross-reference it with a standard copy. I can see it in my mind . . . I see the unredacted version and it is riddled with tritones, medieval suspensions, and chord changes that I am sure make little or no sense to the trained ear. It would be . . . well, *dissonant* would be the most polite description. I think my interest in this piece may just have been a violinist's idle curiosity.

"Then we have *Raudskinna, the Galdrabok of Gottsálkur Nikolásson*. A book of spells, also called *The Book of Power*, but it was also written by the last Roman Catholic Bishop of Iceland, so a possible relic of value, much like the next item, *The Book of Saint Cyprian*."

Flambeau repeated the confession he had made to Father Brown and the Sisters.

"And the last item that I circled, a pristine copy of *The Canticle of Eulalia*. Another relic, presumably connected to the town's church."

"Indeed," said Flambeau. "Legend has it that Eulalia wrote the *Canticle* here in Auseill. It has some local significance concerning her life's mission to do battle with pagan gods. They say the original church bell was stolen by worshipers of Mithras or Saturn."

"So there are three relics in all, each of which has a connection to witchcraft or pagan gods," said Father Brown.

"It makes sense," said Holmes. "I remember noting the connection during the auction, and it cast my mind back to a previous case. I've met Father Damian before, in another time and place."

"And his East European sponsor from the secret society?"

"The Black Hand!" Holmes shouted, sitting upright. "Of course! Unification or Death!"

"I beg your pardon?" Flambeau was flummoxed by the detective's nonsensical exclamations.

"In the months before the assassination of the Archduke Franz-Ferdinand, I was working hard to prevent a secret society of Serbian nationalists, The Order of the Black Hand, from triggering this infernal conflict. They supplied the gun that fired the shot. They empowered the hand that pulled the trigger. The man with Father Damian was Jovan Vojinović, a Serbian *velikaš*, a member of their nobility. He also happens to be a witch of some kind."

"And Father Damian?"

"He used another name, still masquerading as a priest, but he was excommunicated for dabbling in the occult. Father Damian is a fake! I must have called him out, and perhaps named Vojinović as a terrorist. Wine was spilled," Holmes indicated the handkerchief, which was stained, "and then there were two shots. The first struck me in the shoulder while the second struck the Count. The bullets came from a 1910 Browning, the same gun supplied by Franz-Ferdinand's assassin. I am sorry for your loss, M. Flambeau. I did give chase, but in my condition I was unable to gain upon Vojinović.

"A Gendarme and I took a full inventory, and I do recall that no items were missing at that point. The *Gardes* assisted us in securing the Chateau, and I had attempted to track both of the villains in the time that followed. Unfortunately, the evacuation of the town and arrival of the German army superseded my investigation.

"I did manage, however, to obtain your whereabouts, and this additional receipt attests to the second telegram that you received. I then turned my attention to the coming occupation. Thankfully the Count was a very capable man, and the *Gardes* defended the Chateau superbly. At the time I was unaware of the chemical traps that had been set, and I detest the use of such ordnance in modern warfare, but the redoubt held against overwhelming numbers, although we did expect to be overrun by the survivors."

"What happened next?"

"This," Holmes indicated the lint. "Both Father Damian and his companion had rooms in this Gasthof, and I used a secret passage that leads from the Chateau down to the cellar here. While the Germans were busy preparing for their second assault, I was able to examine their accommodation. The only notable clue was a change of clothes in the Serbian's room. On the sleeve of his abandoned jacket I found these fragments of bell-rope."

"So he and Father Damian were ringing in the hours. Why?"

"Practice, I believe. With the evacuation of the town, I should have noticed the bells earlier. No sooner had I deduced that the clue lay within the bells, than they started to peal, and I half-recognised the harmony or, rather, the disharmony."

"Disharmony? The opera music?"

Holmes nodded.

"An approximation of *La Princesse en Jaune*. But tell us about the bell, Flambeau," he said. "There's something special about it. Your father told me, but it would come better from one more familiar with the legend."

"I don't understand," said Flambeau. "We never rang the bell. It is broken. Flawed."

"Of course!" said Father Brown. "The bats!"

"I'm afraid I don't follow," said Flambeau. "The church tower uses a carillon, put in place during a medieval renovation. It was considered bad luck to fit a new bourdon bell, so the church went without for about four-hundred years."

"And then?"

"A *bourdon* became available. It was improperly tuned, so it was moved here just for show. We call it Emanuel, the *Bourdon d'Auseill*."

"Emanuel?" Asked Father Brown "It was a *second* hand bell?"

Flambeau nodded.

"Relocated from Notre Dame Cathedral back in the seventeenth century. The hammer kept shattering, and the story goes that the bell shall never strike until doomsday."

"And strike it did," said Father Brown, "at the end of vespers. Instead of a calling to prayer, it rang out the final cadence of a discordant tune. So low that it could barely be heard, and so dissonant that bats fell dead in the sky, and people lost consciousness. Father Damian could not afford for the German Army to seize his precious booty."

"I tried to warn the Germans," said Holmes, "but I succumbed, just like everybody else. I woke up here, with Damian and Vojinović long gone. Short of a miracle, I suspect that the relics have gone with them."

"Sadly, Mr. Holmes, I think you might be right."

The Westanger Waste
by Kevin P. Thornton

The Ruin of Westanger Abbey, created by the irascible whim of
Henry VIII, had been exposed to the elements since the dissolution
of the monasteries in 1542. Now, 381 years later, it was showing its
age. The interior was rank and damp as if the partial shelter of
damaged rooves and broken casements allowed the worst of the
elements in while letting only the best of them back out again. As a
result, the soft and gentle rains of lyric and poesy had vacated the
gloomy gothic entrails, leaving only mold and rot.

Down below, the newly rebuilt mansion glittered in contrast.
The two men looked down as invitees in robes and sashes,
transported by charabanc and omnibus, swarmed into the building.
A collective of nebulous characters, members of the fourth estate no
doubt, gathered themselves to one side, in a tent. The table was laden
with large draughts of ale as if to attract their attention.

"The Côte d'Azur beckons," said one of the two observers. "Or
maybe the beach promenade of Monaco? We could be there – or at
least I could." He paused to look back down the path. "We could
even be down there, listening to prelates prattle, ministers meander,
and rabbis ramble. It is warm and cozy down there. And yet," he
sniffed disdainfully, "we are 'ere." He said the last in that elegant
way common to his countrymen, the final syllable rising in inflection
as if needing a needling *'Non?'* to complete it. As he did so, he
looked at his companion. The cleric was his friend, but he was also
a man capable of trying the patience of a really patient saint. A Saint
Francis – the one from Assisi. Certainly not Xavier, who was a
Jesuit, and maybe not even de Sales.

"And yet here we are." His companion said exactly the same
words as the other, but the meaning couldn't have been more
different. His answer was in peaceful agreeance, as if the
existentialism of the moment had captured him.

It had eluded Flambeau. "What you have not told me, you
vexatious vicar, is *why?*"

"I am here because I was invited," said Father Brown. "You are
here because I asked you to come with me." It was not a satisfactory
answer, but it was all that was offered.

The man from the Continent sniffed the air suspiciously. "Everything is damp," he said, "like a village of old thatched cottages filled with spinsters in tweed skirts, gossiping until they die. Cold and clammy and . . . ." Words failed him.

"Damp?" supplied Father Brown.

"Yes," said Flambeau, gloomily.

"It is raining," said his companion.

"It is always raining in your country. That is why everything is damp."

"*Quod erat demonstrandum.*"

The two men seemed to have little in common. The Frenchman was taller, dressed in a stylish coat with a rakish hat and gloves of the finest leather. Had he been English, he might have been accused of preening. As he was French, his apparel was perfectly acceptable.

The other man seemed to wear everything slightly askew, as if he had dressed a minute ahead of himself. His clothing was well made but worn, patched in some places, like an old soldier's uniform. Black suit sagging ever so slightly, well-polished shoes with new heels and old soles, and a Mackintosh that kept out most of the rain. The whole was topped off with a wide brim hat that tried in vain to divert the water off his back.

"I thought the *cappello romano* should only be worn with a cassock?" said a voice from behind.

"It is a matter of practicality. A *biretta* offers no protection."

"It is a small sin," said Sherlock Holmes. "I'm sure your god will forgive you. Father Brown, it is as always good to see you. Perhaps the umbrella you are holding would be more efficacious were it open and above you."

Father Brown looked at his hand holding the parapluie as if it were a miraculous appearance. Holmes had never seen the priest un-ombrelled, but he could not ever remember him using it without at least a reminder. On one occasion, the Frenchman had seemed to need to re-instruct him in its operation, so vacuous were his efforts.

When their paths had first crossed, Holmes thought Father Brown's behaviour to be a trick – a subterfuge to disconcert and disarm. It was only when he recognized the keenness of the priest's mind that he had realized it was no act. "He is so focused," he said once to Watson, "that it's as if in noting the peculiarities of his surrounds, he sacrifices the mundanities of normal life."

Watson thought at the time that Father Brown was the only other man Holmes had ever treated as his equal. "His deductive prowess," the detective had continued explaining, "is more inductive

327

than I would normally care for, but he follows the form and failings of human behaviour so well that, had he done this for a living, he would have been my nearest rival. His ways, in the hands of any other, could not have been trusted, and they should not work, but he is never wrong."

"Never?" Watson had said.

"Not that I have ever seen. He is able to place himself in a miscreant's mind so thoroughly that he can predict exactly what they will do. Such a skill makes catching criminals easy. You go to where they are going, and wait for them to arrive."

"Sometimes they don't arrive," Watson had answered, ever loyal, "because you, in chasing them using your own ways, would have already caught them."

Holmes smiled ever so slightly as he remembered that conversation. He turned as he heard his friend arrive behind him. Watson was a bit more solid than when they had first met, yet still as stolid as ever. His walking cane was less a gentleman's accessory nowadays and more a necessary evil, in particular clambering up the hill to see the ruin. Otherwise, he was still the same old Doctor Watson, and his eyes lit up as he greeted old friends.

"Father Brown, it is good to see you again. And you too, Monsieur, still free and clear to come and go as you wish. That is truly good news."

"Thanks to my friend here," said Flambeau pointing at the Padré, "and it is good to see you too, Doctor. It is true what you say: The police no longer hound my every step. Just as you, Doctor, cure the ailments of the physique, the good Father heals those of the soul. When he led me to the reasons why I did what I did, that was when I learnt how to not do so anymore. And now, I am a reformed man."

"We haven't forgotten your Damascene conversion," said Holmes. "You are lucky Father Brown is your friend. I would probably have had you arrested."

"You would never have caught me," said Flambeau.

Doctor Watson sighed. Father Brown smiled. It was the briefest glimpse of joviality from him. Like Holmes, the cleric never seemed to find much to delight him, present company excepted.

Flambeau spread his arms as if to embrace Holmes and Watson, and was amused as their English reticence staidly stepped them back. Instead he gestured at the surroundings.

"There is a perfectly good, overtly tasteless building down the hill with one resident, clergymen from fifty beliefs, and people waiting to ply us with food and drink. Yet we are standing on this mound looking at this wreck of an abbey in the middle of a squall. Why?"

"It is hardly a squall, Monsieur," said Holmes. "In Sussex, this would be no more than a fresh day. And we are here because of this." He extracted a gilt-edged invitation from inside his coat. "I assume you received one as well."

"I did," said Father Brown, producing an identical card from inside his outerwear. The two men briefly compared them. "Identical," said Holmes, holding it for all to see. It read as follows:

> *In the ruinous abbey, find a surprise.*
> *Watch for a murder, a feast for your eyes.*
> *With a room full of clerics, there are secrets and lies.*
> *Death's on the menu, surely that's no surprise.*

"And it was attached to an invitation to whatever-this-is?" asked Flambeau, gesticulating in the general direction of below.

"An inter-disciplinary conference," said Father Brown. "Such events have become popular in these inter-bellum years, The trade union protests of last year have put the landed gentry on edge, and some of them choose to spend their money trying to find spiritual solutions to a material world."

"Inter-bellum?" said Watson. "I thought we had just finished the war to end all wars?"

"There is always another to come," said Flambeau rather gloomily. "In the meantime, if you are poor, you pray. If you are rich, you create a gathering such as this in the hopes that others will pray. They never work. They are the indulgences of people with too much money. Look at the title of this. '*A Convocation of Deitic Believers Hastening Towards A New World Peace*'."

"*Deitic* is an unusual word," said Father Brown "I assume it is meant to be a form of deity, but I have never seen it used this way."

"The invitation to a murder shows similar grammar limitations," said Holmes. "The poetry, and I use that description loosely, has no rhythm. There is the repetition of surprise for no obvious reason other than the lack of either imagination or thesaurus, and it is vague to the point of calumny. Yet it achieved its goal. It brought the two finest detectives in the land to this event."

"I thought my invitation had to do with my vocation," said Father Brown, "and that the poem was a joke in poor taste."

"Maybe there are more detectives here," said Flambeau. "Is your club of excellent detection limited to two? Are there not others?"

"I checked on some of the pretenders," said Holmes. "Our Belgian friend is on the Continent, and Pons is on holiday in Northumberland. There is also a woman in St. Mary Mead who is remarkably astute, but she wasn't contacted either."

"There is an older student at St. Ignatius College," said Father Brown, "although he is little-known right now. And as you know, the second son of the Duke of Denver has shown some talent. There are others as well, but I didn't see any when I arrived. Holmes?"

"Naught but a plethora of prelates gathered in the great hall," he replied. "There's a display in the library of building material, slate and such, but as to detectives, none but ourselves."

"*In the ruinous abbey, find a surprise,*'" said Father Brown. "If there is no surprise to be found here, maybe it is elsewhere."

"The promise of a murder has gathered us here," said Holmes. "Let us return to the event itself."

The Westanger mansion was a ninety-room monstrosity that mixed the worst of Georgian style and Edwardian excess, commingling in a display of overt wealth and covert taste.

"What do you know of the host?" said Father Brown.

"Dufford Hradsky, recently entitled as Viscount Westanger," said Holmes. "His grandfather made his money on the gold reefs of the Transvaal. The son nearly lost it all. Dufford, the third generation, has made it all back and more. He was in manufacturing during the war and is now trying to buy respectability."

"There was a story in *The Times*," said Watson, "that the Viscount had taken his money out of munitions and into construction."

"That is either very noble or very cynical," said Flambeau. "It is the type of tale that might indeed create the opportunity for a Viscountcy. I hope he did well before he changed. If he continues in the building trade, he will need help. His taste – " He gestured at the building. " – is execrable, *n'est-ce pas*? It looks like a wedding cake, this house. Maybe he should go back to munitions, blow it up, and start again. When we walked through, even the runners and rugs were all piggledy-higgledy."

Watson bit back the correction. He knew Flambeau could speak perfect English and mangled it only to tease.

"There was a single stretch of carpet that was not perpendicular," said Father Brown.

"And there seemed to be more salesmen than clergymen," continued the Frenchman. "There were side rooms filled with the wares of construction and repair, and little men in tight collars with order books in triplicate. It would appear Hradsky realizes there is money to be made in church roofing. May I see that poem again?"

Father Brown handed him the copy. "It has placed us at the edge of the Abbey, yet there is no murder. Have we been summoned to prevent one?"

"If so, by whom?" asked Holmes. "Such fore-knowledge would suggest the errant poet is complicit in whatever is to happen." He looked around. The ruins of the abbey were on top of a tor that overlooked Chez Westanger. The Abbey loomed over the mansion below, which had been built on the site of the former monastic cloisters.

"Father," Holmes said, "if we are not up here to actually see anything – "

"Then maybe we are here to be seen," said the priest. "Perhaps it is time to rejoin the luminaries below."

Holmes rarely reacted to feelings. He was a creature of science and logic. Nevertheless, as they walked down, he was disturbed by their vulnerability at the top of the hill – Flambeau ahead in pursuit of creature comforts, Watson pretending to take his time so his old body could negotiate the slope with more ease.

"I believe we are being watched," Holmes said to Father Brown.

"I felt it too," replied the priest. He didn't expect an answer from Holmes, so after a few more steps he said, "Maybe, when we feel something, it is nothing more than a cumulative effect of all our experience and learnings. An instinctive rather than a spiritual response."

"That is an interesting analysis," said Holmes. "We were clearly not directed to the top of the mound as targets. The war has left maybe a thousand marksmen in England alone who are capable of shooting at us out in the open like that – the most logical reason to lure us up there – yet none took their chance."

"It is a puzzle," said Father Brown. "Perhaps we should send a few telegraphic queries to other detection specialists of note, to inquire as to whether they received an invitation?"

"I did that," said Holmes. "In addition to the ones we mentioned, I checked my list and sent out fourteen queries. Nobody else was invited."

"What about the 'Montenegrin', as we shall refer to him?" asked the priest. "Is he still wandering the world, seeking further education? I'd heard he plans to settle in New York?"

"When I was his age, my mind was focused on learning all I needed to know to be the world's greatest detective. Even now there are a hundred topics related to our work that, given the time and inclination, I could write substantive dissertations about. If the young man to whom you allude were ever to write anything, it would likely be an analysis of Bosnian beer or bilaterally symmetrical sub-tropical flowers. He is brilliant, that one. He has the intellect of his Uncle, yet sadly none of his purpose."

"None of his purpose *yet*," said Father Brown gently. "And judging by your comment, you have him to thank for your knowledge of orchids. His interests also interest you."

Holmes nodded, acknowledging the prelate's perspicacity. "Which does leave the question: Why were we both invited? No disrespect, Father Brown, but they hardly need both of us. And neither of us is known for our cooperative work ethic."

"Maybe whoever sent the invitations was unsure of himself and didn't know if we would show interest. And yet, the posing of an ecclesiastical mystery of some sort is more likely to gather me in than not."

"Maybe whoever sent the invitation to you wasn't aware of your availability, so he or she has covered all bets. This person doesn't know you well enough to realize the relative freedom you have. Most priests are tied to their post – a parish, a service institute, the staff of an egotistical archbishop. Our inviter didn't know if you would come, so he sent me an invitation as well, not realizing that I was more unlikely to respond."

"And how are your bees?"

"Largely self-sufficient, which is why I was able to fetch Watson and come to this intrigue."

"Indeed," said Father Brown. "Which still doesn't explain your equanimity in the face of such a shallow premise. Why did you agree to come?"

"Because I knew that *you* would," said Holmes, "and it has been too long since I last saw you. Also, in the years since you reclaimed your companion Flambeau – via a pardon for his sins – to the side of the righteous, I'm now able to be in his company without being seen to consort with a criminal."

Watson had caught them up, and as he passed them he whispered, loud enough for Father Brown to hear, "There is no one more self-righteous than he who declaims the self-righteousness of others."

They had reached the levelled-off area in front of the house. It had not yet been laid with a driveway or formal garden, so in an effort to disguise the unfinished nature of the edifice, the caterers had spilled out in front of the entrance. Tenting and bunting had been used to create extra social areas, and Flambeau had already headed to the nearest one in search of liquid fortification. Watson followed, reasoning that a heartwarming measure of *Uisghe Beatha* from the Highlands was exactly what was needed to fight off the chill weather.

Holmes and Father Brown followed leisurely in their wake. Holmes looked around as they ambled. He noted everything, but he was obvious in his observations. Father Brown was not as obvious, yet Holmes knew he had noted the same troublesome discrepancies.

"You see the same as me," said Holmes.

"I believe so," said Father Brown. "The setup is drab. The bunting does not celebrate. Much expense has been spared. I believe when my fine French friend comes back, we will find the fare not to his favour."

"It is odd," said Holmes, "that such a man, one who measures himself by the opinions of others, has fallen short on this demonstration of largesse."

"What did it say in his *Who's Who* entry?"

"Not very much," said Holmes. "Which is surprising. If you take the time to fill in the application, it is generally because you wish to be seen in a good light. There are gaps in his *curriculum vitae*."

"Education?" asked the priest

"Not listed," said Holmes. "Nor are his interests, clubs, family, or occupations, save businessman. It was as if he was told he needed an entry in *Who's Who*, but not why."

"What's missing may be more important than what is there," said Father Brown.

Holmes concurred. "With the exception of historically interesting people, one's entry is generally a waste of time."

"Yet you looked up Hradsky?"

333

"Only because the nature of a person's entry tells me a lot about him. The Viscount doesn't have the typical trappings of wealth. He has a large house, with drab canvas entertaining areas. He has set up a conference of the great and good, yet also invites the worst of the newspapers. I saw the hacks who are here. They are journalists on their last legs, many of whom haven't written sober copy in years. It would seem the ambitions of the Viscount are beyond his abilities and pocket. Even the entry in *Who's Who* tells us that Viscount Westanger needs a good assistant so he can go about doing whatever it is business tycoons do."

They were at the tent into which Watson and Flambeau had disappeared. The doctor was standing in front of a brazier, warming one hand and holding a glass of brown liquid in the other.

"How is the whisky?" said Father Brown.

"It takes the chill away," said Watson, as always loathe to offend.

Flambeau, on the other hand, seemed to delight in the opportunity. "What is this?" he asked the server. "I know it is supposed to be whisky, but what is it actually?" The server had no answer, so Flambeau turned, looking for a larger audience, and found his friends. "This is not potable," he said. "It would take two miracles from the wedding at Cana to rescue this – one would not be enough. As for the food . . ." He was prevented from opining on the *hors d'oeuvres* by his friend whispering to him momentarily. Flambeau looked around as Father Brown spoke. "Yes," he said. "I see it now. That explains a lot. But what does it mean?"

"I suspect we will find out soon enough," said Holmes, and as if in answer, he was interrupted by the sound of a rifled bullet. Watson and Flambeau crouched by instinct, seeking non-existent cover. Holmes closed his eyes and replayed the sound. He turned to look outside the shelter up to where he believed the shot had originated, only to see Father Brown already staring at the uppermost embattlement of the mansion.

In explanation, the priest said, "I saw the muzzle flash."

"It sounded like a *sharfschutzen* rifle," said Holmes. "A Mauser 98, most likely. They have a distinctive crack." To Watson's raised eyebrow he explained, "I made a study once."

"Of course you did."

"It was indeed a Mauser," said the priest. Flambeau, joining them said, "Your studies were much more close, *mon Padre, non*? The Ardennes, was it not? 1915?

"1914," the Prelate replied. Then, "The shot was not aimed at us."

"Its consequences were," said Holmes. "Let us see who has died. Whoever it was is the reason we are here."

As they neared the house, people came out and began to mill about in that exclusively English way, torn between not wishing to do something, yet feeling that something should be done nevertheless.

The four friends ignored the millers-about and moved through the crowd with purpose towards the mansion entrance. As they drew near, they were approached by a man dressed in a morning coat with ridiculous silken spats on fine leather shoes, and a hairstyle slicked back in such a manner that the rain seemed to accelerate off it. "Mister Holmes. Father Brown. I am so glad you are here. Someone has just tried to shoot one or our guests."

Holmes ignored the outstretched hand while Father Brown slid by in his shadow. Flambeau, coming up behind, shook it and said, "And you are – ?"

The welcome diminished as he replied, "I am Viscount Westanger."

"So not the butler then. *Enchanté.* I am Hercule Flambeau, and my friend here is Doctor Watson. If you will excuse us – " He waved in the direction of the small gathered crowd. " – we have matters to attend."

"But I'm the Viscount," their welcomer repeated.

"Congratulations. 'Ave you been shot?"

"Well, no."

"Then for the moment, Vicomte, we have no further need for you. We will call for you if that changes." With that Flambeau swept Doctor Watson along with him. "Prissy, pernicious prig," he said. Then, "You may use that in your next tale, *mon amis.* And I said *prig*, not *pig*, although in this case I suspect they are interchangeable."

They caught up with Holmes and Father Brown to find nothing more than a bullet hole in the marble floor. Nearby, dressed in peacock finery of woven silk and a cashmere coat, a man was cooling himself with a folding fan. "It was me," he kept repeating. "The bullet was meant for me." He was surrounded, at a distance, by other religious people who seemed anxious to seem well-meant. Father Brown hovered on the edge of the crowd, listening without being noted or noticed.

335

The peacock man with the fan had sat down as if the effort of the day were too much. "Mister Holmes. Mister Holmes," he said again. "I have been shot at."

"Have you?" said Flambeau. "And you are?"

"I am Swami John," he said, as if it meant something. Even among those gathered, there was no startled recognition, no shock that a vital part of their congregation had been attacked. All bar one.

"Swami John," said Viscount Westanger. "My word, that is a terrible thing to have happened. It must be the fascists, or the communists."

"Don't forget the trade unionists," said Flambeau. "There are lots of -*ists* that you did not list. What about the capitalists? Or the Arabists, archeologists, the scientists? It could be anyone. It could be no one."

"But what of the shot at Swami John," said the Viscount. "There is the mark where it struck." The damage to the floor was presented as if in undeniable evidence of malfeasance. Holmes examined it in passing as he walked over to where the men of the press had gathered. It was clear that, like the Swami, they recognized him. Although he had been retired for many years, his fame and striking appearance made him easy to remember, even among the most soused of them. Holmes moved among them, asking questions and receiving answers that seemed not to surprise him, Father Brown appeared by his side. The two of them walked back to Swami John, who was in full voice lamenting his near-death experience. If he thought that this would gain him some measure of sympathy, he was wrong. The varied religious representatives of the conference were retreating back to their events – some to various lecture rooms, others to the displays of building materiel, rain gutters, and tiling.

"The damage to the floor is odd," said Father Brown.

"Indeed," said Holmes. "What do you think of the Swami?"

"In his finery he looks like Joseph from the book of Genesis," said the priest. "It is surprising the killer missed, if indeed the shot was aimed anywhere. He would be an even easier target than the two of us on the hill." He moved over to the side of the stricken mendicant.

"How are you feeling?" he said to him. "Several of our compatriots saw you slip on the carpet at the sound of the bullet. Have you recovered?"

"I will survive," he said as if he disbelieved himself. "And you are?"

"Father Brown."

336

"Were you all the Papists could send? What an insult to the Viscount."

"We are not part of the conference," said Flambeau. "We are here to save you. The question is from whom? Who would wish to kill you? Who are you?"

"Who am I?" he said. "I am the Grand Wazir Swami John Ryukyu of Sassania. I was invited to be a keynote speaker by the Viscount, as I am from outside the formal religions of our time. Lord Westanger felt I could offer a new view on World Peace." He paused, as if expecting the priest to bow his head in mutual prayer, or at least applaud. Father Brown remained still, listening carefully with such a hint of philosophical beatificism upon his countenance that it encouraged the Swami, and his tale continued. Holmes meanwhile sent Watson on an errand, and when the Doctor returned with an uncorked bottle of Welsh whisky and two glasses, he warned Holmes away from the contents. Holmes poured a glass for the Swami, who engaged with it enthusiastically, despite its industrial aroma.

The story was as the detective expected and while the priest continued with the supposed victim. Holmes asked Flambeau and Watson to head upstairs towards where the shot had come from. "Be careful," he said to them both. "Whoever is up there is armed."

The Viscount had disappeared for the moment, and as Holmes listened in part to the Swami's conversation with the priest, oiled by the whisky, he understood why.

"The Swami's real name is indeed John," said Father Brown some minutes later. The subject in question had by now inhaled most of the bottle with well-practised ease and was snoring gently in the armchair. "John Roker, from Camden. He is an out-of-work actor, hired to play this part. The original instruction called for him to be of gentle religious persuasion."

"Let me guess," said Holmes. "The Grand Wazir, and the Ryukyu of Sassania inventions, were all his own." Father Brown nodded, then continued. "He says he doesn't know who hired him, only that there was money in the envelope, and a promise of more to come."

"Everything about this is amateurish," said Holmes. "It is a risk to hire an out-of-work actor in such a manner. Most would drink up the offering and not do the job. As it is, that may have been better. Roker playing Swami Ryukyu isn't a well-thought-out plan. There is no mystery here, Father. It is just a waste of our time."

337

"It would appear so," said the priest. "The poetic invitations were the unfortunate first clue. I wonder what would have happened had we not accepted."

"He would have moved down the list," said Holmes. "It is clear that he wanted the press here to create a news story, yet once again the planning was incomplete. No journalist of note would take a ride out to an event such as this. There are at the moment twenty stories happening in the capital, as they do every day, and the real news reporters are in London covering those. They have no time for such a jaunt, and none of these hacks will be capable of writing a story by the time they travel back.

"And what was the tale that has been laid out in so clumsy a fashion?" he continued. "Attempted murder at religious conference?" He paused as he watched the priest looking around. The rooms off the main hall were all assigned to various events, equally divided among discourse and demonstration.

"It can't be," said the priest. "And yet it is." He turned to his detective friend. "Do you know what the single biggest problem the religious world has to deal with?" He continued without giving Holmes the chance to answer. "More than prejudice, or differences of belief. More than issues of faith, or congregational cant?"

"Buildings," said Holmes.

"Exactly. I speak only from the perspective of one religion, but I have never yet met a parish priest who is not struggling either with a building fund or a repair fund. What if all this," he said, waving his hand gently to encompass the surrounds, "is not about saving the world, but saving his business?"

"But it is so amateurish," said Holmes,

"That is what nearly caught us off guard," said Father Brown. We are so used to dealing with the most extraordinary mysteries. Inventive criminal minds, complicated strategies and plots, twists and turns."

"I assumed that we would be up against a cunning plan by the sharpest of villains, merely because of the calibre of detectives invited," said Holmes. "Whoever created this myth reached too high on too many levels, and succeeded on only one: Getting the two of the finest detectives of their generation to come to his party." He saw the priest wince slightly. "This is no time for false modesty, Father Brown. Now that you have unwrapped the motive, we must decide what crimes have been committed, if any."

"Look who we have found," said Flambeau, returning. He had the Viscount grasped firmly around his bicep with one hand and was

338

carrying a long rifle with a modified sight in the other. Watson was leaning on his walking stick and Holmes felt guilty for taxing his friend so – the stairs would have tested his old injuries. Still, Watson would not have thanked him for any mollycoddling.

Flambeau had frog-marched Westanger across the hall and propelled him into the seat next to the sham Swami. It was this that saved him from the detective's ire, for the Viscount looked at the drunken actor, patted him on his shoulder, and said, "Poor John. Once again I have asked too much of you."

Even the unperturbable Father Brown seemed fleetingly surprised.

"John worked for me before the war. He was my personal secretary, and the finest organizer I had ever worked with. He was the brightest and best of them until he came back. He had nearly a year in the trenches, then two years in hospital, but they couldn't fix what they couldn't see. I don't know what he saw there, what horrors invaded his mind, but he tries to bury them with drink."

"Is he the reason you moved away from arms manufacture to construction?" said Father Brown.

"He is the most obvious of many. When he came back, it was obvious he couldn't work to the same high standard. He couldn't even go near his old office at the munitions works. Then he just disappeared."

"Until you found him again. Did you try to rescue him? Give him something to do?"

"How did you know?" cried Westanger.

"Because of all this," said Holmes, gently gesticulating around him. "Once the facts become clear, it was easy to deduce what happened. You found your friend again and tried to bring him back to work for you. Maybe you tried too hard, maybe you fixated on your change of business, reasoning that a change into construction would mean your friend could come back and work for you."

"A noble idea," murmured Father Brown.

"It didn't work," said Westanger. "Munitions are easy to sell. You make what a government wants and they give you a contract. Construction is hard work, and I found out I'm not a very good salesman. Also," he sighed, "whatever has happened to John, he can't work anymore. I will look after him as much as I can, but his astuteness has fogged over. As you can tell."

"You asked your friend for an idea," said Watson, "and he came up with this?"

"He'd seen all these meetings and conferences in the news," said Westanger. "He thought we could make sales this way. But he couldn't follow through,"

"And you started to run out of money," said Flambeau. Before Westanger could ask, he said. "Shocking whisky, drab design, hideous food. Even the press you bought came too cheap."

"Building such a mansion must have cost you," said Father Brown.

"It cost too much," said Westanger. "And one of the contractors was below standard, making mistakes. But you can't quit on your own home, not if you are trying to make your way in the building world." He pointed at his ersatz bullet mark in the floor. "That was a wayward hammer, dropped by one of his workers. By the time it happened, it would have been too expensive to repair, and I was running out of money. Then John said it looked like a bullet chip, and, well, one thing led to another."

"It doesn't look anything like a bullet chip," said Holmes, "and it is insulting to think we wouldn't see it for what it was. Did you fire the gun? The Viscount nodded. "Next time, scatter some smaller chips near the mark." Westanger looked shamefaced. The Frenchman started laughing, and the sound was so jarring even Father Brown was nearly startled.

"*C'est* impossible?" said Flambeau. "Oh my word, that is too funny. So all of this – the terrible rhymes attached to an invitation sent to these two detecting marvels – all of this started because a worker cracked your marble floor and it looked like it could have been caused by a bullet. You created a crime for what reason? To get in the news? To sell ceilings. *Mon Dieu*, it is crazy! Did you not think that these two would see right through your unsubtle subterfuge? Even Doctor Watson hasn't been fooled by this."

Father Brown stopped his friend with a gentle hand on his arm.

"I am not sure how creating a crime and hoping it would make the papers is supposed to help," he said.

"*Meme la mauvaise presse fait la grande publicité*," said Flambeau. "Or some such. I believe it was Voltaire who said it. There is no such thing as bad press."

"I thought it was Oscar Wilde," said Watson.

"John said it was Mark Twain," said Westanger, "but yes, that was the idea. What seemed like a good idea at the time has proved to be embarrassing and disgraceful on my part." He held up his hands as if to be cuffed. "Please, leave John out of this. He is not to blame. His ideas would never have seen the light, were it not for me."

There was a silence for a moment. Everything depended on Holmes. The great detective looked at his companions. He could read them. The priest had more compassion than a convent, John Watson represented all that was good in an Englishman, and as for Flambeau . . . well, Holmes was forced to admit to himself that the Frenchman's heart was in the right place.

"This has been most annoying and a waste of my time," said Holmes. "But it is fortunate I have it to waste. I see no reason to pursue this further. Clearly Viscount Westanger's actions, misguided as they have been, aren't of malice born. I believe if we take our leave, we can make the last train to London, Simpson's still has fresh Dover sole on the menu. Let that be our goal."

The gratitude on Westanger's face was obvious to even the hardest of hearts.

"Thank you. From the bottom of my heart, I thank you, and I apologize for a list of mistakes on my part that misused your time and station in life. You could have punished me and ruined me, yet you have chosen not to. You have given me a chance and I shall not waste. Please, let me pay for your dinner. My account at Simpson's is still clear."

"*Non, mon amis*," said Flambeau. "You carry on selling your tiles and bricks and not-whats. One day when you are a success, we shall remind you of this promise."

As Flambeau walked towards the exit, arm-in-arm with Watson, they could hear the Doctor's voice rumble, "*What-nots*, Hercule. Not *not-whats*. W*hat- nots*."

"*Pfft*," said Flambeau. "*Pomme de terre, pommes de terre.*"

Holmes and Father Brown followed. "You seem to have something on your mind," said the detective.

"Do I?" the priest replied. "Whatever is it?" They continued on their way, leaving the Viscount sitting next to his snoring friend.

"Do you think he'll make it?" said Holmes.

"I think his idea was good, but his execution unsound." They continued on and the priest said, "I'm glad he did so. It was good to see you, even under such strange circumstances

"Likewise," said Holmes, uncomfortable yet comforted.

"Oh that's what it was," said the priest. "It was *Barnum* – the origin of the quote. It wasn't about bad or good press."

"No," said Holmes. And he said, "It was – " at the same time as Father Brown said "It was – ": "'*I don't care what the newspapers say about me as long as they spell my name right.*'"

"Barnum," said Father Brown.

"Phineas Taylor," said Holmes.

"Indeed."

Father Brown
Confronts the Devil
by Hugh Ashton

It was in that period following the Great War that the events related here took place – that time of moral doubt and uncertainty that followed the great bloodletting of the nations, itself succeeded by a virulent plague that rivalled those experienced by Egypt at the time of the Exodus. Men's souls and consciences were sorely tried, and ancient beliefs and practices that had remained dormant stirred once again, and rose to the surface to challenge the beliefs that had been held for so long.

Father Brown, whose flock at that time was in the East End of London, did not regard himself first and foremost as a detective. What he had achieved in this regard, he saw as the result of his experience of human nature gained as a parish priest, tempered with common sense. He was happily free of the opinion, shared by many who adorned their cards with the title of "Detective", that he was of a caste and quality that placed him above other men.

In this, he was comforted by the ignorance of his parishioners, the majority of whom remained unaware of the fact that their parish priest who celebrated Sunday Mass in a perfectly satisfactory, but less-than-exciting fashion, was the man who had been largely responsible for the arrest and detention of the man known to the popular press as The Shoreditch Strangler, whose exploits had given a vicarious thrill to half of the inhabitants of the metropolis.

The sermons that Father Brown preached to his flock, while perfectly orthodox and competent, and of a nature that could never be taken as heretical, nonetheless failed to stir the passions of his listeners as they might have done had he regaled them with examples drawn from some of the more lurid cases with which he had been involved.

Indeed, so detached was Father Brown from those who referred to themselves as "private detectives" or "investigators" that he was surprised by the nature of the request made by a visitor to his South London parish one spring morning.

"Doctor Watson?" said the little priest. "Ah yes, I recollect the name. I believe there was something about a dog in the West

Country some years back. A matter of inheritance . . . ." He smiled. "Forgive my little jest. How are you? I trust that you and Mr. Holmes are both in good health, though I would have supposed both him – and you, come to that – to be long retired by now. I am sorry if I appear to you to be a little abstracted at present. My mind is currently partly concerned with a matter of some urgency. Now I come to think of it, you may well be of assistance to me."

"Oh?" enquired the other, eyebrows raised.

"Well, it's only a small thing, but Molly Donnelly's little boy has a nasty cough. She's one of my parishioners," he explained apologetically, "and I was wondering where I could find a doctor who would be prepared to examine the child for little or no financial return."

Watson shifted in his seat. "Well, I, er – "

"Splendid!" said the priest. "Come along, now. It's only just around the corner, and it won't take a minute. You can tell me on the way what you have come about – if it's not too personal, that is." Despite Father Brown's small stature and unprepossessing appearance, it seemed that the other was being swept along by a force of nature that could not be withstood, and the two visited the Donnelly household, where Watson examined the infant and prescribed a course of medicines for which, following a brief consultation with Father Brown, he produced the money from his own pocket.

The two men left Mrs. Donnelly's effusive thanks and returned to the study in Father Brown's house.

"I do apologise," said the priest, "for presuming on your good nature just now, but the problem of little Declan has been on my mind since it was brought to my attention yesterday evening, and it simply seemed like Providence that you came in just now. Now, what can I do for you in return?"

"I come not on my own account," replied Watson, "but on behalf of Holmes. You referred to the matter of the Baskerville family in Devon, and you may be also aware that he has handled matters of great delicacy for some of the highest in the land. You were yourself concerned with some of those cases, were you not?"

Father Brown said nothing, and his round moonlike face showed no change of expression.

"It is on one of these cases," said Watson, "that your assistance is sought."

Father Brown shrugged. "I am at a loss as to why you feel that I may be able to provide some assistance on such a matter."

344

"There are other aspects to the case, which Holmes will be better qualified than myself to answer. Come, let us go to Baker Street." When Father Brown appeared puzzled, Watson explained. "Following his retirement to Sussex, Holmes retained the use of his Baker Street rooms for those occasions when he needed to return to the capital. He's waiting there now." He raised a hand as he stepped into the street. "Cab!"

The priest's round face broke into a smile. "Not a hansom cab? I seem to remember in your accounts of Mr. Holmes's cases that a hansom cab was your invariable mode of transport within the city?"

"Since the War, it has proved almost impossible to find a horse-drawn cab. As a doctor, I heartily approve. The dung and other nuisances associated with horses have disappeared. And speaking as a lover of machinery, I confess to being fascinated by motor-cars."

"Do you know," mused Father Brown, as the ill-assorted pair entered the taxi that Watson had hailed, "that this is the first time in a number of years that I have ridden in a motor-car. The last occasion was, I believe, a visit to the North."

"Then how do you move around London?" Watson asked.

"Oh, by omnibus. One meets such interesting people there. Why, only last week I found myself sitting next to a man who, by the time the 'bus had reached Holloway, had informed me of the three burglaries he had committed the previous week."

"Good Lord!" exclaimed Watson. "And you handed him over to the police?"

"Oh no," smiled Father Brown. "I handed him a far stiffer penance. I extracted a promise that he would go to the houses he had robbed, confess his crimes, and restore their property to them."

"And do you really believe he would do that?"

"Of course. He struck me as being an honest man who knew the difference between good and evil. In fact, he confessed to me at the end of our little chat that he had really no idea why he had committed those burglaries, and the fact that he had committed them at all weighed far heavier on his mind than the possibility of his arrest and conviction."

At length the taxi drew up outside 221 Baker Street. Watson paid off the driver, and he and Father Brown mounted the step to the front door.

"I do hope that man's little daughter recovers," the little priest murmured almost absent-mindedly. "I shall pray for her when I next say Mass."

345

"What are you saying?" asked Watson as he unlocked the front door and flung it open.

"Oh, the family photograph by the driver of the taxi we have just taken, and the medicine on the seat beside him: Only prescribed for children with the chicken-pox. A very unpleasant condition, as I am sure you are aware."

"Indeed," said Watson, ushering his guest up the seventeen steps leading to the rooms currently occupied by Sherlock Holmes, and bearing the designation of 221b Baker Street.

Father Brown stood politely outside the door leading to the sitting room, until Watson opened it and waved the visitor inside.

Father Brown's first impression was one of tobacco smoke that had permeated every surface of the room and its furnishings, depositing a yellowish-brown film over every object there, seemingly including the man who half-lay, half-sat in an armchair by the fireplace, smoking a clay pipe that in its own turn would add a layer to the ubiquitous almost archaeological film.

The second impression was one of disorder. Papers, envelopes, and newspapers, seemingly scattered at random, covered the floor. Father Brown, whose preference was for order, found himself disturbed by the sight as he picked his way delicately through the mess, placing his feet carefully on the islands of carpet that were visible at intervals in the sea of paper.

Watson wordlessly indicated a vacant armchair, which Father Brown was presumably to occupy, and perched himself on a dining chair on one side of the room.

Father Brown silently lowered himself into the chair and studied the figure facing him. It had been a while since they had seen each other. Though reclining, Sherlock Holmes's figure was an imposing one. The eyes at first appeared closed, but closer study revealed that in fact they were hooded, and their owner was intently observing his visitor. Only the wisps of pipe smoke that emerged from his mouth and nostrils at intervals, and the occasional movement of the clay pipe held in the long slender fingers, gave any indication that he was awake.

Father Brown was used to these long silences on the part of others. Very often they preceded some startling confession, or an announcement which might have raised the eyebrows of a man less familiar with the world and its follies than Father Brown. Nor was this occasion an exception.

After a few minutes of silence, Sherlock Holmes spoke.

346

"Father Brown, do you believe in the Devil?"

"Do you mean as an abstraction of evil, or as a distinct personality, like you and me?"

"As a person."

The little priest considered the question gravely. "I cannot say that I have ever encountered the Devil other than when he has entered into a person's soul. Evil, like good, needs an agent for its expression, else it is no more than an abstraction. But perhaps, Mr. Holmes, you do not believe in souls?"

Sherlock Holmes was wan. "I was raised in a religious family, Father. As many young men do, I suppose, I turned from religion at University, telling myself that I had little use for fairy-tales. Now, at the figure of threescore years and ten, I find myself re-evaluating my position." He paused, took a drag on his pipe, and chuckled. "I am sure that this is a story you have heard many times before."

Father Brown said nothing, but nodded silently. He had learned over the years how to draw speech from others without speaking himself. As if recognising this, Holmes smiled for the first time since their meeting. "I remember your methods, Father, from our previous work together. I will continue. My faith has been shaken – or perhaps it would be more accurate to say my *lack* of faith has been shaken. Doctor Watson here probably informed you that I have been retained on a case of the gravest importance. At first it appeared to be a relatively simple matter – albeit one at the very highest levels of our government – but it was clear to me within a day of starting my investigation that there was more to this ghastly business than I could have foreseen." He paused, and fixed the priest with his eyes. "What at first sight might have seemed to be a simple, if dastardly, case of passing our nation's secrets to another Power, seems now to have taken a new and diabolical – and I do not use that word lightly – turn. Watson, will you be kind enough to pass the book in question to the Father, please?"

Watson rose from his chair and handed across a slim paper-bound volume to the priest who examined the cover, which depicted a pentacle and the title *Satanus, Salvator Mundi*, with the author being given as Hermes Trismegistus, before laughing softly.

"'*Satan, the Saviour of the World*' – Do you really find that amusing?" Holmes asked. "Do you not find it heretical? Dangerous?"

"It is potentially dangerous, yes, in the way that a barrel of gunpowder is dangerous. For most people, a barrel of gunpowder is something for which they have no use. For a few anarchists, it is a potential means of destruction – assuming that the anarchists have the knowledge to use it as such. It is not the book itself which is dangerous. It is the uses to which men may put the book."

"And the author?"

"As I am sure you are aware, Mr. Holmes, the name is a pseudonym, being the name of a legendary founder of alchemy and hermetic wisdom. I take it that you are aware of the true identity of 'Hermes'?"

"I am, and it saddens me to say that it is one of the present government. Though he currently holds no position in the Cabinet, he is highly favoured to be promoted to high office very soon. You will pardon me if I do not yet mention his name."

"It would probably mean little to me if you did," answered Father Brown. "I take very little interest in such affairs. Indeed, were you to demand the name of the current Prime Minister from me, I might well be hard pressed to provide an answer." He paused and stared reflectively at the handle of his large umbrella, which had accompanied him on his journey to Baker Street, before opening the booklet and glancing through its pages. "All tediously familiar stuff, I am afraid. I confess that I long for some originality in these matters. These are all things we learned in seminary which have been in circulation for hundreds of years."

"I beg your pardon?" It was Watson who spoke. "You learned all these things in your seminary?"

"Of course we did," said the priest, almost impatiently. "How can you expect to defeat evil if you have no understanding of it? But tell me specifically how I may be able to help you."

"The person in question, the author of this little volume, whom we will refer to as 'Sir X', is critical of the current economic system. He claims to be a follower of the German so-called philosopher Karl Marx, and from there, has made himself an ally of the gang of Russians calling themselves Bolsheviks who have taken over Russia. There are also some unsavoury rumours connected to him with regard to his possession of personal information which certain of his colleagues in government would prefer to keep hidden."

"Many passages in the Bible advise many of the same changes to society as does Marx," commented Father Brown mildly.

"You are surely not in agreement with those Russian monsters?" Watson sounded incredulous.

"Not at all. Marx and those who follow him are strictly earthbound and are concerned merely with the things of this earth. The Gospels point us to something above ourselves. But I take it that this mysterious Sir X has access to secret papers, perhaps in his role as an assistant to the Foreign Secretary, or some similar functionary, and has made copies of them to pass to his fellow worshippers of Marx in Moscow?"

As Father Brown continued his recital of what he believed had transpired, the expression on Sherlock Holmes's face changed to one of shocked surprise. When the little priest had paused for breath, the detective's tone was one of incredulity.

"How the Devil – I beg your pardon, Father. I mean to say, how in the world could you possibly know that?"

"Oh," said Father Brown modestly, "I am afraid that my work as a priest sometimes brings me into contact with some unsavoury characters and I learn a few things from them. From there, it is merely a matter of using one's knowledge of human nature to reconstruct the hidden events. Surely you function in much the same way, Mr. Holmes, when you work on your problems?"

"I prefer to employ the scientific method," the detective replied coldly. "I find the presence of emotions and other feelings in a case to be a hindrance to its solution."

"The question is," Watson intervened, in a seeming attempt to prevent friction between the other two, "what comes next. Holmes and I have met Sir X – "

"Perhaps, since Father Brown appears to know so much about this case already," Holmes said, with more than a hint of sarcasm in his voice, "we may dispense with the pseudonyms and name Sir Charles Hawke-Banks."

Father Brown said nothing, but nodded as if to confirm his earlier deduction.

Watson continued his explanation. "As I was saying, Mr. Holmes and I confronted Sir Charles at his home yesterday evening. It was a somewhat frightening experience." He paused, as if expecting some signal from his visitor, inviting him to continue, but there was none forthcoming. "A manservant opened the door and, though we had not announced our visit in advance, surprised us by telling us that we were expected by Sir Charles, who was awaiting us in a room that he termed the Lower Library. He led the way to a door at the back of the house, which was reached down a small flight of stairs, and then knocked on the door in a distinct rhythmic pattern before leaving us. I noted that the man appeared to be ill at ease as he approached the door, and left us with what appeared to be unseemly haste."

349

Holmes took up the story. "I was, of course, familiar with Sir Charles's appearance – indeed, I had dealings with him during the Great War, when I was assisting the Government with various matters. In fact, Sir Charles had had occasion to consult me on some matters concerning Russia. Let me add a little detail by way of explaining the relations that obtain between Sir Charles and myself: At the time when he was enquiring about these Russian subjects, I confess that I had no knowledge of his political leanings or his sympathy for the Bolshevik cause.

"I will add, however, that at the time some of his queries struck me as being a little out of the ordinary. After the signing of the Brest-Litovsk Treaty, some of the lines of his questioning seemed to indicate that there was an ulterior motive to his enquiries. However, it was not until last week that I became fully aware of the reasons for them, when I was shown a copy of a report of the Bolshevik Government in Moscow containing passages which were word-for-word copied from a Parliamentary Commission on the state of our Navy.

"There is only one place from which Moscow could have obtained this information. Sadly, there are more such papers in existence, and there is good reason to believe that copies of these will also be on their way to Russia, if they have not already left the country. That, Father, is an example of the way in which I reach my conclusions. Typically, the motives for a crime become clear after the identity of the malefactor has been revealed – that is to say, the means and the opportunity have been established. With the greatest of respect, I do not see how you can use the motive for a crime as the means of identifying the malefactor. But," he conceded after a pause and a drag at the foul-smelling pipe, "it does appear that you do use this method with some success, if the accounts of your cases are to be believed."

Father Brown allowed himself a small self-deprecatory smile at these words of the older detective, but said nothing, and waited patiently for the story to continue. It was Watson who took up the tale once more.

"The door to this cellar was opened, and Sir Charles stood before us. He was dressed in a kind of dark robe of heavy material, adorned with golden symbols, similar to those in the book you have just seen. When we entered the chamber, we were greeted by the smell of some sort of bitter-smelling incense. The room was dimly lit by a few flickering torches, whose light revealed dark wooden furniture with what appeared to be primitive carvings.

350

"Directly before us was what appeared to be a ghastly parody of a church altar. On it stood an inverted cross, with a five-pointed star over it. Two human skulls, which had been adapted to form candlesticks for two black candles, stood at either side of it. Behind it was a painting which appeared to be of a man, but with a goat's head."

Father Brown laughed. "The usual nonsense," he proclaimed with a smile.

"I assure you, Father," said Sherlock Holmes, "that the overall aspect was quite unnerving. I cannot but confess that it momentarily struck me with fear."

"In my case, it was more than momentary," said Watson. "I do not mind admitting that I was somewhat overcome by the atmosphere."

"No doubt the incense was drugged," suggested Father Brown.

"That's as may be," said Watson. "I can only tell you of my own reactions. I had no wish to investigate the cause of my sudden weakness."

Father Brown said nothing, but continued to look almost abstractedly at the Persian slipper by the fireplace, which appeared to contain something dark and mouldering. "I know that I am very slow," he said at length, "but I am afraid I still fail to understand exactly what it is that you require of me."

"What we require of you, Father," said Watson, "is to visit Sir Charles and retrieve the papers believed to have been copied."

"Surely they are in the hands of the Bolsheviks by now?" asked Father Brown. It was Holmes who shook his head and answered him.

"The authorities are well aware of the situation," he explained, "and have placed a watch on him. Any attempt to contact the Bolshevik agents in London – and yes, there are many who are sympathetic to the cause – would immediately be forestalled. It would create too much of a scandal if he were to be confronted and arrested publicly. It requires some tact and discretion in the handling."

"And you find yourself unable to do so?"

"Ah," Holmes answered. He seemed slightly embarrassed. "Let me continue the narrative. Sir Charles, for it was undoubtedly he, addressed us.

"'You dare to meddle in my affairs, Mr. Holmes,' he told me in a voice that seemed to come from deep within him. 'Or rather,' he continued, 'these are not *my* affairs, but the affairs of the whole world. You believe that I have passed certain papers to Moscow, do you not, and am preparing to pass some more?' I nodded my assent. 'I will tell you now quite frankly that I did and I have every intention of doing so again.'

"'Then you are a sympathiser to the Bolshevik cause?' I asked.

"'I support them, and I wish their cause to succeed, yes. And you wish to hinder their progress, in the interests of what I assume you call decency and law and order, I take it?' I remained silent. 'I will take your silence as assent. You are prepared to cease this persecution?' Again I remained silent. "In which case, I have no alternative but to call down the curse of His Satanic Majesty upon you!"

"He drew himself up to his full height and proclaimed a string of Latin of which I can only give you an approximate translation, my Latin being more than a little rusty. 'I invoke you, ye one! Regal and majestic! Glorious splendour! I invoke you, mighty arch-daimon! Denizen of chaos and Erebus, and of the unfathomable abyss! Haunter of depths! Murk enwrapped, scanning mystery, and protector of cults! Flame-fanning terror darter! Heart-crushing despot! Satanachia of daimons! Invincible Lucifer! Hear the prayer of your humble servant that this man, Sherlock Holmes, and the other, John Watson, may be so gnawed and devoured by the Hounds of Hell that they may find themselves unable to bear their torment, and will cease their persecution of myself, your servant. This I request in the name of Beelzebub and the demons that surround your throne and praise you.'

"Having delivered himself of this, he threw back his head and gave a mocking laugh. At that moment, all the torches and candles were extinguished, leaving only a faint glow from the door, which had been left slightly ajar. Watson and I scrambled up the stairs and out of the house as fast as was possible." Holmes's pale face was flushed, and his breathing was irregular as he concluded his recital.

It is perhaps a matter for regret that Father Brown's giggles were faintly audible, despite the handkerchief with which he had covered his face. Nonetheless, he presented a serious expression to the detective when the handkerchief was removed.

"Have the Hounds of Hell been bothering you and preventing from obtaining the papers yourselves?" asked Father Brown. He looked around the room in an exaggerated fashion. "I see no trace of any infernal canines here."

"They are metaphorical," said Holmes impatiently.

"As is the curse itself," replied the priest.

"I wish I could believe that it was all a figment of our imaginations," said Holmes. For the first time in the conversation, his tone became almost pleading. "However, both Watson and I, on comparing notes, have suffered from nightmares which have been remarkably similar. And yes," he added, holding up a hand, "I am well aware of the powers of auto-suggestion as expressed by alienists. I confess to you that both Watson and myself are more than a little disturbed by what we have experienced."

"I have no wish to enter that house, or to meet that man ever again!" Watson declared emphatically.

"Whether or not the curse actually exists," replied Father Brown, "I take it that you believe that I am able to visit this man's house, discover the papers, and then retrieve them and bring them to you?"

"Precisely," answered Holmes, with a smile on his thin lips. "You have it exactly."

"In which case," said Father Brown, "fools must rush in where angels have already trodden."

Father Brown stood outside the front door of Sir Charles Hawke-Banks's Georgian town house, in a corner of a London square which seemed as far away from the tales of devilry described by Sherlock Holmes as one could imagine.

The window-boxes on every side were a blaze of scarlet geraniums, and the steps leading to each front door appeared to be scrubbed to within an inch of their stony lives, to the extent that Father Brown was almost afraid of disturbing their celestial state with the soles of his all-too-terrestrial boots.

He had heaved on the bell-pull, causing a deep tolling within the depths of the house, which reminded him of the funeral bell of the church in his first parish.

The door opened, and a lugubrious footman, on hearing Father Brown's name, surprised him somewhat by saying that Sir Charles was expecting him before ushering him into the house.

If Father Brown was expecting to be received in an Englishman's idea of a Satanic temple, his expectations were dashed when he was shown into a light and airy drawing room, furnished in a light floral chintz, with a cheerful fire blazing in the grate.

Sir Charles, dressed in more traditional garb than the velvet robe in which he had received Sherlock Holmes and Dr. Watson, advanced smiling, his hand outstretched.

"Father Brown. I have been expecting you."

Father Brown, while attempting to return the handshake, managed to fumble with his umbrella, dropping it on the floor, and somehow in the confusion of his bending down to retrieve it, in the course of which his glasses fell out of his top pocket, hands were never shaken.

"I take it, of course, that you are here at the request of Mr. Sherlock Holmes, whom I had the pleasure of entertaining the other day?"

Father Brown confirmed that this was the case.

"And the purpose of your visit is to retrieve the papers that I abstracted from the Ministry?"

"So you admit it?"

"Admit it? I glory in it. Passing these to my dupes in Moscow will be my act of homage to my master."

"Your master being the Devil?"

"You may term him so. I prefer to style him as Lucifer, the bringer of light, and as Baphomet, the embodiment of all the opposites in nature."

"And what do you expect to gain in return," Father Brown asked. His question appeared to be genuine.

"Why, *power*. Power not only in this nation, but power over all nations of the earth. And of course, with such power come riches."

"And with riches comes happiness?" prompted Father Brown.

"I expect so."

Father Brown's only response was to shake his head sadly.

"You are sceptical," the other laughed. "No doubt you believe in the myth of holy poverty?"

"I do, and I believe that holy poverty – that is the choice to reject the riches of this world, as opposed to the cruelty of involuntary poverty – may be a path to salvation. But I do not believe that riches on their own are the road to damnation. That only comes with the abuse of riches."

"You amuse me, Father Brown," said Sir Charles. "Tell me – how do you intend to force me to give you the papers? Have you bell, book, and candle to hand in order to cast my soul into Hell?"

"I do not need that. You are perfectly capable of making your own path there. Rather than casting you into Hell, it is my duty to extend a hand to you to pull you out of the pit you are digging for yourself."

"You may save your energy," Sir Charles answered with a mocking laugh. "I am so steeped in the worship of my master that you may believe that he dwells in me. I mean no offence to you, but

354

were you the most devout man of your faith, you would be unable to save me, as you term it. For me, I choose my own path."

All the while he was speaking, he moved closer to Father Brown, towering over the little priest, so that his face was within inches of the top of the other's head. His eyes blazed with the light of fanaticism, and even Father Brown, accustomed as he was to many forms of intimidation, found himself involuntarily shrinking and taking a step backwards.

"You amuse me, Priest," said Sir Charles. "Do you wish to make a bargain? A wager, if you will?"

"Explain," Father Brown replied, and there was a confidence and air of command in his words that seemed to take the other aback.

"Sit, if you would, and I will explain the rules of my little game to you." When both were seated in armchairs facing each other, Sir Charles continued. "The papers which I took are in this house. Clearly, I am not going to tell you where, but I will give you a sporting chance. The whole house will be opened for you to search where you will, from attic to cellar. You will have – let me think – twenty minutes to find them. If you do, I will confess myself beaten, and pursue the matter no further. I will call off the curse that I laid on Holmes and Watson. Wait – " he said, as an idea appeared to strike him. "Not only will I do these things, but I will resign my seat in the House and my position in the government, and I will leave the country."

"You seem very confident that I will not find the papers," said Father Brown. "I have your word that they are in the house?"

"You have my word."

"And if I do not find them in the agreed time?"

"Then, alas, I will be forced to unleash the full powers of my master upon you, and Holmes and Watson too, of course. Not the whole power of your Church will be sufficient to withstand his attacks on you, and those around you. I need hardly remind you of his strength and power. And," he added, almost as an afterthought, "the papers will, of course, be sent to Moscow."

"I see."

"Well, do you accept the challenge?"

"Of course," answered Father Brown.

"In which case, since I have no wish to hamper your search unnecessarily, I must give orders for every door, cupboard and drawer in the house to be unlocked. I trust you do not mind a wait of a few minutes while all is prepared?"

Father Brown gave his consent, and Sir Charles rang the bell and issued commands to his servants.

After about fifteen minutes, during which Sir Charles smoked a cigar, offering one to Father Brown, who politely declined the offer, the servants returned with the news that all locks in the house were now released.

"And if you should discover that by some mischance a lock has been left fastened," Sir Charles told Father Brown, "you must announce it at once, and the wager will be declared null and void. I shall remain in this room. However, if you should wish to conduct your search here, I will immediately withdraw to another chamber. Twenty minutes was the time we agreed, was it not?"

"It was."

"You must return to this room with the papers in your hand within twenty minutes. Agreed?"

"Agreed," said the priest.

"Then let us start now."

Eighteen, nineteen minutes passed, during which time Sir Charles remained, as agreed, calmly smoking a cigar.

He was examining his watch, and counting off the remaining seconds when the door burst open, and the little priest's ridiculous figure burst in, a sheaf of papers clutched in his hand.

"I am most terribly sorry to have kept you waiting," said Father Brown, "but after I'd found the papers – these are they, are they not?" Sir Charles, after a cursory glance, confirmed this with a nod. "After I had found the papers, I chanced upon a little book, and I started to read it. And I'm afraid that it was so interesting that I completely forgot the time." He produced a small leather-bound notebook from beneath the papers.

Sir Charles turned pale. "My account book!" he exclaimed.

"If you care to term it so, yes. A list of all those whom you have ben blackmailing for the past ten years or more, together with their secrets, and the sums they have paid to you over the years. And some letters tucked into the back cover, which I did not trouble myself to read. In the interests of quiet living, I feel that they should disappear." And, almost quicker than the eye could follow, Father Brown flicked the notebook into the fireplace, where it immediately started to burn.

Sir Charles watched in stunned silence for a few seconds as the flames licked at the paper, and then frantically scrabbled with the fire-irons, attempting to retrieve the book, but he was too late to save more then a few charred fragments of paper and the spine of the notebook.

"You win, damn you!" he spat out. "I will keep my word. I will lift the curse on Holmes and Watson, and cease from any persecution of you. You may read of my resignation and my leaving the country within a few days. Good day to you." He rang the bell for a footman. "Thomas, Father Brown is leaving."

The priest allowed himself to be shown to the front door. As he walked down the street he glanced upwards at the window of the room he had just left, where he could make out the face of Sir Charles glaring down at him. There was a spring in his step as he made his way to Baker Street.

"Where were the papers?" asked Sherlock Holmes when Father Brown had related his experiences at Sir Charles's house. Somehow, though, he had failed to include in his recital where and how he had discovered the papers, which he had handed to Holmes.

"In the place where I expected them to be," said Father Brown. "Or rather, they were not in the places where I expected them not to be."

"Explain yourself," said Watson. "I am puzzled."

"Well, it occurred to me that Sir Charles was making my task too easy. He made a point of the fact that all the drawers and doors in the place were to be unlocked in order to assist me in my search. Why, I asked myself, would he do that, if the papers were indeed to be found in such a place?"

"I follow your reasoning," Holmes smiled. "You looked in everywhere that was not locked."

"Hardly that. It would be a place where the servants would not enter."

"The cellar!" exclaimed Watson. "His 'temple'!"

"Precisely. I had only to look behind the painting of the goat-headed creature to discover a niche containing the missing papers, and the notebook with the evidence of blackmail. This was a place where servants would not be admitted, and I feel sure that he was of the opinion that the place would instill sufficient fear in me to prevent my entrance."

"He was mistaken, then," Holmes smiled.

"He was indeed. A priest's place is with sinners. It is not the healthy who need a doctor, but the sick, as our Lord said."

"I trust that you don't include us in that category," said Watson laughing, "since you are with us now."

"I will merely remark that I would like to see you and Mr. Holmes at Mass from time to time to time," replied the priest mildly. "I have, however, one further question for both of you: You, Mr. Holmes, and you, Doctor Watson, are both known to me as rationalists and materialists. I cannot seriously believe that either of you are so frightened of a few scraps of cloth and some phrases of bad Latin that you are unable to proceed with the case."

Holmes smiled. "My dear Father Brown, please allow me to explain the small deception to which you have been subjected. While it is true that both Watson and I were at least momentarily disconcerted by Sir Charles's theatricals, I felt that it was at the very least unlikely that he would ever consent to hand back the papers, or to consent to a search. In any event, I was reluctant to obtain a warrant for such a search. I am afraid, my dear sir, that your slightly unprepossessing appearance and manner would lead him to offer you a challenge – a challenge which you would accept. With your proven record of insight into men's hearts – You see, I do acknowledge these things and these methods have their place. – where you would best him. And so it proved," he concluded, drawing on his pipe.

Father Brown took in all this seemingly unmoved. "I have to agree that you were right to withhold your true motives in bringing me into the case. Were you to have told me, I do not think I could have played the part that I did. Nonetheless, I have to regard your lack of truthfulness as a sin – a venial sin, to be sure, but still a sin."

"And now," said Sherlock Holmes, seemingly ignoring Father Brown's last comment, "it appears that Sir Charles will no longer be a danger to our society – thanks to you, Father Brown. Did he give you any clues as to where he might be going?"

"He did not. However, I trust that, wherever he has fled," mused Father Brown in a voice that he might or might not have intended to be heard, "the young man will repent of the most terrible of his sins."

"You refer, of course," said Holmes, "to the atrocious actions in betraying his country."

"Oh no, not at all." Father Brown shook his head gravely. "I refer to the sin of pride."

"Pride?" exclaimed Watson. "What had he that was deserving of pride?"

"Setting himself up to play the part of the Devil on Earth, he imagined himself to be more wicked than the mass of humanity. Is that not pride? Damnable pride?" He stood up and left the room.

As Holmes and Watson looked out over the street, they caught sight of Father Brown, who looked up at them, waving his umbrella in farewell, and they watched silently as the little priest's almost comical figure slipped into the crowds thronging the London street in his quest for an omnibus.

About the Contributors

Dale Ahlquist is President of the Society of Gilbert Keith Chesterton and Publisher and Editor of Gilbert magazine. He has written six books on Chesterton and has edited 18 books of or about Chesterton's writings. He is also the founder of the Chesterton Schools Network.

Hugh Ashton was born in the U.K., and moved to Japan in 1988, where he remained until 2016, living with his wife Yoshiko in the historic city of Kamakura, a little to the south of Yokohama. He and Yoshiko have now moved to Lichfield, a small cathedral city in the Midlands of the U.K., the birthplace of Samuel Johnson, and one-time home of Erasmus Darwin. In the past, he has worked in the technology and financial services industries, which have provided him with material for some of his books set in the 21st century. He currently works as a writer: Novelist, freelance editor, and copywriter, (his work for large Japanese corporations has appeared in international business journals), and journalist, as well as producing industry reports on various aspects of the financial services industry. However, his lifelong interest in Sherlock Holmes has developed into an acclaimed series of adventures featuring the world's most famous detective, written in the style of the originals. In addition to these, he has also published historical and alternate historical novels, short stories, and thrillers. Together with artist Andy Boerger, he has produced the *Sherlock Ferret* series of stories for children, featuring the world's cutest detective.

Mike Adamson holds a Doctoral degree from Flinders University of South Australia. After early aspirations in art and writing, Mike secured qualifications in both marine biology and archaeology. Mike has been a university educator since 2006, has worked in the replication of convincing ancient fossils, is a passionate photographer, master-level hobbyist, and journalist for international magazines. Short fiction sales include to *Metastellar*, *Strand Magazine*, *Little Blue Marble*, *Abyss*, and *Apex*, *Daily Science Fiction*, *Compelling Science Fiction*, and *Nature Futures*. Mike has placed some two-hundred stories to date, totaling over a million words. Mike has completed his first Sherlock Holmes novel with Belanger Books, and will be appearing in translation in European magazines. You can catch up with his journey at his blog "The View From the Keyboard" *http://mike-adamson.blogspot.com*

Brian Belanger, PSI, is a publisher, illustrator, graphic designer, editor, voice actor, and author. In 2015, he co-founded Belanger Books publishing company along with his brother, author Derrick Belanger. His illustrations have appeared in *The Essential Sherlock Holmes* series, *The MacDougall Twins with Sherlock Holmes* series, and *Scones and Bones on Baker Street*. Brian has published a number of Sherlock Holmes anthologies and novels through Belanger Books, as well as new editions of August Derleth's classic Solar Pons mysteries. Brian continues to design all of the covers for Belanger Books, and since 2016 he has designed the majority of book covers for MX Publishing. In 2019, Brian received his investiture in the PSI as "Sir Ronald Duveen". More recently, he created the logo for The ACD Society and designed *The Great Game of Sherlock Holmes* card game. In July 2022, he played Sherlock Holmes onstage in "Yes, Virginia, There is a Sherlock Holmes" and "Sherlock Holmes Goes West." Brian has been narrating Belanger Books' audio releases since April 2023. Find him online at: *www.belangerbooks.com*

Derrick Belanger is an educator and also the author of the #1 bestselling book in its category, *Sherlock Holmes: The Adventure of the Peculiar Provenance*, which was in the top 200 bestselling books on Amazon. He also is the author of *The MacDougall Twins with Sherlock Holmes* books, and he edited the Sir Arthur Conan Doyle horror anthology *A Study in Terror: Sir Arthur Conan Doyle's Revolutionary Stories of Fear and the Supernatural*. Mr. Belanger co-owns the publishing company Belanger Books, which has released numerous Sherlock Holmes anthologies including *Beyond Watson, Holmes Away From Home: Adventures from the Great Hiatus, Sherlock Holmes: Before Baker Street, Sherlock Holmes: Adventures in the Realms of H.G. Wells, Sherlock Holmes and the Occult Detectives, Sherlock Holmes and the Great Detectives*, and *Beyond the Adventures of Sherlock Holmes*. Derrick resides in Colorado and continues compiling unpublished works by Dr. John H. Watson.

Gustavo Bondoni is a novelist and short story writer with over three hundred stories published in fifteen countries, in seven languages. He is a member of Codex and an Active Member of SFWA. His latest novel is a dark historic fantasy entitled *The Swords of Ras*na (2022). He has also published five science fiction novels, four monster books and a thriller entitled *Timeless*. His short fiction is collected in *Pale Reflection* (2020), *Off the Beaten Path* (2019), *Tenth Orbit and Other Faraway Places* (2010) and *Virtuoso and Other Stories* (2011).

Chris Chan is a writer, educator and historian. He works as a researcher and "International Goodwill Ambassador" for Agatha Christie Ltd. His true crime articles, reviews, and short fiction have appeared in *The Strand, The Wisconsin Magazine of History, Mystery Weekly, Gilbert!, Nerd HQ*, Akashic Books' *Mondays are Murder* web series, *The Baker Street Journal, The MX Book of New Sherlock Holmes Stories, Masthead: The Best New England Crime Stories, Sherlock Holmes Mystery Magazine*, and multiple Belanger Books anthologies. He is the creator of the *Funderburke* mysteries, a series featuring a private investigator who works for a school and helps students during times of crisis. The Funderburke short story "The Six-Year-Old Serial Killer" was nominated for a Derringer Award. His first book, *Sherlock & Irene: The Secret Truth Behind "A Scandal in Bohemia"*, was published in 2020 by MX Publishing. His second book, *Murder Most Grotesque: The Comedic Crime Fiction of Joyce Porter* was released by Level Best Books in 2021, and his first novel, *Sherlock's Secretary*, was published by MX Publishing in 2021. *Murder Most Grotesque* was nominated for the Agatha and Silver Falchion Awards for Nonfiction writing, and *Sherlock's Secretary* was nominated for the Silver Falchion for Best Comedy. He is also the author of the anthology of Sherlock Holmes stories *Of Course He Pushed Him*.

Gilbert Keith Chesterton (1874-1936) *Father Brown Chronicler Emeritus* If not for him and Sir Arthur Conan Doyle, this anthology would not exist. Chesterton was an English writer, literary and art critic, philosopher, and Christian apologist. He was well-known for his essays, novels, verse, and short stories, and he wrote over one-hundred books. He is remembered and honored for the purposes of this collection by being the man who introduced the humble and quiet Father Brown,

Roman Catholic priest and detective, to the world by way of fifty-three short stories. Amongst a plethora of clue-finding detectives, Chesterton wrote of solving mysteries by intuition and empathy. *Pray for the Souls.*

Craig Stephen Copland confesses that he discovered Sherlock Holmes when, sometime in the muddled early 1960's, he pinched his older brother's copy of the immortal stories and was forever afterward thoroughly hooked. He is very grateful to his high school English teachers in Toronto who inculcated in him a love of literature and writing, and even inspired him to be an English major at the University of Toronto. There he was blessed to sit at the feet of both Northrup Frye and Marshall McLuhan, and other great literary professors, who led him to believe that he was called to be a high school English teacher. It was his good fortune to come to his pecuniary senses, abandon that goal, and pursue a varied professional career that took him to over one-hundred countries and endless adventures. He considers himself to have been and to continue to be one of the luckiest men on God's good earth. A few years back he took a step in the direction of Sherlockian studies and joined the Sherlock Holmes Society of Canada – also known as The Toronto Bootmakers. In May of 2014, this esteemed group of scholars announced a contest for the writing of a new Sherlock Holmes mystery. Although he had never tried his hand at fiction before, Craig entered and was pleasantly surprised to be selected as one of the winners. Having enjoyed the experience, he decided to write more of the same, and is now on a mission to write a new Sherlock Holmes mystery that is related to and inspired by each of the sixty stories in the original Canon. He currently lives and writes in Toronto and Dubai, and looks forward to finally settling down when he turns ninety.

Sir Arthur Conan Doyle (1859-1930) *Holmes Chronicler Emeritus.* If not for him and G.K. Chesterton, this anthology would not exist. Author, physician, patriot, sportsman, spiritualist, husband and father, and advocate for the oppressed. He is remembered and honored for the purposes of this collection by being the man who introduced Sherlock Holmes to the world. Through fifty-six Holmes short stories, four novels, and additional Apocryphal entries, Doyle revolutionized mystery stories and also greatly influenced and improved police forensic methods and techniques for the betterment of all. *Steel True Blade Straight.*

Brett Fawcett is a humanities and Latin teacher at the Chesterton Academy of St. Isidore in Sherwood Park, Alberta. He lives with his wife and son in Edmonton, where he is a member of the Wisteria Lodgers (The Sherlock Holmes Society of Edmonton). He vividly remembers the first time he finished reading the Sherlock Holmes stories in Grade 6 and has been a student of Holmesian literature and scholarship since then. He is also a frequent author of columns and articles on topics like theology, education, and mental health, as well as the occasional mystery story.

John Linwood Grant is a writer and editor who lives in Yorkshire with a pack of lurchers and a beard. He may also have a family. He focuses particularly on dark Victorian and Edwardian fiction, such as his recent novella *A Study in Grey*, which also features Holmes. Current projects include his *Tales of the Last Edwardian* series, about psychic and psychiatric mysteries, and curating a collection of new stories based on the darker side of the British Empire. He has been published in a number of anthologies and magazines, with stories range from madness in early Virginia to questions about the monsters we ourselves might be. He is also co-editor

363

of *Occult Detective Quarterly*. His website *greydogtales.com* explores weird fiction, especially period ones, weird art, and even weirder lurchers.

Jason Half is a writer and educator whose short fiction has appeared in *Alfred Hitchcock's Mystery Magazine* and in the anthologies *Noir at the Salad Bar*, *Terror at the Crossroads*, and *Landfall: Best New England Crime Stories*. A passionate reader and reviewer of Golden Age Detective fiction, Jason has also contributed to *The Best New True Crime Stories* series and maintains a tribute website for British mystery author Gladys Mitchell at: *www.gladysmitchell.com*

Paul Hiscock is an author of crime, fantasy, horror, and science fiction tales. His short stories have appeared in a variety of anthologies, and include a seventeenth century whodunnit, a science fiction western, punked fairytales, and numerous Sherlock Holmes pastiches. He lives with his family in Kent (England) and spends his days taking care of his two children. He mainly does his writing in coffee shops with members of the local NaNoWriMo group or in the middle of the night when his family has gone to sleep. Consequently, his stories tend to be fuelled by large amounts of black coffee. You can find out more about Paul's writing at www.detectivesanddragons.uk.

Naching T. Kassa is a wife, mother, and writer. She's created short stories, novellas, poems, and co-created three children. She resides in Eastern Washington State with her husband, Dan Kassa. Naching is a member of The Horror Writers Association, Mystery Writers of America, The Sound of the Baskervilles, The ACD Society, The Crew of the Barque Lone Star, and The Sherlock Holmes Society of London. She's also an assistant and staff writer for Still Water Bay at Crystal Lake Publishing. You can find her work on Amazon.
https://www.amazon.com/Naching-T-Kassa/e/B005ZGHTI0

David Marcum plays *The Game* with deadly seriousness. He first discovered Sherlock Holmes in 1975 at the age of ten, and since that time, he has collected, read, and chronologicized literally thousands of traditional Holmes pastiches in the form of novels, short stories, radio and television episodes, movies and scripts, comics, fan-fiction, and unpublished manuscripts. He is the author of over one-hundred Sherlockian pastiches, some published in anthologies and magazines (such as *The Strand* and *The Best Mystery Stories of the Year 2021*) and others collected in his own books, *The Papers of Sherlock Holmes*, *Sherlock Holmes and A Quantity of Debt*, *Sherlock Holmes – Tangled Skeins*, *Sherlock Holmes and The Eye of Heka*, and *The Collected Papers of Sherlock Holmes*. He is the winner of two first-place fiction awards from The Arthur Conan Doyle Society and the Nero Wolfe *Wolfe Pack*. He has edited over sixty books, including over five-dozen traditional Sherlockian anthologies, such as the ongoing series *The MX Book of New Sherlock Holmes Stories*, which he created in 2015. This collection is now at thirty-nine volumes, with more in preparation. He was responsible for bringing back August Derleth's Solar Pons for a new generation with his collections of authorized Pons stories, *The Papers of Solar Pons* and *The Further Papers of Solar Pons*. Pons's return was further assisted by his editing of the reissued authorized versions of the original Pons books, and then several volumes of new Pons adventures. He has done the same for the adventures of Dr. Thorndyke, and has plans for similar projects in the future. He has contributed numerous essays to various publications, and is a member of a number of Sherlockian groups and Scions, as well as The Mystery

Writers of America. His irregular Sherlockian blog, *A Seventeen Step Program*, addresses various topics related to his favorite book friends (as his son used to call them when he was small), and can be found at *http://17stepprogram.blogspot.com/* He is a licensed Civil Engineer, living in Tennessee with his wife and son. Since the age of nineteen, he has worn a deerstalker as his regular-and-only hat. In 2013, he and his deerstalker were finally able make his first trip-of-a-lifetime Holmes Pilgrimage to England, with return Pilgrimages in 2015 and 2016, where you may have spotted him. If you ever run into him and his deerstalker out and about, feel free to say hello!

Jen Matteis is a professional writer and editor who lives in California. Her articles have appeared in numerous daily, weekly, and alt-weekly newspapers, along with several magazines. When not writing for work, she writes for fun: Lovecraftian horror, overly ambitious fantasy, adventures with Sherlock Holmes, and more. Find her online at *www.jenmatteis.com*

The son of a policeman, **Adrian Middleton** has been a father, a journalist, a bouncer, a barman, a civil servant, a tabletop gamer, and policy adviser, a publisher, a freelance consultant and a business district manager. Throughout all of these identities, he has been a writer of weird and speculative fiction, including *The Moriarty Paradigm*, a series of steam-punked Sherlock Holmes stories, and *Tales of Old Horne*, the folkloric adventures of a twentieth-century witch.

Robert V. Stapleton was born in Leeds, England, and served as a full-time Anglican clergyman for forty years, specialising in Rural Ministry. He is now retired, and lives with his wife in North Yorkshire. This is the area of the country made famous by the writings of James Herriot, and television's *The Yorkshire Vet*, to name just a few. Amongst other things, he is a member of the local creative writing group, Thirsk Write Now (TWN), and regularly produces material for them. He has had more than fifty stories published, of various lengths and in a number of different places. He has also written a number of stories for *The MX Book of New Sherlock Holmes Stories*, and several published by Belanger Books. Several of these Sherlock Holmes pastiches have now been brought together and published in a single volume by MX Publishing, under the title of *Sherlock Holmes: A Yorkshireman in Baker Street*. Many of these stories have been set during the Edwardian period, or more broadly between the years 1880 and 1920. His interest in this period of history began at school in the 1960's when he met people who had lived during those years and heard their stories. He also found echoes of those times in literature, architecture, music, and even the coins in his pocket. The Edwardian period was a time of exploration, invention, and high adventure – rich material for thriller writers.

Kevin P. Thornton was shortlisted six times for the Crime Writers of Canada best unpublished novel. He never won – they are all still unpublished, and now he writes short stories. He lives in Canada, north enough that ringing Santa Claus is a local call and winter is a way of life. He has contributed numerous short stories to *The MX Book of New Sherlock Holmes Stories*. By the time you next hear from him, he hopes to have written more.

Joseph S. Walker is an active member of the Mystery Writers of America. His fiction has appeared in magazines, including *Alfred Hitchcock Mystery Magazine*,

Mystery Weekly, and *Dark City*, and in anthologies such as *Seascape*, *Day of the Dark*, and the MWA collections *Scream and Scream Again* and *Life is Short and Then You Die*. In 2019, his story "Haven" won the Al Blanchard Award, and his story "The Last Man in Lafarge" won the inaugural Bill Crider Prize for Short fiction. He lives in Indiana and teaches college literature courses. Follow him on Twitter (*@JSWalkerAuthor*) and visit his website at: *https://jsw47408.wixsite.com/website*

Also from Belanger Books
Edited by David Marcum
Holmes Away From Home:
Adventures from The Great Hiatus
Volumes I and II
*With Forewords by Mark Alberstat, Ron Lies, and David Marcum,
and an Afterward by Derrick Belanger*

Volume I – 1891-1892
The Final Problem – by Sir Arthur Conan Doyle
Over the Mountains in the Darkness – by Sonia Fetherston
An Englishman (or Two) in Florence – by David Ruffle
The Secret Adventure of Sherlock Holmes – by Diane Gilbert Madsen
The Harrowing Intermission – by Craig Janacek
The Adventure of the Indian Protégé – by Jayantika Ganguly
The Incident at Maniyachi Junction – by S. Subramanian
The Adventure on the Road to Mecca – by Deanna Baran
The Adventure of the Dragoman's Son – by John Linwood Grant
A Murder on Mount Athos – by Katie Magnusson
The President's Roses – by Stephen Seitz

Volume II – 1893-1894
The Adventure of the Old Brownstone – by David Marcum
The Adventure of the Flaked Breakfast Cereal – by Mark Levy
For Want of a Sword – by Daniel D. Victor
The Case of the Fragrant Blackmailer – S.F. Bennett
A Case of Juris Imprudence – by Robert Perret
A Most Careful, Strategic, and Logical Mind – by Derrick Belanger
The Aviator's Murder – by C. Edward Davis
The French Affair – by Mark Mower
The Woman Returns – by Richard Paolinelli
The Adventure of the Melting Man – by Shane Simmons
The Adventure of the Empty House – by Sir Arthur Conan Doyle

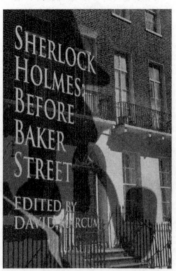

Also from Belanger Books
Edited by David Marcum
Sherlock Holmes and Doctor Watson:
The Early Adventures
Volumes I, II, and III
With a Foreword by David Marcum

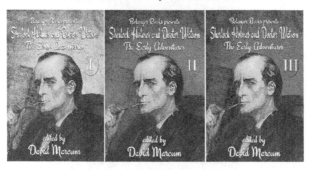

Volume I
A Study in Scarlet (An Excerpt) – by Sir Arthur Conan Doyle
The Adventure of the Persistent Pugilist – Thomas A Burns, Jr.
The Two Bullets – David Marcum
Brother's Keeper – Robert Perret
Bad Blood at Barts – Harry DeMaio
The Inside Men – M.J.H. Simmonds
The Adventure of the Villainous Victim – Chris Chan
The Cable Street Mummy – Paula Hammond
The Piccadilly Poisoner – Roger Riccard
The Adventure of the Modest Inspectors – Derrick Belanger
The Case of the Melancholic Widow – Deanna Baran
Angelique – by Mike Hogan

Volume II
The Adventure of the Substitute Detective – I.A. Watson
The Adventure of the Resident Patient – Sir Arthur Conan Doyle
The Locked-Room Mystery – D.J. Tyrer
The Adventure of the Missing Shadow – Jayantika Ganguly
A Diplomatic Affair – Mark Mower
The Adventure of Stonehenge in London – GC Rosenquist
The Doctor's Tale – David Marcum
The Finding of Geoffrey Hobson – David B. Beckwith
The Adventure of the Last Laugh – Tracy J. Revels
The Penny Murders – Robert Stapleton
The Disappearing Debutante – Stephen Herczeg

Volume III
The Adventure of the Three Fakirs – Annette Siketa
The Mystery of MacLean House – Kevin Thornton
The Adventure of Percival Dubois – Ian Ableson
The Distressing Matter of the Missing Dispatch Box – Will Murray
The Disappearance of the San Sebastiano – S.F. Bennett
The Adventure of the Speckled Band – Sir Arthur Conan Doyle
The Case of the Missing Waistcoat – Emily J. Cohen
The Mystery of the Missing Will – Tim Gambrell
The Adventure of the Persecuted Accountant – Arthur Hall
The Bizarre Challenge of Strange Mr. K – GC Rosenquist
The Broken Watch – M.J.H. Simmonds
The Colchester Experiment – David Marcum

Also from Belanger Books
Edited by David Marcum
After the East Wind Blows:
WWI and Roaring Twenties Adventures of Sherlock Holmes
Volumes I, II, and III
With Forewords by Nicholas Utechin and David Marcum

Part I: The East Wind Blows (1914-1918)
His Last Bow: The War Service of Sherlock Holmes – Sir Arthur Conan Doyle
The Rescue at Ypres – David Marcum
The Silent Sepoy – John Linwood Grant
The Odd Telegram – Kevin P. Thornton
The Adventure of the Synchronised Pup – Wayne Anderson
The Conundrum of the Questionable Coins – Will Murray
The Intrigue of the Kaiser Helmet – Shane Simmons
The Adventure of the Floating Rifles – John Davis
The Adventure of the Singular Needle – Andrew Salmon
The Singular Case of Dr. Butler – Paula Hammond
The Adventure of the Incomplete Cable – Dan Rowley
The Case of the Despicable Client – John Lawrence
The Adventure of the Absconded Corpse – I.A. Watson
Checkmate – Robert Stapleton

Part II: Aftermath (1919-1920)
The Old Sweet Song – Margie Deck
The Seventh Shot – Paul Hiscock
The Adventure of the Suicidal Sister – Craig Stephen Copland
The Curse of the Roaring Tiger – Nick Cardillo
The Search for Mycroft's Successor – Chris Chan
The Case of the Purloined Parcel – Naching T. Kassa
The Game at Checquers – Roger Riccard
The Adventure of the Swiss Banker – Frank Schildiner
The Adventure of the Confederate Treasure – Tracy J. Revels
The Adventure of the Resurrected Brother – Arthur Hall
The Adventure of the Grave Correspondent – Robert Perret
The Austrian Certificates – David Marcum

Part III: When the Storm Has Cleared (1921-1928)
The Adventure of the Silver Screen – Gordon Linzner
The King of Devil's Horn Prison – Derrick Belanger
Lights! Camera! Murder! – Sonia Fetherston
The Lonely Cavalier – Tim Gambrell
The West Egg Affair – Joseph S. Walker
The Curious Case of President Harding – John Lawrence
The Odd Event – Kevin Thornton
The Adventure of the Second Body – Stephen Herczeg
The Case of the Troubled Policeman – Daniel D. Victor
The Unpleasant Affair in Clipstone Street – David Marcum

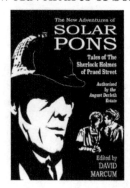

Also from Belanger Books
Edited by David Marcum
The Meeting of the Minds:
The Cases of Sherlock Holmes
and Solar Pons

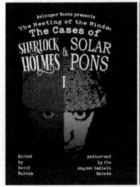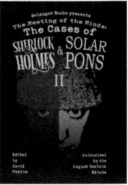

Part I:
The Serpentine Angel – Sean Venning
His Last Bow *Redux* – Sir Arthur Conan Doyle and David Marcum
The Adventure of the Duplicate Detective – Thomas A. Burns, Jr.
The Toledo Dagger – John Linwood Grant
The Case of the Broken Needle – Naching T. Kassa
The Adventure of Yesterday's Morrow – Andrew Salmon
The Bizarre Adventure of the Octagon House – David Marcum
The Croaking Creeper – by Derrick Belanger

Part II:
The Case of the Learned Linguist – Mark Mower
Doctor Parker's Patience – Harry DeMaio
The Adventure of the Perfect Murder – Nick Cardillo
The Norbury Adventure – Thaddeus Tuffentsamer
The Poison Child – Jayantika Ganguly
The Adventure of the Wisconsin Hodag – Chris Chan
The Adventure of the Retired Beekeeper – David Marcum
The Adventure of the Retired Judge – Stephen Herczeg
The Sorcerer and His Apprentice – Robert Stapleton
The Adventures of the Illiterate Informant – I.A. Watson

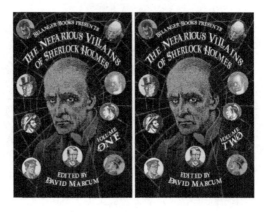

Belanger Books

Printed in Great Britain
by Amazon

23944610R00215